Necessary Evil

The Hunters: Book 1

R. A. Owen

Written Ingenuity

First Edition 2022

Print ISBN- 979-8-9872228-0-5

Ebook ISBN- 979-8-987-2228-1-2

Front and back cover design-Canva

Book design-Atticus

Author-R.A. Owen/Written Ingenuity

TRIGGER WARNINGS

I write for mature readers only.

This is a dark romance.

This book contains descriptive torture, detailed violence, graphic sexual encounters, vague details of child abuse, attempted rape, blood, and murder.

This book is written about Milly's past and present....

PAY ATTENTION TO THE CHAPTER TITLES!

This is book 1 of **The Hunters** series.

Contents

1. Present Milly   1

2. Past Milly 12-years-old   9

3. Present Milly   15

4. Past Milly 12-years-old   21

5. Present Milly   25

6. Past Milly 12-years-old   29

7. Present Milly   33

8. Past Milly 12-years-old   40

9. Present Milly   47

10. Past Milly 12-years-old   51

11. Present Milly   54

12. Past Milly 13-years-old   66

13. Nikolaj   71

14. Past Milly 15-years-old   82

15. Present Milly   90

16. Past Milly 15-years-old   101

17. Present Milly 108

18. Past Milly 18-years-old 117

19. Present Milly 124

20. Past Milly 19-years-old 132

21. Nikolaj 139

22. Past Milly 19-years-old 143

23. Present Milly 149

24. Past Milly 19-years-old 156

25. Present Milly 163

26. Past Milly 22-years-old 172

27. Present Milly 177

28. Present Milly 181

29. Past Milly 22-years-old 186

30. Present Milly 193

31. Past Milly 22-years-old 202

32. Present Milly 211

33. Present Milly 216

34. Past Milly 24-years-old 233

35. Present Milly 243

36. Past Milly 24-years-old 258

37. Present Milly 272

38. Past Milly 24-years-old   287

39. Past Milly 24-years-old   302

40. Present Milly   310

41. Past Milly 24-years-old   318

42. Present Milly   325

43. Present Milly   332

44. Present Milly   339

45. Present Milly   349

46. Present Milly   355

47. Present Milly   365

48. Present Milly   378

49. Present Milly   393

50. Present Milly   398

51. Present Milly   405

                                            414

Social media   415

Acknowledgements   416

Special notes   417

Present Milly

Chapter 1

THE ROOM FILLS WITH the screams of agony reverberating off the walls.

I watch, waiting for the initial shock to fall, staring at him. Tom Kraft. His face is distorted with pain as he screams for any help that may hear him.

His bleeding left hand lay limp, tied at the wrist to the arm of the chair.

Blood runs down the leg of the chair and pools around his severed pinky lying on the floor.

I scan his partially naked body, curious how much torture he could handle and how I'll push his pain limits before killing him.

FUCK TOM KRAFT!

I walk toward him, his eyes filling with fear, and his body whips around, trying to get out of the chair. His breathing is heavy as he starts to plead the useless shit I always hear...."please don't hurt me!"...." I'll do anything!"...." I have a family!"

All his cries fall on deaf ears. I crouch down in front of him, grab his ring and middle finger, push them together, and then cut them off at the knuckle of the hand. Letting them fall to the floor as his blood squirts on my hands.

The sound of his screaming fills the room again. I take this opportunity to cut the pointer and thumb off before he quits for a breath, and they land on the fingers lying on the floor.

Standing, I look back at the tall men that watch me. The men look like gods towering in the shadows. Every feature on them is chiseled to perfection. Nikolaj Fedorov and his business partner Demyan Morozov-my new bosses.

On either side are their two bodyguards and two cleaners. They all are enormous in stature and not to be fucked with. six men that would make anyone in Tom's situation lose hope and shiver in fear.

I walk toward the table by Nikolaj and Demyan. Their arms crossed over their broad chests, and their perfect muscular physiques test the endurance of their black suits.

Their gazes lock on me as I grab the knife from the table behind them and turn back to Tom to serve him what he deserves. Sick Fuck!

His head is bobbing from nausea, panic, and loss of blood. I straddle his legs, tied with barbed wire at the ankles to each chair leg, grabbing his hair and jolting his head upward to look at me as I hover over him. He whimpers, not able to form a word, moaning in agony.

"Do I have your cooperation yet, Tom?" I ask as I gently run the blade of my knife around the edge of his face, studying him.

Finally, he musters the words, "what do you want?!"

Stepping away, I lightly touch the fingers on his right hand. He flinches and starts begging me to stop. I slowly walk around him as my fingers gently glide up his right arm, turning as I reach his back.

I'm now facing Nikolaj, Demyan, and the other men by their sides, as they watch me, curious about what I will do to Tom.

I allow my right hand to stop and rest on his shoulder. My left hand, holding the knife, rests on his other shoulder. "I need to know about Lazlo," I say, then take a deep breath and rotate my head to loosen my neck.

This fuck isn't going to tell me anything easily, but I'll have fun torturing it out of him.

Tom starts to panic again as my right hand starts to squeeze his shoulder. "I don't know about Lazlo. Please don't do this!" He starts to cry.

Why do they always cry when it's time to face the consequences of their actions? Such a pussy bitch!

"You keep saying that," I groan. "You know this can easily be done by just giving me the information I want, but don't get me wrong," leaning down to his ear to say, "I enjoy the hard way." Nipping at his ear, then I slightly bend over his left shoulder and move my face for him to see in his peripheral vision.

With his attention on me, I move my hand with the knife off his shoulder, flip it then slowly push it into his left eye, causing him to scream again. I stare at the blood covering his face and my knife while I wait for him to calm down.

"Ready to talk yet?" I ask, but he just moans and thrashes. "Very well!"

I pull the knife out of his eye and step to his left side as my right hand still follows lightly on his skin. I stop at his hand with no fingers, tap the top of it as a reminder of what I am capable of, then lift my hand off him.

He starts to kick and jerk in his seat, and it appears his fight mode has activated. What a foolish asshole!

"Tommy, Tommy, Tommy, do you feel that? That's adrenaline kicking into fight mode." I tilt my head looking down at him. "Funny how adrenaline can make us think we have power, maybe feel invincible, fearless, even feel the hope of survival, but it's all bullshit!" I snarl, then squat down in front of him.

His glare at me makes me chuckle. "I'm not the reason you're here. You are," I say as I start running my thumb up the blade of my knife, flip it for a better grasp, then slide the knife up Tom's right leg.

He squirms and grunts, and his breathing becomes heavy. I hold the knife to the outline of his dick showing through his tighty whities.

"Tom, why are you protecting these people?" I ask, then glance around. "I don't see them here to protect you! So, tell me, how do we get in contact with Lazlo?"

He squirms as he yells, "I don't know anything. NOTHING!"

I roll my eyes, annoyed at the same song and dance these assholes give every time we capture them. As if I'm just going to let them walk out because they say they don't know anything.

"I already know what you do, Tom! I just want to know how you contacted Lazlo for arrangements," I say as I shrug, still holding the knife against his dick.

"I don't know what you're talking about. I don't know what you want! I don't know who fucking Lazlo is!" Tom screams as he strains against his restraints, then starts crying.

I say calmly, "the hard way. Okay. Well, TOM, let me help your memory. You torture, hurt, and rape people for fun. Especially kids."

His eyes widen as he continues to try to jerk out of the chair.

Pushing the tip of the knife down into the small skinny shaft of his dick just enough to make his blood visible through his underwear, making him freeze.

Still crouching in front of him, I continue, "you would get kids to trust you, then you did horrible things to them. You even paid to hurt people. Sound familiar?"

He looks between me and the knife poking his blood-soaked briefs into his dick. His eyes are filled with fear. I lean my elbows on his legs and say, "I'm sure you're wondering how I know. Allow me to clarify. You took videos of your sick acts as trophies, then saved them to your home computer. You fucking idiot!" I pull the knife out of his dick and stand.

He lowers his head, sobbing, I'm sure from getting caught, not out of remorse.

My patience is gone now. "You seem to need some help talking." I raise the knife and stab it into his dick. He violently buckles and thrashes in the chair, and I withdraw the blade and quickly plunge it into his right hand and twist it.

"Anything you want to say now?" I ask, but he only screams.

Leaving the knife in his hand, I turn back to the table and grab a surgical scalpel. I'm going to skin this fucker alive. They always seem to talk when I'm skinning them.

As I turn back to Tom, Nikolaj grabs the inside of my arm, pulling me into his muscular chest with a thud. His powerful grasp makes my body crave him. In his thick Russian accent, he says into my ear, "hurry this up!" His breath on my skin gives me goosebumps. Letting me go with a jerk, his intense stare has me frozen and staring back at him.

Demyan catches my attention, standing slightly behind Nikolaj and glancing at the scalpel. "M, we have to go. We have a lead on McGriffith. This fuck doesn't know anything," he calmly says-another Russian and slightly more approachable boss. Sinfully attractive and as desirable as his counterpart.

"FINE!" I say through my teeth, roll my eyes toward Nikolaj, then drop the scalpel on the table to pick up a buck knife. "Tom, it's your lucky fucking day," I angrily yell, "guess we ARE doing this the easy way."

I walk back to him, straddling his legs, lift his head by his hair, and sneer, "quickly dying is too good for you, but orders are orders." I wink, then draw my face close to his and snarl, "I'm going to watch your pathetic life leave your body, you fucking piece of shit!"

I raise the knife high, then slam it into his neck over and over as his skin rips apart, and his blood covers my hands and clothes, solidifying why black clothes are our go-to apparel.

After his last breath, I step back, turning to face my bosses. "There, I'm fucking done!" I yell out in a tantrum, spit on Tom's dead body, then drop the knife to the floor.

The two cleaners, Jason and Henry, are suited up in their hazmat suits, face masks, gloves, goggles, and hoods. They start their duties of cleaning the mess and making sure this never happened.

The meticulous attention to detail they must take to cover our assess does not go unnoticed. The bosses pay them very well to ensure the best job is done.

Jason hands me a towel to wipe the blood off. "Throw it in this bin when you're done," he says to me through his mask while pointing to the plastic bin he just wheeled over.

Henry hands me a plastic package with neatly folded clothes in it. "Put these on; throw the old clothes in the bin." I nod in understanding.

Changing out of bloody clothes with an audience is nothing new to me. I tore my shirt off, exposing my black bra, tattoos, scars, and the blood from Tom.

I wipe as much blood off as possible, throw the towel in the plastic bin, and then put on a long-sleeved black shirt. Next, I remove my shoes, socks, and pants, exposing my black panties.

I look around the room to see all the men turned away from me except Nikolaj. He's watching the men ensuring no one turns around too soon. He is a brute asshole most of the time, but he does have some gentlemanly qualities.

I wiggle my ass in his direction as I pull up my leggings and look over my shoulder to see his reaction, but he isn't looking at me.

Throwing the shoes down to the floor to kick them on, I throw my old clothes in the bin, then walk over to the bosses.

The three of us walk to the two black Mercedes Benz G63 AMGs by the garage door. These vehicles ensure our safe travels home. The floor can withstand an explosion with tinted windows, security cameras, and bulletproof, and only tractable by the bosses' men.

Sven, Nikolaj's guard/driver, opens the back passenger door for me. I smile at him as I slide in. Nikolaj gets in on the other side, holding his phone to his ear and speaking in Russian.

Behind us, Demyan gets in the front seat of his SUV while his guard/driver, Gus, gets into the driver's seat. We pull out of the warehouse garage door, off an abandoned loading dock in a decrepit industrial area.

I glance at Nikolaj, a godly specimen of a man with absolutely no patience for me. He is 6'6, and in his 30s, with an overpowering muscular physique, dark wavy shoulder-length hair, a close-kept beard, brown eyes, scars on his visible body, and tattoos that cover his neck, forearms, and hands.

Unfortunately, the only skin I've ever seen is what sticks out of his suit. I wouldn't complain if I got to see more, but he loathes me, so I don't see that happening anytime soon.

My phone dings. Nikolaj glares over at me, and I sink into my seat, staring at my phone. I glance at him, still on his phone, and he directs his attention away from me.

It's a text from Demyan, *'scum are not worth more than a bullet. Don't waste your time on people who can't help you. You still did well'*.

I text back, *'Thanks'*, set my phone on my lap, and stare out the window.

Watching the world pass by in silence, wondering who the next asshole we capture will be. How many sickos do I have to hunt and kill before we get to Lazlo?

Past Milly
12-years-old
Chapter 2

THIS LIFESTYLE ISN'T BY choice. You don't wake up one day with the desire to torture bad people. It's caused by deep dark memories that eat away at you, leaving nothing but anger and hate.

I had a fantastic childhood growing up in Rivers Bend, Iowa. I was an only child. My parents were my world.

I was eight years old when my grandmother told me my dad had died in a car accident earlier that day. He went to the store to get me some ice cream because I got all the spelling words right on the test.

My mother pushed me away when I tried to hug her. She said, "if you weren't born, my husband would still be here!" Then she walked up the stairs and slammed her bedroom door shut.

My grandma stood with me in the kitchen, putting her hands on my shoulders, "grief is different in everyone. Let your mother be, and she will come around." Except she never did.

Grandma stayed a week with us but had to go back home after Dad's funeral. Mother didn't say a word to me. She bought a liquor bottle, which was the end of life as I knew it.

She drank so much that she lost her job, bills piled up, and there was no food in the house. She never looked at me. She didn't care anymore.

Grandma was too sick to take me in, so whenever she called to check on us, I would tell her everything was great. I lied to her about everything in my life because I never wanted to worry her. I'd make up a life a grandmother would be proud of, and she was proud of me; in my fake life.

Mom lost the house, then we ended up in a shit motel. Mom got a new boyfriend named Skip, and Skip got mom hooked on drugs.

I came home from school one day to find Skip alone. Mom went to the store to get more liquor. Skip walked across the room to me, then rubbed his finger on my cheek. I glared up at him. I hated that man with every bone in my body. Then he tossed me on the bed.

After his assault, he sat up to have a cigarette. The shame and embarrassment I felt didn't end there. Skip abused me whenever he could, even if my mom was asleep in the next bed. Not that she would have done anything to stop him.

After two years of Skip's abuse, I finally broke. I packed my few belongings and acted like I was going to school.

Mom ignored me, as usual. After four years of her hating me, I never expected her to acknowledge me.

Skip licked his gross lips, winked, and said, "can't wait to see you after school."

I shut the door to the room and felt the morning breeze on my skin. What the hell is a 12-year-old going to do on her own? I thought to myself and started to walk across town, passing every place I would see when I was with my dad. He would take me everywhere with him and tell me stories of his childhood.

I walked past a small grocery store where we would get sodas from time to time. I noticed a lady, older, standing by a blue truck. She was stunning, and next to her was an older man, just a little taller than she was. He has jaw-length brown hair and a beard. He was loading groceries in the truck.

She looked right at me. Nervousness and guilt set in, and my mind panicked.

Does she know I skipped school and that I'm running away?

Can she read my mind?

My anxiety grabbed hold of me, and I picked up my pace. I didn't look back, but I knew she was still staring at me.

Turning on the side of the grocery store building, I ran down the hill behind it. In the far distance were tents the homeless used to sleep. Mom and I slept in the tents many times.

That was my destination until I figured out where else to go.

I was standing down in the valley, still far from the tents. I just stared at the shit hole I never wanted to see again, but there I was.

A gentle voice behind me said, "hello." I turned to see it was the lady from the truck.

I defensively yelled to her, "I didn't do anything," and started marching toward the tents.

She calmly said, "I know, but you look hungry. I just want to give you this sandwich and juice."

I stopped dead in my tracks. I was hungry. I hadn't eaten since yesterday when I grabbed a half-eaten slice of pizza out of the garbage at school.

I turned to face her with my guard still up, "what do you want from me?"

"Nothing," she said, holding a prepackaged sandwich and a bottle of orange juice up in the air toward me.

"If I take those, what do I have to do for you?" I asked suspiciously.

She furrowed her eyebrows, and a confused look crossed her face. She said, "nothing, just take them." I slowly walk back to her, cautious of her hands and my surroundings.

Grabbing the items from her, I jumped back and turned on my heel to start walking back toward the tents.

"Do you want to go there?" She asked, still staring at me and pointing to the tents.

"I don't have a choice," I snapped, not facing her this time.

She pleaded a little louder, startling me, "possibly! Listen..." I turned to face her. "Sit here with me. Just for a minute, so I can make sure you eat those." She pointed to my hands, then continued, "if you go down there with food and juice, you know damn well someone will steal them from you."

I knew she was right, but could I trust her? I looked over my shoulder at the tents and back at her. I took a few steps toward her and asked, "are you going to hurt me if I sit with you?"

"NO! What? I just want to make sure you eat," she said, shocked.

I nodded, walked back to her, and sat on a nearby bench. I put my bag down on the ground, then started wrestling with the sandwich packaging.

She gently grabbed it from my hands, saying, "I'm Mary. What's your name?" Then handing back the sandwich.

I took a close look at her features. Her brown eyes looked gentle, like my grandma's. Her very curly hair was pulled back into a scarf, and her beautiful brown complexion gleamed in the light shining through the trees. I started to relax just a little.

I took a bite of the sandwich, and with a full mouth, said, "Milly." I couldn't take my eyes off of her. She was beautiful.

She rested her head on her hand and her elbow on the corresponding knee, tilting her head slightly to look at me, then chuckled. "Milly! I like that name."

She lifted her head back up, took a deep breath, and crossed her legs while staring out into our view of trees, grass, a small pond, and homeless tents.

"What are you running from, Milly?" She asked as she looked around, squinting from the sun hitting her eyes.

I stopped chewing, and I felt my face go flush. "Why do you think I'm running?" I asked, with a mouth full of food. I finally swallowed, and I sat staring at her.

She turned her head to look at me and smiled. I could tell she knew the answer already.

"My mom and her shitty boyfriend, Skip," I blurted out.

She laughed, "I know all about shitty boyfriends." She looked at me, winked, and smiled. "But it must be pretty bad for you to risk skipping school to get away?"

"You have no idea, Mary." I half smiled at her.

Just then, I heard footsteps wrestling in the leaves behind us. Mary turned slightly. "Ah yes, well, Milly, I have to go," she said.

I looked back to see the man from the truck standing a few feet behind us. I looked back at Mary, nudged my head, and whispered, "shitty boyfriend?"

She laughed, "no, wonderful husband," as she glanced back at him.

My eyebrows bunched, and I took another bite of my sandwich as I turned to face him better.

He smiled at me. His smile looked kind, unlike Skips. I studied him for a second while I finished chewing my food.

"I'm Jared," he said while doing a single wave with his hand. I turned back to Mary without saying anything to Jared.

She adjusted her position so she could face me better. "Milly, I understand your situation, but please don't go to those tents. Nothing good happens in those tents, especially to kids. You can come to stay with Jared and me. We have plenty of room in our house. You will be safe with us. Then we can figure out this whole 'Mom and Skip' thing," she pleaded.

I stared at her. I contemplated my choices. 1. Skip, 2. Homeless, or 3. A chance.

I nodded slightly, grabbed my juice, and another half of my sandwich, and said, "okay."

I wondered why she would care what happened to me when she didn't even know me. Are these people my saviors or my newest enemies?

Jared walked closer and asked, "can I put your bag in the truck?"

I leaned down to grab the bag, handed it to him, and walked beside Mary to the blue truck.

I quietly sat as we pulled away from the store and hoped that the further I got away from Rivers Bend, the better I would be.

Present Milly

Chapter 3

SVEN PULLS THROUGH THE massive iron gates into the compound, consisting of 500 acres of land, completely enclosed with tall concrete walls. The iron gate is the only entrance and exit of the property. Guards constantly walk the grounds all day and all night. Cameras at every angle imaginable. No one gets in or out of here without being noticed.

The car stops by the steps leading up to the 32,000-square-foot mansion's front entrance. Nikolaj and Sven get out; I linger in the backseat, as instructed numerous times before, until Sven opens my door, then I step out.

Nikolaj is already headed up the stairs on his phone-as always.

I look back at Demyan's car as he and Gus get out. Demyan yells to me, "M, you did good tonight!" I nod while looking at the stairs as I walk to the house. Demyan's not far behind. The wind is in the right direction, and I get a whiff of his cologne, and it's so good.

"Don't you have your place in the compound?" I joke, not turning around.

"Yeah, but Niko and I have work to do tonight," he responds, and I can tell he is smiling.

Demyan is handsome!! He's early 30's, about 6'4", muscular, blue eyes, light brown hair, longer on top, styled back and a little toward the side; his full beard is clean, extra short length, his jawline is perfect, and his smile exposes straight white teeth. His personality is of a gentle but deadly lion, and he keeps the peace between Nikolaj and the world.

I walk through the huge black double doors into the foyer with gray marble floors that line this entire level of the mansion. To my right is a very long wall adjacent to the garage, and just after that, the basement stairs that lead to my office and the weapons room.

The door straight ahead, slightly to my right, is Nikolaj's office. I watch as he walks in, taking his jacket off as he passes the threshold of his office. I could see every detailed muscle under his shirt as he moved.

The room next to his, slightly to my left, is the meeting room/library. We don't use the space often, but it is big enough to accommodate the entire crew working here.

To my immediate left is the dining room, with four tall white columns creating the illusion of boundaries. There are two massive wooden tables, each with 12 chairs. On the backside of the dining room is a kitchen the size of a small house.

I've been here three months, and this place still blows me away in sheer size.

Demyan walks up to my side, brushing his shoulder to mine, saying something. "I'm sorry, what?" I ask, drawing my attention to him.

"My place is much cozier. You should come over sometime," he says with a smirk.

He is devilishly good-looking, so mesmerizing, and very charming. Making being stolen from my life a little easier.

"Yeah. Okay," I say, and just like that, he's on his way to Nikolaj's office. I smile slightly, then head to the basement stairs.

Eight thousand square feet in the basement, the first door to the right leads to the weapons room, and my office is further down the hall to the left. We hack, hunt, and make gadgets for whatever mission or assignment the bosses are doing or for our enjoyment.

We're nerds!

I open the door to the office. Four thousand square feet of computers, trackers, burner phones, cameras, monitors, speakers, recorders, all the cool gadgets we make, and everything we need to make them. To the right of the door is a vault where we keep all the files of the bosses' cases, assignments, and blueprints, plus the records of the sick fucks I hunt and kill. If their story intertwines with someone else we are looking for, we'll need to revisit their file.

Three others are working here right now. Theo, Daniel, and Vance. "Working hard, fellow nerds?" I ask with a scoff.

"You mean sexy nerds," Theo chuckles as he walks to his desk.

Theo is a robotics engineer and wicked smart. He can create just about anything you ask him to, but he's goofy, and his social skills are; well, he's the most intelligent dumb guy I've ever met. He's 34, has blonde hair, blue eyes, a medium build, and is a goofy guy from Denmark.

Vance is leaning over Daniel's desk analyzing something when he looks up and says, "how did it go, kiddo?"

I rub my forehead with my forearm and say, "cut short, but the guy is dead and can't hurt anyone else." I sit at my desk, lean back in my chair, and watch Vance walk over to me.

Vance is our oldest nerd. Heavier set, dark brown curly-haired-Italian father figure. He's one of my guys and a long-time friend, handpicked by me to work here.

He reaches the side of my U-shaped desk, standing inside the opening by my chair, looking at me; he squints, and raises an eyebrow, "okay, kiddo, what's wrong?"

I roll my eyes at him and adjust my position in my chair, "I'm 24, not 12 anymore. I'm not a *kiddo*!" I turn my head away from him and fumble with my computer. He chuckles; it makes me smile.

Vance and I are very close. We just understand each other, which makes us inseparable and protective of one another.

Sitting on my desk with his feet dangling above the floor, "well?" he whispers.

"Vance, you're being protective," I whisper back, looking at him with a smirk.

"Milly," he says a little louder and sternly, "did the job get done?"

"Yes! I already told you that!"

He leans down, gets closer to my face, and demands, "then why are you pouting?"

"I'm not pouting!" I mock him with a scowl.

"I've known you too long. You're a shitty liar!"

I act offended and shocked at his words, then slightly tip my head side to side. He's right. "Uuugh," I grunt out.

I lean my torso into his left leg, wrap my hands around his calves and rest my left cheek on his lower thigh. He puts his hand on my head and scrunches his fingers in my hair.

"I want to go home, to be honest! I don't want to be here anymore. I don't want to do these jobs under the bosses' supervision," I mumble as my cheek pushes my lips to the side of my face.

Vance grumbles in his throat and takes a deep breath, "we can't go home, kiddo. I told you this was the consequence before you barged into their warehouse," Vance quietly says.

"I know. I should have listened to you. Regrets, right?" I huff out, then say, "the bosses just want to kill them and get it over with, Vance. None of the assholes I've hunted since being here have suffered. They all get easy, quick deaths because of Nikolaj and Demyan."

I turn my head, so my chin rests on Vance's left knee. He pats my head like a dog, but it's comforting, so I'll allow it.

Staring down at me, he says, "the bosses have jobs to do, too, kiddo. We have to do what they say. You're lucky to be able to hunt and kill; you're welcome, by the way."

"Okay fine, I'm pouting!" I close my eyes. I'm exhausted from torturing Tom.

He laughs softly and confidently says, "I know!"

Switching his tone, "dead is dead, kiddo. Our goal is to ensure these sickos don't hurt anyone else. You did that. Be proud of the work you got to do tonight."

I sit back up and toss him a fake smile. He nods, amused by my ability to try and be proud of myself. "Now, close the file, shower, and get to bed. You're a mess," he stands, motions to my computer, then walks back to his desk.

I move all of Tom Kraft's files to an external drive to store in the vault.

"Holy Milly! You look like shit," Daniel spits out, laughing as he hands a file to Theo. Daniel must have found his way back to reality, being I have been in the room 10 minutes, and he's just now noticing me.

"Oh, be nice, you ass. Milly's been working and killing people. You should know better than to mouth off to a killer," Theo jokes.

"You should see the other guy. He's in pretty rough shape," I confess, pressing my lips together and raising my eyebrows at Daniel jokingly.

"You'd never hurt your favorite basement office co-hacker, would you, Milly, old pal," Daniel pleads sarcastically. He knows I'd never hurt him. We've grown too close.

"Never!" The sweet, sentimental reassurance I offer him seems to clear his worries.

Daniel is a 31-year-old nerd from Compton. He is slightly shorter than me, skinny, wears big circle glasses, is super bright, and obsessed with celebrity news. He has the biggest crush on Demyan, and Theo gets on his nerves by giving him shit about it. Even though they bicker all the time, they are inseparable.

We all form unusual attachments to this lifestyle.

Past Milly
12-years-old
Chapter 4

WE PULLED UP TO a huge old house in the middle of nowhere, surrounded by trees.

Jared parked on the side of the house, next to a door.

I got out as soon as I saw the other two open their doors. Realizing I didn't finish my sandwich or juice, I quickly drank the juice and shoved the remaining half of my sandwich into my coat pocket.

Jared chuckled behind me, which startled me. "There is more food in your future, child!" He said, "you don't have to worry about that."

We entered a kitchen with an island in the middle of the room. There were windows on one side of the kitchen and a table with six chairs in front of it. Glancing around, I noticed a more oversized table in the next room. Everything looks older but clean and fancy.

Mary and Jared put away the groceries as they glanced and smiled at each other in passing. They sure smiled a lot.

"Milly, how old are you?" Mary asked.

"12".

"Oh! That's such an important time in your life. The last year before you're a teenager!"

I put my head down and rubbed my shoes lightly on the floor, "I don't know."

Mary stood on the opposite side of the island from me. "Milly, whoever hurt you is long gone now. We will protect you," Mary said caringly.

"Why? You don't even know me!" I snapped in a mumble.

Filling the teapot in the sink on the island, not missing a beat, she answered, "I already told you-yes I do!".

Mary looks up at me. "Rough childhoods are nothing new in this fucked up world." She turned the knob on the gas stove and clicked until it lit and said, "in this world, there's a lot of evil, and that's why there's a necessary evil."

She turned back to me and tapped the top of the stool motioning for me to sit. She walked to the fridge and grabbed a juice and an apple, then sat on the seat beside me while handing me the food and drink.

"Necessary evil?" I asked, confused.

"Some people follow all the rules and do their best to be good people. Some people do bad things because they want to hurt innocent people. Some people hurt those that hurt innocent and good people. That's a necessary evil." She adjusted on the stool and laughed as I took a bite of the apple, and juice splattered all over. She grabbed a napkin by the sink and handed it to me.

"Think about war. It's never a good thing, but there are usually two sides. One side tries to dominate or destroy, while the other tries to save and protect. War is dark, no matter what, and anyone involved in war has to do bad things. The difference is one of the sides is doing bad things for the betterment-the good of the situation. Those people are the necessary evil."

Jared spoke up, and I jumped, forgetting he was in the room, "sometimes you have a choice where you want to be. Sometimes fate puts you where she wants you in life."

I turned on my stool to face him and asked, "what are you two?"

Jared fiddled with the placemat, took a deep breath, looked at Mary, and said, "we are the necessary evil that protects good people worth protecting."

Mary explains, "we do bad things to bad people because they do bad things to good people."

"Okay, I get it now. Like cops, but not cops, cool!" I said, shrugging my shoulders and taking a bite of my apple.

I've seen a lot of shitty stuff in the last four years, so these people weren't scaring me with all this good and evil talk.

Jared said, "well, let's get dinner started. It's already four, and the chicken isn't going to cook itself."

"Four!" I yelled in a panic and jumped off my stool. "I'm dead! Skip is going to kill me! I have to go!"

Jared stared at me. Mary walked to me slowly and grabbed my shoulders. "Milly, I told you no one would hurt you anymore."

"But you don't know, Skip. My mom doesn't care if I'm alive, but Skip is horrible. He likes to hurt me."

Mary darted a look at Jared, then left the room. "What if I told you there is no way Skip will ever get to you again? Would you feel safe then?"

After a long pause, I said, "I wish they were dead! I hate them!"
I started crying-not a little cry, but a body-shaking, snot-dripping
ugly cry. She caught me as I crumbled and led me to the floor softly.

I heard Jared say something to her, but I was too wrapped up in
my crying to make it out. I felt her nod against the top of my head,
and then I saw Jared walk to the side door in the kitchen, and my
eyes closed when the door clicked shut.

"Where is he going?" I asked quietly.

Mary answered calmly, "necessary evil!"

Present Milly

Chapter 5

SHUTTING THE VAULT DOOR, I see Daniel standing beside me. "What?" I asked him suspiciously.

"I'm on this McGriffith case for the bosses," he says, looking over his shoulder to make sure no one can hear him. Daniel only looks into the bosses affairs, so if anyone knew I knew something I shouldn't, they'd know who told me. The bosses are not particularly keen on me knowing anything about their business or affairs. I'm the black sheep, cast out, the intruder.

"Yes, I know!" I say with a bit of sarcasm. Clearly, he's working on a case for the bosses. It's his only job besides messing around with gadgets with us.

"Well, there's some weird shit I found, but I doubt the bosses will tell you. I think you should know."

"Okay, like what?" I ask, tipping my head down to get closer to him.

"Quick run down because you need a shower-you stink," he says while waving his hand with palm side out in a figure-eight manner.

My eyes widen, and I jerk my head toward him to signal him to hurry up.

"McGriffith had a bunch of rape cases filed against him over the years, but none made it to court. Two accusers were found dead, but the deaths didn't point to McGriffith. The rest of the women received huge lumps of money from anonymous sources," he whispers slightly, rubbing his hand on the nape of his neck.

I furrow my eyebrows and continue to listen to him.

"I just thought it might be something you are interested in since you hunt assholes like this," he says with a shrug.

"I'm interested! Put a copy of everything you found on my desk, and I'll look at it later," I instruct. He nods and walks back to his desk.

"You two don't work too late," I say to Theo and Daniel as I head to the door with Vance on my heels.

We walk down the hallway leading us to the stairs to the main level. To ensure no one overhears us, we don't say too much to each other at this point. We don't wholly trust everyone in the mansion.

Nikolaj and Demyan must have trust issues, as well. Otherwise, why do all their exceptionally talented people and the house help have to live here in the mansion?

The entire 2nd floor has eight rooms, like mini apartments. The four corner apartments have two bedrooms and two bathrooms. The four middle flats have an open concept, so everything is in one giant room except the bathroom has walls and a door. All eight have a kitchen and a balcony.

Nikolaj has the entire 3rd floor to himself, and Demyan lives in a separate house in the compound. I've walked by it a few times but never been inside.

"I'm going to grab a bite really quick." I motion to the kitchen.

"Fine. I'll make you a sandwich, kiddo," Vance says. No matter how old I get, he will never quit calling me that or insisting on cooking for me.

I rest up against the island in the middle of the kitchen, interlace my fingers and rest my head down on my joined palms, regretting my decision that caused us to be here. Vance palms the top of my head as a sign he understands my pain.

He turns to the fridge to collect the food, then places it all on the island. It doesn't take him long to whip up the sandwiches. We eat them in complete silence, just gazing at each other.

After cleaning up, we head upstairs to the second floor. "Vance, you are the best! Thank you for being here for me," I sincerely tell him.

He's been my rock for so many years, and even though I recently made the biggest mistake of my life, he still stayed by my side.

"I wouldn't want to be anywhere else, kiddo."

We have middle rooms on the left side of the hallway. Vance's room is the first door we stop at, and he says, "get some sleep," Vance says while opening the door to his room.

"Good night, best friend," I say, and he chuckles. I walk away and hear his door click shut and lock.

My room is simple. A couch, two end tables, a king bed with two nightstands, a small table for two, a dresser, and a small bookcase. The kitchen and a small table to my right. The living room area and bedroom area are to my left. The bathroom sits adjoining a wall to the kitchen. On the other side of the bathroom, by the outside wall, is my dresser and an open walk-in closet. The balcony door is on the left side by the bedroom area, with huge windows on each side.

I kick my shoes off by the front door and head to the bathroom. The shower warms up while I stare at myself in the mirror, thinking back to a time when this life was more straightforward.

The hot water runs over my body, washing the dried blood splatter that seeped through my clothes while ending Tom Kraft's life. While washing my hair, I'm startled by a forceful knock at my door.

Past Milly
12-years-old
Chapter 6

TWO WEEKS LATER.

I was in Heaven!

Mary homeschooled me and taught me to cook, clean, and garden. She liked to do those things, so she knew how to do them well.

Jared taught me how to play catch with a baseball, and he bought me a fitted mitt.

Mary took me shopping in a city I had never been to. Chicago. She bought me so much stuff I wondered when she would run out of money.

We painted the room they gave me, and she picked out a Walnut bedroom set.

The entire house was done perfectly, like something you'd see in a magazine. Jared prided himself that the house was "over 100 years old and still solid!" he always said. It was as huge as it was beautiful.

I was allowed in certain rooms of the house, and others were locked. The attic was where Jared worked, so I wasn't allowed up there, nor in the basement.

I was content with how things were going, but I couldn't help but wonder when it would all fall apart and their dark secrets would come out.

I was sitting on the porch one fall afternoon, letting the wind blow on me as I embraced the sun's heat.

Jared was just getting home from running errands in Chicago. I saw something jumping around in the truck. Jared was trying to hold it still.

Mary came out of the house and said, "what did he find now?"

I smiled at her, and she glanced down at me, looked back up at Jared, and her eyebrows scrunched together.

"Jared Benecelli, what the hell is that?!"

Jared got out of the truck with a chuckle, and a four-legged creature hurled out after him.

"It's a puppy!" I yelled as I jumped up and started running to meet it.

Mary shook her head in defeat.

Jared explained, "he was just walking on the side of the road. No collar. Nothing. He's just a puppy, and he's friendly. I couldn't just leave him there."

Mary groaned, "unbelievable! You are... such a softy!". He laughed and nodded in agreement.

"What's his name?" I asked.

"I don't know. He's going to grow to be a huge dog. Just look at those paws!" Jared said while kneeling beside the puppy and petting his back.

I studied the dog over, trying to think of a name. "What about Bear?" I said, "because he has all the colors of every kind of bear, and he's going to be big."

This little puppy started to lick Jared's face uncontrollably with brown, black, and white all in his fur. "Bear fits! He's about to lick my face off!" He wrestled the puppy off of him, then got up to retrieve the groceries from the truck.

From then on, Bear followed me everywhere. He slept in my bed, ate all the time, and chewed on everything. Mary even fell in love with Bear, too.

The night the people that stayed in the three locked rooms came back was the first night in weeks that I felt scared and nervous. The fear and anticipation of meeting them stressed me out. The questions piled up in my head.

What if they were like Skip?

What if Jared and Mary took me just to hurt me?

Jared met Bear and me in the upstairs hallway. "Ready, kiddo?" he asked.

"For what?" Preparing for the worst to be said. This life is too good to be true, and tonight must be the night it falls apart.

"Once everyone gets here, the peace and quiet we have come to love will be gone!" He smiled, put his hand on my shoulder, and led me down the stairs to Mary in the kitchen.

After 20 minutes, we heard cars driving up the road, then car doors slamming, talking, and then they were on the porch. The door flew open, and five people walked in.

That was the night my life changed forever, but I didn't know it at the time.

Present Milly

Chapter 7

ANOTHER KNOCK AT THE door.

"YEAH, HANG ON!" I snap, stepping out of the shower and sliding my robe on.

All I want to do is wash Tom Kraft's blood off of me, then go to bed.

FUCK!

I head to the door, annoyed and ready to yell at the impatient person continually knocking. I pull it open, and my words catch in my throat.

Demyan is standing there. "Hi," I say, annoyed but simmering down.

He devilishly smiles, eyeing me up and down, "we need to see you in Nikolaj's office."

"You're a boss. Can't you just tell me here?" I question him as he stands there with his hands in his pockets. The thought of walking back downstairs and dealing with Nikolaj's attitude mentally exhausts me even more.

"Now, Milly," he demands, and I can't help but smirk. He's fucking hot when he orders me around. I'm definitely demented for thinking my captors are sexy.

"Okay! Can I get dressed, or is this a clothesless occasion?" I inquire sarcastically, leaning my shoulder against the door frame and giving a wink.

He eyes me for a second time, licks his lower lip, then says, "clothes, for now, and hurry up," then walks away.

I grab sweatpants and a tee shirt. Barefooted with wet hair, I walk down to Nikolaj's office and knock.

"Enter!" he growls. He's always crabby, especially when I'm around. I've watched him freely talk to everyone, but when I walk in the room, he becomes a quiet asshole with a glaring problem.

I walk in, close the door, and admire the hand-carved bookcases and desk as I walk toward Demyan and him, and say, "you needed to see me, Boss...and Boss."

"SIT!" he barks, motioning for me to sit by Demyan in the chairs in front of his desk.

Nikolaj is at the mini-bar pouring an amber-colored drink into his glass, then walks over to fill Demyan's glass. Never offering me any.

"What is it you need?" I ask hesitantly, watching his every move. His movements are flawless and precise.

He sits at his desk, takes a drink, and proceeds slowly and angrily, "I need you to be a target for the McGriffith mission tomorrow night. We need him alone," he pauses, leans toward his desk, and continues with more anger in his tone, "you will have to seduce him to get him alone. I don't care what you have to do. Just get him somewhere private. We'll take him from there." He leans back in his chair, eyeing Demyan, then drinks the rest of his scotch.

I adjust nervously in my seat. I never take the lead or bait. Hell, I've never directly worked on the bosses' cases before. Usually, I just work on my stuff or help Theo and Daniel with the gadgets.

"This is Aanya's job," I blurt out. I'm not trained to be bait. I'm trained to hunt and kill from the darkest corners of the shadows.

"Aanya's been shot and needs to recover," Demyan says, laying his hand on the armrest of my chair. I look down at this hand, then up at him as I process what he just said.

"Shot?! When? Who?" I ask as the questions keep piling up in my head.

"Damn it, Milly!! We don't have to tell you everything! You are our only option, so you are doing it!" Nikolaj unleashes. Standing, he throws his glass against the wall, smashing it into pieces.

"You are meeting with my team tomorrow morning to get you...." He looks me up and down while I'm sitting in the chair. With a disgusted look says, "...ready for the gala. And for FUCK'S SAKE, take this seriously!" He storms out of the room.

I look at Demyan. "What the hell did I ever do to him? The guy hates me!"

Demyan stands, motions for me to stand, and we walk to the office door. "He doesn't think you should do this job," he clarifies, and I feel his hand lay on the small of my back. It sends tingles down my legs, but it's not enough to distract me from what was just asked of me.

"Oh, so he thinks I'm going to blow it!" I nod and move away from his touch.

"Yes and no. You don't have a certain Je ne sais quoi. You're a hunter, a killer, not bait." He moves his hands to his pockets and steps toward the front door.

"Oh, comforting. So good behind the scenes, but I don't have what it takes to get a man's attention! Got it! Thanks, Demyan! Thanks for that!" I start to walk to the stairs that lead to my room.

"Milly, listen," Demyan says, "get some sleep. Tomorrow you are going to nail this mission. Show him you are the best at everything!" He turns on his heel and walks out the front door. I give him a stank eye until the door is shut, then walk to the stairs. I think of all the ways I could mess this up and how much more Nikolaj will hate me if I blow this, and we don't get the target in our possession.

Starting the shower again, I stand there, letting the water run down my hair and skin, thinking about what they asked.

Because of everything that happened to me in my childhood and the life I chose as a kid, I've never had a boyfriend or dated. I'm a virgin, well, on my terms. I don't count what Skip did to me as losing my virginity.

Am I even capable of seducing a man?

What Daniel told me this evening in the basement makes it sounds like Trevor just takes what he wants, seduced or not. Maybe I'll be lucky tomorrow night.

I finish my shower, get dressed, and then go to Vance's room for some advice, but I see a bag on his bed as I walk into the room.

"Where are you going?" I ask, scowling at the suitcase, then at him.

"Jared needs me for a little bit. Hopefully, it will just be a week. I'll be back before you know it, kiddo. What's up?" He asks as he goes back to packing. Vance was allowed to keep his outside phone when I came here, sparking a small drop of jealousy in me that he could talk to Jared without me.

"Well, now I'm sad you're leaving, and I'm going to make an ass out of myself tomorrow," I grunt and sit on the edge of his bed.

"You are going to do a great job, Milly," he claims, walking back to the bed and packing some clothes into his suitcase. He stops to hold my chin and smiles.

"You know about tomorrow?" I ask.

"Of course! Well, I mean, I just found out. Demyan came here to tell me about Aanya and asked if I thought you could do it, and of course, I know you can," he boosters and flips the suitcase shut, and zips it.

Vance thinks I can do anything, but I'm afraid he might be wrong this time. He knows about my past experiences, so I'm not quite sure where he is getting his optimism.

"Oh. Why didn't you warn me?"

"He went straight to your room after leaving here, and Jared called right as he left. I figured you could handle the conversation on your own." He winked at me and set his suitcase on the floor.

"Okay, well, if you think I got this handled, then I must be able to!" I sarcastically laugh, get up, and turn to walk out and back to my room.

"Milly, you can do this!" he cheers. I smile at him, close the door, and head back to my room.

I lay in bed tossing and turning, thinking about how it's been 12 years since I came into this life and three months of imprisonment at Nikolaj and Demyan's compound.

I'm good at hunting people, hurting bad people, protecting good people, and being a ghost. Seducing people or even just dancing? Not on my list of things I can do.

We danced in the living room for Mary and Jared's wedding anniversary, and Rosco said I looked like a fish flopping out of water.

I'm 5'7", have a curvy and athletic build, long auburn hair, fair-skinned, and brown eyes, and nothing special about my looks. I just use minimal makeup, and my hair is always in a messy bun or messy ponytail. I don't draw attention like other women.

I'm generic and not McGriffith's type.

I can't compete with Aanya. She's 5'9", has legs for days, cinched waist, long perfect brown hair, big brown eyes, and her Indian accent just purrs from her lips. She always looks like a supermodel, even in sweatpants, a tee shirt, and a ponytail. She's the kind of girl that makes other girls question their sexuality.

Then it finally sinks in; Nikolaj thinks I'm too basic. He knows that no matter how much lipstick I put on, I won't get McGriffith's attention, and the mission will be a failure. He knows he is relying on someone who cannot deliver results. This is going to give him another reason to hate me. My heart sinks, and tears well up in my eyes.

I'm sure he would rather Aanya do this assignment because I would rather Aanya do this assignment, but we're both shit out of luck.

The only reason the bosses picked me to do this job is that Aanya and I are the only two women who do this kind of work for the bosses.

I need to focus on how to get McGriffith to notice me.

Think Milly!

I'm seriously fucked, and not in a good way.

FUCK!

Past Milly
12-years-old

Chapter 8

"Everyone, meet Milly!"

They all turned toward me, my skin felt like fire, and the absolute intensity of their eyes on me made me wish I could magically have sunk into the floor.

The woman gave a furrowed brow glance at the men. "You all act as if you've never seen a child up close!" She barked, lifted her hand, and stated, "I'm Grace. It is so nice to meet you."

She smiled, shook my hand then turned her attention to Mary on the other side of the island. "What's cooking, Mar?"

All the men just said "hi" from a distance, and after a few awkward seconds, they turned back to Jared to talk.

I sat on the stool beside the island alone, watching all this playing out in front of me.

Sadly, I can't remember having family over when my dad was alive. I know we did, but the memory is long gone.

Mary and Grace were chatting in the kitchen when the heavier guy walked to the stove, looking at everything that was cooking.

"Is it to your standards, Vance?" Mary laughed.

"Smells great," he said, then planted a kiss on Mary's cheek.

"It should. I had the best teacher in the world," she bantered.

"I wouldn't say I'm the best, but good, yes!" He laughed.

"Hey, kiddo, I'm Vance." I turned to the island to see him standing at the sink, washing some green plants.

"Hi. What is that?" I asked, staring at the plant, trying not to be nervous around all these people.

"Parsley. For the sauce," he said while nudging his head in the direction of the stove. "Mama always used fresh ingredients. So, I always use fresh ingredients." He reached down into the cabinet on the island and brought up a cutting board and knife.

"I'm Jared and Frank's oldest brother," he said while cutting the parsley.

"Frank?" I asked since none of the men had introduced themselves to me.

"The goofy-looking guy by Jared," he pointed with the knife. I turned slightly and saw the goofy-looking guy looking at us.

"Hey, just because I got my looks from mom's side doesn't make me goofy-looking," Frank said.

"Yes, it does!" Jared laughs while nudging him on the shoulder and messing with his hair. "Grace, how did you fall for a weirdo like Frank?!" Jared yelled out.

Without hesitation, Mary answered, "the same way I fell for your goofy-looking ass, Jared!!" Everyone laughed, and Jared nodded his head, glaring at his wife.

I turned to Vance, putting the parsley in the boiling sauce on the stove. He returned to the island, sat on the stool beside me, and cracked open a beer.

"Mary has told me about you, or at least the details she knows," he said while adjusting his leg and wiping some lint off it. "So, Milly, tell me your story, or at least what you want to tell me."

I looked at him and wondered if I told him the truth, would he run? Will they kick me out? Would there be consequences for telling my horrible truth?

"Or not, Milly. I will never say you have to do something," Vance said, leaning down toward me, "but if you ever want to talk, I'm always here for you. You are important to Mary and Jared. We are a family here, and if you accept all of us, we can be your family, too."

I smiled at him, then looked around the room at all the people. "Will I be safe?" I asked as I leaned in and whispered to Vance.

A confused look crossed his face, then he said, "of course, Milly, you are safe. We are your family now and always. Bonus, I'll teach you how to cook, just like I did my brothers and their wives." He chuckled, looking at Grace, who turned around and smiled at him, then glared after she heard his comment.

"I could cook before I meant you, Vance!" She said as her face distorted with a cringe.

"Making ramen noodles is not cooking!!" Vance said, shaking his head.

"Shots fired!" Frank yelled out from the back and made a whistling grenade sound. The room erupted in laughter, and I felt a smile form on my face.

I looked up at Vance as he was laughing at the situation, and I realized he reminded me of my dad. He was kind, caring, and funny. Everything my dad was, or at least what I think I can remember of my dad.

The placemats were set, and the food was arranged in the middle of the table. Mary and Jared each took a seat at the ends of the table. I sat on Mary's right, Grace was on Mary's left, Vance sat to my right, Frank sat to Grace's left, and two men I hadn't talked to yet sat on the last two open chairs on either side of the table.

Vance nudged me, "these two goofballs are Adio and Rosco." They both looked at me and then nodded their heads.

"I'm Frank." The man by Grace said with a smile. "Vance and Jared's baby brother and Grace's husband."

"Hi," I said quietly. I looked around the table, and Vance said, "One weirdly happy family."

We ate salad, pasta, and bread. It was so good. Vance started to tell me about his time growing up with his Italian family. His Mama, Nonna, and Bisnonna were always cooking, and they never let the men in the kitchen, except Vance. He learned all the good stuff, he called it, from the women in his childhood.

He talked about his wife, Evelyn. She died 10 years ago from cancer. They had three kids. Two boys, all grown now with wives of their own, but no grandkids. He told me about their jobs and lifestyles. Sadly, he told me his daughter died at 15, but he didn't go into detail about her.

I asked Vance, "where is everyone from?"

"Frank, Jerad, and I are from New Jersey. Our Bis BisNonna and Bis BisNonnio immigrated to Philadelphia in 1886. Later moved to South Jersey, where all our family has been since. Grace and Frank are married-no kids. Mary and Jared are married- no kids- but you know that already."

He smiled and pointed to Rosco. "Rosco is from Jersey."

"Oh, like you!" I said.

"No Jersey, the largest of the Channel Islands, between England and France," he replied.

"Oh. I guess I have a lot to learn." I smiled and looked down at my lap.

"The trick to learning is wanting to learn," Vance nudged me.

"No one wants to learn in school, Vance," I said with a chuckle.

"True, but you have to learn for the life you want, and that's why you should want to learn." He went all nerdy on me when I thought I'd like him.

"Okay, what about Adio?" I asked.

"Adio is from Jamaica. Montego Bay, to be exact."

I asked, "how did everyone become a part of this family?" The table got eerily quiet.

Mary answered, "well, Milly, we work together." I nodded, content with that answer.

"Some are better at working than others!" Adio joked while pointing to Rosco.

"Bullshit! You couldn't hit a fly on the wall with a car!" Rosco snapped.

Grace yelled out, "We all know women do it better!"

The room ignited an uproar of competition of who did what better. Everyone was yelling over everyone else.

Vance finally got everyone to calm down and looked at me as he shook his head with a grin.

Rosco blurted out, "when do we start training the kid?" Dead silence again. My stomach dropped, and I felt like I was in trouble.

"She has the best team for training," Frank said.

Grace said, "I don't want to encourage anything, but it never is too soon to start training Mary."

"I know," Mary replied to Grace.

"Don't worry. I'll be by your side every step of the way," Vance said in my ear as he put his arm on the back of my chair.

Jared says, "of course, we should start training her! Milly, do you know any languages besides English?" Jared asked.

"No," I answered and slid down my chair a bit.

"Grace knows more than anyone here, so she will teach you languages," Frank added.

I looked at Mary for approval.

She said slowly and quietly, "Milly, I hoped you would have a normal childhood from here on out, but if this is what you want, then we will start training."

She adjusted her position and said, "you will need to learn languages, fighting, self-defense, technology, weapons, disguises, and all the things the dark world requires of you."

Her voice cracked, and she paused for a second. When she composed herself, she continued, "in time, you will learn how to kill people. Are you ready for that?"

My face must have given away my overwhelming fear.

Vance leaned toward me a bit, "you okay, kiddo? You can wait or not do it at all. Your choice."

Was I okay? I didn't know.

Was she serious? Milly, focus! Everyone is staring at you.

"I'm okay," I whispered.

"Unfortunately, what we do is not a pretty business," she leaned in and grabbed my hands in hers. "We are the judge, jury, and executioner."

Grace joined in, "saving those who don't have the power to save themselves is the reward in this business. Nothing better than telling the victims they don't have to be afraid anymore. We don't stop. We don't accept defeat. We'll hunt the world. We never lose, Milly."

Vance said, "that's why we are family. We have each other's back and fight together."

I was ready not to be the victim anymore and to help others. "When do we start training?" I asked.

"Tomorrow," Vance said.

I looked around the room at all the people, my new family.

I barely remembered my family before Dad died. I was happy back then, or maybe it was a dream. Perhaps I was never a happy child, or maybe it was a faded memory.

Either way, I wanted the happiness I felt that night, and I'd do whatever I had to.

Present Milly

Chapter 9

I DON'T SLEEP AND probably look worse than I ever have. I walk out of my room as ready for the day as possible.

When I reach the main level, I see a group of people standing in the foyer. Tons of cases and people bringing clothes racks into the hall.

WHAT THE FUCK IS GOING ON?

Gus and Sven bring in more containers as everyone else is working on bringing them into the meeting room.

Theo walks up behind me and nudges my shoulder, "well, Cinderella, are you ready for your dress-up day?"

"Fuck yourself, Theo!" I snarl jokingly at him, not taking my eyes off the commotion.

"Good Luck," he laughs, walks toward the basement stairs, and turns back to me to make a sarcastic face and waves. I mouth the words *fuck you* to him before he turns to walk down the stairs.

I see Nikolaj standing at his office door, arms crossed over his chest, wide stance, and glaring at me. He motions slightly with his finger for me to come to him.

I lift my chin, take a deep breath, and walk over.

What could this asshole possibly want already?

He looks at me from head to toe as I walk over to him. Judgy fucker!

Leaning close to my face, he grabs my chin and growls, "you do as you are told, exactly how you are told to. Don't fuck this up!" Letting go of me with force, he walks into the meeting room.

I follow close behind, like the excellent prisoner I am.

He speaks Russian to the people there, unaware I know what he is saying. He tells them to make me desirable at whatever cost. So, he thinks I'm undesirable. Well, fuck him.

I reveal my secret by replying in Russian, "udachi v prevrashchenii etogo utenka v lebedya!" I glare at the back of Nikolaj's head, wanting to rip his hair out.

He whips around, grabs my shoulders with a squeeze, leans into my face, his long curly hair falling to his temples, and gritting his teeth. "Is this a joke to you? Your self-pity is not welcome here! McGriffith's attention requires certain standards, so take this seriously!"

I'm not sure why but my body enjoys his aggressiveness, his breath on my face, and the smell of his cologne.

How can I be so turned on by someone I hate so much?!

He leans back up, straightens his suit jacket, and brushes past me as he walks out of the meeting room, into his office, and slams the door shut.

I look at all the people in the room, staring at me, as I'm covered in embarrassment and dread.

Demyan walks over as tears start pooling in my eyes.

"He's fun," I say as I choke back my emotions and try to cover my shame with humor.

"Milly, there are many things you don't understand about Niko. Just focus on becoming a woman McGriffith would pursue," he smiles, pats my arm, and walks out of the room.

I huff out a breath and head over to the crew who intend to make me perfect.

I'm sitting in the chair, watching two people running around me with hair color swatches and makeup palettes.

Another person took my measurements and is going through rack after rack of clothes looking for a dress for tonight.

Straight in front of me is my etiquette coach, Tilda. She's teaching me everything: dinnerware, manners, walking, talking, carrying myself, AND flirting.

I'm fucking terrible. I am out of my comfort zone, and it shows. This is all new to me. I've never had to go to this extreme to hunt someone before.

After a few hours of chaos, my hair is done. I look in the temporary mirror they placed on the wall. My auburn hair has highlights around the face, cut in layers, but still long. They curled it and pinned one side away from my ear with a diamond clip.

Ty, the makeup artist, is working on me now. Plucking, smearing, blotting, blending color after color, brush after brush.

How long is it going to take me to wash all this off?

OH MY GOD! He just glued lashes to my eyes! I can't quit blinking at the feeling of something glued to my lashes.

He snaps, "stop blinking!!! You'll get used to them! Just give it a minute!"

They all laugh as my embarrassed self slouches in my chair. Fuck this sucks!

The next up to make fun of me was the clothing lady, Amiee.

She measures me again, makes a bunch of faces, and says, "I don't think I have anything that will fit you properly. I wish I knew your measurements beforehand; I could have made you bigger clothes."

WOW! That was fucking brutal.

Ty steps up to my side, "Amiee, you're such a bitch! Look at these curves!! This girl is sexy. Ty's got you, baby!" He pats my shoulder for reassurance, looks me up and down, stares for a second, then swishes his hips to the clothes racks.

He throws clothes off the racks, and Amiee looks distraught at the mess, but he doesn't care. He brings me a few dresses to try on, but will they fit?

I can't handle being embarrassed any more than I already am.

Dove helps me get my dress on so I don't ruin my hair.

NOTHING WORKS!! If it's not the fit, they disapprove of the tattoos and scars on me. This is a lost cause.

Then, he comes over with a deep wine-colored wrap-style satin dress, a small collar, long sleeves, slit all the way up the left side to the panty line, the neckline drops down into a *v*, and miniature train on the back.

"Try this, Milly." He looks confident in his choice, making me more nervous. Finally, it's on, Dove nods in approval, and I turn to the group.

A look of satisfaction crosses their faces.

"Beautiful!" Tilda says.

I slip on a pair of golden strap heels that wrap up my calves. Amiee hands me a small golden clutch, and they slide on some bracelets, a necklace, and earrings. I'm ready!

Past Milly
12-years-old
Chapter 10

Day one of my training.

Everyone was going over what they did and what they were going to teach me, but I couldn't keep up with what they were saying. It all mingled together and became a blur. Complete information overload.

"Breathe, kiddo. Training takes years! You don't need to know everything right now," Vance told me.

He was right! Training did take years!

The first year was learning languages with Grace and fighting skills with Adio and Rosco.

We trained from 4 am to 6 pm. 4-10 fighting, 10-11:30 shower and lunch, 11:30-6 languages, and Mary homeschooled me (math, science, and history) during meals and from 6-8. By 8, I was dead and in bed.

This was my schedule every day, over and over and over, for an entire year of my life. It was a lot for a 12-year-old to handle, but it was better than what I was going through before I moved in with those people.

Grace was patient when teaching me. She knew so many languages, but she said it wasn't overnight. Twenty-three languages! That's what she knew, and my goal was to learn how to read, write, and speak each language. She said learning the accents is essential because no one doubts your story with the correct pronunciation. She purposely mixed different languages to test me, confuse people, or when she was mad. Especially when she was mad at Frank. He would call her his spitfire Latino mama.

Adio and Rosco were teaching me fighting skills. Boxing, Wrestling, kickboxing, MMA, we worked on martial arts- Judo, Karate, Muay Thai, Jiu Jitsu, and military combat-Krav Maja- or as Rosco put it, Kick-Ass arts.

Rosco said it takes time to master everything and to always get back up and try again. Never accept defeat.

By the end of year one, Grace would quiz my language skills while I trained to fight to make sure I could handle the pressure of using the correct accents and language in intense situations. I never complained out loud about the pressure they put on me.

Adio and Rosco pushed me some days, but I never lost my composer.

They taught me that a calm head stays focused.

I never tried to show emotion because Adio said leading with emotions was why mistakes were made.

They taught me how to use various weapons, from swords, hands, nunchucks, throwing stars, knives, and guns. Anything they could think to use, we used. The poor trees around the property took beating after beating, slash and slash, and stab and stab.

Mary's only rule was that I was not to get hurt.

Well, I did get hurt A LOT!

Adio and Rosco were great teachers but didn't know how to do it gently, just in full force. I had the wind knocked out of me so many times. It was better to know how it feels to be hit in training, so I could become aware of how to react in a real fight.

Their best advice was just don't get hit. OBVIOUSLY!!

Present Milly

Chapter 11

I'M STILL IN THE meeting room finishing up some etiquette things with Tilda when Daniel and Theo walk in to put trackers on me. We always did this with Aanya, so I knew the drill.

"Wow, you look gorgeous!" Theo exclaims in a goofy tone with a wink while he sets the gear down on the table beside me.

"Just get this over with," I grumble with an eye roll.

"Apparently, you don't like your look," Theo points out. He's right. This whole day has been exhausting, and I haven't even started the mission yet. I feel entirely out of my comfort zone.

"This isn't me," I mumble. I don't want to discredit all this team's hard work into my appearance today, but I'm not a glamor girl.

Daniel starts to place a tracker and whispers, "you do look great, but I think you always do," flashing a half smile.

After everything is set on me, Theo confirms, "you are trackable, but just remember you won't have any communication or audio,"

"Okay, let's get this over with," I say with a heavy breath. I grab my clutch off the table, take one more look at myself in the mirror, and nod in approval. It might not be me, but I will embrace the look for tonight.

Gus stands by the door waiting for me to be done getting pampered. He is dressed in his usual black suit, white button-up, and black tie. I walk toward him, and he gestures to the door saying, "your chariot awaits milady!"

"Don't be a dork," I cringe, making him laugh. He has one arm stretched out straight through the threshold and the other behind the small of his back and waits for me to walk out the meeting room door before he follows. As I walk, my dress flows over my lower body, and the slit shows my entire leg with every left step.

"Didn't you like your dress-up day, Cinderella?" He jokes, catching up to my strides and getting a kick out of my misery. I snap a look that could set him on fire, but he laughs harder and shakes his head.

We walk straight toward the front door, bantering with each other, when Demyan yells, "you clean up nice, M!"

The tone of his voice sends chills down my spine. I look over my shoulder and notice how handsome he looks in his black tux, a single-breasted 5-button vest, white shirt with black buttons, black bowtie, and black leather double monk-strap dress shoes.

Then I look over to see Nikolaj standing next to him, and I feel a gasp in my throat. *Holy fuck*! He looks sexy in his black tux, double-breasted 6-button vest, a black button-up, and black tie with a clip and collar chain. He seems more fuckable than he usually does.

Maybe a tag team should be how I lose my virginity.

GODDAMN IT, MILLY! I think as I squeeze my eyes shut for a brief second before pulling them off my bosses and turning back to catch up to Gus.

Making it outside, Gus holds his arm out for me while we walk down the stairs.

Sven holds the door open on Demyan's Mercedes Benz GLC 43 Sedan., and Gus guides me as I start to sit in the backseat, but then Tilda and Amiee run over in a panic about wrinkling the dress. Gus and Sven can barely hold back their laughter while I watch, confused, as the two women fluff and fold my dress as I slide into the car.

Waiting for the door to close, I run my hands over the dress to feel the smooth fabric when the light from the house is blocked. I look up to see Nikolaj, looking godly, kneeling in the car's opening.

What does he want?

Is he riding with me?

He leans into the car, scanning me from head to toe when his intoxicating scent hits my senses, and I gasp in a breath.

Quickly, I look away as my core starts to tingle from his presence so close to mine. His hand curls around my jawline, forcing my face back toward him, and we lock eyes. His skin is warm, his grip gentle but demanding, and my pussy rebels as I feel my wetness pooling.

"What?" I choke out in a whisper, staring into his deep brown eyes. He licks his lower lip pulling it between his teeth, making me wonder if he knows what my body is doing because of him.

"We're going to be late," I whisper nervously.

Curling his fingers under my jaw, he slides his thumb over my chin, and pulls my mouth open slightly. He stares at my mouth. I study his facial features, then he looks into my eyes. My body reacts even more, and goosebumps cover my arms. He releases my face and stands as my gaze follows him, then shuts the door, leaving me staring at him through the window with a soaked pussy.

Biting my lower lip, I can still feel his touch, which makes me want more.

What the fuck was that? I think to myself.

The car drives away from the house, and I try to get my head in the game. Taking a deep breath, I focus on the task at hand. Getting McGriffith to notice me. Something tells me the crew did their magic, or why else would Nikolaj come to the car and touch my face with wanting eyes?

"Nervous, Milly?" Sven asks, looking at me through the rearview mirror.

"No," I lie and turn my gaze to the window to my right.

"Well, you look nervous," Gus jokes as he turns his head around the side of the front passenger seat.

"Thanks, Gus. Makes me feel all warm and fuzzy knowing I look nervous," I laugh and rest my head back. "I just hope McGriffith takes the bait," I wishfully say.

"You are the bait, Milly," Gus points out as he turns to face the front again.

"No shit!" I sarcastically exclaim, turning my head to look out the window.

"You'll do great," Sven tries to reassure me, then says, "he will notice you. Even the bosses noticed you." I give him a sideways look and scowl.

We reach the gala. All the people there are dressed like royalty. Cars are all over the place. Nausea hits me. I don't do *people* things without Vance, and now I'm going in alone to be bait for some douche fuck that I know nothing about.

"You've got this, Milly," Gus cheers, turning toward me from the front passenger seat.

Sven opens my door, then tells me not to puke as he helps me out of the car.

I look around, taking the scene in while discreetly fixing my dress. Then, I noticed Nikolaj's G-Wagon parked right behind us. As Demyan and Nikolaj get out, they are instantly swarmed by beautiful women, touching them, giggling, and throwing themselves at my bosses. Nikolaj hands the valet his keys and then talks to the women.

Why am I jealous about this?

Shaking it off, I start walking up the stairs to the entrance of the building.

I spot a couple of men looking at me as I walk past them, which boosts my confidence.

I walk into the hotel, where I'm directed to the doors that lead to the gala. Taking a deep breath, I decide that I am going into this room like I own the place. Confidence!!

I walk through the doors, grab a glass of champagne from the server, and look around as I glide through the room. People are dancing, drinking, gambling, and talking. I pace slowly around the room like a tourist, taking in all the event's glory. The crystal chandeliers, the tables with tall floral arrangements, ice sculptures, musicians, the smell of food, and a million and one different perfumes and colognes.

I feel a brush on my lower back and a breeze runs across my shoulder blades.

I expected it would be Sven or Gus, but the man who stepped to my side was more petite, with salt and pepper hair, glasses, butt chin, and pencil-thin lips. Trevor McGriffith!!

"Beautiful, isn't it? Almost heavenly," he coos with a smile, then turns toward me.

"Stunning," I reply with a smirk, keeping eye contact with him. I study his features and stature. Sizing him up if I need to defend myself.

He shifts his weight, adjusts his glasses, looks down at the floor, and my gaze follows his movements. He's trying to act shy. Probably to give me the illusion he is harmless, but I know better. I may not know the details of his crimes, but I know he is not harmless.

"What's your name?" he asks, drawing his attention back to me.

"Angelica," I answer with a slight accent I learned from Grace but inspired by Rosco.

"Where are you from, Angelica?" he inquires, stepping a tad closer, trying to sensualize his gaze.

I reply, "Jersey. The Channel Islands."

Daniel told me Trevor likes powerful women. Confident women. Women who don't bullshit. He acts shy until he gets them trapped, then he does anything imaginable to make them feel worthless, used, and beneath him. Sometimes, he will have other men hiding in his room to help abuse these women.

Daniel didn't disclose the details of what he did to the women. I didn't have time to read the file Daniel left me, but I'm assuming it's a small dick complex. Either way, I need to act like the woman he would be looking for. I take control of the situation and brush my free fingers on his hand, resting on the railing overlooking the dance floor.

"What's your name?" I ask him, even though I already know.

"Trevor," he nods and pushes his glasses up his nose. He avoids eye contact with me for long periods of time. A tactic to show submission. He's trying to get me to trust him.

"Where are you from, Trevor?" I ask, leaning in a little.

He stutters and chuckles, "Chicago."

I smirk, look down, then back up at him to comment, "Chicago is a very nice city!"

"You've been there?"

"A few times," I explained. Finishing my champagne, I tip my glass at him and give him a raised eyebrow and a wink to signal I want another. He jumps right on it and catches the attention of the server walking by.

I turn to scan the room for Demyan, Gus, Sven, or even Nikolaj, but no one's in sight. They must be ready and waiting for me to bring him out. They fucking better be anyway! I turn my attention to the small man standing next to me again. He hands me my glass, and I down it in one pull. His eyes get wide at the act, but when my eyes snap back to him, I can see a faint evil in his gaze. Time to do what I'm here for. Time to get Trevor out of sight and into the hands of my bosses. I take a step closer to him, my right leg touches his body, and I seductively ask him if he wants to get out of there as I run my hand around his waist.

"Yeah, I have a suite upstairs," he replies, sounding like a giddy schoolboy.

"Lead the way," I commanded, grabbing his hand to follow him to the back entrance of the gala room. We get to the hallway, the doors shut behind us, and the party sounds are now muffled to us. Trevor leads us down the hall, glancing back at me continuously until we reach the elevators. He impatiently pushes the button to go up.

Why isn't anyone here to catch this asshole?

Do I really have to go upstairs with him?

The doors slide open, and for a split second, I contemplate beating the shit out of him and waiting for the bosses to catch up to us. Too late, Trevor pulls me into the elevator and the doors shut.

My heart starts to race as he comes toward me, grabbing my waist and pushing me against the wall. His tiny body pressed against mine. He slams his mouth into mine and kisses me, almost as if he's trying to lick my face off.

I need to keep his attention long enough for the bosses, wherever the fuck they are, to catch up. So, I allow him to continue. He moves his tongue across my lips, teeth, and into my mouth. His tongue tastes like fish, and his teeth hit against mine as he roughly kisses me. I feel gross.

I unbutton his coat and loosen his bowtie as he kisses my neck. His hand moves up my thigh, curling around to grab my ass cheek under my dress, and I hear fabric tear.

This fucker just ripped my dress!

FINALLY, the doors open. Trevor pulls away, grabs my hand, and practically runs to his room while dragging me with him. He pulls out the key card, winks at me with a shit grin, and taps the lock.

I can't even fake sexy with him anymore. I'm disgusted. I'm pissed that the bosses weren't there when the elevator doors opened. I'm panicking internally because I refuse to let this fucker touch me anymore.

He walks in first and holds the door open for me. I still don't see the bosses, Sven or Gus, down either direction of the hallway. The tracker I'm wearing better fucking work, but just in case, I discreetly throw my clutch against the outside wall by his door, then I walk in slowly and cautiously.

I scan the room. I don't see any signs of someone else in the room with us, not even the men that are supposed to grab Trevor.

Did I miss something?

Where is everyone?

I've never been bait when hunting someone, and I've never been alone with the one we are chasing.

What if the bosses don't find me?

Survival kicks in, I can hear my heart pounding in my ears, and my throat goes dry. I make my move.

I move to Trevor, blocking the door open with part of my body. I run my hands up his arms to the buttons of his shirt, then rip it open. Buttons fly everywhere. I slowly move my hands up his exposed chest to his neck. He moans slightly, never breaking eye contact. My hands touch the bare skin of his neck and wrap around it.

"Do you like to be choked, Trevor?" I whisper sensually against his lips as I tighten my grip around his neck.

Before he can answer, I pull him close to knee him in the balls. He tries to push me away, but my grip stays tight around his neck. He hits at anything he can; my arms, face, torso, and kicks at my legs. I dig my fingers deeper into his skin to keep my grip tight.

I kick his knee back, hyper-extending it, and he grunts. I can see his movements slow as he starts to go unconscious. I don't want him dead, but I want him to pass out.

I hear something hit the door beside me, then Trevor is ripped from me with a jerk, and I see him slammed to the floor, and a huge body lands on top of him, pinning him to the floor. It takes a second to realize it's Nikolaj.

I want to yell at him for taking so fucking long to find me, but I stand down as relief covers me. I lean against the door to catch my breath and watch Nikolaj restrain Trevor.

Trevor groans, "what the fuck, you stupid whore!?!" Barely composing himself, he continues, "you're fucking crazy!" His eyes widen when he realizes I'm standing at the door and not the one on top of him. Nikolaj punches his face, then sits up on his heels when Trevor stops fighting him. Trevor lets out a cough while rubbing his neck and face.

Nikolaj looks at me, jumps up, charges me, grabs my arm, and gets my attention off Trevor. He doesn't say a word, but the look he is giving me is full of concern. I nod to let him know I am okay. He turns toward Trevor just as he sits up on the floor.

Trevor sees us, "look, man, it was the whore's idea to come up here! I'll pay whatever she costs." He hoists himself up to the seating position and chuckles, "but I want my time with her. I'm going to fuck the attitude right out of her."

Nikolaj grabs Trevor by the neck, hoisting him up from the floor. He is no match for Nikolaj's towering height and overall size. Trevor fights to be put down but to no avail.

Nikolaj punches him in the gut, then growls in Trevor's face, "she's not a whore. She's mine!" Then drops him to the ground with a thud and kicks him in the face. Trevor falls back, unconscious.

I hear running in the hallway, and as I turn to see what it is, Demyan, Sven, and Gus come running into the room. They assess the situation.

"Take him to the warehouse!" Demyan orders, kicking Trevor in the ribs.

I stay at the door, watching the men pull Trevor from the ground and drag his unconscious body out of the room.

Nikolaj stops by me and asks, "are you okay?" Scanning my face and body, I'm assuming he is looking for wounds.

"Yes," I answered with a shaky voice. My whole body is starting to shake uncontrollably. I've never had this reaction before, but I've never done a mission like this.

After his evaluation, he steps closer to me and says, "you shouldn't have left the gala!" His big strong hands gently rub down the sides of my face and rest, cupping under my jawline as they tip my head toward him. He looks different right now. Caring.

"You told me to do whatever I had to to get him alone," I whisper, "and don't fuck up!"

He growls as his jaw ticks, tipping his head up toward the ceiling, then back down, pushing his forehead to mine. This is not the first time he's forced his forehead into mine, but this is the first time it's done gently and with care.

"We weren't ready for you to leave," he explains, then pulls his head back to look into my eyes.

"I don't have an earpiece, remember?" I shrug, looking up at him. "Plus, you were distracted by the car with all the women trying to get to you," I sadly joke to try to ease the situation.

He looks at me with confusion in his eyes. "Distracted? Never from you," then clenches his jaw and asks, "did he touch you?"

"Yes," I reply as an obvious point. "But that was the job, right?" I ask, trying to brush off the memory, but my head starts to race through the night's events. It starts to sink in that they weren't ready. I walked out of the gala with a serial rapist, and the men had no idea what was happening. They did lose me for a bit.

What if they didn't find me?

What would have happened to me?

My anxiety starts to rise, and I feel a flood of emotions consuming me. Without a moment's thought, I find myself wrapping my arms around his waist and laying my head on his chest to hug him.

I feel him tense up. This is wrong. I shouldn't be hugging him. I instantly want to pull away, but my body won't let me. I need to know I'm safe. I need to calm the memories that are starting to haunt me.

Then I feel him wrap his arms around my body and squeeze lightly.

I take a deep sigh of relief and melt into him. I don't care how much this man and I hate each other; I need him to just hold me right now.

"Let's go home!" he commands gently against the top of my head while stroking my hair.

Past Milly
13-years-old

Chapter 12

A YEAR LATER.

Vance exclaimed, "kiddo-it's been exactly one year today since we met. So, I have declared this your Rebirthday." He laughed as he put a party hat on my head, adjusted the strap under my chin, and nudged my arm.

"What? What is a Rebirthday?" I asked with a confused look as I fiddled with the uncomfortable strap of the hat.

"The day your new life started and when we all officially became part of your life," he answered as he reached to hug me.

Everyone yelled out, in a not-so-unison way, "Happy Rebirthday, Milly!" They all brought out their gifts from under their chairs. How did I not see gifts under their chairs when I walked into the dining room?

"Oh, Thank you!! But I don't need gifts. I have everything I could ever want here at this table," I choked out, holding back tears.

The past 12 months had been the best I had ever had. Well, that I could remember. The memories of my father were fading into a black abyss in my head. Making me question if some of the things I remembered really happened or if they were part of the fake life I told my grandma.

Adio chimed in, "today is really for all of us. We are celebrating our greatest adventure. You! Enjoy your Rebirthday, Mouse."

Adio and Rosco called me *Mouse* because I was quiet and sneaky when fighting. Also, I was good at hiding. I could crawl into some of the smallest spots, and they would always walk by, not noticing me.

During dinner, I stayed silent and listened to everything, taking it all in. Always know your surroundings-Rosco 101-listen to everything and everyone—even the ones you trust. Rosco had told me story after story of people turning on him and how he always has his guard up with everyone. Trust issues.

The talk turned to arguing about who did what better, so I decided it was time for me to leave. I stood, cleared my dishes, and headed to the kitchen. I heard someone follow me, and when I looked back, I saw Frank. I've talked to Frank only a few times since I met him. He was always busy looking into people and hunting predators. Evil never took a break.

"I remember when Vance and Jared started doing this business," he started to explain, and I looked back at him. "They both had military training. Vance was a weapons specialist. He was a sniper in the Marines. Jared was Special Ops. They were fearless and deadly," Frank said and laughed, shook his head, and started to wash dishes.

He handed me the towel and ordered, "you dry and put away." I nodded and took the towel from his hand.

He continued, "they were real-life vigilantes, and I knew I would join them one day. I didn't want their long military careers, though. I wanted to be as good as they were, just not put in the time they did."

He looked at me, winked, and inquired, "sound familiar?" He handed me another dish, and Mary brought more dishes from the table.

After she walked out of the kitchen, Frank continued, "they started training me when I was 17. I fought them all the way, too. Eventually, I saw results from all my hard work, which drove me to work even harder. It took years, Milly. To be honest, you never stop training. You have to keep up with everything you learned so you don't get rusty. You must keep learning new things to be a step ahead of everyone. It's frustrating some days but always worth it. The most important lesson I have learned in all my years doing this is patience." I turned to put the dishes in the cabinets and the silverware in the drawer, all while I hung on every word Frank said.

He handed me the last plate when I asked, "how did you all meet Grace, Mary, Adio, and Rosco?" I walked to the cabinet, put the dish away, and walked back to the island to hear the story.

He leaned his hip to the counter and explained, "Mary was Special Ops. Grace was a Marine. We acquired Adio and Rosco through other military correspondence Vance and Jared have."

Frank told me more details about each person. Grace was older than him. She was just starting the Marines when Jared retired. They didn't know each other then, but after Grace became a considerable asset in foreign affairs, Jared snatched her up.

Frank and Grace worked together for three years before dating; the rest was history. Jared and Mary dated from when Vance was in the Marines. Mary was older than Jared, too.

"What happened to Vance's daughter?" I asked. Frank stopped, looked into the dining room from the island, and stepped closer to me.

"Vance doesn't like to talk about it, so I'm surprised he told you he had a daughter." He took a deep breath and whispered, "her name was Rachel. She was 13 when she was murdered 18 years ago. That's when Vance started doing this business. He was looking for the piece of shit that killed his daughter. When Jared found out what Vance was doing, he wanted in. They searched for weeks and found the guy, a child rapist just out of prison, but no one knew he was staying in Vance's neighborhood. They captured him, took him to an abandoned building, tortured him, then killed him. They decided that was their purpose. To ensure no one's daughter or son would be hurt by assholes who couldn't control themselves. Rachel was four years younger than me."

I made a face because why was he so much younger than his brothers?

He rolled his eyes as if he knew what I was thinking, "I'm the oops baby," he laughed, then explained, "my parents were done after Jared, but then I came along. I joined Vance and Jared right after they killed that guy. Our parents never suspected anything. They were proud of their military sons. I was a tech nerd, building gadgets and computer smart. It didn't take long for our parents to know I would be just as great as my brothers." He moved from the sink to the other side of the island, then stopped to say, "I taught Jared and Vance computers, so I did teach them stuff, too." He smiled, patted the top of the island, and said, "good job with dishes, kid."

He turned to walk back into the dining room with everyone else when I blurted out, "How old are all of you?"

He stopped, looked over his left shoulder, and said, "too old some days."

Nikolaj

Chapter 13

PULLING AWAY FROM HER embrace, I grab her hand, leading her out of the room.

She bends down to grab her clutch, and I pull her close as she stands back up. Her eyes never leave the ground as we walk down the hallway to the elevators.

"Are you okay, Milly?" I ask, trying to be gentle enough not to scare her while fighting the urge to want to wrap her in my arms and carry her. "Did he hurt you?"

"No," she says so quietly that if she hadn't slightly shaken her head, I would never have known what she said.

Shock must be setting in.

We reach the elevators. Once the doors close, Milly gently pulls her hand away, which I allow, since she can't get hurt in here with just the two of us.

"Good thinking with your clutch. Very clever," I explained to her. She just nods as she stares at the golden mirror doors.

I can't keep my attention on her for long. It's just her and me here since Demyan and our men are headed to the warehouse with Trevor.

I must stay alert if someone else tries to get on our elevator.

McGriffith is a middleman to us. He has always been a shady piece of shit, but he got us top dollar on our merchandise, so we kept him around. Four days ago, a shipment of ours went missing. We tracked it to McGriffith. He's not stupid, and he knew we were looking for him. He went into hiding, or so we thought. We were told he was expected to be at the gala tonight, and we knew that was our chance.

Daniel told us Trevor was a serial rapist, so we knew we had to lure him in. The plan was to use Aanya for bait, but that quickly changed when she was shot earlier last night, working another case for us.

I focus as the elevator nears the lobby floor. Trevor always has his men nearby, and I'm sure they knew he was going upstairs with her, and in his long absence, they are bound to go looking for him. This means if they spot her with me and not him, they will figure out we have him and attack us.

I won't risk losing her again.

When the doors open, I grab her hand and hold it tight. I see in my peripheral vision that she is looking up at me, but I keep my eyes forward, looking out for trouble.

I quickly guide her through the crowd, stiffening my arm to my torso, keeping her close to me. My 6'6" height towers over everyone as I charge through the crowd. Every person here knows of me and my rather unorthodox approaches to resistance, so most people step out of our way, and the ones that don't move get shoved out of the way.

A man bumps into Milly. Fucking piece of shit! I turn my glare back at him and sneer, "fuck off," as I pull her closer to me. She grabs my forearm with her other hand and grips it tightly.

In our quickened pace, I feel her leg rub against mine with every step. I would embrace her touches in any other circumstance, but this is survival mode to get Milly back to our safe compound.

Finally, the outside doors are within mere feet of us, and I plow through them, pulling her with me. Relieved to see the valet already had my G-wagon ready. Demyan must have called it for me.

The kid tosses me the keys. I grab Milly's arm and pull her in front of me to shield her from everyone. I push my chest into her back, pushing her to the car door, then I open it for her. She turns and looks up at me with her big brown eyes.

I put my hand on the top of the car frame and leaned into her. "Get in," I growl.

She adjusts her dress to sit in the passenger seat. I step into the door's opening, lift the remaining body of her dress, and set it in the vehicle. Leaning in and looking over her visible body for wounds. I grab her seatbelt, reach over to buckle it, and notice her dress is ripped higher at the slit on her hip. A fire lights in my veins as I rub my finger over the torn threads. Motherfucker ripped it!

"I'm okay," she whispers in my ear while she lays her hand on mine, touching the threads. Her voice is sensual music in my ears. Her breath on my neck is heavenly. I turn to look at her face. She cracks a small smile, then nods.

I step back, close the door, and stare at my reflection in her tinted window. I'm getting too close to her. I need to gain control of myself. I'm her boss. She's off-limits.

I jump in the driver's seat, struggle to avoid looking at her again, and speed away. We stop at the red light a few blocks from the hotel. I can't help myself. I look over at Milly, staring out the side window. I wonder if she has never been put in a similar situation. Vulnerable. Alone. Forced to seduce a sick fuck like McGriffith.

I've done so many bad things in my life that I'm numb to many situations. I can easily disassociate myself after the crime, and easily move on with my life. I suppose that makes me a monster.

I find myself wishing to know what's going through her head right now. For me, she put herself in harm's way to play bait in a mission she knew nothing about. She did exactly what I told her to do. She even let a man violate her because I told her to do whatever she had to do to get him alone. A comment I regret saying to her.

The light turns green. I speed the few blocks to the interstate ramp, onto the highway, and quickly switch lanes until I reach the fast lane. We blow past vehicle after vehicle. We have a 45-minute drive to our compound, leaving plenty of time for someone to get to us if we are being followed. I weave through the cars, jumping lanes and paying attention to the cars in the rearview mirror for anyone trying to keep up with me. Nothing. We are in the clear and can relax a bit, but I refuse to slow down.

I look at her as she silently watches the cars we pass and fiddles with her fingers. I reach over to her, slide my hand under hers, then she laces her fingers in mine.

"Thank you for finding me," she whispers, but there is a slight hint of anger in her words. It makes me want to pull her onto my lap, caress her face, hold her and keep her safe.

She has every right to be mad. Mistakes were made tonight, and it almost cost us, Milly. She wasn't to be out of our sight. Things happened so fast. We weren't entirely in place when I saw her walking out of the gala with Trevor. I radioed my men to follow her, but we lost her at the elevators.

I took the next elevator while Demyan waited to radio me what floor they stopped on.

I charged out as soon as the elevator doors opened, but I didn't see them. My anger stoked, thinking I may have lost her forever. I looked down the hall to my right, and that's when I saw her gold clutch by a door. I ran in that direction, saw the door being held open, and then heard the commotion coming from inside the room.

When the threshold is in my sight, I see her choking Trevor. I knew she wouldn't go down without a fight, but it made me wonder what he did to her to make her unleash on him.

He was hitting her arms, trying to claw at her face, and kicking her legs. It did something to me. I charged into the room, grabbed him, and ripped him away from her. The cocksucker didn't stand a chance against me. I wanted to kill Trevor right then and there.

A calmness fills me as we pull up through the gate to the mansion. I watch it close behind us, and the guards resume their positions. The vehicle tires roar on the long paved driveway. Milly pulls her hands free of mine, and I already miss the feeling of her skin on mine. I look over to see her looking at me with a half smile.

"I'm fine," she says, sitting up taller, like the mansion gives her comfort.

We pull up to the main stairs of the mansion, she adjusts to open her door, but I order her to wait. She knows my rule about her door, but she continually tries to break it. She sits back and snaps her eyes to glare at me. I laugh inside my head. My little pissed-off

Milly. She's always trying to be so strong. One of the reasons I desire her.

As I get out of the G-wagon, I button my suit jacket and walk around the vehicle. My eyes don't lose sight of her for more than a few seconds. I open her door. She hesitates for a second, then shifts her legs to get out. I hold my hand out to help her, which she accepts like the good little darling she is. When she steps out, she stands so close to me that I can smell her scent, like a sweet flower; it makes my cock twitch.

"I'm fine, really. I don't need to be babied," she snaps, with a glare on her face. I chuckle inside. My sweet Milly, be mad at me all you want as long as you're here with me and safe under my protection.

I move my hand from hers and run it down her face. Her skin is so soft and warm. Staring into her deep brown eyes, I lean in a bit toward her, stopping just by her face, letting my lips hover closely to hers.

I want to tell her she's beautiful.

I want to kiss her full lips.

I want to taste her on me.

I want to bend her over this car and fuck her so hard that she has no choice but to scream my name.

Sadly, I can't do any of it.

I move away from her and motion toward the house. She slowly starts to walk to the stairs, but when she realizes I'm following her, she tries to get further ahead of me. An impossible task given our height difference.

I walk behind her to watch the satin dress hug her body. Her ass slightly jiggles with each angry step, and her leg peaks out the side as she holds her dress up to avoid tripping on it.

Fuck, she's beautiful!

I want to grab her and show her she's mine. My cock wants her to know who she belongs to. It wants to feel her cummimg all over it while I pound into her sweet pussy.

She reaches the front door, but I grab the handle before she can. Opening it, she lets out a huff as she walks past me. I catch the scent of her hair.

My phone rings. FUCK! I hate the interruption from Milly's presence, but it's Demyan.

"What?" I snap, answering the call but not taking my eyes off her. She walks to the stairs that lead to her room, then glances over her shoulder back at me with a grin.

An invitation to her room, maybe?

Then she rounds the corner to walk up the stairs, entirely out of my sight.

"Hey, are you there, Niko?" Demyan asks.

"Yeah! What!??" I snapped.

"What do we do with McGriffith?"

"Make him sit! I'll be there later." I hang up and head to my office as I take off my suit jacket. I'm going to kill that motherfucker slowly to ensure he feels every ounce of pain.

Laying my jacket on the chair in front of my desk, I walk to the mini-bar and pour some scotch as I loosen my tie with the other hand. I grab the glass, throw my tie on my jacket, and round my desk to sit in my chair.

Scanning the notes left on my desk, I see a note from Theo. *Aanya is home and going to make a full recovery!* Good news for us, but the fuck who shot her is a dead man walking.

I rub my hand on my forehead as I tilt my head back against the headrest, rotating the chair to face the floor-to-ceiling windows overlooking the gardens and pool.

What would Trevor have done if I didn't get there in time?

What if we couldn't find the room?

Could Milly have continued to fight him?

I didn't want Milly to do this job. I wanted her here and safe.

Milly has been here since the night she came into our lives three months ago. The night we had Seth Jones in the warehouse.

She snuck in, bypassing all our guards outside like a ghost and walking into the room Jones was in. She was right behind me when we finally noticed her.

Chuckling to myself at the memory, I take another mouthful of scotch, swish it around my mouth, then swallow.

Continuing my mental stroll down memory lane.

Milly's about a foot shorter than me.

Her tactical clothes were tight as they hugged every curve her body was blessed with. She was a sight to see with her perky breasts, thick curvy ass, reddish hair, and beautiful face staring at me.

She was upbeat and naive to where she was and who she walked in on. I underestimated her at first, but she proved to be fierce.

The events that followed her interrogation were not my finest moments.

I wanted Milly, so I took what I wanted.

She tried to leave, just like it wasn't a big deal. I motioned for Sven to knock her out.

I brought her to the mansion, gave her a room, and waited for her to wake up. Demyan and I took turns watching over her, not that our men aren't honorable, but because she was clearly trained to escape, and we didn't want that.

The next day Milly woke up like a pissed rabid dog. She was strong, quick, and fought with no mercy. But we expected it after watching her skin a man's arm.

It took both Demyan and me to restrain her and calm her down to talk.

I laugh to myself at the memory and take another drink of scotch.

We weren't going to let her leave. She's too valuable an asset.

We made a deal with her. Anything she wanted, but she couldn't leave.

She obviously didn't know what power she had at that time. She requested Vance come to stay with her and that she could still do her 'hunting' from our compound.

We're bad guys, yes, but not ones that tolerate sick fucks like that walking around.

Conditionally, we agreed to both, but I would have given her anything to be here.

She is my obsession now. I crave her. Desire her, but I cannot let myself have her. She would be a weakness if anyone wanted to get to me.

Demyan and I spent too long and sacrificed too much to let it all crash down because of one woman.

We are the heads of our family businesses, both legal and illegal. We expanded our products, businesses, and clientele, becoming very successful at what we do. This created many enemies that would kill what we love to get to us.

We sent our families to safer places. We agreed to build this compound to protect us, our staff, and now to keep Milly safe.

Her presence around here, however, has been a challenge to me. The harder I try to avoid her, the more bitter and angry I become with the burden. I try to tell myself it's easier to ignore, avoid her, and pretend she doesn't exist, but I catch my eyes involuntarily following her whenever she's around. My self-control is weakening.

I dream about her.

Fantasize about her.

She is everything I have ever thought I would want in a companion.

Making it impossible for me to want to fuck anyone else for the last three months. Before Milly, I would fuck escorts almost every night at Demyan's hotels and clubs. It was easy, mindless, with no emotion, no attachment.

They would do whatever I asked them to do, and some of the things I asked of them tested the limits of pain and pleasure. Some backed out, and some pushed through because they wanted to be mine. Unfortunately, there was no chance of them being more than a fuck for me. I would parade them around on my arm at clubs and brothels because I didn't care who saw them with me. I didn't care who would use them as a target, thinking they could get to me. I wouldn't give a shit about a dead escort.

But Milly is unique, making her the biggest target for someone to get to me.

She is the woman I cannot have and must always be safe, even from me.

I drink the remaining scotch and slam the glass on the desk—time to deal with McGriffith.

Past Milly
15-years-old

Chapter 14

ANOTHER TWO YEARS OF training.

I can read, write, speak and match the accents to nine languages.

My self-defense lessons are impeccable.

Adio brought his brother, Linford, from Jamaica, to be part of the business. Linford was two years older than Adio but taller, more muscular, and funnier.

He helped me become a quicker and quieter fighter.

We would run around in the trees behind the house to train. Linford would hide in branches and jump down on me.

"Pickney, you're not doing so good!" He would get up laughing at me.

"I think you are cheating!"

"How? I have the same trees you have. It's not cheating when I'm just smarter!"

I hated when he said that; obviously he was smarter, but he didn't need to rub it in.

Vance hated it when training would get too rough on me. He always knew when to check on me, and I was usually bleeding when he did.

There was one day that was different from all the other days.

"Kiddo, you're bleeding," Vance exclaimed and pointed to my temple as he walked over to Linford and me.

Linford said, "all part of training."

"Take it easy, Linford! Train her! Don't kill her," Vance snapped.

Linford chuckled, wrapped his arm around me, and said, "sorry, Pickney."

"I can handle it, Vance," I grumble, "you're too protective."

I wanted to know everything about our business, even the pain. The pain and the cuts helped me control myself, so I could stay focused.

Vance shook his head in disapproval, then demanded, "let's go to the house for dinner."

Walking to the house, Linford and I wrestled around and charged one another. Vance walked behind us, calling us children, and told us someone would get hurt. He was such a father to everyone.

We sat at the table. Linford threw a napkin at me, and when I went to throw it back, Vance yelled, "Milly!" I jerked in my seat, set the napkin on the table, and glared at Linford, who was laughing at me.

While eating, Rosco and Adio got back from recon. Vance walked over to them, discussing the night's events. I didn't know much about recon or the steps involved in hunting. Mary hid some things from me because I was still young.

The night talk was above my level, so I decided to turn in early.

While lying in bed, dead tired, there was a knock on the door.

The door creaked open, the hall light shone into my room, and I heard Vance's voice ask, "hey, kiddo, you up?"

"Yeah. What's up?" I turned on my bed to face him.

"I thought since I have to do some recon tomorrow, you might like to join me. Start learning something new," he explains while leaning against the door frame, with the hall light illuminating my room.

I jumped up so excited and yelled, "YES! YES!! I would love to go!! You're really going to let me go with you?"

"Yeah! Mary said it was ok. Besides, I think you need a break from getting your butt kicked!" He laughed while pointing to my bruises, scrapes, and cuts.

"Hey, I'm good at fighting for a 15-year-old," I slouched, tried to defend myself, then sat back down on the bed.

"Stay humble, kiddo. Just because you're good doesn't mean you're the best. Even if you are the best, don't tell yourself that. Egos can drop a person to their knees even if their opponent can't," he explained, and pushed off the door frame, grabbed the doorknob, and started to pull the door shut.

"That doesn't make sense, but ok," I said quietly, rolled my eyes, and laid back on the bed.

"Now go to bed. I'll get you up at 6 am," he ordered and shut the door to my room.

I was way too excited to sleep, though.

6 am

Vance walked into my room. "Get up, kid. We leave in 30."

I jumped up, got dressed, ran downstairs to eat, ran back upstairs to brush my teeth, put my hair up in a ponytail, and got my shoes on. Then, I went back downstairs to do my chores for Bear.

Finally, I was ready! I stood by the door and looked at the clock to see it was 6:15 am. Ok, I was a little ambitious but excited to do something new that day.

Vance walked into the kitchen to grab a cup of coffee and looked at me weirdly, "You do know how to tell time, right?"

"Yes! I can't help it. I'm excited," I explained and resumed waiting. He nodded while walking out of the kitchen.

"I'm not leaving without you, so you don't have to stand there," he said over his shoulder.

"I know. I'll wait here, though," I replied cheerfully.

He stopped and turned toward me and verified, "did you eat? Brush your teeth? Do your chores for Bear?"

"Yes, to all," I said proudly.

"Good!"

It took forever, but 6:30am finally came.

Vance motioned toward the door, saying, "let's go!"

I was so excited I could have peed!

OH MY GOD!!

"I have to pee," I yelled out.

"What? You stood by the door for 15 minutes," he replies, stunned at the news, and holding the door open. I hear the birds chirping, and a cool breeze hits my face.

"I know! I'm so sorry. Please don't leave me," I begged him.

He smirked and said, "no worries. I'll be in the car."

I did my deed and ran full bore to the car. I got in, huffing and puffing as Vance stared at me. I sat and stared out the window briefly before I looked over at Vance.

He had a dead serious look on his face, then asked, "you, ok?"

"Yes," I said, smiling, and got my seatbelt on. He smiled, shook his head, and started the Suburban.

Vance had some serious patience. He said he had to; growing up with Jared and Frank was a test. He called them ding dongs. The stories those three have, it's a wonder how they all survived their childhoods.

We parked by a beat-up tan and brick building at about 7:05am. All the surrounding buildings were brick and older as well.

We were just sitting there, waiting. Vance told me to be quiet and watch for a man and a girl about 8. He was bald with glasses, and she had ear-length blonde hair.

We waited and watched. 30 minutes went by, and no one came out. Then 40 minutes. 50 minutes. An hour!

NOTHING!

That didn't seem to bother Vance at all. He just sat, watched, and waited, but I was bored! I played with the visor, the locks, and the windows and buckled and unbuckled my seatbelt about a thousand times.

"Stop and be patient," he firmly stated without looking at me.

Finally, they came out of the building. I didn't say anything. I just tapped Vance's hand as he told me to do. He said commotion in a car draws attention, so everything must be subtle. He nodded at my gesture.

They got into an older blue Jeep parked three cars ahead of us. Vance waited for them to stop at the stop light, about 50 feet from where they were parked, then we pulled out to follow them. My heart was pounding, but Vance seemed relaxed and calm.

The blue jeep turned right and then into the gas station a few blocks away. We followed him into the parking area. Vance told me to stay in the car, and he got out.

The man noticed Vance right away. Who wouldn't? A tall, heavy-set Italian man doesn't blend in with the crowd.

Vance said something to him. The guy smiled, gestured, and pointed a couple of ways. Vance nodded and walked back to the car.

"What was all that?" I asked, turning my body to better face him.

"I asked for directions. The man will lead us to where I want him to go."

"Oh! This is awesome," I said excitedly.

The man came back out, waved to Vance, and Vance waved back.

We followed the guy's car. Left turn. Right turn, then straight. We headed down a road with no buildings. Up ahead, there was an area that looked like old buildings. The guy stopped in front of the last building, and we pulled behind them.

Vance walked to the car, and the man rolled the window down. I saw Vance extend his hand as if to shake it. Instead, he grabbed the guy, and Vance's head went into the car's open window, then he threw the keys out behind him.

Rosco, Adio, and Linford came running out of the building. Vance wrestled the guy, and he opened the door. Rosco grabbed the guy and pulled him out, kicking and yelling.

I saw movement in my peripheral on the right side, and I snapped my head in that direction to see Grace. She was opening the passenger door of the jeep. She led the girl to the seat behind me, then got into the driver's seat herself.

We took the girl to a residential neighborhood. Grace got out slowly, staring at the house as she stood outside the open car door. She leaned in, looked to the back seat, and asked the girl if it was safe to go home. The girl nodded and started to cry.

I looked to see a man walking out with a look of confusion on his face.

Grace shut the door and walked over to him. I don't know what she said, but the guy started to cry and fell to his knees.

A lady came running out of the house as Grace returned to the car. She opened the door, and the girl jumped out and ran to the people.

I assumed they were her parents. They hugged and cried.

Grace said something to the man. He stood, shook her hand, nodded, then she turned to the car and got back in.

As she adjusted in her seat, I said to her, "I have so many questions."

"I bet you do. We have the drive home to discuss it, so start asking," she replied, looking over her shoulder for cars, then pulled onto the road.

I asked her every question possible.

How did they know the girl was kidnapped?

How did they know those were the girl's parents?

How did they know where the guy lived?

How did they know he would be leaving his place around that time?

How did they know his car?

His looks?

How did they know it was the right girl?

What was Vance doing with him?

What was that building they were at?

She answered every one of my questions without getting annoyed or frustrated. She told me to ask Mary for more details because Mary had the final say in how involved I got at the time. I was, after all, the child SHE saved.

Mary and Jared met us on the porch when we pulled up to the house. Grace told Mary, "it's taken care of." Mary nodded.

Jared asked me if I was ok, and I smiled and said, "yes!"

How could I not be ok? That girl was back with a loving family because of the heroes of my new family.

Present Milly

Chapter 15

2 A.M., AND I'M still awake.

The events from the night before are still swirling in my head.

I text Vance, *'missing you. When are you coming back?'* I know it's late or early, depending on how you look at it, but at least he knows I'm awake, so if he does want to call me.

I climb out of bed. My head is pounding, but if I can't sleep, I might as well see what I can find out about McGriffith and if he is associated with Lazlo.

The Lazlo case has been a struggle for years. It's impossible to track down anyone willing to give out information so we can shut Lazlo down.

As I walk by Nikolaj's office, I think about how he acted. He's always cold-hearted and a brute asshole, but last night he was different. He was gentle and caring, and it confused me even more.

Reaching my office, the other five desks in the room are unoccupied since it's not our standard time to work. My desk sits by the vault on one side of the room, along with Daniel, Theo, and Vance. On the opposite side of the room are Nikolaj and Demyan's desks. Sometimes the bosses work down here, but they primarily work in their own office upstairs.

The walls here are lined with locked cases for all our spy toys, as Theo calls them. Monitors cover the wall by Nikolaj and Demyan's desks so they can see the grounds' perimeter and inside the mansion's common areas.

I sit at my 'u' shaped desk, turn on my computer and four screens, then open the bottom drawer of my desk to find the file Daniel left for me with all the details he collected on McGriffith. It doesn't take long for me to read through the file. Daniel was looking at stuff for the bosses, so he wouldn't focus on what I would look for, but it's a good start.

Daniel said there were accusations against Trevor of rape, but the court dropped charges, the victims received substantial checks, or the accusers were found dead. The man is a serial rapist with deep pockets and friends in high places.

Why would someone protect Trevor?

What business did the bosses have with Trevor?

They weren't looking at McGriffith for his serial rapist tendencies, so what was so crucial that Nikolaj and Demyan would give this case to Daniel?

Daniel's job is to protect Nikolaj and Demyan's business from being hacked and ensure big deals and trades don't happen without their knowledge.

Sick fucks like Trevor are my territory. I hunt them. I kill them. This case should have been mine.

Was Aanya shot because of Trevor?

Why did Jared need Vance this week of all weeks?

I throw my head to the back of my chair. I'm frustrated with all the unanswered questions. I feel so out of touch with everything going on here.

At least with my family, we kept each other in the loop. As I got older, we had no secrets because we trusted each other.

Here there are only secrets. There is no trust. Frustrated, angry, and sick of this fucking place! I slam my hands down on my desk and stand from my chair.

I need coffee.

It's 4 A.M.

The house is quiet, and I make my way to the kitchen. The coffee brews as I stand there, hands pressed against the counter and my head hanging between my shoulders.

I pour my mug of coffee, twist on the cover, and walk out of the kitchen. I hear the front door open as I pass through the dining room. I stop to see who it is, and Nikolaj walks in, still in his tux from last night, followed by Demyan, Sven, and Gus.

Nikolaj stops when he sees me standing there watching him. He has his everyday *fuck you* look on his face, but even mad, he looks delicious.

The memories of how he touched my face last night, his smell, his eyes, and the way he held my hands all the way home make my pussy tingle.

Demyan stops beside his business partner, looks over and sees me, and asks, "don't you sleep!?"

"I should ask you the same thing," I smirk and start to walk toward the basement stairs, slowing my steps when Sven and Gus catch my attention as they walk past me without saying a word.

They looked exhausted. I assume they are going upstairs to their rooms on the second floor.

What did they do to McGriffith that they are getting in so late?

I draw my attention back to Demyan and slowly walk past him as I say, "guess I'll go back to work." He nods and heads in the direction of Nikolaj's office.

I see Nikolaj still standing by the front door. His eyes follow me. He slowly steps in my direction. I slow my strides while I stare at him. He's making me extremely nervous.

Does he want to talk to me?

Should I say something to him?

His eyebrows pull closer together the closer he gets to me. Nope! I'm not saying a word to him, and I can't imagine he has anything to say to me. Obviously, he was only nice to me last night, and I shouldn't think about it anymore.

What an asshole!

His eyes lock on mine as I pass him.

"Great, the asshole version of you is back. Lucky us," I spit out, then break our stare, and head downstairs as I cringe, thinking, '*What the fuck was that, Milly? Control your word vomit!*'

Getting back to my desk unscathed, I sit down and drink my coffee. The warmth runs down my throat as the bitter taste coats my tongue, and I relax a bit. I live off coffee. It's like air to me.

I fumble with my pen. I should get back to work, there is so much to do, but I cannot get that asshole out of my head. He's such an asshole! A sexy, mysterious asshole!

I smelt his cologne when I walked by him upstairs. His rolled shirtsleeves showed his muscular tattooed and scared forearms, and his tux jacket was hanging over his shoulder with one very thick long finger.

His hands are enormous, and I couldn't help but compare the difference in size when he was holding my hands in the car. Nikolaj made me feel amazing last night, the way he had my face in his hands at the hotel, pulling me through the crowd, and when he said 'she's mine' to Trevor.

I can feel myself getting wetter the more I think about him. I lean back in my chair and wonder, how can a man I hate so much who also hates me make me feel so goddam aroused?

I lick my lips, focusing on the wetness in my panties as I run my hand gently down the front of my shirt. Well, no one will be down here for a while. I walk to the bathroom behind my desk, lock the door, and stand in front of the counter.

I spread my legs wider and unzipped my pants. Reaching my hand down into my soaked panties, I massage my swollen clit up and down. My other hand is under my bra, pinching my nipple, sending a bolt of electricity straight to my pussy. I run my fingers around my nub with more pressure and steady strokes.

I watch my movements in the mirror, feeling sexy as I fantasize that Nikolaj will catch me in the act. He'll kiss my neck while he shoves his fingers into my wet pussy that's aching for him as I rub my clit. I change movements and massage long strokes from my clit to my entrance, teasing it with the tips of my fingers. The wetness smacks between my fingers and center. It doesn't take long for my body to explode, relief consumes me, and my body feels electric.

Maybe now I can get some work done.

After I've composed myself and washed up, I open the door to return to work, but to my surprise, Nikolaj is sitting on my desk.

His long thick muscular legs spread wide, hanging mere inches above the floor. He's slightly leaning forward, his white dress shirt is unbuttoned three buttons to expose his tattooed chest, while his palms wrap around the edge of my desk. His hair is now in the sexiest man bun I've ever seen, and his eyes snap to mine.

"Hey," I cough out, "what's up?" I try my hardest to look normal, not like I just fucked myself in the bathroom to a fantasy of the man sitting in front of me, but I'm sure my flushed cheeks are a dead giveaway.

"You left this in the car," he says in a sultry voice, moves his hand to his side, and picks up the clutch I used last night. The look on his face makes me think he knows what I just did.

"Oh, thanks," I say as I walk closer to my desk but avoid getting too close to him. "Just leave it there," I directed, trying not to stare at his perfect body while pointing to the space beside his thigh.

"Come take it from me," he says with a deep, demanding, raspy voice. He sits up straight and pulls the clutch close to his lap.

"Um, ok," I say suspiciously, then slowly move directly in front of him. If I step closer to him, I will stand between his legs.

He rests the clutch on his thigh as he seems to be eyeing me suspiciously. I start to panic inside. "Thanks for bringing it to me," I say as I reach out further for it, but leave my feet planted on the floor in front of him.

He glances down at my hand, then back to my face, and curls his index finger, beckoning me to step closer. I do as I'm directed out of curiosity about where this is going. I'm standing so close to him that all he'd have to do is close his legs to trap me. He leans forward a little, keeping eye contact with me, and takes a deep breath. My eyes involuntarily widen, and my face turns red. His eyes move slowly down my body, studying every feature I have, then he slowly blinks his gaze back to mine.

He moves the clutch closer to me, and I slowly put my fingers around it, and he runs his fingers over mine. Goosebumps cover my body as his fingers glide between mine while we both still hold the clutch. He pulls his hand away from mine and draws them to his face. He runs it over his beard, ensuring his fingers pass his nose, then takes a deep breath.

Is he?

Can he?

I step back, keeping my eyes on him, and without a word, he gets up and walks out of the office.

Oh my fucking god!

Mortified, I slam myself down in my chair, relieved he left.

He's so intense, maybe crazy, but definitely intense.

I rub my hands over my face and take a deep breath. Good, I only smell soap. I shake my head to clear it. Back to work!

Hours go by.

I keep hitting dead-end after dead-end with McGriffith and Lazlo.

I've tried calling Vance four times and sent about 14 text messages with questions, but no response.

What the hell, Vance?

Where are you?

I'm getting worried.

COFFEE BREAK!

I need more coffee.

I know, this time, I'll see someone in the kitchen because it's 7:30 A.M.

Theo and Daniel are in the kitchen bullshitting as those two lads always do. I walk in, saying, "good morning, nerds!"

"Oh, Milly! Great! Settle something for us," Theo says with an over-enthusiastic voice.

"Ok, what?" I ask, cringing, as I pour coffee into my mug.

Daniel says, "it's dumb. Save yourself," then shakes his head before taking a drink of the liquid heaven he makes himself every morning. He has a sweet tooth, and his coffee shows it.

"Shut up, you twat," Theo snaps, turning to me, and kindly says, "sexiest actor alive!" Lifts his eyebrows with big eyes and holds his hands out like he is giving me something.

"What?" I asked, confused.

"Keep up, Milly! Who do you think the sexiest actor alive is," Theo replies.

I make a face at both of them. "This is what you waste your time talking about?"

"I guess," Daniel jokes as he sits on the stool by the island and takes another drink of coffee.

"Listen. Daniel says Ryan Reynolds, but he's every human being's sexiest man. So, Daniel has to pick someone else," Theo rolls his eyes in a huff.

"I see. Ok. Theo, who did you pick?" I ask, with my mug to my lips.

He stands proud, then says, "Idris Elba!"

"Yeah, that's a good one," I say after taking a sip of coffee. "Ok. Daniel, who would you pick if not Ryan Reynolds?"

He thinks for a minute and says, "Oscar Isaac with a beard, but not without." I nod in agreement with his decision. Daniel is very particular about things, so it wasn't out of character to hear his preference for a beard over not.

"Theo, why do you care about the sexiest actor, anyway?" I ask, moving to the end of the island by the dining room.

"I'm trying to have a connection with Daniel that doesn't just consist of tech stuff."

"Ok, and talking about sexy men is your way of what?" I ask with a suspicious side look at Theo.

Daniel moves to my side by the island and nudges his head toward Theo to show his profound interest in the answer.

"Daniel! I'm trying to bond with you! I want to be your friend! Quit blocking me," Theo says with desperation and slams his hands on the counter.

"Theo, I'm more than just a gay hacker! I have hobbies!" Daniel snaps, shakes his head and takes a long drink of his iced coffee.

"First, Theo, you two are inseparable, so I'm going to say your friends. Second, Daniel, you have hobbies other than being a gay hacker?" I ask sarcastically and furrow my brows. "Who knew," I add, then turn to leave before the discussion gets heated again.

"WAIT! You have to tell us who has the better choice of man," Theo blurts out.

"Facial hair always," I reply while looking over my shoulder at the men standing in the kitchen.

Daniel does a little excited dance, and Theo's face goes sad, so I stop to say, "Idris Elba has facial hair, so I think you both are right."

Then continue walking to the basement stairs as I hear Theo and Daniel saying something about having to pick one and it's unfair to walk away from them.

I catch a glimpse of Nikolaj standing inside his office doorway, reading a file and wearing his usual black suit that hugs his body perfectly.

I pick up the pace before he sees me, convinced he knows what I did downstairs, and that's embarrassing as fuck.

I get to my desk, relieved I wasn't spotted by the boss man, then get back to work. Hearing the door open, I assume it's Theo and Daniel, so I don't look. Instead, I continue clicking away at the keyboard.

I see someone sitting on my desk from the corner of my eye. I see Nikolaj with one leg resting on the desktop, the other still firmly planted on the floor, and he is leaning toward me, resting his forearm on his thick thigh. I turn my chair to see him better. I can't get any words out because I don't know why he's back at my desk and what he wants to talk about. I sit quietly, staring at him.

"Thank you for what you did last night," he says, in the same kind voice he used on me in the hotel room. "I don't always express my appreciation when I should. So, Thank you." He nods a single time but doesn't move.

"Yeah, no problem," I finally stuttered before realizing I was leaning closer to him.

Quickly I turn to start working on my computer. I can sense he is still sitting there, but I don't want to look back at him out of sheer embarrassment about my word vomit earlier, what I did in the bathroom, and my obscene thoughts about him.

He stands and pats my upper arm, making me jerk a little. I look at him to see that his eyes aren't their typical intense *hate* stare but a softer, sexier gaze.

He turns and walks toward his desk. I guess he's working down here today. This should be interesting.

He stops, looks over his shoulder, and says, "I'm glad to hear you like facial hair."

I slump in my chair, trying to hide my face behind the four monitors on my desk. What in the actual fuck is going on?!

Past Milly
15-years-old
Chapter 16

I WAS SITTING ON one of the fallen trees behind the house when Vance walked up, "hey, kiddo. Are you okay?"

"I have questions," I stated, looking up at him.

"Of course you do. I figured you would. Can I sit?" He motioned to the section of the tree beside me.

"Of course, besty!" I laughed. Despite the age difference, Vance knew he was my best friend since we were practically inseparable.

Vance was special. I imagined I was the best chance at a daughter he had, and he was the best chance at a father I had.

"Should I ask questions, or do you just want to talk to me?" I asked with a wink.

"I'll talk," he said, "ask questions if you need to, kiddo."

"Okay," I snuggled into him, and he wrapped his arm around me. I could hear his heartbeat with every breath he took.

"You know the bad people we hunt. They hurt kids, well they hurt anyone they can, but mostly kids," he said gently against the top of my head.

I don't know if it was his accent, Jersey shore style, or calming, deep voice, but nothing could get my attention away from Vance when he talked.

"Jared, Frank, and I cyber stalk these bad guys. We go through everything we can find about them online. Nothing can be hidden from us," he said and chuckled. He shifted his position to face me. "We even look into extended family and friends. Once we have all the information we can find, Rosco, Adio, and Linford run recon."

"We were doing recon today," I said and adjusted to face him better.

"Well, that's all it was supposed to be, kiddo, but I didn't think he would talk to me at the gas station or bring me to the shop."

"Shop?" I asked.

"Yeah. Where we take bad guys for questioning or just to get rid of them." He looked at me. I know he was wondering if I could handle this information or not, but I can.

I eagerly said, "keep going, Vance!"

"Okay. Okay," he grunted and moved from the fallen tree to the ground.

"That tree hurts my ass!" We laughed, and I moved to the ground with him.

"Where was I? Oh yeah," he said, nudging me. "That's when we follow bad people. We get sight of them, learn their everyday movements, and take note of anything we couldn't see in cyberspace. After that, we all group up to form a plan and then get them. Running errands is the code for that."

"Why codes?"

"Because we are not the only hackers in the world, and some governments have hackers, too," he said. He changes his tone and says, "look, kiddo, everything we do is ugly, and there are things you will see and do that you will not be able to forget. The anger will become acid in your veins. Your heart will burn with fury. But seeing our vigilante justice being done and children getting to go home reminds us that what we do is for the better cause. Even if it does kill our souls. That emotional moment when people are vulnerable to us because we brought their loved ones home. That reminds us we're human. That feeling brings us back to a softer side of this darkness. We do this for the love that still exists in the world. Sometimes, though, loved ones don't get to go home. Sometimes we fail." His face ached when he said it like demons and ghosts of the ones that got away haunted him.

"How many bad guys have gotten away?" I looked at him sadly. I didn't like when he was sad.

"Too many. Sadly, it will happen to you, too. It will haunt you forever, knowing those assholes get to hurt more innocent people." I leaned into Vance to side-hug him.

"You're still my hero," I softly said, and I felt his smile on top of my head.

Vance said, "come on, time for you to see the attic." I couldn't contain my excitement as we walked up the stairs that led to the attic.

I looked around and saw computers, monitors, desks, chairs, and whiteboards with tons of writing. The room was filled with high-tech equipment, and it looked like everything was on and running with a purpose.

Jared was at the desk in the back corner of the room with headphones on, and on the screen were green squiggly lines.

Frank was writing on a whiteboard, and Adio, Linford, and Rosco watched. Another whiteboard had names and lines drawn between the words putting them together.

Vance stopped to talk to Frank. I stood there, taking in the room in its entirety.

Jared walked over to me, "hey, Milly. Fancy seeing you here. Come on, I'll show you around." He motioned for me to follow and brought me to the desk he was just sitting at.

"Here, we listen to any recording we can get our hands on. Voicemails, video calls that were recorded, and phone calls. We analyze words, and codes, take out background noise, remove extra voices, enhance a voice or sounds we can't quite make out." He pulled out the chair, and I sat down. "Here is what I'm working on now." He put the headphones on me and another pair on himself. He pushed play, and the green lines started to move.

"Do you also need salt and sugar?" a woman's voice asked.

"No, just the flower, fresh this time," a man said.

The woman replied, "sorry, we're out of fresh."

"Fine, put it on my tab," he said.

She came back a few seconds later and snapped, "no tab. You must pay your old tab first."

The man sounded irritated now, "Bullshit! I just paid. I did my job, and that was the deal."

She returned to the line and said, "this is the last transaction you are allowed to put on your tab. Your job was incomplete. You must pay upfront IF you are allowed to buy again."

Jared stopped the tape.

"What are they talking about?" I asked.

"They are using codes, so they don't get caught doing illegal stuff. Many people use codes to keep outsiders from figuring out their conversation."

"So, in this case, salt and sugar are drugs, and a flower is a female," I guessed.

"Exactly," Jared smiled. "For a 15-year-old, you catch on to this stuff quickly."

Probably because I was around this stuff constantly with mom and Skip. Plus, I didn't have friends my age to distract me from it.

"This woman is part of a sex trafficking and drug ring. She's the middleman. The one who gets people what they want by getting it from a supplier," he said.

"Okay. The debt? He doesn't pay, so he is required to do something for her or the supplier?" I asked.

"Yep. But it sounds like the job wasn't done properly."

Jared told me about deciphering codes and what he had figured out about the phone call. He clarified that *flowers* meant a young woman, *fresh* meant a virgin, but the girls they had were not virgins. Salt meant cocaine, and sugar meant meth. Her threat about 'IF' he was allowed to buy from there meant if they didn't kill him first.

Jared stood up, saying, "this is only part of what we do. The part you didn't hear on the phone was the drop-off and pick-up location."

We walked over to Frank and the other men, and Jared continued the tour. "Over here, we figure out where and how we get these assholes. The goal is to get the delivery person, too, but that doesn't always work. The delivery person is quick and usually undetectable. That's why we have to be steps ahead of them. They might say 6 pm on the call, but delivery might be made hours before. They will drug whomever they are dropping off, so it looks like a homeless person sleeping. That's when these three knuckleheads come in," he said as he pointed to Rosco, Adio, and Linford.

Frank took over, "sometimes parents are looking for kids, sisters are looking for brothers, or friends are looking for friends. We have hunted for people who've asked, and we've hunted because we get a lead. We kill sick fucks. We also take whatever money and assets we can get from the cocksuckers and give it to the people they hurt, but we keep some for ourselves. We need to survive, too. It's not just sex victims we help, either. We help anyone that needs us. We just particularly like to torture and kill sex predators."

"Like Mom and Skip?" I asked, and they all got quiet and looked at me.

Vance walked over to me and set his hand on my shoulder, "Milly, we save people. We saved you."

"I know. I know what you had to do to save me, too. Someday, I would like to know how. That probably makes me weird, but they hurt me for so long. I just want to know they had to hurt, too." A tear fell from my eye. Vance hugged me.

Adio said from behind Vance, "we didn't know you at the time, Milly, but just know we did right by you. That's all you should know about that particular situation."

Adio walked around Vance, positioned himself right in front of me, and looked into my face. "Innocent people like you are why we go into the dark alleys. The reason we aren't scared of the boogie man. We are the demons that hunt and haunt. Milly, the day Jared called Rosco and me to tell us we had to grab your mom and Skip was the first time I heard actual emotion about a case in Jared's voice. That's the day I knew you were more than just a victim. You were a new member of our family. We all stayed away, so you could have time to acclimate with Jared and Mary. We watched from afar until we could come home."

Vance didn't break his stare, "are you okay, kiddo?"

"I'm more okay than I've ever been. Thank you all for everything you have ever done for me." Vance hugged me, and everyone else smiled.

"Enough with the mushy shit. Let's get back to work," Rosco said as he cleared his throat, and it broke the emotional tension we felt talking about my past.

Present Milly

Chapter 17

THEO AND DANIEL FIND their way to the office a few minutes later with Demyan in their company. Guess both bosses are working down here today.

Great. I looked at my phone to see Vance hadn't texted or called me, so I texted Vance again. I'm really getting worried about him. He always texts me back, at least.

I really miss him, it feels like he's been gone forever, but he just left yesterday. Sadly, he won't be back until Thursday, which leaves me alone for another six days.

We've been working for a few hours hovering over a table in the middle of the room, and today is like every other day, including the usual bickering between Danial, Theo, and me. Three creative, stubborn minds working together are bound to cause some tension and drama.

We never take it personally with each other, and this is when Vance calls us toddlers and yells for us to stop.

After last night's events, we decided to make a pair of earrings to help Aanya stay in contact with the bosses during a mission. They have to have an undetectable earpiece and microphone. We have to figure out how the pieces can hide in the ear from the earrings, but we cannot use significant technology, so the range of communication will be low. Not like Aanya is out of range of anyone.

The Entire time we are working, I can't help but feel embarrassed. I'm not easily embarrassed, but Nikolaj has me twisted. He can go from brute asshole to gentle giant in a blink of an eye, and I'm sure he caught me this morning in the bathroom. Honestly, everyone fucks themselves now and then. There's no shame in it. So, I need to forget about that and focus on my work. Except Demyan's been looking at me weirdly. Did he tell Demyan?

Great, now I'll dwell on that for the rest of the day. I just need to get through today.

The day becomes night, and we are getting worn out. Theo yells to the bosses, "I'm done for the day. Heading out if that's okay?"

Yelling is typical since the room is so big, and sometimes we just don't want to walk across to the other side.

"Me too!" Daniel says.

"Have a good night, gents!" Nikolaj says, not looking from his desk, and Demyan makes a quick wave. I'm done too, but I am determined to learn more about Lazlo.

My family has been looking for Lazlo for two years. Frank says the Lazlo cases are the worst they've dealt with. The intel or lack of it, the dead-end clues, and the endless trail of murdered abuse victims.

The only evidence we have to tie the cases together is the business cards we found at each crime scene. A red circle card with a gold square design, and on the upper right side was a 2-digit number in black. Unfortunately, we have been unable to track anything down about the card, not even where they were printed.

Demyan walks by me, "M get some rest. Pretty sure you didn't sleep at all last night. Call it a day!" He has a flirty smile, and the way his eyes wander down my body hints to me that he may have a sexually aggressive side.

"Yeah! Just finishing up some things, Demyan," I answer with a smirk.

Demyan seems to flirt with everyone, including me, but I suppose it comes with the territory of looking like a Greek God. Walking over to my desk, he rests his hand on the back of my chair and leans in to see what I'm working on.

"Lazlo?" he questions, looking down at me. He continues, "that's not an easy job." He stands and starts walking to the door.

I watch him. "Do you know anything about Lazlo?" I ask, hoping he would say McGriffith said something.

He stops, turns to me, and clarifies, "no, just what you have told me and three months of watching you work on it."

I wanted to ask him about McGriffith, but he was out the door before I got the courage to say anything. I know Nikolaj is still in the room with me, but I'm not asking him anything in case he switches personalities again.

Staring at my computer, my brain fills with overwhelming frustration for Lazlo and McGriffith, worry for Vance, embarrassment for myself, confusion for Nikolaj, and sadness at being away from my family.

I hate that I am stuck here.

I hate that I can't call anyone except Demyan, Vance, and Nikolaj.

My computer is continuously monitored, so I can't talk to my family without the bosses knowing.

I can't leave.

I can't do anything except sit in this house and work.

I've trained for 12 years to be what I am, but now I'm a prisoner.

Anger and frustration build inside me, and it feels like fire! Before I know it, I throw my pen on the desk and march toward Nikolaj's desk.

WHAT THE FUCK AM I DOING?

I start pleading with myself to stop, but my legs keep walking.

I'm halfway between my desk and Nikolaj when he looks up to say, "have a good night!"

This is it! My chance to back the fuck out of this stupid tantrum and abort the mission. I can just turn away and go to my room.

NOPE!

My legs are still walking. This is mutiny.

I reach his desk, my heart is pounding, and my face is red hot.

Then my mouth betrays me, and I blurt out, "Why the fuck won't you let me go?"

My eyes widen, and my throat goes dry.

"What?" he asks, not even looking up from his desk.

"You tore me from my life and insist I stay here! WHY?" I snap, stepping to the edge of his desk.

"Because we may need your abilities, and we don't know how much you pretend not to know about us," he explains and sits back in his chair.

I grow more enraged. "What the fuck does that mean? I told you and Demyan I wasn't looking for you two that night. I had Jones in my sight at the hotel when you grabbed him. I needed to talk to him. Your business isn't important to me."

His voice becomes loud and deep, making me jump a little when he says, "you're here because you walked into the wrong fucking warehouse that night. You are here until we say you can go. I allow you to do your work when it doesn't interfere with my business. That's more than generous. Now go." He motions with his arm for me to leave. His eyes burn into me, but I will not back down.

"Why didn't I get the McGriffith case? He's a serial rapist. That's my territory." He puts his pen down lightly, stands from his chair, buttons his jacket then comes within a foot of my face. His height towers over me. My knees shake, but I don't budge.

"I don't have to explain anything to you. Whatever Trevor has done in the past has nothing to do with me, dushka," he tilts his head toward me, and I want to punch this fucker in the face.

He just called me DUCKY in Russian.

"Ducky?!" I ask, gritting through my teeth.

"Da! You called yourself a duck yesterday, dushka." Does he think he's funny right now?

"I was talking about the ugly duckling!" I slightly shake my head. UNBELIEVABLE!

I'm trained to deal with assholes, to not take it personally, but I'm going to kill this motherfucker for making it personal. Remember what Adio would tell me repeatedly, never fight with emotion.

I take a deep breath to calm myself. I shake my head slightly and say, "fuck this," with a smile and turn to walk out.

I'm only a few feet from the door when I feel Nikolaj grab the back of my neck, spin me around, and pull me toward him.

"What?!' I snap, annoyed.

Trying to jerk out of his grasp and take a step away. He grabs my upper right arm with his right hand and pulls me, so my shoulder is at his chest. I try to pull my arm from his grasp, but I can't.

His lips get close to my ear, and he says in a low, rumbled voice, "you can't really be that unhappy here? Are you that spoiled that you don't know how good you have it?"

I glare at him and sneer, "you know nothing about me." I hold my stare for what feels like an eternity.

He pulls his head back a little, and his eyebrows push together. He explains, "you have everything you could need here, but you complain about wanting more."

I turn to face him, asking, "why do you hate me? I never did anything wrong to you." I realize this isn't going to go anywhere, so I admit defeat. "Never mind. I'm sorry I snapped at you. It won't happen again. Can I go now?" I sarcastically spew out.

He looks my face up and down, then lets go of my arm. I linger for a second. There are so many things I want to say to this fucker, but instead, I shrug my shoulders, decide to save my breath, and quickly turn to walk out.

"Wait," he says while stepping to block the door from me.

There is a moment of hesitation before he wraps his hands around the sides of my neck and comes in for a kiss.

Shock fills me, making it impossible to pull away, or maybe I don't want to. His lips are soft and gentle as they caress mine.

He slowly pulls away and looks into my eyes. I gasp in a breath, then he kisses me again. He moves one hand to my lower back, pulling me toward him. I place my hands on his hips. His kiss is slow and caring. I've never felt something so amazing, but this is not the right thing to do. He's my boss. He's with Aanya, isn't he?

He tilts his head to get a better angle at my mouth, but I pull back and quickly whisper, "I'm not who you want."

"What?" he says, his head still close to mine. I feel his breath on my face, the warmth of his skin on my neck, and his other hand firmly wrapped against me.

"I'm not Aanya," I whisper, looking down at his chest, and this time he pulls away a little with a confused look on his face.

"Aanya?" He asks, and I start to second-guess my presumption of them being a couple.

"Yeah. Aren't you two together?" My hands move from his hips to his chest to push him away.

He tilts his head, moving closer to my face, not letting me push away, and says, "Aanya has a wife. We work together and have for a long time, but there is no sexual attraction between us." I stop pushing away from him and stare at him. He's not with her. I can be with him guilt-free. WAIT! He's my boss. He hates me. If we do this, he will hate me even more and make my life more miserable than it already is. I can't risk that.

"You still don't want me, Nikolaj," my voice faint as the words came out. I stare into his chestnut eyes a second longer, then push against him again. This time he releases his hold on me, and I step away from him. This is for the best.

"Very well. If that's what you want. I never have and will never force a woman to be with me," he says, turning on his heel to walk toward his desk.

I pause for a second.

Do I really want him to stop?

He'll hate me more if I do let him continue. Men like him don't fuck people they hate, especially if they are a virgin. I slowly turn to walk out of the room.

Once clear of the door, I run up the basement stairs and bolt it to my room. I slam the door shut and lean my back against it.

Standing there for a second as I process everything that just happened.

HOLY SHIT!!

I smile a little, then head to the bathroom to shower.

While the shower heats up, I stare in the mirror, still smiling. That was the most amazing kiss I've ever had. That's not saying much; the only men I kissed before were for work or unwanted.

I still feel his hands touching my body.

My lips still tingle from the kiss.

My body is craving him.

I should go back downstairs to Nikolaj.

NO!!

He's my boss. He hates me. There are too many reasons not to go back to him, so I'll just please myself, then go to bed.

Removing my clothes, I gently run my fingers over my perky nipples, down my stomach, embracing my soft skin. I glide my hands back up to my nipples and pinch and rotate them between my thumbs and fingers, sending excitement through my body.

I could only think about Nikolaj's hands on me, being pulled into his firm chest and beard rubbing against my ear and neck when he called me spoiled. Somehow, I'm not even mad anymore. He can call me whatever he wants as long as I can feel him on me again.

I keep my right hand on my nipple, moving my left to my sensitive, swollen clit peeking out between my wet folds.

His kiss made me ache for him, and if he could do this to my body with a kiss, what else could he make me do?

My mind races with every sexual act I can think of him doing to me, and my left hand picks up speed.

I stop, put my hands on the counter, and lean forward. Maybe I should go downstairs to let Nikolaj feel what he did to me. Let him finish me.

STOP MILLY!

You're a fucking virgin! STOP!

I get in the shower and rub my clit again as my other hand resumes teasing and pinching my nipples.

Just as the sensations collectively build in my core, I hear a knock at the door and grunt in annoyance. Every goddamn time I want to shower, I get interrupted.

I shut the water off. Grab my robe, head to the door, swinging it open in frustration.

Past Milly
18-years-old
Chapter 18

I SPENT THE NEXT three years training and working in the attic.

The fighting was fun, but Linford added weights to help strengthen my muscles, and I was always sore.

I learned another nine languages and got to do more recon. I was getting good at what I did.

After six years of training, I felt pretty confident, or at least I thought I was.

My 18th birthday was the first time I got to experience what we did from beginning to end.

I got to ride with Adio in one car while Rosco and Linford were in the other vehicle.

It was 9pm, and we sat outside an apartment building and watched for Terry Krause to come out. He was in his late 20s, olive skin, black hair, brown eyes, 5'9", and 212 pounds.

He had a reputation for heading to the bars about this time to find a drunk lady to take home and sexually assault her and her kids (if any), then leaving after knocking them all out.

Adio was ready to kill him, but we couldn't risk being seen under streetlights, so we waited in the shadows.

Finally, he came out wearing dark jeans, a white tee shirt, and a brown leather coat.

He took the sidewalk, and we followed slowly in the car. Adio called Rosco and Linford to tell them he was on the move.

We watched Terry for a few nights, and he always took the same path to the downtown bars.

Terry started to cross a dark alley when Linford, dressed head to toe in black, grabbed him. Adio sped up to park in front of the alley to block the view from anyone looking. Linford knocked Terry out, and Rosco helped shove him in the trunk.

Then we drove to the shop.

Frank, Vance, and Jerad were waiting by the big garage door for us to show up.

Frank shuts the door after both cars pull in.

Rosco opened the truck, Adio grabbed Terry's arms, and Linford grabbed his legs. They set him on the chair and tied him up.

The three Benecelli men stood around a table discussing the acts in the case and how to handle that scumbag.

I was told to stand off to the side and take in as much as I could.

Vance grabbed a chair and flipped it back, so he was sitting facing Terry. Rosco, Adio, and Linford stood at Terry's back.

Smelling salts were used to wake him up. He was given a minute to come around, then realized what was happening. He started yelling to let him go. No one said anything. They just let him rant.

Vance leaned in a little and quietly told him to listen close. Terry got a pissed look on his face but did quiet down. Vance asked a series of questions to ensure we had the right guy.

Terry refused to answer, but Rosco pointed his gun at Terry's head, which seemed to get him talking. Finally, he verified who he was. Vance stood and gave Frank and Jerad the 'okay' to start.

Terry's eyes looked all over and stopped me. "What the fuck? You sick fucks bring your kid here?!"

Adio punched him in the face, and he whimpered from the hit.

Vance called me over to the table, and we went through Terry's phone and saw pictures of his victims and texts he sent to the families he hurt, threatening them to keep quiet.

Terry managed a small strip mall on the North end of the city. His Facebook page looked welcoming, which made him more dangerous because he baited families into letting him in their lives.

Jared stepped to the table and said, "here we go, Milly. Don't feel like you have to do anything or even watch if you don't want to." He smiled, gave me a thumbs-up, and walked back to Terry Krause.

Adio was the lead of this case, which meant he was the one who decided and handed out the punishment.

Adio asked more questions about particular women, families, and a motive. Terry didn't answer any questions, so Adio kept punching him.

Terry was bleeding from his nose and mouth, his left eye was already swelling shut, and he was missing some teeth. He started to beg for mercy. Called himself a sick man. Promised to get help.

Adio replied to him, "you are not a man! There is no help for you!" Adio's Jamaican accent got very thick when he was angry, and his voice got deep, like the Devil was coming out to grab Terry's soul.

"Please stop," Terry begged.

"You showed no mercy to those mothers begging for their children's safety! You didn't show mercy when those kids screamed and cried for you to stop!"

Terry started to cry, "I'm sorry!"

"Not yet; you're not!" Adio headed to the table to pick up a knife. Milly, want an anatomy lesson?" He smirked, flipping the knife.

"Yes," I said, maybe too excitedly. I looked at Vance and Jared for approval, and both men nodded.

I had been training for six years to be there that night.

I followed Adio over to Terry. Linford, Rosco, and Frank adjusted their positions to ensure I wouldn't get hurt if anything went wrong.

It annoyed me; I wasn't a child anymore, I was ready, but they were just doing what family does.

Adio smiled at me and said, "if you need to walk away, just go ahead. If you don't want to do anything, then don't," he winked at me and moved to the side of Terry, grabbing the top of his ear, and with a quick movement cut Terry's ear off. His screams of pain filled the room. Adio dropped the flesh to the ground.

"Do you want to do the other side?" he asked. I stared at him, the knife looked at Terry, then I shook my head.

"I can try," I said with a bit of nervousness in my voice.

"Okay, mouse! Whenever you are ready. Just remember, we are just taking out the trash! He has been proven guilty of doing horrible things, and this sick fuck deserves to suffer. When he is dead, the world will be a little safer," Adio said.

I grabbed the knife and walked over to Terry. Grabbed the top of his ear, pulled it forward to expose the skin attached to his head, then lined the blade up with the crease.

"You are all the sick fucks for letting a kid do this! YOU'RE FUCKING NUTS!" Terry screamed out.

Angered that he would call my family '*nuts*'. I sliced the knife into his skin and pulled back to continue cutting his ear off little by little. He screamed so hard his voice shook.

"Good job, mouse! Take your time. The slower you go, the more misery he will be in," Adio said like a proud uncle.

The ear was cut off, and I threw it to the ground.

Adio took the knife from me, smiled, then said, "that's enough for you for one night."

Disappointed I didn't get to do more cutting, but this was my first time, so I went back to observing.

I watched as he shoved the knife into Terry's shoulder behind the clavicle. He screamed and tried to break free from the chair.

Adio pulled the knife out, then wiped the blood with a cloth. "The knife gets slippery when it's covered in blood," he clarified.

Then turned to continue the punishment. Adio stabbed, cut, burned, and punched Terry. His skin was raw, bleeding, cut off, and sizzled black, and as time passed, his screams became softer.

Blood covered all the men that stood around Terry.

I stood next to Adio as he worked, learning everything he said and did.

No one was afraid of cops showing up. We had all the time in the world, and it was open season on Terry Krause.

Vance said all the research they do in these cases would find a place in their heads, and taking time to punish those people helped get it out of their heads and kept the demons at bay.

Terry couldn't handle much more. Adio knew that, so he straddled Terry's legs, grabbed his hair, and forced his head back to look up at him.

"Look at me, Punda," Adio growled through his teeth, "I want to watch the life leave your body!" Then he slit his neck open, holding his head, and leaned closer to Terry's face. Staring into his eyes until Terry went limp.

Adio dropped the knife and stepped back.

Frank was on the phone, "it's time," he said, then hung up.

Adio nodded at me. "You okay, Mouse?"

"Of course, I am," I said and smiled. He started wiping his hands on a cloth.

"Cleaners?" he asked, glancing at Frank.

"Already called," Frank said.

They collected paperwork from the table and shoved it in a brown cardboard box.

Adio finished cleaning himself up, and Linford patted his brother's back. Rosco palmed my head.

Frank and Jared got into their car, Adio and I got into ours, and Rosco and Linford got in their vehicle.

Vance was standing by the dead body.

"He always waits for the cleaners to show up," Adio said.

Even after we'd pulled out of the shop, I stared at Vance as he closed the big door.

"Is he coming soon?" I asked Adio.

"Yes. Vance is very good at what he does and will be back home before you know it."

I stared out the window, worried.

Nothing about the night bothered me but leaving Vance scared me. I trusted Adio, though, so I tried to relax on the way home.

Trust! I hadn't used that word in a long time, but I trusted all of them, even if they had blood on their hands.

Present Milly

Chapter 19

TO MY SURPRISE, NIKOLAJ is standing outside my door, leaning against the doorframe, with his suit jacket unbuttoned.

"Yes?" I ask suspiciously. He slowly looks me up and down. "I was in the shower," I explain while covering up more with the robe.

"Hmm," he growls as he barges into my room, looks around, and finally darts his attention back to me. "Do you have an STD?" he asked nonchalantly.

Offended and annoyed, I slam my hands on my hips and answer, "what? NO!"

Who does this asshole think he is?

"Unless I'm reading your reaction to me wrong, I'd say you want me. So, tell me, Milly, why do you say I don't want you?" He asks, not moving a muscle. His stare intensifies, and I can feel my face blush, my throat dry, and my brain cloud over.

"What?" Confusion crosses my face.

"I won't repeat myself." He steps closer to me and puts his hands in his pants pockets. His stance is wide, his body within a foot of me. My breathing becomes heavy. He towers over me, and his body radiates '*fuck me*' vibes. I feel my pussy, still soaked and swollen from the shower, aching for his touch.

I shift my weight between my feet, trying to discreetly rub my thighs together to ease the desire aching at my center. I'm too embarrassed to confess how bad I want him and that I'm a virgin, so I quietly say, "I don't know."

"Not an answer," he persists, still staring at me.

I feel the pressure to say anything just so he would leave, but do I really want him to go? I should just let this happen. It would feel so good.

So, I asked, "why did you kiss me?"

He answers as he steps a couple inches closer to me, "I think you're sexy when you're mad. I wanted to taste the anger on your lips." His tongue darts out and licks his bottom lip then curls his lip in between his teeth. The gesture hitches my breath in my throat. I watch as he drags his teeth against his full bottom lip as it pulls out.

Shocked, I choke out, "what? That doesn't make sense." I give him a sideways look. "You're confusing me," I growl. I've spent all day stressed about this guy, and now he will make it all worse with that answer.

I step closer to him, now only a few inches separate us, and point my finger at his chest. I feel his thick tight muscles flexing under my touch. I focus on the tick of each flex. I wonder what he looks like shirtless. I feel my cheeks flush.

Shaking my head to clear my thoughts, I ask, "are you insane? Like clinically insane?" He straight-faced looks at my finger against his shirt and seductively snaps a look at me. I can only imagine what he's thinking, and I quiver at the thoughts that race through my head.

WAIT!

Is this turning him on?

I pull my finger off him and take a few steps back, and he watches me like I'm prey.

Agitated, I explain, "you go from being an asshole to me all the time, despising my every move to kissing me in seconds. Don't get me wrong, I liked the kiss. It's the best I've ever had. But you hate me. Remember?!" I look at the floor, shaking my head as confusion covers me. I feel him step closer, but I cannot look up at him.

"Maybe I don't hate you. Maybe I like watching you squirm when I'm around," he says, and I snap a look back at him. He cocks an eyebrow and takes another step closer. His feet are on either side of mine, his hands still in his pockets, and his body barely touches mine. His face looks down at mine, and he asks, "so, you liked that I kissed you?" He has a devilish grin on his face.

"Yes, no, I mean...." I stutter in a whisper. I roll my eyes and tilt my head to the ceiling. I drop my gaze a little to look up at him, then gently explain, "look! I'm not that experienced in doing.... I spent half my life training and hunting. There wasn't a lot of time to...."

I cringe, then finish saying, "you seem very experienced. Women flock to you. You're sexy as fuck! Who wouldn't want to fuck you? That's intimidating to someone like me."

I shrug my shoulders, let my arms fall to my sides, and groan, "UGH! I need to get dressed. I'm not having this conversation with you when I'm half-naked." I step away from him but miss the presence of his body against mine.

I walk to my closet and see Nikolaj make his way to the mini-bar. I was hoping he would find his way to the door to leave. I don't know how much more embarrassment I can take.

He starts shifting through my liquor bottles. "Flavored vodka?" He glances at me over his right shoulder with a look.

"What? Isn't Vodka a Russian liquor? Don't knock the flavors until you try it," I scoff as I grab a shirt and sweatpants from the shelf, then walk back to the room, holding them tight to my chest.

He walks over to me, looks over my face, brushes the back of his fingers over the robe on my upper arm, then his eyes follow the movements of his hand. I get instant tingles throughout my body.

Watching his face, admiring the perfection before me, his fingers take my chin, and he says, "show me what you did to yourself in the bathroom this morning." He leans closer, his lips almost to mine. "I heard you breathing heavily, and then you made a squeaking sound. It's all I've thought about all day."

His lips fall onto mine, his beard against my face makes my body vibrate, and the warmth of his hand on my chin makes me melt.

I'm not even ashamed that he knows about this morning. I'm turned on that he knows. I want to show him what I did. I want to tell him that I thought about him catching me in there and finishing me off.

He brushes his tongue over my lips, parting them and forcing his tongue into my mouth. It's soft as it caresses past mine.

His hand grabs the back of my neck, and his other arm drops around my waist as he pulls me tighter into him. The height difference between us is minimized as he pulls me up to my tippy toes.

His smell is intoxicating, and the taste and feel of his mouth on mine make my pussy clench with desire.

I drop the clothes and wrap my arms around his waist and up his back. I can feel his muscles through his jacket and shirt, and the urge to rip his clothes off to see every inch of him fills me. He feels so good as my hands rub his back and sides.

He kisses me with desire as he pulls me into him more. I moan into the kiss, and he devours my mouth while his beard tickles me.

I'm ready for him to take me. Just throw me on the bed and ravage me, but he pulls away, and my head follows him a little, desperate for more.

He rubs his thumb over my bottom lip, red from his kiss, while supporting my chin again. "Interesting," he says, studying my face.

I can't even muster any words. My excitement turns into confusion. I bite my bottom lip and nervously ask, "What?"

Worry crosses my face.

Was I terrible?

A feeling of overwhelming self-doubt starts to engulf me.

He brushes a piece of my hair from my face, leans in for another kiss, then I blurt out, "I'm a virgin!" My body feels like it dropped 20 stories, and I squeeze my eyes shut for a second.

He stops mere centimeters from my lips, pulls away from my head, and a mortified look crosses my face as I open my eyes to look up at him.

Can the ground just swallow me whole now?!

"A virgin? Fuck..." he growls, looking away to the side of him. I knew it. No man like him will ever want a virgin. I let embarrassment take over, and I shove him away.

Standing a few feet apart, I fiddle with my robe straps and look at the pile of clothes on the floor. He needs to leave. This has been the shittiest day ever, and I want it over.

I look up to tell him to leave, but before a word escapes my mouth, I see a smile form on his face. A full-on smile! I've never seen him smile before. It was perfect! His full lips. His perfect teeth. I realize he's looking at me like I'm the best thing he's ever seen.

He's fucking sexy!

Charging toward me, wrapping his arms around my body, he slams his lips into mine. This time he kisses me fiercely, like a wild animal. Like he just caught his prey.

I stand on my tiptoes, wrapping one arm around his neck while the other palms his chest. He splays his fingers across my upper back, and his other hand moves down to grab my ass.

He pulls back, grabs my hair, and yanks my head back to look at him. The lust shines through his eyes before he nips my bottom lip and lets his tongue takes my mouth. The taste of him stimulates my taste buds again. His full soft lips work over mine, and I get lost in the feeling of Nikolaj Fedorov, the man I fantasized about so many times.

He works his way down my chin to my neck, kissing every inch of my skin. His beard rubs against me, and the sensation is overwhelming with pleasure. I turn my head toward the side of his to smell his hair, this new urge of desire fills me, and I moan into his ear as his lips and beard work the sensitive skin in the crook of my neck, then his hold on me tightens on my ass, and he pulls my hair harder, stretching my neck further.

He devours my skin, kissing, biting, licking, and edging me closer to climax.

I grab hold of his shirt, and my other hand grabs the back of his head as he moves my robe off my shoulder and makes his way to my collarbone, rubbing his teeth the length of it.

I moan louder as his touch makes my entire body tingle. He smiles against my shoulder before running his teeth back until he reaches my neck again, then his tongue licks up my throat, over my chin, and he bites it lightly.

My breathing is hard and heavy. I'm aching for Nikolaj to feel every part of my body.

His huge hard cock is pushing against me through his pants, making me want to pull it out so he can fuck me.

I move my hand down his torso to his belt buckle, and he lets out a growl in his throat before saying, "no!" Rubbing his cheek on mine, his beard sends electricity through me.

He whispers in my ear with a profoundly seductive, raspy growl, "I don't want your virtue tonight, but I will be the one taking it when it's time. You're mine now!"

Gently, he kisses my neck while running his fingers up my arm to the other side of my neck, and I can't help but quickly gasp in at the excitement he makes me feel. He returns to my face, resting his forehead on mine for a second, then turns and leaves without a word.

I'm left panting, aching, and soaked between my thighs.

HOLY SHIT!

WOW!

Back in the shower, as the water runs over me, I rub my hands over my nipples, twisting and pulling. I slide my hand down and start rubbing my swollen clit to the thoughts of the man I desperately desire.

Wishing he would come back into my room and find me touching myself to his memory.

I kneel in the shower, slide a finger inside my wet folds, let out a slight moan, then slide in another. I thrust them in and out while my finger and thumb rub my clit.

Grinding against my fingers, I think how much I wish it was Nikolaj. The kissing, the way he made me feel, the feeling of him in my mouth, and his beard tickling me. How I can still feel him on my lips and skin.

Just as my movements increase in speed and hardness, I cum! Bolts of electric vibrations course through me as my body jerks, and I moan loudly in relief.

I slide my two fingers out, leaning forward as my hand holds my balance on the shower floor. I rub my clit slowly as I come down from the orgasm, then stand to finish my shower.

Lying in bed, all I can think about is him. Looking at the clock, it's only 8 pm.

I fuck myself to his memory again. This time using the toys in my bedside drawer.

This goes on a few more times.

Orgasm after orgasm, fucking myself to Nikolaj's hold he had on me earlier.

After I'm satisfied enough, I finally fall asleep.

Past Milly
19-years-old

Chapter 20

ANOTHER YEAR WENT BY.

I could read, write and speak 20 languages with corresponding accents. I hunted bad guys alongside my family. I was taught to hack and search for information. I learned torture techniques along the way.

I was sitting at my desk when Jared walked over and handed me a file and explained, "it's your time to shine, Milly. It's yours to take the lead on." That was the first case I got to lead. Taking the lead was a big deal, meaning I was the head of operations for that case. I was responsible for finding out as much as possible about the target and who they knew. I was in charge of recon, creating a plan, directing our people, and executing the plan. The fun part was taking the target to the warehouse, where I could decide how they were tortured and for how long.

I grabbed the file with a massive smile on my face, and Jared continued, "you have all of us to help you with this, so if you need anything, let any of us know. Good Luck!"

"Okay! Thanks," I said. He nodded and returned to the table to sort the evidence in another case we worked on.

I stared at the closed file for a minute. I couldn't believe they trusted me with this.

"Open the file!" Linford yelled from across the room, then said, "that's step one!"

"Hilarious, Linford," I sneered with a sarcastic smirk.

I laid the file on my desk and opened the cover. It was still a surreal feeling that the case was all mine to handle. The inside of the file had a picture of a woman. Shannon Thompson. The card Vance filled out was attached to the opposite side of the folder. 34, Caucasian, blonde hair, brown eyes, 5'1", 102 pounds, lived in a trailer park with her 13 and 14-year-old daughters.

Prostituted herself for drugs. Worked on the corner of Quick Pick gas station on St. Hilanes Ave. Accusations of prostituting her 13 and 14-year-old out for debts she owed.

I spent the better part of the day trying to find all the information I could on her. Jared always said even if it seems like enough information, it's not. Keep looking until we know we have found every possible piece of data we can find.

No mistakes allowed!

I searched for two days straight.

The guilt of giving Shannon an extra two days with her daughters was setting in, and I grew impatient.

"Vance, this has to be enough. We have to get her and save her daughters," I protested, resting my head on my desk. He sat beside me, massaged the back of my head, and leaned on my desk with his elbow.

"Listen, kiddo, you can't cut corners here. If mistakes are made, we could be found out, go to prison, or be hunted. I am not ready to risk this family of ours because you feel guilty," he explains firmly with a huff.

I rolled my eyes and said, "I've been searching day and night for anything. I know everyone in her family, her family's friends, and their employers" I pulled my head up and interlocked my hands, and begged him, "let me call a meeting. Let me make a plan with the guys. Let me start following her. Let me do recon on her! Please!"

"Let me see your file," Vance snapped. He was annoyed with my begging, but I didn't care. I tried to be patient, but I knew what those girls were going through, and I couldn't help them soon enough. He had to understand we needed to act now.

Linford said I was too impulsive in training, and maybe he was right, but the guilt was consuming me.

"Look, kiddo, I'll let you call the meeting with the team, but you need to take every precaution to protect our family. Understood?!" Vance commanded.

Vance had never doubted me, and I know they took weeks of searching, but the memories of what I went through with Skip were flooding my head, and all I wanted to do was save these two girls like my new family saved me.

We decided to execute the plan and grab Shannon that night.

10:30 pm-With all my men stationed and ready, Rosco and I headed out to follow Shannon.

She stood on the corner with a few other prostitutes. Each looking for their next trick. Shannon staggered drunkenly and high as fuck to every car that pulled up in front of her. She would lean into the car window and then get into the car. We followed every time to ensure Shannon wasn't returning to her place. Within 30 minutes, she'd be back on the corner and looking for her next trick. She did about eight tricks in the time we watched her.

We decided that was enough of her and went to her trailer to check on her daughters. We turned into a run-down trailer park. Our blacked-out Audi A8 was quite the sight in that area, and we knew we would draw attention if we weren't careful. We shut the lights off and slowly crept along the road until we parked in front of trailer 48. I sat there and stared at the run-down shit hole, no lights on, and trash laid outside. I shook my head in disbelief.

"What do you want to do, boss?" Rosco asked while he leaned forward on the steering wheel to get a better look at the trailer.

"Please don't call me boss. I'm just hoping not to screw this up and cause more shit to happen to the girls," I smiled, never letting my eyes stop scanning each window.

Adio grabbed my arm, my attention turned to him, and he tilted his head with a smile. "Milly, we are in this together. There is no way you are going to screw this up. Not without our help," Adio joked in his lame way to try and assure me it was going to be okay. I turned my head back to the trailer and nodded.

"Call Grace and Mary. Tell them to get here to take the kids to safety."

"How do we know the girls are in there?" Rosco asked as he bobbed his head around to better see the trailer and its surroundings.

"We don't, but from what I have learned about her, she doesn't let the girls go anywhere, so they have to be in there. We need to get them out. They can't endure this torture any longer," I said while rubbing my lips against my knuckles. I heard him pick up his phone, and the screen dimly lit his face.

I told Rosco, "tell them their grandparents are 40 miles away. I left their number in the glove box of Mary's car. Call them and tell them what is going on."

"Okay, Milly," he said. Grace answered, and Rosco explained everything. She told him they were on their way, and he hung up.

"Rosco, I need to go check on them," I said. My heart was pounding, and anxiousness fluttered in my stomach. It was killing me to wait for a second longer. He pulled the car into a vacant driveway just a few trailers down. We snuck up to Shannon's trailer, peeking through the windows as we went. No signs of anything.

Rosco picked the lock, and I watched him closely to learn. After he got the door open, we slipped inside and pulled out our guns as total darkness met us. We gave our eyes a second to adjust, then moved forward through the trailer.

We found the girls in the side bedroom, curled up on the bed. They looked rough and damaged. The way I looked when I was 12. I took a deep breath, shoved my Glock into the back waistband of my pants, and walked into the room.

"Milly?" Rosco whispered firmly as he tried to grab my arm.

Jennifer, the oldest girl, woke up and grabbed her sister. "Get away," she screamed.

"Listen, Jennifer and Amanda! I'm here to help," I calmly explained. Mary taught me to be gentle to others in times of fear. "I'm not going to hurt you. I'm here to get you away from this hell your mom has put you in," I say as I slowly step toward them.

"You don't know anything about us," Jennifer snapped and pulled her sister into her tighter to shield her.

Not the reaction I was looking for, but I continued calmly, "yes, I do. I was you. I have been in the exact same spot you have been in." I stepped closer. They both stared at me for a moment.

We heard footsteps in the living room. Rosco held a hand up to signal us to wait and be quiet. I motioned for the girls to cover under the blankets. They must have sensed concern from us because they did what I asked without a fight.

Rosco walked to the living room with his gun drawn, and I pulled my Glock out and stood guard in the girls' bedroom.

The footsteps got closer, then he disappeared into the living room around the corner. I stepped out into the hallway to see if I could see him.

After an intense moment, I saw a shadow on the wall. I pointed my gun toward the living room, then Grace walked into sight and flipped on a light. I lowered my weapon, told the girls it was okay to get up, and turned on the bedroom light.

"This is Grace. She is going to take you to your Grandparents," I said as Grace followed me into the room. I tucked my gun into the back of my belt.

Jennifer said, "we haven't seen them since Amanda was a baby. Do you think they remember us?"

A tear ran down her face. Grace quickly wiped it away, telling her their grandparents were awaiting their arrival and they couldn't wait to see them.

Jennifer smiled and excitedly rushed Amanda off the bed and to the dresser. Grace and I helped the girls pack while Rosco kept watching for Shannon.

With Grace's car loaded, the girls were buckled in and ready. I told them to stay with their grandparents and that we would check in on them soon.

Grace pulled out of the driveway, and the girls were on their way to safety.

Rosco and I waited at the trailer for the piece of shit mom and whoever she brought home with her.

Nikolaj

Chapter 21

IT TOOK EVERYTHING I had to walk out of Milly's room.

She's innocent!

She's right; I am intimidating.

I like it rough.

I like the pain and the pleasure of sex.

I don't want to hurt her the first time she feels me inside her, but I don't know how much I can control myself.

Hearing her in the basement bathroom was enough to crack me. Her heavy breathing, the wet smacking sound her fingers made while stroking her wet pussy, and the little squeak she made when she came.

It was all so fucking sexy. I wanted her to keep going so I could walk in on her and fuck her. I wanted to lick her pussy off her fingers as she screamed my name while I pounded into her on the counter, but I refrained.

I needed to smell the sex on her fingers, so I made her come close to me to take the clutch. I didn't get the smell I was hoping for, but I was content to just rub the fingers that brought her so much pleasure just a few minutes ago.

I came straight to my place and jerked off afterward, but I couldn't get her out of my head. I definitely couldn't keep my eyes off her all day. I imagined her tiny fingers rubbing her swollen clit and soaking in her wet cunt as she moaned in pleasure. Her ass jiggled deliciously under her black leggings as she walked around. It made me want to spank her to see her skin turn red from my hit.

When I saw her storming to my desk tonight, I tried to stop her from getting too close. The torture I endured watching her all day had me barely holding on to my self-control. I knew her sexy tantrum would be the thing that broke me. She's so fucking sexy when she's mad. I had to have her after that. I couldn't let her go without tasting her.

It was absolutely out of line for me, as her boss, to do, but I didn't care. I didn't expect her to pull away, bring up Aanya, or leave, but I'm glad I followed her to her room to clear it up. Her kiss was surprisingly stiff at first. That's when I figured out she probably hasn't kissed very many people in her life, but fuck was I shocked when she told me she was a virgin! A fucking virgin! I have so much to teach her and many ways to destroy her body. The thought of her innocence makes my cock twitch knowing I will be the first she will feel on her and in her.

Standing outside the door, I place my head against the frame.

I wonder if she is touching herself right now.

I wonder if she would let me eat her wet cunt I've been obsessed about.

I shake my head a single time.

NO!

If I eat her sweet pussy, I'll fuck her mercilessly into two pieces. That's not fair to her. She needs to be eased into sex with me, gentle and slow, allowing her body to stretch to my extra-large size.

Frustrated, I walk in, kick the door shut while ripping my coat off, then my shirt, and throw them to the floor, all while I stalk to the shower.

I let the water run all over me before I grab my solid cock and squeeze. Putting my hand on the shower wall, I start rubbing up and down my shaft and massaging the sensitive ridge around the head.

I can still taste her sweetness in my mouth and feel her soft skin. The way she moaned in my ear from kissing her neck makes me wonder what she would sound like screaming my name.

My strokes get faster, my grip tightens, and I throw my head back a little as I grunt out with my orgasm. Cum falls to the shower floor, and I slow my strokes. Breathing heavily as my dick throbs in my hand. But it desires more than my touch. It desires her hands, her mouth around it, her sweet cunt pulling it deep into her.

GODDAMN IT!

I want her now!

My cock wants her now!

It wants to feel Milly from the inside.

I let out a deep frustrating growl and start stroking again. I feel my core tighten as my hand strokes up my sensitive cock, my jaw tightens and ticks, and my body jerks as I reach the point of exploding.

"FUCK," I moan and let my head fall to my forearm, resting on the shower wall tiles. My dick is jerking uncontrollably, the head is red from the friction, and it cums again.

My strokes slow, and I take a deep breath to try and calm my lust for her.

I pull my head off the wall and continue my shower. I know deep down I should be fighting my urges for her. I know I should not pursue her any further. I should stop this madness and let her resume thinking I hate her.

I have to stop this urge before it consumes me.

It's dangerous to want her.

It's dangerous to let myself have her.

When she's around me, my vision and thoughts are clouded.

CONTROL YOURSELF, NIKOLAJ!

Or Milly will have to leave.

Past Milly
19-years-old
Chapter 22

WE SEARCHED THROUGH THE trailer house while we waited. Rosco told me stories of other cases they had and gave me some ideas about how to torture her.

"No piece of shit should die unpunished," he said.

I stared at a cross on the wall. "How can someone like her have a cross on the wall? Not that it surprises me. This God didn't help me when I needed it, so I can't expect him to be there to help anyone else," I said.

"I don't believe in that organized religion. I don't believe there is a heaven or hell," Rosco said.

"You don't believe in God?" I ask, scanning through the pictures on the wall.

"I don't trust that God," he said as he gave the middle finger to the cross on the wall.

"What do you believe in?" I ask as I turn toward him.

"I believe many things. Not really the place to get into what I believe, though." He stopped and walked to me. "I believe I was given my life and ability to help protect others. Evil is not just bad. Evil can also be good. One day I'll explain all of this, but right now, we need to set up for her to come home."

Headlights entered the trailer park. We assumed it was a false alarm like the other 10 times, so Rosco went to the back of the trailer. Except it wasn't a false alarm.

"Rosco," I whispered loudly down the hall.

He came to me, looked toward the window, and nodded.

We went into the girls' room. I shoved some pillows on the bed to look like Amanda, and I slid in to be Jennifer. Rosco covered me with the blanket, then hid in the closet directly at the foot of the bed, leaving the sliding mirror door open a little.

The front door opened. I heard talking. A woman, assuming Shannon, and three different men she brought home.

My blood boiled. I couldn't think about what Shannon was planning. I had to stay focused.

They turned on the music. I heard one man ask, "does anyone want a beer!" They all said yes in their own way.

The woman said, "Leech, you got any stuff?" She was slurring and sounded fucked up.

"Of course, baby! I need my payment," the douche named Leech said.

"She's sleeping, I'm sure. I'll go check," Shannon replied.

I heard her walking back to the room while the men started to get rowdy and loud, then she stumbled into the room.

I already had my Glock pulled out with the suppressor still on.

She struggled to the bed, tripped, and caught herself at my feet. I'm not surprised she didn't figure out it was my combat boots she landed on, not bare feet.

She's fucked up out of her mind.

She started patting my legs. "Jennifer, sweety! Mommy needs you to do something for me. Amanda, you too. Come on, girls. This is the last trick today, promise."

TODAY?!!!!!

WHAT THE FUCK?!!!!!

She reached for the blanket that was covering the pillows beside me. I heard Rosco say, gritting his teeth, "Quiet, cunt!"

I removed the blanket and stood up, pointing my gun at her face. I didn't say a word.

"Who are you people?" She mumbled with her eyes hardly open. "Where are my daughters?" She asked and rubbed her dirty hair.

"Far from you," I sneered at her.

Rosco pulled the cap off a needle and shoved it into her neck.

Usually, we don't drug them, but we couldn't risk making noise or being detected because we wanted everyone she brought home. She passed out and fell on the bed.

I looked at Rosco and held up three fingers. He nodded and led the way out of the room.

We stayed in the hall so as not to be seen before we could evaluate the scene in the living room. Rosco peeked around the corner to get the placement of where everyone was sitting. He used his left hand to signal where I should go then he was gone.

"Are you fuckers ready to party?!" Rosco asked the pieces of shit in the living room. I follow; our guns were drawn and pointed right at the assholes.

One man was sitting on the couch in front of the window, another was on the floor by the coffee table getting Blow ready, and the third was in the chair closest to me.

Rosco made his way to the other side of the room and stood by the kitchen.

The man on the couch yelled, "what the fuck, man? What do you want?"

The man on the floor reached to his side. "Don't fucking do it," I snapped.

"Hey baby, just be chill. I'm sure we can work something out." He tried to smoothly talk to me. He blew a kiss when he was done, and vomit climbed up my throat.

"Tonight, isn't your lucky night, *baby*,'" I said with my teeth grinding together. "Hands up douchebag!"

"We are all going to take a little joy ride," Rosco said. He was relaxed and calm.

The guy on the floor smirked at Rosco, "I call the whore," then pointed to me.

The guy in the chair tried to bolt, and I wrapped my left forearm around his neck. I slammed him back into the chair and tightened my squeeze around his neck with the chair between us. I had the leverage at that point because he couldn't kick or jerk me off of him.

I grabbed my gun and pointed it at the guy trying to climb over the couch toward the closed window behind it. "SIT THE FUCK DOWN, OR I'LL KILL YOU HERE AND NOW!" I yelled.

I looked up to see Rosco pistol-whip the guy on the floor repeatedly.

"We need to get out of here," I said to Rosco as he stood up from the knocked-out drug dealer.

He walked over to the man on the couch. "Please, man! Please don't! I have a family."

"Should have thought about that before you came here to hurt innocent kids!" Rosco slammed the needle into his neck, and the man slowly went to sleep.

The man in the chair was out, too, but to be sure we wouldn't have any issues getting them into the car, we injected the last two men.

"See, I'm good at this! I took out three to your one," he bragged.

"You injected two of them, so that doesn't count. So, we are even!"

"BULLSHIT! You're a sore loser! Just because I work smarter and not harder doesn't mean they don't count."

I put my gun away and shook my head at him, "okay smart guy, how do we get all four of these people into your Audi A8?" I asked him.

"You're the lead. It's your problem," Rosco joked.

What a smartass! "Go get the car," I ordered while shaking my head.

We got two into the trunk and two in the backseat. The man on the couch was a severely heavy guy; I just wanted to kill him there, so we didn't have to deal with him, but Rosco said that's evidence, and we can't have that.

With everyone loaded, we drove off out of the trailer park. The car started to stink with the assholes in there.

Rosco told Vance we were on our way about ¼ mile out.

We pulled into the shop and the door quickly shut.

Vance opened my door when the car stopped. "Are you okay? Are you hurt?"

"No. I'm fine, Vance," I replied and smiled.

"How many did you get?" Vance asked while looking in the car, then over at me. I held up four fingers.

"Holy shit, there were four people there?" Frank said while joining us by the car.

Adio and Linford opened the trunk to drag the two men out. Rosco and I struggled with the two in the back seat.

"How the hell did you get them all in here, just the two of you, without being seen?" Adio asked while struggling to get a guy out of the trunk.

"Not easily," I grunted as I tore Shannon from the car.

We finally got all four of them tied to chairs, then we waited for the fun to start.

Present Milly

Chapter 23

I STRETCH TO FIND the edge of my comforter. Flipping it back and swinging my feet to the floor.

What a beautiful morning!

Looking at my phone, still nothing from Vance, but I text him anyway.

I grab some clothes from the closet and head to the bathroom. I brush my teeth, use the toilet, and then get dressed.

My bra slides off the counter when I grab my panties. I bend down to grab it, then BANG; my head hits the corner of the marble counter. I lose my balance and my face slams into the counter's edge.

Dizzy, I sit on the floor and feel a warmth on my cheek. When I pull my hand away from my face, I see I'm bleeding.

Jumping to my feet, looking in the mirror, completely naked, my head is definitely bleeding. I grab the first aid kit out of the vanity drawer, hold some gauze, apply pressure, and secure a band aid to the wound. I ended up changing the gauze three times before the bleeding stopped.

Heading downstairs, I mentally prepare myself for whatever shit talk Theo and Daniel will give me when I hear a woman talking in the meeting room. It's Aanya. I stare into the space while I walk by to see Nikolaj and Demyan talking with her.

I don't say anything.

I just keep walking.

I hear Demyan yell my name. I turn to see him running out of the meeting room. "M, your head is bleeding," he says, then he grabs my face in his hands, analyzing my left temple.

"Yeah, I...Hi, Aanya. How are you feeling?" I ask with my face still in Demyan's hands.

She smiles and says, "I'm sore but healing nicely. You, on the other hand, WOW!"

"Oh, no, this is nothing," I say, trying to downplay the situation, but I touch my head and realize I'm bleeding again. "I hit it this morning," I say, staring at the blood on my fingers.

Nikolaj stares at me with his usual *I hate you* look he always has toward me.

Great!

Last night meant nothing. He's like Dr. Jekyll and Hyde, two personalities in one body, and he's completely unpredictable.

"You need stitches. Let's go!" Demyan grabs my hand and leads me to the kitchen.

He guides me to a stool by the island and sits me down. Adjusting myself on the seat so I'm comfortable, he slams a medical kit on the island beside me, making me jump.

It's much more advanced than my tiny first aid kit in my room. He grabs the stool beside me, moves it closer, sits down, grabs my legs, and turns me toward him.

We are sitting extremely close.

I see Aanya walk into the kitchen, and Nikolaj is leaning against the column between the kitchen and dining room.

I guess last night was a mistake, so I'll take the win; I got to kiss him and forget about anything else. I roll my eyes to look away from him.

Demyan places his hands on my cheeks and tilts my head down. "How exactly did this happen?" He asks, then starts to dig through the kit.

I see Nikolaj take a few steps toward us, then I glance back to what Demyan is doing and answer, "clumsy!"

"Obviously! Keep talking, M," Demyan demands.

"I bent down to grab something and misjudged the distance to the counter corner."

"Ok. And this?" He rubs his finger down the line bruise giving me goosebumps from his gentleness.

"I guess I hit my head hard enough to make me stumble, then hit my face on the edge of the counter." I turn my head away from him to see Aanya pouring coffee, then sliding me a cup across the island.

"We've all done that, but maybe not to that extreme," she says and laughs.

"Ok, stitches time. Ready?" Demyan adjusts himself, his legs are on either side of mine, enclosing me between him, and his feet are resting on the rungs of my stool. His face is right in my face, and I can feel his breath on my skin.

If Nikolaj is over me, I'll maybe fuck this boss.

Wow, Demyan smells good.

I try to look around to not stare at him, but he is a sexy ass man. My god, Russians make men differently.

He sets a cloth on my lap and tells me to hold still. I feel a prick in my forehead.

"This should help dull the pain when I stitch you up," he says with his head slightly tilted up, concentrating on what he is doing.

"You're stitching me up?" I ask, surprised. He just smiles and continues working on my head.

Aanya says, "I have to go, but I'll see you all soon." She rounds the island.

Demyan turns slightly to say goodbye.

"Take care, Milly!"

"You too, Aanya." I watch her walk over to Nikolaj. She puts her hand on Nikolaj's chest, he smirks, and a tiny bit of jealousy hits me; then Aanya walks out.

I jerk and tense at the first poke of the needle going through my skin and squeeze my hands into fists on my lap.

"Hold still, M, or I'll tie you up!" He winks with a smile.

"Warn me next time. That hurts," I scoff with a chuckle.

"I said it would dull, not numb completely," he says slyly.

Nikolaj smoothly glides closer to us, staring at Demyan's work, then locks eyes with me and scowls.

Should I say something to him or just sit here quietly?

Another poke through my forehead and I pull back a little and wince.

"M," Demyan snaps. I hold back the tear about to escape from my eye and nod. "Niko, you may have to hold her down," Demyan barks as he adjusts his position closer to me, pinning my legs together with his.

"I'll stay still," I assure him while looking at Nikolaj. Although, thinking about Nikolaj holding me down and Demyan......

STOP MILLY!

I roll my eyes and clear my thoughts.

I concentrate on holding still while Demyan finishes tying up the second stitch before he starts to laugh. "Glad you found something to stare at!"

I realized I was looking at his dick area mere centimeters from my knees the whole time I was concentrating.

I stutter my words out, "No! No, I was just concentrating so I wouldn't move. I'm sorry."

I whip my eyes over to Nikolaj, whose eyes are now filled with anger as he stares at me. "What? Why are you always so pissed at me?" I ask.

I need to work on my word vomit control when I feel embarrassed.

I see Demyan look up at Nikolaj and then back to me. Nikolaj walks to the opposite side of the island without answering my question.

I ignore my urge to keep asking, and instead, I stare at my coffee cup.

Trina and her husband, Sasha, walk into the kitchen. "Oh lord, what is going on with her?" Trina asks.

"Just stitching up a clumsy lady," Demyan says.

Trina and Sasha laugh and continue on their way to the rest of the kitchen. They are the house cooks and live in the corner room on the other side of the hall from me.

Demyan finishes up the final stitch, grabs a band aid, and puts it on my temple. He holds the sides of my face and tilts my head down a bit to kiss the band aid. My heart stops, my core tingles, and my cheeks blush.

"There, all done," he says while adjusting his footing to stand up.

"Thanks!" I jumped up, panicked, and grabbed my coffee.

I attempt to walk out, but Demyan catches me by the arm and hands me a bottle of ibuprofen.

"Thank you again," I say, then glance at Nikolaj and speed walk down to the basement office.

"Good morning, nerds," I say, trying to act normal, hoping they won't make a big deal about my face.

"Good morning......What the hell happened, Milly!" Daniel stops what he is doing and starts walking over to me, and Theo follows suit.

"Tell me, the other guy looks worse?" Theo says sarcastically.

Daniel looks at the band aid, then asks, "fight or clumsy?"

"Clumsy," I reassure him.

"True Milly fashion," Daniel says while nudging Theo.

"Go back to work, assess," I say while turning toward my desk. I glance at my phone for Vance, but still nothing. I text him about my head and go on with my day.

I have been studying this file on my desk for about an hour.

Theo and Daniel are arguing over their everyday stuff. Daniel likes to get involved with Theo's projects but usually only tells him what he is doing wrong. He swears it's only to help Theo, not piss him off, but I know better. They end up bitching and complaining about each other like toddlers.

I usually don't let them get to me, but my head is pounding, and they are not helping.

"Shut up! You two are acting like goddam children!" I yell out! They look at me with surprised looks on their faces.

"Well, someone is in a mood," Theo spouts out, and both turn away from me. I dig out the bottle of ibuprofen Demyan gave me and take two.

"Sorry, guys. I just have a headache."

"All is forgiven!" Daniel smiles and turns back to Theo.

Today is going to be a long ass day.

Past Milly
19-years-old
Chapter 24

WE'VE LOOKED THROUGH EVERYTHING the men had on them. The big guy had a wallet. His ID said James Henry Johnson, so we called him JJ. The other two didn't have anything.

The one I choked in the chair looked homeless. Probably a runaway 10 years ago.

Leech was a small-time drug dealer with a bad habit of getting paid with sex, and it didn't matter what age. We contemplated dropping him off with his supplier with a note of ways he collected payments from customers, but we didn't want to see him back on the streets. He would die that night, and we would be the executioners.

We didn't know the homeless man, so Vance suggested just shooting him in the head since we still had three more douche fucks to deal with.

With the suppressor in my left hand, I grabbed my Glock, and Vance stood to my right side. He had a hard time not coaching me through things. Such a father figure.

"Point to the forehead," Vance directed.

"I know, Vance," I replied.

This fucker was just sitting there, knocked-out, with no idea what would happen.

"Slowly pull the trigger," Vance said.

I pulled the trigger, and the guy's head flew back and down again.

"Good job, kiddo," Vance said to me.

I looked over to see Shannon awake.

"Showtime," Vance said as he raised his eyebrows and smiled.

Linford moved the dead man away from the group. I stood in front of Shannon. She whimpered through the gag in her mouth. I crouched down on one knee to better make eye contact with her.

"Shannon Thompson, correct?" She just looked at me. "I want to talk for now, okay?" I asked her.

"Don't give them options." Frank cut in. I put my head down, then to the side to look over my shoulder where Frank stood. I took a deep breath and nodded.

"Shannon, do you know why you are here?" She shook her head slowly to say '*no*'. I stood back up.

"It's one thing to fuck your life up, but to take your daughters down *Bullshit Avenue* with you...well, there are no words to describe how shitty of a mom you are." I snarled, and she started to cry. "Stop crying. You don't get to cry!"

Frustrating, knowing that she was only crying because she got caught.

I had looked forward to that night since I was handed the case. That was my redemption for what my mom did to me.

"Do you know these two assholes over here?" I pointed to JJ and Leech.

She nodded yes.

"How about that asshole over there?" I grabbed her head and pointed it toward the dead homeless guy still tied to the chair. Her eyes got wide.

"That's what's going to happen to all three of you tonight. YOU won't die so quickly." I grinned, then noticed the other two men started to stir and wake up.

"Oh good, it's a party now," Adio said.

Vance took off his coat to roll up his sleeves and mentioned in my ear, "Kiddo, First, we want the names of all the other people she paid with her daughters."

I took my coat off and picked up my first weapon from the table by Jared. I was nervous, but I didn't want to show it. No mistakes were allowed! "Vance, do this with me because I don't miss anything."

Adio, Linford, and Rosco each stood behind one of the chairs. Jared sat on the stool by the table, trying to figure out everything he could about JJ and Leech. Frank listened to our interrogation as an extra set of ears. Vance was by my side.

"Let's start with Shannon," he said while pointing for me to lead the way over to her.

"I want to know every name of every person you let rape your daughters," I said while getting into her face.

Rosco removed her gag. "Fuck you! Stupid Bitch," she screamed and spit on me.

Vance's eyes turned black as he filled with fury and said, "that's a fucking mistake!" Then motioned to Rosco, who hit the back of her head with his gun.

"Stupid acts have stupid consequences. Now answer her question," Rosco snarled in her ear.

The two other men were screaming and jerking in their chairs, trying to get free, but Adio and Linford held them down. Vance motioned for me to continue.

"You have no allies here, Shannon. No one even knows you're missing," I pointed out demeaningly. "You are nothing to anybody. But you have a chance to do something good."

"What do you want from me?" She asked, defeated, knowing she was not getting out of there in one piece.

"Names," I said calmly as my brows furrowed, and I cocked my head to the side a bit.

She just stared. I grabbed the pliers from my pocket and hooked her lip piercing with them. She moved around, trying to get out of the plier's grasp.

Rosco grabbed her head to hold it in place. I ripped the piercing through her lower lip with a tight grip on the pliers. Blood poured down her chin as she screamed.

"Names," I yelled at her this time.

She cried and begged, "Please don't do this!" I wondered if her daughters begged her not to let people hurt them.

"Give me names, and maybe I'll end it quickly," I bargained.

"Why do you care about my daughters," She stammered the words out while blood spattered with every word.

"Someone has to. Those girls you had deserve a shot at a good life. Despite their shitty mom," I snapped at her.

"Had?" She asked as her voice shook.

"They are safe now," Vance said, "far away from you!"

"Save someone else's daughters or sons. Give us names," I pleaded with her.

"Will you let me go if I do?" she asked. Did she really think she would walk out of there alive?

"Help us catch these people," Vance said as he knelt in front of her.

"Why? No one cared about me," she whined.

"You don't get to ruin your daughters' lives because you hate your past." Vance followed as he stared at her.

"You should do better for them, Shannon." He showed her a picture of her daughters. She just stared at it with no emotion.

"I'm dead anyway, right?" She asked softly, then looked up at me.

"Do something good for the world before you die. Give it a few less sick fucks to worry about," I said.

Vance walked to me; she glared at me and shook her head, angry with herself for caving.

"Your high has worn off. You will feel everything I do to you," I reminded Shannon. "Make it quick for yourself."

"Fine," She snapped.

Frank grabbed a chair, sat by her, wrote every word she said, and recorded it in case we needed it later. Jared started looking up the collected names.

I moved to Leech while Frank and Jared worked with Shannon. His eyes filled with tears. "Please don't," he mumbled through his gag.

I leaned into his face, with my forehead pressed against his, "You're fucking dead! Fuck you," I snapped in a whisper, then turned to Vance and Linford.

Both stood to the sides of Leech.

Jared yelled from the table, "don't waste your time with that loser. He's a piece of shit but not worth our time."

I nodded at Linford, and he grabbed Leeches head and snapped his neck.

Shannon screamed as she looked in our direction.

JJ was screaming in his gag. I looked over at him, "shut the fuck up," I snapped.

Maybe it was because I was full of anger, or perhaps it was because that case hit close to home, but I wanted to hurt those people, to make them suffer, but instead, I had two easy kills!

Vance grabbed my arm and pulled me to the side.

"Breathe, kiddo! There are so many more assholes to hurt. Sometimes we end some fast and sometimes slow. The less information they have to give us, the less time we waste on them. Pull it together, Milly!"

He said my name. He never said my name. "Look, kiddo, this isn't your past. It's about the victims of each situation. Think of them, not you."

"Okay. Sorry Vance," I said quietly. He squeezed my shoulder, and we went back to JJ and Shannon.

Frank said, "she can't think of anything else." We looked at two notebook pages, front and back, with names and details of people.

"Is this everything?" Vance asked Shannon. She nodded. Vance quickly pulled out his gun and shot her in the face. I looked at him.

"Kiddo-stay focused," he warned. I was fucking pissed. I wanted to hurt her more. I wanted to give the girls some kind of justice for their mother's actions, but Vance shot her.

I walked over to JJ. Resting my hands on his forearms resting on the chair, I asked him, "Why?" He started to cry. Adio stepped to JJ's side to remove his gag.

"I don't know," he said.

"Not a good enough answer! Do you know anything that can help us find the names on the list?" I ask.

"No, I just met these people tonight. I paid for Shannon, and she told me she had something better at her place." I pulled my gun out of the back of my pants and aimed it at him.

"NO! PLEASE, NO! I'm a sick man. I'm sorry! Please! I.." I shot him between the eyes. No thought. No emotion.

Vance walked over to me while I still had my gun pointed at JJ, "Good job, kiddo!" I heard Jared on the phone with the cleaners.

We packed everything we needed from this case and loaded up the cars.

I wanted to wait with Vance for the cleaners, but Rosco pulled me to the vehicle. "Las, let's go. Vance will be fine. You need to be safe."

Back at the house, I sat quietly watching for Vance. "He's okay, mouse," Adio said. Then headlights were coming up the driveway. Vance! I met him in the doorway.

"You okay, kiddo?"

"Yep! Just worried about you," I smiled, and he chuckled.

"I'm always good." I threw my arms around his waist to hug him.

"I can't lose you, Vance," I mumbled into his chest.

"You won't," he said, then kissed the top of my head.

Present Milly

Chapter 25

THE DOOR CLICKS OPEN, and Demyan walks in. "How's the head, M?"

"Hurts, but fine!"

"Good. Don't forget your pills." I pick up the bottle and shake it at him, then Nikolaj comes through the door, and I turn myself back to the file I was working on, trying not to make eye contact.

Leaning my head in my hand, a file lands on the one I am looking at. I looked to see which asshole dropped it, and there stood Nikolaj. Of course.

"I need this done now! All the information you can get about Leone's Shipping Company. Business and personal lives of everyone in that file," he says firmly and demandingly.

His voice is rough, demanding tone makes my body rebel against me, and I feel my center reacting to him.

"Ok," I whisper while looking up at him. He nods one sharp nod, then walks away.

As he walks to his desk, I watch his perfect ass in his black suit pants. My mind races to how he made me feel last night and how his beard tickled me. I squeeze my thighs together to ease the building ache for him.

MILLY, GET IT TOGETHER!

Then I realize Nikolaj is giving me one of his files. One of his business files. He's trusting me with it. I adjust in my seat, trying to hold my smile and open the file.

The Leone family. four-generation shipping heirs. If I've learned anything from Frank and Jerad about multi-generational businesses, they are good at hiding what keeps them going, legal and illegal. I'm good at finding things that aren't supposed to be found for the Leone family.

Time to do what I do best. I search, stalk, scroll, and hunt. Click after click after click, typing continuously. All four of my screens have a purpose right now.

I spend the next few hours searching for all the obvious starting points. Social media, news, public records, business records, anything that came up with the Leone name attached.

I started to dig deeper into all the men, but they are old school and try to stay away from any modern technology. That makes finding information on them harder, but not impossible.

Luca Leone and his father, Matteo Leone, are the original owners of Leone Shipping Company. They keep off the grid. They don't have social media or online subscriptions; they don't even have email addresses.

Luca's son Anthony and his three sons run the business now, well, two of the three sons. Anthony has some online news subscriptions and an email account, but it's full of junk mail, and nothing has been sent out of that account. He does have a couple unpaid parking tickets, but that's it.

Their taxes look shady, but anything government related isn't worth the risk of us potentially getting caught.

These three men don't make waves or draw attention to themselves. Anthony's two older sons, Luca and Matteo, named after their elders, live the way of their elders, except they stream TV. They don't have any social media.

The youngest of Anthony's sons is Enzo, an apparent black sheep of the family. He was not loved, and it shows.

He's all over every social media there is. He has picture after picture of himself. He is also a frequent visitor to many *quick fuck* apps. I scroll through all his accounts, and none of his social media accounts have a picture of him with a partner.

That's weird, considering he likes his *fuck* apps.

I get to it-his home computer. This wasn't as hard as I figured it would be. He had basic cyber security that you can download for free. Either his family didn't love him enough to get him a good security setup, or he didn't care.

I see nothing really out of the ordinary at first glance. A lot of dick pics. His small skinny dick with a small mole or skin tag on the shaft, making it easy to id if need be. He has an abnormal amount of his dick pics saved to his computer, thousands of pics.

GROSS!

I search for another level of his computer, one not obvious to the world, and you must be trained to navigate. I see a single file on this hidden level. It's password protected but easily deciphered, considering all his passwords are the same.

Sexmachine69!

Such a confident idiot with a tiny pecker. I click to open the file and freeze, stunned at what it contains. 757 files in this folder. Each file is labeled with a name, date, and age. The first file is named Lisa-3/20/2010-15 years old.

I quickly push my chair back, aggressively pull open a drawer, and fumble to grab a flash drive before sliding back to my desk to start downloading all the files.

I wait impatiently at how long this is taking. What if the folder is set to self-destruct when tampered with by an outside source? My fingers start tapping on my desk, I feel my face tensing up, and I let out a low annoyed growl.

I looked around the room to see if anyone had heard it. My impatience has drawn Demyan's and Nikolaj's attention. They both are walking toward me now. I turn to my screens to see someone is using my hacked computer.

Who the fuck is using it?

The bosses stand behind me but don't say a word. They just study all my screens.

I connect to the webcam of the hacked computer to see who it is. We get a view of 34-year-old Enzo Leone staring at his laptop. He looks nervous.

Does he know I'm in his file?

There is no way he is tech-savvy with the basic factory shit he has on his computer. I lock his folder with a new password, so he can't access the pictures anymore.

Finally, the folder is downloaded. I jump up and throw the drive to Daniel and demand, "tell me how many files are on that drive?" He nods and runs to his computer.

I'm determined to do justice for all of Enzo's victims. I screenshot Enzo's face.

I'll get this motherfucker tonight and make him pay.

Then I'm out of his computer before being found.

I jump past Demyan and run to Daniel's desk. No one's saying anything. They're just letting me work.

Daniel says, "one folder appeared."

"Click it," I demand as I stand next to him, watching his computer. 757 files load up.

"Great! Click on the first one. I need to see if it's Enzo in any of those pictures!"

Daniel follows orders, and just as the pictures load, then grunts out, "what the FUCK! JESUS CHRIST!"

He jumps off his chair, and I jump in without hesitation, turning back to the screen. I scroll quickly through the pictures until I see a man in a mirror with his victim under him. I click the image to see he's looking at himself in the mirror, so I zoom in.

It's Enzo!

I meet the bosses back at my desk. Theo comes over, but Daniel sits on Vance's desk in a trance staring at the floor with his hands fisted together over his mouth.

I'll deal with him in a minute.

I look at each boss before talking. Nikolaj has his usual *fuck you* look, so I'll just focus on Demyan. I sit, turn my chair a little to angle toward Demyan, and say, "Enzo is a child rapist. 757 files are hidden in the folder I found. Each could be a potential victim, considering they all have names, ages, and dates. I opened the first file and found a picture of Enzo's face, proving he was guilty. So basically, whatever you want from the Leones, this is your leverage because they would want this covered up. There's nothing on any of the others. They all keep their lives quiet. THIS! They would pay to keep out of the news."

Demyan looks at Nikolaj and says, "blackmail!"

I shrug and say, "basically."

"Good job, M," Demyan says to me with a smile and a wink.

I smile, proud of my work until I notice Daniel still on Vance's desk. I walk over to him, sit down, and rub my hand over his back.

"I'm sorry, Daniel! I should have never had you look at those files."

He looks over at me. "I've always known shit like that existed, but you never think you would actually have to see it. I hate that I saw it and that it happens." Daniel takes a deep breath and continues, "I'm glad you do what you do, Milly. I just have so many questions or maybe statements. I don't know. I can't wrap my head around any of it." He rubs his forehead and looks down again.

"You don't have to," I say, and now Theo is crouched in front of Daniel. "Let's have dinner tonight. The three of us. You can ask me anything you want. No holds barred, or we can talk about anything else. Whatever you want. Ok?"

I nudge Daniel, which makes him smile at me and say, "deal! 7 work for both of you?" Theo and I nod at each other, then at Daniel.

"7 it is," Theo says.

I walk back to my desk, noticing Nikolaj has placed himself on the empty spot of my u-shaped desk and Demyan opposite him. They are looking at all the information I printed on the Leones and the screens.

My chair is now slightly behind them. I take my seat, look over at Demyan and apologize, "sorry, family first." He nods in agreement.

Nikolaj, sitting on my desk, puts his shoe on the arm of my chair and turns my chair toward him, and pushes it back a little further, so now I have no choice but to look at him, too.

"OOOKkayyy! I'll face you, too," I say with big, annoyed eyes.

"Good," Nikolaj snaps!

Demyan asks most of the questions regarding the shipping company. I show and explain everything I found out. Making sure to offer equal attention to both bosses.

"I did notice that all six men have the same meeting date in their calendars. Tonight. Is that with you two?" I asked.

"No," Nikolaj says while crossing his arms.

I nod, move closer so I can type, and Nikolaj removes his foot from my chair.

I wonder if Demyan sees how he acts around me.

"Here it is," I say as I pull the information up on my screen.

Demyan leans in, and Nikolaj leans over me and looks from over my shoulder, holding the back of my chair.

I can smell both their colognes, and it gives me tingles in my center. I can feel the heat from their bodies on me.

I look at Nikolaj to see his beard trimmed and perfectly combed. I gaze at his fierce jawline, and the memories of him kissing my neck flood me.

"Milly," Demyan firmly says, and I snap my attention to him.

Nikolaj looked back at me like he knew I was staring at him.

My face turns red, and I stutter to compose myself. "Yes. Sorry. As I was saying. The meeting is tonight. All six men will be there. This is surprising since Enzo has never been invited to meetings per the past calendar attendee lists. So, we can try to get into any tech they have in that room, or you guys can just go down there yourselves." I look between the two bosses.

"Let's watch from here, but have someone ready to go to the building," Nikolaj says to Demyan.

"Done. Let's go eat. I'm starving," Demyan says while walking to the door. "Come on. Lunchtime," he yells to Theo and Daniel.

"Niko, coming?"

Nikolaj nods and follows.

"Let's go, M!" I get up and follow everyone.

I never eat with the group. Why was Demyan so insistent about all of us going to eat together?

Theo and Daniel lead us to the stairs, followed by Nikolaj, then Demyan and I walk side by side.

"Have you heard from Vance?" I asked Demyan.

"No." He pauses for a second, then says, "you two are really close."

"Yeah, he's like a father to me."

"What happened to your real father?"

"He died when I was 8."

"I'm sorry, M! What about your mom?"

I shrug, look over at Demyan and answer nonchalantly, "oh, Vance killed her and her boyfriend when I was 12."

My face slams into Nikolaj's back as he stops dead right in front of me on the stairs and looks over his shoulder at me.

"Sorry, I wasn't watching," I apologize, and he turns to finish the staircase, but I don't move.

"Wow, he's intense," I say quietly, and Demyan laughs.

"Come on." He nudges me up the stairs.

The kitchen smells fantastic, but it always does. Trina and Sasha are the best cooks. I glance at all the people in the dining room talking to each other.

"Is there something going on?" I ask Demyan.

"No, just lunchtime. Everyone comes in for it. YOU don't, but everyone else does," he explains, then chuckles while elbowing my arm.

The dining room gets chaotic, with everyone getting their food and finding somewhere to sit.

I take this opportunity to sneak behind one of the columns that separate the dining room from the foyer and bolt to the basement stairs.

I don't do crowds, especially without Vance.

Once I'm at my desk, I call Vance.

No answer.

Past Milly
22-years-old

Chapter 26

TIME PASSED ON.

Year after year.

Case after case.

We hunted all over the country. Florida, Arizona, California, East coast, West coast, North, South, then other countries- France, Jamaica, Jersey, and Canada.

We were frequent fliers.

Things were getting more and more complicated with the new technology that was coming out. Making it harder to track some but more accessible to follow others.

More people had been recruited with backgrounds in combat, war, military, law enforcement, and other experiences that could have helped us. All those people wanted was to help stop child abuse, domestic abuse, sex crimes, and trafficking by stepping up to fight with us for our cause.

Vance had set up divisions worldwide, and each division had a 'go-to' or boss. Vance was the US boss and worked in close contact with all of them.

There were 183 people who all worked in the US, and Vance had assistants who helped manage them. They were divided up into 13 coalitions throughout the US. Each group had a group of states to take care of.

Frank geared his attention mainly on the dark web. He had a ton of people in other countries that worked with him. They tracked anything and everything.

Jerad searched for transactions involving human trafficking, solicitation for sex with minors, accusations of rape, and domestic abuse. Our coalition had one rule-Do not hurt innocent people.

Adio, Linford, Rosco, and I were joined by Terrell, Rosa, Kit, Luna, and Dominick. Adio was put in charge of all eight of us. He also organized hunts throughout the country.

We were all ghosts. Declared dead in everyday society. Our identities were erased, we were untraceable, and we used fake IDs when flying.

We were the hunters in the dark, and no monster was safe from us.

It had been 10 years since that day Mary and Jared saved me.

I never thought I'd make it to 22 years old back then.

Well, technically, I didn't. Jared produced a death certificate for me. It said I died at 12 years old, and the cause of death was murder.

He presented it to my grandma, acting like a detective. When she asked what happened, he told her my mother and Skip had killed me, and they were on the run.

He told her my body was very mangled and recommended a closed casket. He warned her not to view my body.

From a distance, I watched the beautiful funeral she had for me. The absolute devastation I watched her experience broke my heart.

Jared returned to her a few days later to tell her my mother and Skip were found dead in a burned-up car.

He said she didn't even look sad, more like relieved.

She asked what had happened. Jared told her the toxicology report said there was a ton of drugs and alcohol in their systems, and they were alive when the car started on fire, but they couldn't get out.

"So, they burned alive?" She asked him. Jared nodded, and she said, "good, they deserve to burn in Hell."

When my grandmother didn't want mom's body, Jared had his guy cremate her and skip, throwing the ashes in the garbage.

Good to have connections in funeral homes and cemeteries.

I know what happened to them, and Jared wasn't lying. They were fed a ton of drugs and alcohol. Vance, Jared, Rosco, and Adio crashed their car and started it on fire. They were alive when they began to burn.

I would go to my grave from time to time. I liked to see my grandma there, and I sat behind a nearby headstone to hear her talk to my gravestone. She would tell *me* everything going on in her life and stories of her past that she probably would have said to me if I had been around her growing up.

She died when I was 19.

Vance helped me plan my attendance at her funeral. We waited until everyone left the viewing the night before, and the funeral home director, a friend of Vance's, let us in to see her.

She looked so peaceful, but I know the last of her life was filled with guilt and regret because of me.

I cut a piece of her hair off. I wanted her with me for the rest of my life.

We watched them bury her in between my father's headstone and mine.

I visited her whenever I could, and Vance always came with me. I'd tell her everything I was doing. The truth of what I was doing, about my new family, the hunting, and the killing.

My whole life was consumed by horror and death. Every tattoo Linford has given me was about death, demons, devils, angels, and gods.

It was hard to believe in just one religion with all the different cultures and religions. Our beliefs were not a concern for any of us.

We were all a team, and we were protecting the innocent victims we saved.

We were a united force and invisible to all. If we needed or wanted your skills, we would find you.

Frank found two events advertised in code on the web. Both were in Arkansas, a day apart and within an hour of each other.

It crossed his mind that they could be set up by law enforcement, but it was improbable.

The first event, in code, was advertising to rapists. Frank said it's probably an event put on by RRP-Rapists Rights and Privileges. These fucks think it should be legal to rape someone as long as they do it on their own property. Dumb fucks! That one was on a Friday.

The second event was also in code, but Frank could make out the lingo for sex trafficking minors. That one was on a Saturday.

We don't know how many people had seen the advertisements or how many could make out the codes. Vance prepared for the worst and called in people from other parts of the US, Ireland, Italy, and Africa. They had big teams, and Vance knew they would be able to send people over to help.

Lara was the head of the division in Ireland. She had ties to the Irish mafia, and she had 70 people under her that did what we did. She brought 20 people plus herself.

Dante was the leader of the Italian division. He had 30 people who worked under him, bringing 11 plus himself.

Mazi was the leader of the division in Africa. He had the most people under him, 270 to be exact. He had assistants that helped him keep tabs on his country. He brought 50 people, plus himself and an assistant.

The US was able to get 44 people to join us in Arkansas.

It was a 2-day hunt. 120 of us needed to get in, get the job done and get out unseen. No pressure.

Present Milly
Chapter 27

'*FUCK VANCE! WHERE ARE you!*' I text him.

It's been three days.

Vance always keeps in touch when he leaves me. I want to call Jared, Mary, Adio, or anyone from my family. I need to know Vance is ok, but I cannot risk Nikolaj or Demyan finding out about them. As far as they knew, it was just Vance and me. We have been cautious not to mention our family, and this is not the time to disclose them.

When Vance leaves, he tells them it's to hunt someone, which isn't a lie; just how many are hunting isn't disclosed.

They trust Vance but not me. I'm never allowed to leave without Nikolaj or Demyan. I guess it's because I'd be untraceable if I got away from them.

Looking over the information, I collected today on the Leone family, when I remember to wipe the pictures off of Daniel's computer. I pull out the drive and head back to my desk as the door clicks open, and Theo and Daniel walk in.

"Just taking that shit off your computer, Daniel," I clarify to Daniel.

"Thanks. Hey, the bosses were looking for you all lunchtime," Daniel says.

"What? Why?"

"We don't know, but Nikolaj didn't look happy." Theo shakes his head.

"Does he ever," I snapped.

My phone vibrates. I excitedly grabbed it, thinking it would be Vance. Demyan texted, *I need you in my office, now.*

'Ok,' I text back and head upstairs.

I knock on the office door and wait. No answer. I text Demyan, *'I knocked!'*

'Not Nikolaj's office. Mine!' Then I heard a click in the meeting room, then I saw Demyan walk out of the back corner of the meeting room.

"Seriously!? You've been here three months, and you don't know where my office is?" He asks sarcastically as he stops by the meeting room table with his hands on his hips.

"I figured you shared it with Nikolaj."

"No, come on." He waves to me to hurry up.

His office is much simpler than Nikolaj's office.

"I didn't know there was even a door back here," I say as I look around the room.

"Sit," he says while pointing to the chairs in front of his desk. "Where did you go at lunch?" He places himself in front of me and partially sits on his desk.

"I wanted to call Vance. I'm worried," I reply.

"I was hoping to talk to you. Get to know you better. You've been here for a while now, but I don't know anything about you."

"There's not much to know," I say nervously. Demyan leans off his desk, touches my stitches with his thick fingers, and runs them down my bruised cheek. "I think there is a lot to know about you, M," he says, staring at my face.

Demyan has always been nice to me, but never this touchy-feely. I pull back in my chair and say, "you called me up here to get to know me better, or is there work to do?"

"All work and no play?" He questions with a smirk. He's charming, handsome, and smells really good.

"Yes. If we talk all day, we'll run out of time to set up for the meeting," I say.

"Another time, then." He smiles and walks around his desk.

"Come here. I want to show you something," Demyan says, curling his finger for me to follow him. I hesitate for a second but then walk around.

Does he know Nikolaj kissed me?

Is this a competition between them now?

I'm thinking too far into this. I lean down to look at Demyan's screen. He shows me a picture of the office room Leones will be using.

BANG! Nikolaj busts through the door, yelling, "did you find her?!"

I stand up straight, wide-eyed, and speechless.

He stalks toward me. "You were told to eat with us," he barked!

"Niko," Demyan motions for him to calm down and continues saying, "let's get this figured out."

"You do as you are told to do," Nikolaj says, pointing at me and then walking to the desk's other side.

I'm furious!

Who the fuck does he think he is?

I want to say so many things to this asshole!

Demyan starts, "we need access to all the cameras, phones, anything and everything you can get into...we want." I nod to Demyan and glare at Nikolaj. "Have it ready by 6pm tonight. Can you handle that, M?"

"Sure can." I smile at Demyan.

He continues to explain that since Enzo is a rare participant in the meetings, tonight is a one-time deal. We need it right the first time. "Got it! I can have this ready in time as long as I get room to work." I sneer at Nikolaj.

"Great," Demyan says, looking between his business partner and me, "well, I don't see this meeting going anywhere, so get out of my office, both of you."

Nikolaj and I glare at each other as we walk out.

Reaching the meeting room doors, Nikolaj leans into me and whispers, "Four! Don't make me keep counting," then walks into his office and shuts the door.

It takes everything I have to not bust through his door and ask him what '*four*' meant.

Present Milly

Chapter 28

IT'S 5PM.

I'm all set up to take over suite 37D on the 37th floor of the Pensacola building at 155 Stateside Avenue. I run a few tests while the room is empty, so we don't get caught if something goes wrong.

My phone vibrates. A text from Demyan, '*My office. Need updates.*'

I walk up the stairs, past Nikolaj's office, and through the meeting room to Demyan's office. His door is open, and he is alone.

"Give me good news, M," he says, smiling and walking around his desk.

"I'm done and ready. Everything is set up downstairs."

"You're ahead of schedule. That's great! I knew you could do it!" He's standing in front of me now, and although he is gorgeous to look at, this is awkward.

"Yep," I exaggerated the pop in the last 'p,' "was there anything else you needed to know?" I ask, hoping I can leave.

He stares at me for a second. "No, I guess. Since you are ready, I'll head down and take a look. I just have to finish a few things.

You can wait here if you want. Grab a drink." He motions to the mini-bar.

"No, I'll just meet you downstairs."

"Ok, but I still want to get to know you. So maybe you'll have dinner with me sometime at my house, and we can talk more personally."

"Sure," I suspiciously sigh, "see you downstairs."

I practically run to the basement. This must be a game between the bosses. What the fuck is going on?

I bust through the basement office door and slam myself down on my chair.

"How do you two work for the bosses! They don't give anyone room to work. It's constantly over my shoulder or going to one office or the other. Nikolaj is always pissed at something." I let a long, loud growl before looking at Theo and Daniel. "Sorry. I just needed to vent it out."

"Ok. But the bosses never bug me when I'm working on stuff," Daniel says.

"Nope, they don't bug me either," Theo says, "maybe they find you irresistible?" He raises and lowers his eyebrows at me.

"Do you want me to punch you in the face?" I ask, gritting through my teeth.

"Nope," he cowers, stops making faces, but sends a shit-eating grin to Daniel.

"Is it because I'm a woman, and they don't think I can do it?"

Neither one answers immediately, but then Theo says, "you are one of two women that work on this side of their business, and the other one is a lesbian. Wait, are you a lesbian, too?"

"No, but I'm seriously considering it if it keeps them off my ass," I smirk. I toss my head to the back of my chair and stare at the ceiling. "I miss Vance."

"Yeah, about that dinner tonight," Daniel says, "you can't get out of it even if you're in a bad mood. Theo and I have questions."

"I figured you would." I laugh and shift forward in my seat." I will answer whatever you ask." I smile, then turn to the door as it opens.

Sven walks in, followed by Gus. "Bosses sent us down for information about the meeting, Milly," Sven says while walking to me. Gus stops by Theo and Daniel to see what they are working on.

"Yep, I'll print a folder," I say. Sven lingers around my desk, touching the magnetic ball display I have.

"If that falls, I will kill you," I say without looking at him. He moves his hands to his pocket, rocking on his heels, and looks around until I am done.

I hand him the file, and he flips through the pages.

"Use the service entrance. There's not a body scan checkpoint there."

He nods, "thanks." He motions for Gus, and they walk out.

Nikolaj comes in before the door closes. Great. Here we go. He walks straight to my desk, stands there looking around at my computers, then looks at the guys working on stuff.

"Good night, gents," he demands toward Theo and Daniel. They nod and start to walk out.

"We're still on for 7, Milly?" Daniel asks.

"I'll be there," I say to them. Then turn to Nikolaj and ask, "where's Demyan?"

"He's going to the building in case something goes wrong."

I pull my brows together, then proceed to explain what I have set up with the headsets, the voice changer, that he will be talking to the group through the phones like a conference call. He seems to understand. I tap into the cameras to watch everyone enter the meeting, but no one has arrived yet.

I hand Nikolaj the headset when he says, "this is your job."

My eyes widened. "What?" I choke out, "you told me to find info and set all this up. You never said I had to do anything with the meeting!"

"Now you do," he says calmly and firmly.

I ask, "what do you want from them?"

"Shipping rights." That short answer makes me turn to him with a confused look.

"That's it? All this so they can ship your stuff?"

"Yes," he answers and runs his hand through his hair.

Turning back to the screens, I see a server walk into the meeting room with pitchers of water, glasses, and a folder for each spot. She lays everything out perfectly.

My heart is racing.

I feel unprepared.

I don't know exactly what the bosses do or why they need shipping rights, but I guess I can bullshit my way through this.

I take a deep breath and let it out slowly. Ok, Milly-you got this, I think to myself.

I put the headphones on and adjusted the computer settings and voice changer settings. Nikolaj sits on my desk with the screen to his right and puts on an extra set of headphones.

"If I need you to help me, will you?" I ask him.

"Of course." He rubs the back of his hand against my cheek. I blush, and he cracks a smile. "Ty tak legko krasneyesh," he purrs as his hand cups around my jaw. I swallow hard and gaze into his eyes.

Past Milly
22-years-old
Chapter 29

FOUR CAMPS WERE SET up within a six-mile radius of the coordinates in the ad. Each of the division leaders took a tent to supervise.

The coordinates lead us to the middle of a cornfield. We would have called bullshit if it wasn't for the 50'x50' section of corn cut down and a single vehicle-width path leading from the highway. We were in the right place.

We set up cameras in the trees. Each of the four camps could see the feed.

We had 12 people set up on tech, 10 were lookouts around the field, and 10 people set up to check the IDs of anyone that came. The rest of us were suited up in full gear, ready to destroy fucking rapists.

6 am Friday.

Lara radioed that a black Toyota Tundra drove into the middle of the area.

We watched the monitors to see a man get out and open the cover to the truck bed. He pulled out two folding tables, letting them fall to the ground.

A van pulled in and parked next to the truck. The driver jumped out, ran to the back of the van, and opened the doors. He pulled out three folding tables.

The two men set up the legs of each table in a line. Then both vehicles left.

"What the fuck? Is there registration for this shit?" Adio snapped.

"It would be easier to get their names, wouldn't it?" Vance joked.

After a few hours of nothing, a man walked out of the corn stalks and to the tables.

A few minutes later, three cars pulled up to the tables, nine people got out, and the three cars left.

Vance sent a car out to follow that convoy. Rosco suggested we start grabbing them before the crowd got too big, but Vance said to wait. There wasn't anything indicating that it was a rape event.

Three more cars pulled in, and nine more people got out. One car opened the trunk, and they grabbed blankets and a 5-gallon bucket.

Those three cars left, and Vance sent another car to follow them.

"What the fuck is in the bucket?" Linford asked.

"I can't see," I said while squinting at the screen.

We watched the 3rd convoy of cars pull in, drop nine people off, then leave, and one of our cars followed them.

"I'm guessing they don't want many cars parked there. That would draw attention," one of the Italians said.

"Where are they picking these people up from?" I asked.

Vance got on the phone with Frank and explained what was happening.

Frank scrambled to see what he had missed about the pick-up location. There was nothing.

"They must have done this before. Those men must have known each other from previous times," Frank said.

"It's fine. We're here, so let's do what we came here to do," Vance said.

"There's not much we can do if they stay off the grid, I heard Frank say through the phone.

"Does anyone know where these people are coming from?" Mazi asked.

"No, we are trying to find out," Vance said.

Lara said, "We will get every asshole that shows their face here, and they will pay for their crimes."

Lara was the great-granddaughter of the former Italian Mafia boss man, Marco Carbone. She was an assassin for her grandfather, Davide Carbone. She was feared by many. She took amusement in hurting people that deserved it. She stepped down from the mafia to do this line of work with us.

"A Convoy is at a run-down motel off highway 319," one of our guys radioed.

"Roger that," another one said over the radio

"A convoy sighted at a motel on Rigered street in Minco."

"Roger that."

"The motels are within 5 miles of here in each direction," Lara said.

"Heading back to the field on Highway 319."

"Roger."

"Where's the 3rd convoy we saw?" Rosco asked.

"Base to Headhunter, do you copy?" Vance asked.

"Headhunter here," a woman said

"What's going on with the convoy?" Vance asked.

"We are driving down county nine. We may have been spotted, so we pulled back some. The car seems to be just driving."

"Head back to base. We will try again when the cars come back," Vance said.

"Roger that," she said.

"Fuck! If they were spotted, they must have told the other convoys," Adio said

"All hunters back to base now," Vance radioed. "Pull back and head to base!"

"Roger"

"On our way."

"If the cars are seen returning to the bases, we will be fucked," Rosco said.

"Too many people lingering around. We are bound to be spotted," Linford said while crushing a paper cup in his hand and throwing it into the garbage.

"Who's not going to see six big green tents set up in the trees around a cornfield?" Rosco joked.

"We're fine! This is going to be fine!" Vance tried to reassure everyone.

We were waiting again.

No action at the field except for the 28 people standing around talking. The man who walked in was constantly on his phone. He didn't seem worried but happy.

An hour passed, three cars pulled in, and nine people got out. The vehicles parked, and the drivers' exited. The same happened with the other two convoys of vehicles. 64 people total.

They all seemed comfortable with each other. Chatting, passing beers, and getting rowdy. It was like a giant frat party.

One of the men moved behind the middle table to get everyone's attention. There were two empty tables on each side of the table the man was standing at.

"Fuck these assholes," Rosco spouted.

"Shut up, man!" Linford slammed his hand on Rosco's chest.

Lara said, "heads up, light gray van heading to the group!"

The van parked behind the man at the table, and a young man who looked to be tweaking got out and opened the two back doors. Four women jumped out in the same messed-up condition.

"Get ready. This could be the reason they are here. Get into position on the field," Vance said.

Adio, Linford, Rosco, and I took a truck to the field. We parked on the main highway by some trees. Adio told us to spread out but stay within sight of each other. We started walking through the field.

Corn stalk after corn stalk hit us. Thankfully there was a good wind to cover our movements. When we spotted the group, we saw them pushing the women around. The women were panicking and crying.

"Tie them up," said the man we assumed was the leader. 3-4 guys wrestled each woman down.

We stood and watched this happen right in front of us. Rage started to consume us.

"Stay calm. Never fight with emotion," Adio said.

"Hold," Vance said over the radio.

"Wait until their intentions are clear! No mistakes," he barked.

The leader starts to talk. "Four seductive vixens are lying here in front of us. We brought them here to prove a point! Women who partake in alcohol and drugs lose control, cannot make decisions and deserve what they get for being irresponsible. They spend all their time flirting, drinking, doing drugs, and dancing their seductive moves to tease men and then walk away. We will not allow this to happen. They can no longer come to our properties and get our hopes up for sexual activities, then change their minds and leave. They walk around like sluts and whores, but cry when they get what they want. No more are we the monsters for taking what they flaunted in front of us. Gentleman, today we show these four sluts what it means to dress like sluts who are drunk and high on MY land!"

The men cheered, and the women screamed and thrashed around to get off the four tables.

Some men removed their clothes, while others cut the clothes off the women. "Today, we all partake in these four whores! Today, these whores will get what they ask for, our attention and intentions! Today we teach these whores that if you show off your assets like a whore on my property, we will do whatever we want with you! It's our right!!"

The first group of men started to approach the tables the women were tied to.

"NOW!" Vance yelled over the radio.

Like a scene from a movie, 150 soldiers charged into the opening of that field.

"GET DOWN!"

"GET THE FUCK DOWN!" We all yelled at these fucks. 64 men knelt in the field with 150 guns pointed at them.

A couple of our people untied the women from the tables.

A van pulled into the field, Vance and Lara stepped out, and Grace and Mary jumped out the back. They ran to the girls and wrapped them in blankets and ran them back to the van. Lara drove them out of the field.

Vance walked over to the men and found the leader.

"Who the fuck are you?" The man snarled.

Vance cocked a grin, "your worst nightmare." Then grabbed the leader's pants from the ground.

"Jeremy Brown. Just the man I hoped you would be," Vance said while looking through the man's wallet.

"All of you are dead today! Rapists have no place in our world," Vance yelled. "Jeremy Brown. Your death will be excruciating."

Adio asked, "what do we do with all these fucks?!"

Vance replied, "kill them, and the cleaners will take them and burn them!"

Vance left with Jeremy Brown and a few soldiers.

It didn't take long to establish order between us and kill the remaining men.

We collected wallets, then faded into the corn back to our bases to tear down and prepare for tomorrow.

Present Milly

Chapter 30

THE TWO OLDER SONS of Anthony, Matteo, and Luca, walk into the room.

"I don't understand why Great Grandpa wants to meet here. His health will barely be able to handle the drive over," Luca says.

"He wants us to be here, so here we are. Just make sure the folders are correct. He wants to go over the final business arrangements," Matteo says.

"Then why the fuck is Enzo coming?" Luca spits.

"He is a Leone, like it or not," Matteo says while sitting down.

"I don't like it! The files look good, brother," Luca says, finding his place next to Matteo. Nikolaj and I watch the brothers make small talk and shift around in their chairs.

It's 5:55pm.

We see Matteo senior pull both big wooden doors and lock them open. He runs back behind the door, and a few seconds later, we see Luca Sr come to the doorway, Anthony is pushing his wheelchair, and Matteo walks in beside them. Luca Jr and Matteo Jr are seen running over to help with their Great Grandfather.

"Hello, boys," Luca Sr says while looking up from his wheelchair and smiling.

"Why couldn't we meet at your house, Great Grandfather?" Luca asks.

"Because I need to get out, and this is my reason to leave!" Luca Sr laughs.

Matteo removes the chair from the end of the table that Luca Sr chooses to sit at. Anthony and Matteo find their spots on either side of Luca Sr, and the others sit.

"Now we wait for the so-called grandson of mine," Matteo Sr spits out.

"He'll be late as always," Anthony says as shame covers his face.

"How are my Great Grandsons?" Luca Sr says, trying to talk as loud as he can with his frail voice.

"Good! Victoria and I are still trying for a baby, but it's just not happening," Matteo Jr says.

Luca Sr nods in acceptance of the answer.

"Leone seed is strong grandson! It will happen. In the meantime, have fun trying," Matteo Sr says, and they all laugh.

"Luca?" Luca Sr directs his attention to Jr.

"Good here! Elizabeth and I just found out she is pregnant again. This is number four," Luca Jr says.

"Great! When she hears Elizabeth is pregnant again, Victoria will think she married the wrong son," Matteo Jr jokes.

"Have Victoria call Elizabeth. Maybe there are some pointers only women know," Luca Jr says, shrugging, and the room fills with laughter.

I'm writing like crazy to keep up with the information I'm Listening to. Nikolaj sits quietly, waiting for the moment to attack.

Enzo walked in, "sounds like the party started without me." The room grows quiet.

"If you were here on time, then you would know what we are talking about," Anthony grits through his teeth.

"Yeah, well, some of us have a life we can't just drop, Father," Enzo says.

"Sit," barks Luca Sr!

Enzo follows orders. Slouches in his chair and looks utterly useless to this meeting.

Luca Sr and Matteo Sr spend the next while discussing what will happen with the business after Luca Sr dies. Everyone, except Enzo, seems to agree with the plan.

Enzo starts stirring in his seat, "this is bullshit! None of the business goes to me?"

The lawyer walks in. "I see you've discussed the hierarchy!"

"Yes, dear friend," Luca Sr says. Motioning for Dean to sit between Anthony and Enzo.

"Okay, well, I'm here to collect signatures and make sure everyone understands how this works legally," Dean says a few things, and Enzo looks like he will kill everyone.

"Wait until the paper is signed," Nikolaj whispers to me.

"All deals made under my supervision will be honored until no longer needed. Understand?" Luca Sr asks.

"We are men of our word, and we will not screw over our business clients just because one of us dies," Matteo Sr says, and all the men nod except Enzo. They pass the paperwork around, and everyone signs.

"Okay, now to the shitty part," Dean says while turning toward Enzo.

"This legal document states that none of the Leone Shipping business is to go to you!"

"What the FUCK!" Enzo jumps from his chair.

"Your lifestyle of partying and recklessness cannot be associated with our honorable business," Matteo Sr says.

"Sit down, Enzo," Luca Jr says, standing, and Matteo Jr follows. The two brothers tower over Enzo. Surprisingly, they have the same parents.

Enzo sits slowly. Matteo and Luca glare at him as they sit, too.

"This contract states you will get $250,000 a year to live off of, but when you die, the payments stop. They do not go to your kids or wife if you obtain any," Dean finishes.

"You're buying me out of business. I'm not even allowed to be a part of it? This is fucked up," Enzo snaps, "and I'm worth more than $250,000!"

I look at Nikolaj, and he nods. I access the phone speaker, and a loud click in the meeting room gets the men's attention. I have the voice changer activated, and I slowly say, "I beg to differ, Enzo."

"Who the fuck is this?" Enzo says. The other men asked the same thing.

"Calm down, gentlemen, and I'll tell you who I am." I pause as they compose themselves, then continue, "I have a business proposition for you, Luca Leone Sr." I notice the lawyer grab his phone.

"Put down the phone, Dean Knoels." They all looked around the room to see how I knew he was grabbing it.

Matteo Sr asks, "you can see us?"

"Yes, no sudden moves or my men will have to intrude on your meeting."

"What do you want?" Anthony asks.

"I want a lifetime of shipping rights."

"Why would we ever do that for someone who can't show their face?" Anthony asks.

"Because you have a problem that I can make go away, and no one will ever know. OR the problem gets leaked, and Leone Shipping is no longer so honorable," I say.

"Blackmail! This is ridiculous," Luca Sr says, shoving a folder away from him.

"No, what's ridiculous is how long it's been going on, and no one stopped it," I yell.

The Leones start to mumble to each other, except Enzo, who sits quietly.

"One of you is an evil man," I sing, "one of you is going to die tonight. The blackmail is for us to keep it from being leaked to every newspaper and every Leone Shipping customer."

"What are you talking about?" Anthony snaps.

Enzo starts to get up. "This is bullshit! I'm out!"

"Sit down, Enzo," I say calmly. Then the two wooden doors open, and Gus, Sven, and Demyan walk in. They have distorted face masks on. I look over at Nikolaj; he has Demyan on speaker, so he can hear everything in his earpiece. They point their guns at Enzo, and he backs up to sit. Our men stand guard at the doors.

"Enzo, look what you made me do. Tsk tsk tsk. Well..." I scoff, "now that I have your attention again, let's get to business. I'm sure you all know who isn't like the rest of you, but do any of you know why?" I pause.

"What did you do, Enzo?" Anthony turns toward Enzo and grits at his son.

"Nothing! I don't know what he's talking about," Enzo says.

"Continue, man, on the phone," Luca Sr says.

"Very well. It started in 2010. Enzo was 20 years old when he started saving pictures." Enzo looks scared of his family that is glaring in his direction.

"What kind of pictures?" Anthony asks. I send a single picture from Lisa's file, using a burner phone, to Anthony's phone. I sent the most recent victim's photo with Enzo's face. His phone dings and he looks down at it, hesitating to pick it up.

"I'd look, Anthony. It's important," I say. He slowly picks up the phone and opens the file.

"JESUS CHRIST, ENZO," he says while slamming his phone down.

Luca Sr grabs the phone but is unable to muster words. Matteo Sr grabbed the phone next.

"Fuck Enzo!" He tosses the phone to Enzo's brothers and then hangs his head in his hands.

With tears rolling down his face, Luca Sr says, "you are no Leone! You're a monster!"

Our men blocked the door as Enzo shifted in his chair, trying to stir up a lie to protect his ass. His brothers look at the phone. Rage consumes them.

After a pause, I continue, "I have 757 files. Each file has 100+ pictures taken. All these files are Enzo's victims." The men are distraught at this information. "We want you to ship whatever and whenever we need you to, no questions asked. In return, we won't leak this incriminating information to the public. Leone Shipping will still be as honorable as before, and we will get what we want. Win-Win. Enzo has to die tonight, of course! We cannot let him hurt anyone else." They look at each other, and Enzo wiggles in his chair.

"Fine! You have my word. We will honor your shipping requests," Luca Sr says.

Anthony stands, "but Enzo dies here and now! You are no son of mine, you sick FUCK!"

Our men are on high alert. This isn't the plan, and at this point, anything could happen.

Anthony motions for his two sons to grab Enzo. Matteo Jr and Luca Jr jump the table and clutch their brother. The brothers hold Enzo as Anthony takes his suit jacket off.

Dean tries to talk him out of whatever he has planned but quits when he realizes his words fall on deaf ears.

Anthony approaches his sons. His deep sad look turns cold and hateful when he makes eye contact with Enzo. He punches Enzo in the face. When the older sons reset their footing, Anthony throws a punch at Enzo's stomach. He crunches in pain and coughs out blood.

"PLEASE, FATHER! THEY ARE LYING!" He pleads.

"Don't call me father," Anthony says while punching Enzo three consecutive times in the face.

"Don't talk to me anymore, you worthless shit," Anthony knees him repeatedly in the balls.

This causes Enzo to lose his footing, so the brothers clutch him tighter to keep him upright. Anthony throws blow after blow to every part of Enzo's body. Blood is splattering all over the four men.

The Elders sit at the table looking in approval.

Anthony steps back and pulls a knife from his leg strap. While walking toward Enzo, he says, "Hell is too good for you. I should let these people take you and torture you until they feel you've suffered enough, but I am too ashamed of you. I need to kill you myself, so I can finally be proud of you for bleeding out and suffering on this floor before you die. You are my biggest mistake Enzo!"

He puts the knife's point to Enzo's throat and pushes in slowly through his esophagus.

"I want you to die a slow, painful death knowing we did this to you," Anthony growls while pushing the knife in as far as he can.

"Suffer, brother," Matteo Jr says, gritting through his teeth into Enzo's ear. Enzo coughs blood out, and it lands on Anthony's face. Luca Jr spits on Enzo's face but says nothing to him.

Anthony pulls the knife out, and the brothers let him fall to the floor. He thrashes and struggles to hold his throat as he bleeds out, and the movements he's going through will only cause him to run out of air faster.

Covered in Enzo's blood, Anthony and his sons return to their seats.

Nikolaj motions for me to end it.

"You'll hear from us soon." Our men turn and leave the room, and I disconnect from the phone's speaker.

"Add murder to the blackmail list," I chuckled, shocked at the events.

"Good job Milly," Nikolaj says. I feel a sense of pride in him, but I will not overthink it. He is too hot and cold.

"Everything was recorded. I'll put it in the vault." Nikolaj nods in approval as he continues to sit and watch the men in the meeting room.

They are crying, confused, and angry.

Mattero Jr is on the phone with someone, but it is quick. Probably their cleaners.

Enzo lay alone, dead, or barely hanging on to life. Hard to tell. His father shows no remorse.

Something tells me Enzo was on a hit list with the Leones, and tonight's evidence made it easier to get rid of him.

Past Milly
22-years-old

Chapter 31

FRANK CHECKED INTO EVERY ID we found in the field that day. He checked bank accounts, jobs, families, friends, criminal history, and any incriminating activity they had been up to.

Some men in that field were doctors, college professors, coaches, and family. Men who lived as wolves in sheep's clothing.

Frank gave tips to local law enforcement in each perps city of residence. Hopefully, the hunt we sent law enforcement on will help catch other rapists and sex offenders.

He would say the guy was on the run with a large amount of money from his account.

In reality, we took the money and sent it to victims of the assholes if we could find names. Otherwise, we would keep it and use it to help stop more assholes. We caught 64 men from 18 states.

The next event was scheduled for the next day, and the house was 20 minutes away.

We had an ally 2 counties over. He said we could tent in his pasture.

Vance decided to send half our people home. "Too many people in the pasture will get attention," he explained.

On the day of the event:

We headed to the event. Our convoy split up, and we ended up a ¼ mile from the house, parked behind some trees. We could hear music from the house. This scene seemed off.

"Vance, what the fuck is this place?" Adio said as we stepped out of the truck.

"I don't know. I'll find out," Vance said.

A few minutes later, Vance got out of the truck. "This is it. They must have started early."

Vance radioed to all of the soldiers. He told us to keep low in the wheat field and get to the house.

I'm not sure what 60-plus people crawling through a wheat field looked like, but the wind helped hide our movements.

We spread out but kept each other in sight. Vance stayed in the truck with Kit.

"This is taking too fucking long," Linford growled.

"Patience, brother. No mistakes!" Adio reassured him.

We got to the edge of the property, surrounded by trees. We were divided into four groups, Alpha, Bravo, Delta, and Foxtrot. Adio, Linford, Rosco, me, and 16 others are part of the Alpha team.

"Advance when ready," Vance said

"Alpha, go," Adio said. The alpha team dispersed onto the property hiding behind anything we could find.

"Bravo go," Adio said. Alphas shuffled to a new spot, and the bravos took our places. That continued until we were all surrounding the house and other buildings on the property.

We stood by the house, waiting for our time to run in. The music stopped. Adio held up his fist to signal for all of us to stay. We started hearing yelling, crying, and stuff being thrown.

Adio gave the command to enter. We entered through windows and doors.

We saw half-naked men and women in the living room and dining room. The kitchen was filthy, and there was alcohol all over. Kids were screaming upstairs. There was a man covered in blood crying by the stairs.

Adio directed some of our people to go upstairs, and the rest of us kept guns on the 15 people in the living room area.

Adio started yelling for everyone to shut the fuck up and pushed his gun into the forehead of the man yelling the loudest.

"Shut. The. Fuck. Up," Adio snarled. He turned his attention to the lady next to the guy. "What's in the basement?" She didn't say anything.

Adio radioed to the people outside. "We need a group in the basement."

"Roger that. On our way."

"Jesus FUCK!" One of our guys came running down the stairs, distraught and ready to kill someone.

Adio stepped back, and Lindord took his place, holding the gun to the man. Adio walked to the soldier. "What?"

"There are dead kids up there," the soldier said.

The man by the stairs started to cry louder. Adio looked down at him. "Whose blood is on you?" The man just cried.

Adio grabbed the man's throat, pulled him up, and slammed him into the wall. "Whose blood is that?"

"I didn't mean to," the man whimpered.

Another one of our men came down. "Sir, all the kids were assaulted and abused. four are dead, and three barely awake. They must have been drugged."

Adio's rage built, and the energy in the room shifted. "FUCK!" Adio yelled. "Base, get in here now," Adio said to Vance and the other leaders.

The man was still crying and was about to pass out from Adio's grip around his throat. He dropped the man to the floor.

"What did you do?" Adio growled.

The man whimpered, "what? I didn't mean to. I just wanted to touch her! Oh, GOD! I fucked up!"

"Adio! Come over here," Vance said.

"Vance, you need to go upstairs and see what the fuck is going on. I'll keep him here," Adio said.

"I don't have to right now," Vance placed his hand on Adio's shoulder. "Just step away before I tell you what they found," Vance commanded.

I stood on the opposite side of the room from Vance and Adio. They were talking very quietly and very close to each other. Adio took off his helmet and face mask.

I've never seen a look like that on his face before. He looked heartbroken, defeated as if whatever Vance said had consumed Adio's mind as an utter failure.

"What the fuck is going on?" Linford asked with obvious concern for his brother.

Adio looked at him, then at me. His face told us that we were too late, and the cost was children's lives.

"What do you want us to do?" Linford asked.

Vance put his hand on Adio's shoulder and said, "tie all these fuckers up in the middle of the room. We're burning them alive!" He turned to the team waiting on the stars, "get the victims from upstairs. Take them to the vans with Mary and Grace. Take the dead to the other van. Be careful with all of them. They've been through enough."

The team headed upstairs, and Vance followed with Adio.

A commotion started, and some soldiers swore and ran back downstairs. Unable to handle the scene upstairs.

We got all 15 people tied up in the middle of the room. They fought, swore, and spit at us, but we still overpowered them. We were an unstoppable force fueled with anger and hate.

A man asked the crying man, "why did you do it?" The man cried harder.

Linford asked the oldest-looking man if there were only 15 people in the house. The man spits in Linford's face.

"That's a fucking mistake," Rosco said. Linford hit the man in the face with the butt of his gun.

I started walking up the stairs when a soldier came running down. "It's too much!" He said as he passed me.

I reached the top of the stairs. Scanning, I immediately noticed four rooms up there to my left, and a bathroom was straight ahead of me. I glanced inside the empty bathroom, blood was all over the tub, sink, floor, and toilet, and there were used condoms in the garbage can.

I walked to the first bedroom and saw four of our people in it. They were wrapping three small bodies in sheets and placing them in black body bags.

I heard one of them say, "looks like an overdose."

I saw Vance and Adio talking in the room's doorway furthest from me. Adio looked up at me and headed into the other room.

The second bedroom was empty.

The third bedroom had Adio and a few of our people getting three drugged victims ready to take to medical care.

I reached Vance. He stopped me at the door.

"Kiddo, you don't want to go in there."

"Vance, I'm here to help."

"I know, but...." He stopped and put his hands on my cheeks, bringing his forehead into mine. "Milly, it's a....." His words lodge in his throat, and he closes his eyes before continuing, "I'm guessing she died from the abuse and beatings."

I placed my hands over his hands which were still resting on my face. He was overcome with hate and sadness.

"Please, Milly, go downstairs. I can't have this nightmare haunt you forever. Let it be mine." Tears pooled in his eyes.

"Of course, Vance. I'll go downstairs." He kissed my forehead, and I headed back downstairs.

"How bad?" Linford asked as he walked over to me.

"Four dead, including a baby. three severely drugged."

"Fuck! FUCK!" He yelled.

We were not used to failure of this caliber. It was too much to take in and understand. Rage and hatred were building inside us.

Linford grabbed one man by the hair and pulled him up slightly. "Who set this up? Who the fuck is in charge?"

He punched the guy until his face was full of blood, dropped his back to the floor, and moved to the next person. No one was talking.

Finally, he walked to the man who was crying. The man who obviously killed one of the kids. "Did you kill the baby?" He looked up at Linford.

"I didn't mean to kill her!" He cried.

"Did you kill the other three?"

"No," he whispered.

"How many people were here?" Rosco asked over Linford's shoulder.

"Just us."

A man from the tied-up group yelled, "shut the fuck up, man! FUCK!"

Rosco walked over to him and punched him in the face. "Shut the fuck up, asshole! Let the crier talk!" Rosco growled.

Linford looked down at the crier. "Keep talking."

The man whispered, "Steve set it up."

"SHUT UP, CHRIS!! YOU FUCK!" the man by Rosco yelled.

"ALL you fuckers shut the fuck up," Rosco yelled at the group.

Linford kneeled by Chris. "Keep talking, Chris."

Before he could say anything, footsteps were heard walking down the steps. Our people were seen carrying body bags. We got eerily quiet at what we saw, body bags carefully carried down the stairs and out of the house.

The footsteps continued, and we saw the three living children being carried down, followed by Adio and Vance.

Vance walked over to Linford. "Anyone talking? Any info?" Vance asked.

"Not really. Just that Steve set this up," Linford answered.

"Who is steve?" Vance asked.

"This fucker right here." Rosco pushed his gun into Steve's forehead.

"Who is this guy?" Vance asked while pointing to Chris.

"Baby killer, Chris," Linford gritted his teeth.

"But he's the only one talking." Vance nodded at this point.

"Ok, Chris. What's this?" Vance asked while he held up a circular red card with squares cut out of it and a 2-digit black number on the upper corner.

"Don't you say a fucking word Chris," one man yelled.

Chris started crying again, then sputtered, "Lazlo's card."

"How do we get a hold of Lazlo?" Vance asked.

"I don't know," Chris whimpered.

"Does anyone here know how to get a hold of Lazlo?" Vance asked, holding up the card for the group to see. No one said a word. Vance leaned down to Chris. "Who's in charge here?"

"Steve," he whispered.

Vance walked over to Rosco, holding a gun to Steve's head.

"Chris, you fucking rat," Steve spit out.

"Steve shut the fuck up," Vance said.

Steve snarled, "I'm not telling you shit, asshole!"

Vance yelled, "everyone out!"

Adio walked in with a gasoline container and poured it everywhere except the group of people.

"They will die slowly, with the fire around them eating at their flesh from a distance. Shoot any that try to run," Adio said over the radio.

After a count to ensure our people were out of the house, Vance threw a match inside the house.

The gas ignited.

We watched and listened to the screams of 15 sick fucks slowly being eaten by the flames around them.

That was the most severe case any of us experienced. That was the case that haunts all of us to this day. Lazlo.

Present Milly

Chapter 32

I SAVE THE RECORDING of the Leone meeting to an external drive and get the gear organized and put away.

Nikolaj watches me while sitting at my desk.

"It's 6:45 pm. I'd better get ready for my date with Daniel and Theo," I chuckle nervously.

"Nervous?" Nikolaj asks.

I lean down to put the headphones in the cabinet and say, "I just don't tell stories of my life, that's all." I stand and walk over to my computer to shut it down.

"Why is that?" he asks.

"Just not something I do. Why don't you talk about yourself?" I ask, standing opposite him to admire how his hair frames his face and how his brown eyes stare at me, making my pussy clench.

"You've never asked me anything about me. Just about my work," Nikolaj says, scanning my face.

Finally, I say, "you know you're not very approachable, right? Plus, I doubt you're an open book." I smirk, then bite my lower lip.

"Come here," he kindly says with a half grin and sultry eyes.

I walk over to him, and he grabs my hand to pull me closer. I rest my hands on each of his thighs.

He leans into me and whispers on my lips, "you did good tonight, Milly."

His lip presses against mine tenderly, moving slowly, and I savor his touch. His hand curves around my neck as he pulls back just enough to focus on my face.

"Thank you," I say with desire in my voice and lean in to kiss him more. He wraps his hands around my face, caressing my jaw with his thumbs, and his tongue slides in, filling my mouth with his taste.

Pulling back slightly, he says, "Ty sladok na vkus! Ty tak lagkokrasneyesh," then smiles.

I slightly cringe. How embarrassing for a grown woman to blush at just a kiss.

"I like having this effect on you," he says and kisses my forehead. "You'll be late for your date." He pushes me back a step while he gets off the desk and stands against me.

"Yeah, I should go," I said, disappointed and breathless.

"I *will* see you later," he says firmly, then leaves.

I wait a few minutes before leaving the room. My head is spinning, and I need a moment alone.

When I gain the clarity to go upstairs to the kitchen, I see Nikolaj's office door is shut.

Daniel and Theo move around the kitchen, laughing and cooking.

"Hey, guys! What's cooking?" I ask.

"Baked chicken, potatoes, carrots, and gravy, baby," Daniel says.

"You're in a good mood," I chuckle.

"It's the wine loosening him up," Theo laughs.

I take a seat on the island. Theo pours me a glass, smirking, "I picked the wine, so I hope you enjoy it as much as Daniel does." Theo nods his head toward Daniel, dancing by the stove.

Smiling, I take a drink, "wow! This is good!" I praise.

Theo nods proudly.

"Ok, so do you want to start asking questions now or when we eat?" I inquire.

Theo jumps in, "now! I'll go first. On the stairs, you said Vance and his brother killed your mom. Explain."

"Wow! Not easing in, are we?" I chuckle. Both men grab their glasses of wine and sit around the island to have a good view of me. I shift uncomfortably in my chair.

"Ok. Well, long story short...." I start.

Daniel cuts in, "not cutting stories short. We get all the details."

"I understand you want all the details, but some are still too painful to go in-depth with. So, can we ease into some of my stories just for tonight?" I ask. Both men nod and lean in to hang on to every word.

I start again, "ok. When I was young, my dad died. My mom went batshit insane. My mom's new boyfriend was a piece of shit. Vance and his brother rescued me and killed my mom and her piece of shit boyfriend." I pause as the men react.

"Holy shit. I'm sorry, Milly," Theo says. Daniel takes a big drink of wine.

"Don't be. I don't want pity. Plus, I would never have met you two if things panned out differently in my life," I say and 'cheers' them both.

Daniel goes to the stove to check on the food. The smell brings me back to when Mary and Jared got me home. We had chicken that night, too.

"What's wrong, Milly," Theo asks.

I snap back to reality. "Oh, nothing. It's just the first night at Jared's house; we had chicken. The aroma is bringing back memories," I say.

"Oh shit, Milly! If I knew, I would have made something else," Daniel says apologetically.

"No! It's a good memory! They became my family," I say.

"I didn't know Vance had a brother," Theo says. I stare at him, remembering we didn't tell anyone about this.

"Well, he's gone now," I say and take a massive drink.

"Food is ready," Daniel says, setting the food in front of us.

"Wow! You're a great cook just by the look and smell," I boast.

"Good job, Daniel! Milly, we are both here for you when you want to talk. I just wanted to say that before we get lost in this amazing food," Theo says.

"AWWWW! Thanks, Theo! You are the best two nerds anyone could ever hope to have as friends," I say and hold up my wine glass.

"Sexy nerds, Milly! You mean to say, sexy nerds," Theo jokes. We start to dish up the mouthwatering food and waste no time shoving it into our mouths.

"Daniel, about what you saw today. I'm sorry. Vance and I all see that stuff, so we are sort of numb to it. Well, as numb as one can be, I guess. We get to kill those fuckers we hunt, which helps us overcome the shit we see. I'm here if you ever want to talk about it. Just know that guy is dead now. He can't do that to anyone else."

Daniel nods and says, "It's ok. I'm glad people like you risk everything to help kill those sick fucks."

Theo blurts out with a mouth full of food, "this is so good."

I spent the next few hours explaining parts of my life that couldn't give away that it wasn't just Vance and me.

I tell them I taught myself different languages, but I know who taught me. Thank you, Grace!

I tell them I taught myself how to fight, but credit will always go to the men who trained me every day for so many years.

They hang on every word I say, not judging me, but in support and understanding.

Like real friends!

Present Milly

Chapter 33

I HEAD UP TO my room after dinner, tired and ready to snuggle into bed for what I hope will be a good night's sleep.

I close my door, kick my shoes off, leaving the lights off with the plan to just walk to bed. When I turn and see someone sitting on the couch with a dim lamp on. I jump back to flip the lights on.

"FUCK," I yell! My heart races a thousand beats per minute.

Nikolaj's sitting on the couch, suit jacket off, sleeves rolled up, his undone tie hanging around his neck, the top buttons of his shirt unbuttoned, and a drink in his hand.

"Flavored Vodka isn't that bad," he jokes, not moving an inch from his position.

"Is that a joke? Are you joking right now?! You scared the shit out of me," I exclaim and slowly walk toward him.

"I told you I *would* see you later," he replies in a low voice. I watch his lips open as he brings his glass to his mouth to take a drink.

I shake my head to focus back on our conversation. "I thought you meant like tomorrow. How long have you been up here?" I ask.

"Long enough," he grins.

I walk to the wet bar, pour myself some Vodka to calm my nerves, and slam it down. The burn down my throat makes my face wince a little and cough in my throat.

"What flavor did you choose?" he asks as he leans over on the couch.

"Ummm, I don't know," I say and pick up the bottle, "Coconut," I answer. I stare at him for a second, fuck, he looks delicious. I quickly pour myself another and slam it again.

"Why are you in my room?" I ask after the burn is gone.

"To see if I like flavored Vodka," he says seductively.

Confusion crosses my face as my breath catches in my throat. I feel my body responding to Nikolaj's low baritone voice.

Is it because he's mysterious?

Maybe because he's the Devil, and I'm under his sinful trance.

I don't care.

I want whatever's going to happen.

Finally, trying to be calm, I stutter, "do you like flavored Vodka, then?" I set my glass down and pour more coconut vodka into it.

"I already told you," he says while cocking an eyebrow, "it's not bad." His eyes are hungry, looking me up and down, then his tongue darts out to lick his bottom lip.

My breath hitches in my throat, and I cough out. I do a quick shake of my head to clear my mind. "Well, I was just going to go to bed. So..." I say, trying to hint for him to leave.

Why did I say that? I don't really want him to leave. My nervousness is getting the best of me.

"Then get in bed," he purrs with that Russian accent and raspy voice. He leans into the crook of the couch and armrest to face me better.

"But you're still here," I nervously whisper.

"...and?" he smirks, slams the rest of his drink, and walks to the bar where I am standing.

Setting his glass down, he leans into me; runs his jawline against my cheek until his lips find my ear. "You, Milly, have earned four spankings today," he growls.

"What?" I choke out and pull away from him. "That's what you meant when we walked out of Demyan's office. four was for spankings?" I clarify in defiance.

He grabs the back of my neck and pulls me back into him. "Yes. I've been watching that ass of yours all day, and now I finally get to mark it," he replies, then runs his teeth over my jawline to my lips.

My pussy is soaked and clenching with anticipation.

I pull my head back, look into his eyes, and bite my lower lip. "What did I do to earn spankings? Follow-up question, do you earn spankings, too?" I ask seductively.

I want him to spank me and to experience it with him, but I won't go down without a fight. I'll make him work for every spanking he thinks he will give me.

He looks at me, his lip slightly jerking in the corner. "Do you want to spank me, Milly?" He asks as his eye twitches slightly.

I blush instantly.

"Blushing again," he practically sings in a low voice with delight. His hand still holds the back of my neck, and he brings his lips close and teases me with anticipation of a kiss.

My body is begging for him, and my mind has submitted to what my body wants.

Finally, he kisses me fiercely, parting my lips with his tongue and taking my mouth passionately, pulling me closer to him.

He grabs my ponytail, yanking it back, forcing my head back to look up at him. "You were so deliciously naughty today," he growls.

Before I can get a word out, he hoists me around the waist and carries me to the tall bedpost. "Hands on the post," he demands while pulling his untied tie off his neck.

He stands in front of me, with the post between us. Grabbing my hands, he pulls them toward him and ties them at the wrist so the post holds me in place.

He walks behind me, pressing his body against my back. He places his hands on my forearms and then runs them up to my shoulder and down my sides. I quiver at his touch.

His thumbs slide under the band of my pants. My body jerks slightly at the new sensation of his touch on my waist.

His breath hits the sensitive part of my neck, and the hairs of his beard tickle my skin. I gasp as he moves his head to my ear and whispers, "there are two rules. 1-you, don't make a sound when we are in your room. 2-Do as you are told. Understood?"

I nod.

"Good," he says and nips my ear lobe.

He pulls my pants down to the middle of my thighs in one swift move, leaving my black thong on.

Kneeling on one knee, his hands run up the back of my thighs and cup my ass cheeks. He lightly bites one cheek, then stands back up.

His mouth finds my other ear, "someday, you will tell me about those tattoos and scars on your legs and ass." I look over my shoulder at him.

He leans down and catches my lips for a quick kiss. "But for now, bend over!"

My arms slide down the post while he pulls my ass toward his direction. I'm bent in half at the waist-completely exposed to him, and nervousness and anxiousness start to set in.

My legs are shaking, but before I can dwell on those feelings too long, he steps to my side and reaches over me to hold my waist. His left hip/thigh pushed into the left side of my torso.

"Remember, not a sound," he warns with a threatening voice.

WACK!

His first hit stings and burns. Oddly filling me with pleasure and the need for more.

"That's for not calling *ME* when you hurt your head," he says calmly.

I look over my shoulder at his body towering over me. My legs are shaking, and I feel them weakening.

WACK!

I wince and try to hide the tear that managed to sneak out. The other cheek stings but aches for more!

"That's for staring at Demyan's cock," he says with annoyance in his voice.

I catch myself before I argue with him.

WACK!

The first cheek is hit again.

The sting intensifies.

I bite my lower lip to hold back the cry of pain and pleasure consuming me.

"That's for disappearing at lunch," he says.

WACK!

The other side hit again.

Both legs are weak.

A scream of aerosol lodges in my throat.

"That's for fighting me all day."

He rubs both cheeks as he pushes his thigh into my side to support my body.

Moving behind me, he guides me back to a standing position. He pushes his hard cock, still trapped in his pants, against my back.

He unties my hands, turns me to face him, then runs his palm on my face.

"Get on the bed," he growls.

My heart is pounding in my chest as I sit at the foot of the bed.

Keeping eye contact with him as I clumsily wiggle my way to the headboard, with my pants now around my knees.

He chuckles and jokes, "very smooth!"

As my back presses against the headboard, I laugh and shyly say, "I didn't think I needed to master the art of moving up the bed, but I'll remember for next time."

"Next time? hmmm...You liked being spanked," he says devilishly.

My eyes widen, but I refuse to let him think he has won this round. "Maybe next time you'll make them hurt," I tease.

"Tsk tsk. The welts on your ass tell me they hurt. Now quiet," he demands, then grabs my pants and aggressively pulls them down, bringing me with them so I'm lying on my back.

I pull my legs together. Completely exposing my soaked vag to someone is not in my comfort zone, even though I want him to see it.

"Uh-Uh! Let me see how wet your pussy is for me," he orders, staring at my center as he adjusts his dick in his pants.

I glance down to see his massive bulge begging to be let out. I lick my lips, and vibrations of excitement cover my body. Complying with his demand, I slowly open my legs again. His eyes are lustful at my arousal soaking through my panties.

He climbs onto the foot of the bed while unbuttoning his shirt, then rips it off and throws it on the floor. His torso and arms are covered in tattoos, scars, and his muscles are exquisitely defined.

My breathing is heavy, and the anticipation of what he will do is killing me.

He sits on his heels, hooking my panties with his thumbs, and with one quick move, he rips them from my body.

I gasp!

He grabs my right leg, whips me over on my side, smacks my ass, then brings my leg back down, so I'm lying on my back again, with my legs wide around him.

"No noise when we...are...in...your...room," he demands.

He runs his hands up my inner thighs but stops, careful not to touch my wet folds. "Hmmmm...so nice and wet," he says, admiring my center, then licks his lips.

Grabbing my arms, he pulls me up, yanks my shirt off, then gently pushes me back down to the bed.

I'm energized with desire as his thighs spread wider while he crawls up me, pushing against the backs of my thighs and moving my legs up while he nestles between them.

He lays his body on me while resting on his forearms, giving me a feeling of his stature. His lips meet mine, and the passion in his kiss takes my breath away.

He leans over to his right forearm and says, "if you want me to stop at any time, just tell me."

I nod, but I don't foresee myself wanting him to stop.

He leans back to me and, slowly but firmly, takes in every bit of my mouth. Breaking our kiss, he works his way down my neck. Kissing and licking every inch of it, then down to my chest.

His left hand slides down my cheek until it reaches the clasp between my breasts and unbuckles it. He gently removes each breast from their lace cups, then grabs one and teases the nipple while taking the other in his mouth.

The pure sensation of it makes me moan and arch my back.

He pulls up so fast, and I'm on my other side in milliseconds. WACK!

He pulls me back into place and hovers over me. "I said no noise in your room!"

My chest is heaving.

My body aching with desire and pleasure.

"This is all new to me. I've never had anyone make me feel this way," I whisper. He grins, then adjusts his body onto me again.

"No one has ever licked these plump nipples before?" He asks, flicking one with his tongue, then moving to suck on the other.

I quietly moan out, "no."

His hand spans the width of my stomach as his mouth follows, licking my skin, and making me quiver at his touch. The muscles of his body contract with every movement showing off his sexy physique.

Against my skin, he asks, "no one has ever touched you?" Looking up at me with a cocked eyebrow and *fuck me* eyes.

"Not like this," I whisper.

He kisses my stomach and sides while his hand moves to play with my breasts. He looks so turned on about being my first.

But is he my first?

Am I supposed to include Skip?

I should tell him about Skip?

Am I a liar if I don't?

Will he think I'm gross if I tell him?

I feel guilty that I haven't told him about my past, and the words come out faster than I could think, "wait!"

I lean up on my elbows. He stays right where he is, nestled between my thighs with his chin resting on my stomach. I hesitate to speak, prompting him to lean up with his hands on either side of me. Looking into my eyes, he asks, "are you ok?"

"I feel you should know something before you go any further." He looks confused, leans up, and sits on his heels. I slowly confess, "I should say I haven't been touched like this consensually...and I'm not a virgin per se...I was raped a long time ago." I nervously pull my lower lip between my teeth and bite down.

He takes a deep breath. The silence is killing me, but it's only fair he knows, even if it means he will walk out.

I break the deafening silence and finish saying as I wiggle to sit up, "so I guess I'm not a virgin, but I am when it comes to having a choice."

It feels like forever before he finally says, "do you want to do this, or would you like me to stop?" Not what I was expecting him to say, but at least he's not running out of my room yet.

"I want this, but you should have a choice if you want to do this with someone damaged like me," I say, leaning closer to his presence.

"We are all damaged somehow, Milly. You should not feel shame for a past you couldn't control." He moves a piece of hair away from my face, then smirks, saying, "I wouldn't be in your room if I didn't want to do this with you."

His low, raspy voice increases my desire, and I move to meet him as he leans closer to me. Melting into him as we kiss, I place my hands on his cheeks.

Pulling away, he says, "now, I'd like to be the first to lick your sweet pussy." He puts his hand on the center of my chest and gently pushes me back down. He adjusts his body between my legs, and with one last look at me, he says, "you're blushing."

Then his tongue laps a single time at my swollen clit, eagerly waiting for him. The sensation is intense as I wrap my hand in his curly brown hair. He licks and gently teases my little bud. Then sucks it into his mouth, and the intense feeling arches my back off the bed.

My head pulls up to watch him as he flicks his tongue and sucks on my clit. I bite my lower lip to hold my moan, letting the excitement consume me, and lower myself to the bed.

He stops. "Did you make yourself cum in the bathroom yesterday?" He asks with his mouth against my clit.

I push myself back on my elbows and seductively answer, "yes."

I can't help but grin because he knows. He smiles as he rests the side of his head on my inner thigh to look up at me. The warmth of his skin and the tickle of his beard are intoxicating. His beautiful brown eyes make me feel like I'm the sexiest thing he has ever seen.

"I stood by the door and listened to you," he confesses, "I just wanted to hear you say it." He gives a quick chuckle and then goes back to sucking on my clit. The feeling makes my head fling back.

Stopping briefly, he asks me, "blushing?"

I feel his thick finger run down my wet slit, stopping at my entrance, then gently sliding in. My back arches up. His thick finger fits perfectly and curls to massage the right spot.

His other hand rubs up my stomach over my breast and pinches my nipple. I rub my hand over his arm and grab my other breast.

Pure ecstasy engulfs me as he slowly slides his finger out and thrusts it back in. His tongue flicks and sucks my clit with no mercy.

I am completely on edge. Making it harder and harder to hold in my moans. I tighten my grip on his hair, trying to channel my desire elsewhere, so I don't make a sound.

I feel a second finger at my entrance, and I brace myself. He slams it in me with the first finger. I let out a throaty scream before I could catch myself.

"Please don't spank me," I plead, breathy and heaving. "I want to cum," I beg Nikolaj.

He says nothing.

The stinging pleasure of his fingers stretching me sends me into complete bliss. His other fingers twist my nipple as I claw into his arm.

His fingers pick up their speed. His tongue is not missing a sweet sensual beat. His movements send me over the edge, and I release an explosion of pleasure. My body shakes and quivers. My pussy throbs on his two fingers.

He licks me slower and lighter while I come down from my orgasm.

Pulling his fingers out, making me miss the fullness they made me feel, he straddles my thigh and pulls his cock out of his pants.

My eyes widened at his enormous cock within my reach. I look at his face to see his beard glistening with my arousal.

He collects my juices from my slit, then begins stroking my arousal on his thick long cock. His hand runs up to the head, gives a slight twist, and moves back down the shaft.

He leans over, mercilessly shoving two fingers back in me, immediately sending pleasure and pain to my core. His thrusts meet the same force as his strokes on his cock. I pull my lower lip between my teeth to hold in my moan.

His thick fingers fill my pussy, stinging in the best possible way as they stretch me again. I run my hand up his thigh and my other down to rub my clit. The harder he strokes, the harder I rub.

Our eyes lock. Our movements match in a harmonious rhythm until we reach a euphoric orgasm. My pussy throbs harder than ever on Nikolaj's fingers as I watch his cock palpate and feel his warm cum fall on my stomach.

Our breathing is heavy, and our eyes linger on each other.

He slowly pulls his fingers out of me, running them over the cum covering my belly, and shoves them into my mouth. "Taste us," he growls. His demanding voice and his dominance over me make me feral. I'll do whatever he wants me to because I want more of him!

I lick every bit of the salty cream off of his fingers. Satisfaction covers his face, and he smiles at my compliance.

"Good! Don't move," he orders while getting off the bed, then walks to the bathroom. I hear him washing up, then starts running the tub water.

Coming back out, sadly, his magnificent cock is tucked back in his pants but still shirtless. He hands me a glass of water that I desperately accept. I lean up just enough to guzzle the refreshing liquid down my throat.

"You moaned! That's a spanking," he demands with a cocked eyebrow. "I was kind enough to let you cum, but now your spanking's due." He takes the empty glass from me, sets it on the nightstand, and flips me to my side.

WACK!

Leaving me in this position, he calmly says in appreciation, "your ass is nice and red." He gently rubs my ass.

I look over to see him admiring his work. He looks at me with fierce eyes.

Still on my side, he leans in, cups behind my neck, kisses me with ownership, and takes my breath away. He's making it known that I'm his.

He tilts his head to mine. "I've wanted to mark this ass for three months," he smiles and nips my nose with his teeth. "Bath!" he orders, picking me up. I wrap my arms around his neck.

He gently sets me in the tub as it fills with water. Sitting on the ledge, he pulls my hair out of the ponytail. "Do you bathe all the women you've been with?" I ask while giving him a sarcastic look.

He chuckles and replies, "I haven't had any ladies I like enough to do this with."

"I don't believe that," I retort. He rolls his eyes before he leans over to grab the washcloth off the counter.

"Don't get me wrong. I have had my fair share of women. Some I would fuck more than once, but never more than twice. I've never brought any of them here, though."

"Where do you fuck them, then?" I ask with sincere curiosity.

He makes a throaty growl of annoyance. Kneels beside the tub and dunks the washcloth in the bath water.

Quietly, he washes my face and works his way down to my chest. He takes his time and kisses every part he can get to.

"Anywhere. They were escorts. They'll fuck wherever I tell them to," he finally says against the skin on my shoulder.

"You only fuck escorts?" I turn my head and breathe in the smell of his hair. Making me crave him even more.

"Da! No attachment and they are *clean*," He washes my arms, running the washcloth up over my other shoulder.

"Clean? You mean..." I start to inquire before I notice his look on me is a warning not to finish the sentence because I already know the answer. I nod with a slight grin. "What am I then?" I asked shyly.

He takes my chin, moving my head to look at him, and sternly looks into my eyes and answers, "You, my sweet Milly, are now my only." He smiles and kisses my forehead.

I feel like a puddle of feelings, the confusion being the major one, but right now, I like my big scary Russian being gentle and talking.

"One day, you will tell me your story, Da?" he asks, scanning my face with a grip still on my chin, and his thumb rubs my lower lip.

"Of course," I say in a pleasured voice as I place a hand on his cheek, running my wet fingers through his beard.

He moves his hand down to my slit, running his finger around my entrance. "Typically, I eat pussy for hours," he sensually states, nipping my lower lip as he slides a finger into me. I take a sharp breath in as his finger fills me again. "But, if I did that with you, I'd have to fuck you. I don't want to fuck you in your room." His lips brush against my ear. "I don't want anyone to hear your screams but me."

He pushes another finger in and slowly moves them in and out. "So, when I do fuck you, Milly," he pauses, grabs a fist full of my hair and pulls my head back, then says, "it will be in my place, where only I can hear you scream my name when my cock slams inside you."

He pushes his fingers into me hard, holding them deep inside me, making me slightly lift up at the intensity of the feeling. I moan quietly in my throat.

"I want you screaming my name when you cum on my cock," he says as he smashes his lips into mine.

Pulling back, leaving me out of breath and craving more, he says with a smirk, "you're blushing again."

"You say some dirty things," I admit in a voice filled with desire as his fingers slowly and delicately start to slide in and out of me.

"I've seen your bedside drawer. You're not that innocent," Nikolaj jokes, then lightly bites my shoulder. His thumb moves to my clit, and he lazily massages it.

I try to hide my face, knowing exactly what he saw in that drawer. "No, you don't get to hide your face," he says as he grabs my hands with his other hand and pulls them away from my face.

His voice becomes seductive when he says, "I want to know everything you do with those toys. I want you to show me how you fuck yourself with them."

He moans into my skin while pushing a third finger into me. I push up from the tub again, arching my back, biting my lip, and holding in my painful excitement. I snap my head at him, and he devours my mouth while his fingers fill me to the max and tenderly fucks me with them. Unable to control it any longer, I moan in his mouth, and his hand releases my chin and takes hold of my entire jawline.

He pulls away, slowly pulls his fingers out, and whispers, "I have to stop."

"Why?" I whisper back wantingly.

"If I don't, I will rip you from this tub, haul your ass upstairs and fuck you until tomorrow," he growls, and his hand palms my thigh and squeezes.

"Would that be so bad?" I ask breathily.

He takes a deep breath as if contemplating his options. After composing himself, he says, "relax. Soak," then leaves the bathroom.

He is set on not fucking me here. It's admirable the restraint he has, but my body is aching for him. The foreplay makes me want to march my ass upstairs as he follows and slide down on his cock. If it will fit. He has the biggest dick I've ever seen.

I lean on the tub's ledge to see what he is doing. I see the comforter fly off the bed. He walks by the bathroom door with his shirt on but unbuttoned and untucked. He comes back with another comforter from the closet and flips it onto the bed. What is it with my bosses making the bed?

He returns to the bathroom, sits on the tub's ledge, and holds his hand out to help me stand up. Nikolaj takes his time drying me off. I take this time to study his features closer.

His brown shoulder-length curly hair is pulled back into a bun.

The scars on his face, hands, and arms.

The tattoos that cover his upper body and neck.

He stands before me and pulls out a shirt hanging from his pocket and puts it on me. I smile and absorb every second of how gentle and caring he is.

He steps to me, his face touching mine. "I will take care of you from now on." His hands interlocked with mine. I melt into him. "Time for bed. You will need your energy," he grins devilishly, "I refuse to keep my hands off of you any longer."

He leads me to my bed with one corner pulled back, and I slide in. He pulls up the comforter, tucks it around me, and rubs the back of his hand across my forehead and down my cheek.

Sitting on the edge of the bed, putting his arm around my waist, he tells me, "three months I watched you. I wanted your smile to be for me, your laugh for me, and I wanted to mark your ass with my hands. I fought myself for three months. I can't fight anymore." He leans down, kisses my lips, cheeks, and neck, then whispers in my ear, "I'm yours. You're mine. All of you."

My stomach flutters, a smile crosses my face, and I rub his hand resting by my side. He leans up. Kisses my forehead. "Good night Letnicha Lola," he whispers and leaves.

Letnicha Lola?! Slavic Goddess that puts love in the hearts of gods and men. My heart melts. I smile as I cuddle up with the comforter.

There is so much about that man that I don't know. He's an enigma and one I am willing to try and figure out.

Past Milly
24-years-old
Chapter 34

It HAD BEEN TWO years since we heard about Lazlo, and we searched the depth of every dark corner to find any information.

We hit dead-end after dead-end.

Whoever Lazlo was, they were way ahead of us. All we knew was Lazlo set up the house we burned down.

How many more places are set up like that?

How many people have been hurt because of Lazlo?

The tension got high between coalitions around the world. Our hunting and searching became aggressive as we crossed turfs in search of sick fucks, abusers, and Lazlo. No one's boundaries were respected.

Vance and the other leaders struggled to keep order amongst the hunters.

Accusations rose that Lazlo could be one of us, which may be how they stayed ahead of us. Those rumors are quickly laid to rest by leaders but remained in the back of our minds.

We were getting eager, hunting with emotion, and mistakes were bound to get made.

We attended parties, clubs, fundraisers, and any place that brought people in. We were looking for a red card.

Vance was very protective of me. He made sure I was out of sight and out of imminent danger. I hid in duct work, dark corners, crawl spaces, and rafters. True to the nickname Rosco gave me, mouse!

The night my life changed again was when we hunted Seth Jones. A man sick enough to be on our radar and a full-time crook with ties in politics, big corp, real estate, and mafia. He had a grotesque personal life and was lapped in the luxury of his blood money.

He RSVP'd to be at the grand opening of Hartiars, a high-class hotel on the outskirts of Tacoma. Rooms on the lower 15 floors were over $1000 a night, while rooms on the upper 5 floors were $10,000 a night.

There had to be more than just beds in those rooms, and we would find exactly what this hotel would be used for.

150 US politicians, celebrities, and other people I didn't recognize were in attendance that night.

Frank and Jared sat in the van, taking names and pictures through the camera system. Vance was giving orders to everyone through their earpiece.

We were all in position. Kit and I were by the side of the elevators. We watched Seth glide through the crowd. He greeted and mingled with everyone at this event.

He was a social butterfly, but then he stopped dead; his face dropped and turned white as he looked at a group of men in a corner. They were tall and very intimidating even to me. Seth turned to his right and walked through a group of people.

He was headed toward the elevator that Kit and I stood by. He looked scared.

"Should I block the elevators and stop him?" I radioed Vance.

"No! Hold your position," Vance said.

I watched Seth get closer and closer to the elevators. He was almost running. I panned back to the crowd to see the four men following him and minimizing the distance between them and Seth.

"Vance!?" I said sternly. We could not let that fucker get away! Why was Vance being so cautious? I was right in line to grab Seth.

"He's being followed. Too risky. Stay out of sight," Vance said calmly.

"I can grab him," I said as my heart jumped out of my chest.

"If the names on the guest list are correct, then those men are no joke, Milly! They are Russian and have ties to the Bratva. They will kill you if you intervene, and it won't be a quick death. Stay put, Milly," Vance commanded. I could hear the worry in his voice, but letting Seth get away just could not be an option.

"I'll be fine," I said.

"Milly..." Vance started, but I took my earpiece out and handed it to Kit. He reluctantly took it, but I could see on his face he was worried.

"I'll meet you at the house," I told him, and patted his shoulder.
"You shouldn't do this," he pleaded with me.
"I'll be fine!"

I followed them. I had no communication or access to my
people. I was alone and slightly scared, but the fear I felt was
overpowered by the need I had to know what Seth knew about
Lazlo.

The men caught up to Seth, and the tallest man slammed
him into the wall. Seth begged them to stop. The tall man said
something about money and fucked up, then punched Seth a few
times and knocked him out.

They dragged him to a black SUV sitting by the side door exit.
After shoving Seth in, they pulled away.

I panned the outside for something to follow them in. I saw a
motorcycle. Thankfully, Rosco taught me how to hotwire, and I
was on the SUV's trail in no time.

I followed loosely as they drove into an old shipping district's
beat-up, run-down garage.

I parked at the end of the street, walked to the building
they entered, and looked around for access. Nothing looked
trustworthy, but there was a vent about 12 feet up.

I climbed some wooden pallets, unscrewed the vent cover,
scanned down the ventilation tunnel, and saw two lights shining
in.

I slipped through the vent tunnel and saw the first light leading
to an office with a desk and a lamp. The room looked empty from
the angles I could see.

The second light was brighter. I crawled to that opening and saw the four men that took Seth and two more men standing by them. Seth was knocked-out and tied to a chair.

"This fucker doesn't have our money or shipment, Niko!"

"Then he will tell us where both are, then we kill him!"

I headed back to the other vent. I opened it and checked for anyone.

No one.

I slid down onto the desk and scurried to the floor. Looking around, I saw it was clear. I took a deep breath and crawled against the wall to the other room where the men were.

I heard the men talking. I heard Seth waking up and asking what was going on.

I waited a few minutes, then I went into the room. I was standing right behind the tallest man when the two men, who were not at the hotel, spotted me.

"What the fuck," they yelled! All the men spun around to me and pulled their guns out. I threw my hands up.

"Hold on! I just need to ask Seth Jones about a name," I said quickly, hoping they wouldn't open fire, "then I'm on my way!"

They stared at me with absolute hatred and waited for the boss to talk. The tall man asked, "who are you, and how many are with you?"

"A ghost, and just me." I admit I was scared, but I couldn't let them see my fear.

After eyeing me up and down, he said, "what name?"

It must have been a good sign that he hadn't killed me yet. I started lowering my arms, but the tall man's face darkened, and he motioned at my arms and demanded, "hands up." I put my hands back up and analyzed my situation. I was unarmed and outnumbered, so I'd do what they asked of me for the time being. I started to regret my decision to go there.

He asked, "what is so important about the name?" My hesitation in answering made him angry, and he said, "I am not a patient man."

He moved closer to me and pushed his gun to my head, and I finally answered, "hunting." My hands were still in the air, and I was vulnerable.

The answer was not good enough. The tall man got furious and yelled, "don't waste my time with one-word answers, *suka*, I will kill you!"

That fucker wasn't going to kill me. He wondered why I snuck into an abandoned warehouse to talk to some low-life. I wanted to test the theory, so I quickly dropped my arms to my sides.

They all jumped.

The man standing slightly to the side of the tall man said, "you'll die if you do that again!"

"I'm not worried," I said since I proved they were interested in my motive. I was not a threat to their money or shipment. And as long as they stayed interested in my objective, I would live.

The tall one grabbed my left upper arm and squeezed with the gun still at my head.

He towered over me, built like a brick fucking house, sexy as hell, but that wasn't the time to admire him.

I tried not to let him see I was in pain. I controlled my expression, looked into his dark eyes, and joked, "now we both have guns pointed at us. Are we having fun?"

He squeezed my arm tighter; I winced at the pain he was causing, pulled it together, then smiled at him as I tried to take back the upper hand. "Drop the guns, and I'll tell you everything," I said.

"I don't negotiate," he snarled at me. He was starting to annoy the shit out of me.

"Fine," I barked at him as I summed up my predicament in my head. I have fought more than six men at a time before, but I was armed. But the men in front of me didn't know if I was armed or about my fighting skills. "I'll fight all of you. I'm *not* worried," I snapped and tried to jerk away from his hold, but he held tight to me.

He looked like he was enjoying hurting me, then he pressed his head to mine. It was a fucking rock. "I'll drop the guns. Humor your request since you took the time to sneak in just to get caught, then I'll take my time killing you," he snarled.

I couldn't take the pain in my arm or forehead any longer. He was so strong. I tried to hide my discomfort but could only muster a low, whispered word, "deal."

He had his men lower their guns and let my arm go. He moved his hands over my torso, down my body, and to each leg. "Like what you feel, big guy?" I asked, then licked my lips.

"You came here unarmed? Foolish," he scoffed as he stood back up and glanced at the men behind him.

"I'm not here to hurt any of *you*. Just Seth," I clarified.

He leaned against the table and crossed his massive arms over his chest. I started to explain, "Seth's a shitty guy. He might have information about an even shittier person, and I need to know what he knows."

The man next to the tall one asked, "how shitty?"

"He hurts kids. Would you like me to go into detail?" I asked.

They looked at Seth with even more anger than before. The tall man motioned for me to proceed over to Seth.

I knew Seth wouldn't give up any information quickly, but it was worth a try to ask him first, considering he was in the wrong spot, as it were.

I walked over to Seth, leaned down to his face, and asked, "are we going to do this the easy way or the hard way?" He spat in my face. I stood back up and turned slightly behind me. "Can I borrow that knife on the table?" I asked the tall man. I walked over to grab it from him while I wiped the spit from my face.

I cut off Seth's shirt to expose his skin. I ran my fingers over his shoulder and down to his clavicle. He squirmed under my touch.

"FUCK YOU!" he screamed at me.

"Shhhhhh," I gently shushed in his ear.

"I'm not telling you shit," he barked. I lined the knife up with his clavicle and sliced the skin that covered it. He screamed and jerked in his chair.

"Uff. Not much for the pain, are you? Would you like to talk to me about Lazlo now, or should we keep going?" I asked him.

"FUCK YOU! FUUUCK," he screamed through his cries!

"Ok," I nonchalantly shrugged, then proceeded to cut the skin off his right shoulder from his clavicle to his shoulder blade. Exposing the muscles, tendons, ligaments, and bone. Blood covered my hands and ran down Seth's body.

Seth screamed and cried the entire time, but I knew he would need more motivation than that to talk to me. I dug the knife into the fresh cut and started to cut the skin from his shoulder down his arm, exposing more of his muscles.

His screams were intense, and his jerking body made it tricky to hold the bloody skin taut while I cut.

After some time went by of skinning him, he calmed down. It must have been his body going into shock and the blood loss that caused him to sit still but quietly moan in pain. He was unable to fight back. His head was bobbing, and he looked like he was about to pass out, throw up, or both.

"Seth.... oh Sethy boy. You can't go to sleep now. You have to tell me what you know," I calmly said to him.

He started to close his eyes, and I flipped the knife and plunged it into his leg, right next to his dick. He screamed from the new intense pain and yelled, "THEY FIND YOU!" He cried uncontrollably as the adrenaline kicked in.

"What the fuck does that mean?" I asked him as I ripped the knife out of his thigh. He buckled and screamed, trying to break his restraints. I waited for the shock to fall to give him a chance to answer.

"If they want to work with you, they will find you," he mumbled through his pain.

"They? There's more than one person," I asked.

He nodded yes. "Lazlo's an organization," he breathed out, barely able to speak at this point.

"Organization of what?!" I insisted as I pulled his head up.

"They get you whatever you want, anything...for a price," he said, then his eyes closed, and he said, "kill me."

"You still have business with these men," I said, then Seth finally passed out from shock.

I walked to the men, placed the knife on the table, and the tall man asked, "who's Lazlo?"

"I don't know, but I have to find out," I said while I wiped my hands on a towel. I was not about to wait any longer, so I threw the towel on the table and headed to the door.

Then it all turned black.

Present Milly

Chapter 35

I WALK AROUND THE kitchen corner to see Theo and Daniel getting coffee.

"Hey, boys," I exclaim energetically. I can't help but smile at the dirty little secret I have.

"Milly Vanilly," Theo jokes while pointing two finger guns in my direction.

"Ah, no. Please don't start using that nickname," I giggle, trying to hide my utter annoyance with the nickname.

"Fine. I think I want to learn Russian, so I can understand the bosses. So, tell me if my Russian accent sounds right," Theo requests. Apparently, he listened to every detail of my stories last night, and I may have created a monster.

"Oh man, this ought to be good. Let's hear it," I imply while I brace myself, and Daniel stands beside me, cringing with anticipation.

"Da yo tag sooger een your covee!" He looks so confident. It breaks my heart to tell him it needs work, but without criticism, there is no growth.

"Um, no. Not quite right, but keep working on it," I snicker. I wonder how Grace taught me all those languages and accents without busting out laughing in my face.

Theo continues to practice his accent on random words when I see Nikolaj round the corner into the dining room, and instantly I stiffen up at the sight of him. I try to avoid eye contact because looking at him will make me smile, and I doubt he wants anyone to know what he did to me last night.

How am I supposed to act around him now?

Is he going to be an asshole?

"Good morning, boss," Daniel cheerfully says, adding more sugar to his coffee, then twisting the cover on the cup.

"Gents," Nikolaj replies with a nod as he reaches the edge of the kitchen. His voice is so exquisitely sensual, giving me tingles all over my body.

He glides to the side of the island I'm on, and I feel him stand directly behind me. The heat radiating from his body engulfs me. Then he kisses the top of my head, moves my hair away from my ear, then whispers as he tips his head down toward me, "good morning." I melt at the feeling of his breath on my skin and the vibration of his voice through his chest pressed against my back.

"Morning," I respond wide-eyed, looking at his hands as they wrap around my waist. I look up to see Daniel and Theo staring back at me in shock and speechless.

I look over my shoulder at Nikolaj. His hair is down today, making him unbearable eye candy. He runs his hand down my hips, then walks around the island. My eyes are locked on him as he pours coffee into his mug. I follow every move he makes until I hear a slight snap to my other side.

I look to see Daniel mouth to me, *'You are telling me EVERYTHING!'* Theo stands behind Daniel with the biggest shit grin on his face. The extended silence catches the attention of Nikolaj, who turns to look at us.

"Well, off to work," Daniel insists, nudging Theo and gawking at me. I squint at them as they turn and head to the basement stairs.

Nikolaj sets his coffee down on the island. His eyes lock with mine, and I feel my center clench. Fuck, he's insanely sexy. This can't be real. I must be dreaming, but before I wake up, I'd better leave so I can remember the look on his face.

"Well, I guess I should get to work, too," I suggest as I push off the island.

"Come here," he orders, smirking at me and his eyes full of lust. My belly flutters. Maybe I'm not dreaming after all. I bite my lower lip while my body internally likes the way he commands me; it makes me feral.

I slowly walk around the island until I'm standing before him. He wraps his solid tattooed hands around my waist and lifts me onto the island. Situating himself to the side of me and pushing my legs together. He reaches his tall body across the island, grabs my coffee, and hands it to me.

His lips brush the rim of his mug, and he says, "first, we have coffee. Then, you can go to work."

"Okay," I whisper in compliance. His cologne infuses the air around me, and his thigh is lightly pressed against mine.

"Did you sleep well?" He questions, laying his hand on my thigh and tenderly squeezing.

"Yes. Did you?" I turn to angle myself toward him, but he stops me dead. He gives me a devilish look and turns my legs back over the edge of the counter, wrapping his hand on the other thigh to pin my legs closed between his hand and thigh.

He leans into my ear, "keep your legs together. It makes it easier for me to resist ripping your clothes off and eating your wet pussy on this island right here and now!"

I choke on my air at his words. The image of him between my legs resurfaces, and I can't help but want to rebel against his orders and force him to eat me out again.

"What makes you think I'm wet already?" I tease seductively, but I know he knows what he does to me.

"Because you're blushing. I'll check if you want me to," he softly solicits, hypnotizing me as he moves to kiss the delicate crook of my neck. His beard tickles me, making me squeak out a little laugh and squeeze my shoulder and head together. He growls against my skin and forces his way further into my neck.

"You say some dirty things," I divulge against the side of his head.

"You have no idea." He nips my ear. My breathing is heavy with desire. I can't help but think about his cock cumming on me last night and his fingers inside me.

"Can I ask you something?" I purr against his ear.

"Da." He lightly bites my shoulder.

I nip at his ear lobe, then ask, "will it fit the first time?"

He pulls back some, bemused, and asks, "will what fit?"

I use my eyes to point to his dick which is already pushing taut against his pants.

He takes a deep breath and cross-examines, "you're more worried about it fitting than hurting?" He throws me an odd look and cocks his eyebrow at me.

"I can handle pain." I turn my head to line up with his face and look into his eyes.

He presses his lips against my forehead, then responds, "I'll put that to the test." He smiles against my head. The movement feels dark and devilish. Like he's picturing all the ways he will try to hurt me. I replay memories of our first few encounters; he is much stronger than me, and I may have just given him permission to prove it.

He looks down into my eyes, bringing my focus back to him, and clarifies, "to answer your question, yes, it will fit. I'll stretch you with my fingers first, which will help with the pain you may have taking my cock into you." He flicks at my lips with his tongue a single time, then kisses my nose. My pussy clenches.

He runs his hand from my thigh to my side, pulls me close to him, and sensually suggests, "unless you want pain. Then I won't stretch you first. I'll just ram inside you so hard, past the resistance your pussy will give me, to the deepest parts of your body. You'll tense up and fight me because of the pain, but it won't stop me from pulling out and slamming back into you hard enough to make you scream for mercy."

I draw in a sharp breath and scan his eyes. He knows what his words and voice are doing to me right now, and I think he likes that he's torturing me with anticipation.

I mutter, "holy shit!" I'm absolutely soaking between my legs, and it's all from his words. I clear my throat and explain, "I like how you felt last night." I lay my hand on his. "One of your fingers equals about two of mine. I've only ever done two of mine, but you did three of yours last night," I explain suggestively and look up at him. "The sting and pleasure it caused me were unbelievably good," I reveal breathily against his lips, then press mine to his.

He groans at the gentleness of my kiss, then pulls back enough to say against my lips, "you won't know how you want to take my cock the first time until we are in the moment." He pulls further back, grabs his mug, and takes a drink.

"About time!" Demyan shouts out! I jump and try to push off the island, but Nikolaj places his hand over my hips and thighs to hold me in place.

"Morning, Dem," he dryly says, then takes another drink of coffee.

As he gets his coffee, Demyan's back is right in front of me. Looking back at us from over his shoulder, he smiles and shakes his head.

"Good morning, you two," he exaggerates as he turns to face us. Leaning against the counter across from us, he takes a drink of coffee and grins while swallowing.

My face is mortified.

"She's blushing, Niko," Demyan chortles. Nikolaj smiles and nods against his coffee cup, aware of my uncontrollable tint taking over my face, then takes a drink.

Demyan shamelessly studies me with a wicked smile. He looks like he's been patiently waiting for this, and now it's open season on Milly.

"Fuck! About time," Demyan vocalizes excitedly with a chuckle. "I didn't think I could handle what an asshole you were becoming," he quips, then adds, "I kept telling you to accept your feelings, bro, but you fought it! Douchebag!"

Nikolaj stands there, drinking his coffee, not caring what Demyan's saying, and still holding me in place.

"Oh, this is going to be a great day!" Demyan sings and starts whistling as he walks out of the kitchen.

"Oh! Demyan!" I shout. He turns to me in a dancing movement.

"Yes, M," he sings.

"Have you talked to Vance?"

"No," he affirms and sombers up.

"Could you call him? He isn't answering the phone you gave him, so I was hoping you could call him on his other number."

"I will. I'll let you know what I find out." Demyan turns back and leaves.

I turn back to Nikolaj, who is now scowling at me. "What?" I ask, trying to figure out what just happened to piss him off.

"Why wouldn't you ask me to call Vance?" He catechizes with a deadly glare.

"Look, I spent three months thinking you hated me, so it's going to take some time to understand what's going on between us," I confess.

"Fair enough," he accepts and adds, "but try harder. I want to be the first person you think of from now on." He smiles, showing his fantastic jawline and perfect teeth. Pulling me into him, then off the island while he kisses my forehead. "Time for work," he orders.

Walking into the basement office, I see Daniel and Theo sitting at my desk, as I knew they would be.

"TALK!" Daniel urges. "Wait, is he coming down here?" he quickly asks.

"No," I affirm, sitting on my desk opposite the two who are eagerly waiting for the details.

"TALK!" He insists again, but louder and more demanding.

"I don't know," I start with a mumble, then shrug. The two men sitting in front of me can see right through my bullshit, and they know I know that.

"Don't give us that shit," Theo wisecracks and nudges Daniel. The impatiently shocked look both men are giving clearly shows I am not getting out of this conversation so easily.

I stammered out the words, "he just started being affectionate."

"Nope!" Daniel asserts, shaking his head.

Theo adds, crossing his arms over his chest, "details!"

"Don't we have to work on something?" I implore, rubbing my hand over the back of my neck and glancing at my computer.

Theo answers in a matter-of-fact tone, "I'm jealous, quite honestly. I wanted Nikolaj to kiss me!" We both look at Theo. This guy says some of the weirdest things, but he's super funny.

"You're not gay," Daniel points out with a sideways glare.

"Doesn't matter! He's a fucking sexy ass man! Demyan, too," Theo expresses with a wink, then drifts into thought. I'm not sure what he's thinking about, but his tongue darts out, and his eyes roll with a slow blink.

"I will never understand you, Theo," Daniel comments, shaking his head and running his hands down his face. The remark snaps Theo out of his daze and back to the conversation at hand.

"Okay, Milly! TELL US EVERYTHING!" Daniel pleads, focusing back on me, "and don't leave out any details, damn it!"

"He kissed me, I liked it, and that's it," I answered. I don't say anything else as I start to slide off the desk, trying to avoid eye contact with either hacker sitting across from me.

"Tight-lipped," Theo affirms, nudging Daniel, shaking his head from side to side.

"Go away, you two," I commanded, pushing them off my desk.

At that moment, Demyan walks in, and a taken-back look crosses his face as he witnesses me manhandling my two co-workers.

"All good, M?" he asks suspiciously as I shove the two nerds away from my desk.

"Yeah. Fine. Just nosey boys here that won't go to work," I titter, and Theo playfully bats at my hand on his chest, pushing him away. My other hand is on Daniel's chest, and he willingly goes in the direction I force him.

"Okay," Damyan says with a dumbfounded look, then continues, "well, I called Vance, but no one answered. I'll try again later. Nikolaj had to leave for the day for business. If you three need anything, I'll be in my office."

"Okay," We all say. Then Demyan leaves.

Today is an easy day. We only have a little work from the bosses, so we tinker with some of our gadgets.

"Goddammit, Theo! If you send that mini fucking drone to hover over my head again, I'll shove it up your ass. I'm trying to work here," Daniel snaps, waving a screwdriver in Theo's direction.

"Oh, you're actually working, you moody American, on what?" Theo retaliates, throwing a crumpled paper in Daniel's direction.

"UGH! You're the dumbest, smartest dickhead I know!" Daniel barks, throwing the wadded paper into the trash and focusing back on his tinkering.

"Are you talking about my dick's head, Daniel? I'm flattered," Theo jokes, batting his eyes and swooning toward Daniel.

"NO! Fuck Theo," Daniel growls and throws his pen at Theo.

"You two are acting like children," I snap, frustrated with the lack of progress I am making researching Lazlo.

"Oh, shove it, you're making out with the boss. You just sit quietly," Theo banters. I glare at him, and he makes a snooty face and draws his attention back to Daniel.

"Yes! I got it!" Daniel celebrates.

"What did you get working?" Theo inquires.

"The spider car!" Theo and I dumbfoundingly look at each other.

"What the fuck is a spider car?" I inquire, lying my file on my desk and walking over to my fellow nerds.

"It's a remote-controlled car that can fold up and crawl into tight spaces," Daniel explains while studying and rotating the spider car.

"Okay smart guy, let's see it work," Theo proposes, putting his screwdriver down, and tries to grab the car from Daniel but fails.

Daniel sets his robot on the floor. "Okay, let me just...." Daniel starts, then fades into deep thought as he pushes the remote buttons. The anticipation is killing us as we look on, waiting for something to happen.

Theo and I watch as the spider car makes a few clicks, then unfolds into a small remote-controlled vehicle.

"Impressed so far," I cheer. The car rolls all over the room, then Daniel folds it back up to crawl around.

"Wow! That is really cool. What would you do with it?" Theo asks, slowly walking over to it to get a better look.

"Well, we could mount a camera on it or a recorder. Anything," Daniel says, picks up the car, and admires his work.

We continued working by playing with our toys until the workday ended.

I head to my room, expecting to see Nikolaj sitting there again, but no one.

After my shower, I crawl into bed and turn the tv on.

Three episodes later of some vampire show that doesn't have my attention, but it's mindless to watch. There's a bang on my door. I jump up, thinking it's Nikolaj coming to make our earlier conversation a reality.

My shoulders drop when I open the door, and I see Demyan standing there.

"Hey," I mutter, then notice Demyan looks sad. Something's happened. "Everything okay?" I inquire, hoping what he has to say isn't as bad as his vibes give off.

"Come downstairs, M," he somberly insists, making my heart sink.

"Did something happen?" I implore, but I'm afraid to hear the answer.

"Come on," Demyan orders, grabs my hand, and pulls me through the hall and down the stairs. His speed is quick and determined. My head is spinning with scenarios, but Demyan is tight-lipped and won't tell me anything.

Standing in the foyer near the front doors waiting, I ask, "what's going on, Demyan?" Before he can answer, I see headlights speeding down the driveway through the glass of the front doors.

"Who is that? Should I be getting ready to fight?" I interrogate as my adrenaline rises.

"No," Demyan sniggers softly, "but brace yourself." I look at him, but he keeps his eyes on the front doors.

My attention draws back to the doors when I hear them click open. Nikolaj walks in, blood covering his clothes, and my heart stops. I slowly start to walk toward him, taking it all in. What job did he have to do that left him looking like this. My breath catches in my throat, then I see others behind him. Looking around Nikolaj's enormous stature, I see Vance behind him.

"VANCE!" I jerk into a run and grab him. He grunts out in pain and tenses up.

"Milly, he's hurt," Nikolaj whispers softly to my side while placing his hand on my shoulder.

"What happened?!" I insist, scanning over Vance and seeing signs of torture. His clothes are torn. He's covered in blood, and his face is mangled and bruised. His arms have cuts and minor circular burns on them. Anger starts to flow like fire in my veins.

Demyan walks beside me, places his hand on my other shoulder, and discloses, "M, I'm sorry I lied, but someone did answer Vance's phone when I called it this morning. It wasn't him, though."

I quickly look back at Demyan, my eyes full of confusion, then I put my focus back on Vance. "Are you okay?" I ask.

"Yes. Just beat up a little," Vance explains with a scoff, then coughs.

"Let's get you to your room," Nikolaj suggests while reaching under Vance's arm to better support him, and Demyan grabs the other side.

I follow as Demyan and Nikolaj support Vance to the elevator, then to his room.

I watch Vance wince as he lays down in his bed. My heart breaks seeing him like this. It hurts that I didn't know what he was going through, so I couldn't help him sooner.

Watching the bosses being attentive to Vance's needs shows a compassionate side of this life that I rarely see. The side that makes us human.

"The doctor will be here in the morning. Just rest now," Demyan insists, taking the glass of water from Vance.

I'm heartbroken as I sit down on the bed by Vance. I lay my hand on his leg, covered by the comforter, and ask, "what happened?"

He moans and adjusts his body for a more comfortable position. "Tomorrow, Milly. I'll explain tomorrow," Vance verbalizes and closes his eyes.

I nod and stand to leave, and Nikolaj places his arm around me as we walk out.

"Come to my office," Nikolaj demands while shutting the door. The three of us head downstairs in silence.

"Please tell me what happened," I plead to both bosses while Demyan closes the office door.

"We didn't know he was in trouble until I called him this morning. Someone had him. Wanted information and money," Demyan mutters, rubbing his forehead and walking toward Nikolaj's desk.

"Sven and Gus went with me to extract Vance," Nikolaj firmly states while ripping his shirt off to put on a new one. My breath hitches in my throat at seeing his chiseled torso covered in dry blood.

"Whose blood is that?" I ask, hoping he killed the fuckers that took and tortured my sweetest best friend.

"They weren't going to just give us Vance, Milly. We had to take him," Nikolaj confesses, shirtless, rubbing his hand on my cheek.

"You went and saved him for me?" I ask, scanning his chest, stomach, and arms for wounds.

Nikolaj chuckles, "no, we saved Vance because he's one of our men, and we like him." He pulls the shirt up his arms simultaneously and jerks his shoulders to move it over and into place.

"I like him, too," I quietly claim and smile at the ground.

"M, the people that took him weren't given a chance to explain anything," Demyan mentions while eyeballing Nikolaj, who is pouring a glass of scotch with his shirt still unbuttoned and slams it in one pull.

"We weren't there to make friends, Dem," Nikolaj contends in annoyance, slamming his glass down and pouring another, then swallowing it in one gulp. Afterward, he pours two additional glasses and fills his own.

"How many were there?" I asked, looking between the two.

"Six, but let's wait for Vance to tell us more," Nikolaj answers while handing me a glass of scotch and one to Demyan. I take a drink, and it burns down my throat, causing me to cough a little. Demyan chuckles as his eyes scan my body, then looks at his drink. Nikolaj smirks at me as I sip some more. I will need scotch to help shut my brain down, so I can sleep tonight.

"Alright, I'm going home!" Demyan announces, setting his empty glass down on the mini-bar.

"Night," I respond and sip more scotch.

"Night, M," Demyan sings as he leaves, almost insinuating he thinks he knows something will happen with Nikolaj and me tonight. The door to the office clicks shut, and I turn to Nikolaj.

"Sorry we didn't check on Vance sooner," Nikolaj apologizes, stepping closer to me and running his hand down my face and hair.

"It's not your fault, but I should check on him," I suggest. I do not want to walk away, but I don't want Vance out of my sight for too long now. I'm afraid something will happen to him.

"Of course," Nikolaj responds kindly as his hands move up and down my arms. "You take care of Vance tonight, but tomorrow night, you're mine."

He grabs me forcefully, pulling me closer to him. I throw my arms around his neck and tippy-toe to kiss his lips. "Thank you for risking your life for Vance." I lay little pecks on his bearded jawline and back to his lips.

"I didn't risk anything," he clarifies, then explains, "most of the men we fought were untrained, easy to kill. They were probably forced to be there. They were scared and died protecting something they probably knew nothing about."

I put my hands on his cheeks and sweetly respond, "thank you anyway."

He smiles, then leads me to Vance's room.

"Good night, Milly!"

"Good night, Nikolaj."

Past Milly
24-years-old

Chapter 36

I WOKE UP IN a large room, lying on a soft bed and still wearing my tactical clothes from the mission to grab Seth.

The two men from the warehouse were sitting by the bed, watching me as they chatted in Russian.

Why were they watching me sleep?

I was not about to get raped, so I jumped up from the bed and tried to bolt to the door. Both men were startled from their chairs and ran to grab me.

I reached the door, but it was locked.

They grabbed me, and I started to kick and punch at them. Getting free, I ran around the room, throwing things at them. Every time they caught me, I broke loose again and kicked and punched them while running away.

I run to the door again, hoping to throw my body into it and break it open. Before I could reach the door, the taller one grabbed me around the arms and torso. I tried to head-butt him, but he squeezed tighter, crushing me. The pain was too much and made it impossible to move.

The other man knelt down to grab my ankles. I used the big guy as leverage, kicked my feet up, and tried to hit the man in front of me, but he quickly moved out of the way.

I felt the hold on me tighten, making it hard to breathe but easy for the other man to tie my ankles with his tie. He grabbed me behind the knees.

I was splayed between the two men, struggling to breathe and in immense pain. I couldn't move, couldn't breathe, but I was sure as shit not going to stop fighting. I used everything I had in me to start jerking my body again.

"Listen," the man holding my knees barked, "we are not going to hurt you, so stop fucking moving." His face was exhausted, and his hair was a mess, but he still looked hot as fuck.

The shortness of breath and pain in my torso was getting to be too much, and I felt my body start to pass out. I stopped jerking. I went limp. I focused on staying conscious. Breathe!

I hoped giving in at that moment would help save my energy for when I tried to escape again. Eventually, they would get tired of holding me, and I would have the advantage of power to get away.

"We just want to talk," the man at my knees explains, "my name is Demyan." His hands gripped my legs tightly and sent chills to my core.

I hated that my body reacted that way. These men stole me! I should not want anything to do with them.

"About what?!" I snarled. The tall man behind me tightened his grip around me even more, which caused me to groan in my throat.

He was going to break every bone if he squeezed any tighter. The tall man stated in my ear, "we'll let go. You will not fight anymore." Something about his breath on my neck and broad chilling Russian accent made my body rebel even more.

I couldn't take any more of his vice grip around me, so I complied and mumbled, "okay."

They set me down surprisingly gently, considering I had kicked, punched, and fought like hell just moments ago.

I walked over to sit on the side of the bed. They sat back in the chairs by the bed and composed themselves.

"Who are you, and who do you work for?" Demyan inquires.

"What's your name?" I cross-examined the tall man who made my body quiver a few seconds ago.

He studied my face for a second and snarled, "we ask the questions, not you!"

I took a moment to think about my options. 1)Comply with their orders and maybe live, or 2) fight and probably die.

I knew two things, they would not just let me go, and I wouldn't go down without a fight.

"I'm Milly," I scoffed in defeat, then continued, "I don't work for anyone. I hunt people who hurt and abuse kids and other innocent people." I bit the side of my lower lip, knowing I had just fucked up badly.

"How many work with you? How many knew you were at our warehouse?" Demyan interrogated, calm and collected, as he leaned back in his seat and adjusted his cufflinks.

Slightly defeated, I softly answered, "no one knows where I was or am now." I tried to stretch out my torso to relieve the ache I was feeling from the fighting.

"How many work with you? How many know you're missing?" The tall man snapped as he leaned toward me and snarled.

"What is your name, tall angry man," I demanded and glared at him.

Demyan intervened in our stare-down, "you don't do jobs like that alone, Milly. So, how many are in your group?"

"Just me," I snapped and whipped a look at Demyan.

The tall man jumped to his feet, wrapped his hand around my neck, pulled me off the bed, and forced my head to his. "This is not a game! Answer," he growled and squeezed tighter and tighter.

Demyan demanded the man drop me, but he didn't.

"Two," I struggled to say. "There are two of us," I could barely get the words out, and the lighted-headed feeling returned.

Demyan moved from his seat, grabbed the tall man's arm, and yelled for him to let me go. When he did, I caught my footing while gripping the edge of the bed for balance.

I rubbed my neck and adjusted back on the bed. "Well, I see who is in charge," I implied sarcastically.

Both men composed themselves again and sat back down.

Demyan insists, "this is not the time to make jokes, Milly. You are the intruder. Now make this easy on everyone and just answer the questions we ask."

Then with a very kind and soft-spoken voice, he continued, "just to clarify, this is Nikolaj. He and I are both bosses. Don't confuse my kindness for weakness, and don't confuse his silence for fear. Clear, Milly?"

I stared at both men, then nodded.

"Good," Demyan expressed his delight in my willingness to do as I was told.

"Who are the other people involved?" Nikolaj demanded.

I cracked my neck and glared up at the ceiling. "My partner is old and just helps me with tech stuff. So, leave him out of this," I demanded, moving my glare to both men.

"Name?" Nikolaj grilled. I stared at him with absolute hate in my eyes. Fuck that guy! Fuck both of those guys!

"You can kill me now. I won't give you his name," I contend.

Demyan adjusted in his chair, then explained, "Milly, obviously you have skills, so killing you isn't really on our agenda, but keeping you around is. We may need someone with your abilities in the future."

I nodded. "Then you don't need the other person. Just me," I suggested, trying to get them to drop it.

"Name," Nikolaj snapped again.

"NO," I snarled.

He moved to the edge of his chair, and I moved to the edge of the bed. I saw a movement in my peripheral, and I glanced at Demyan.

As he leaned back in his chair, Demyan said, "I already helped you once. You give me no reason to help you twice."

Nikolaj stood before me and ran his finger over the area where he choked me, growling, then warned, "final chance."

I didn't move or say a word. I refused to put Vance in harm's way.

He grabbed my neck again, stared into my eyes, and observed, "so naive to think we won't hunt your partner down. Let us see, you were at the grand opening, da? Cameras there will have footage of inside and outside the hotel. We'll see how many were really with you."

I could hardly breathe but couldn't let them find our whole crew. I hoped Vance would understand. I closed my eyes in total defeat and regret. "Vance," I muttered.

I was dropped down on the bed but crumbled to the floor. I laid my palm on the floor, leaned on my arm, and hung my head low. I saw Demyan stand and walk to my side by Nikolaj.

Why did I go against Vance's orders?

"Last name or phone number?" Demyan asked, looking down at me.

Nikolaj returned to the chair with a satisfied look and ran his hand through his beard. "I'm sure our office would be an upgrade for you and Vance. So, either let us call him or give us a last name to find him," Nikolaj insisted and adjusted his suit jacket.

It felt like everything was going in slow motion. I knew I was ruining Vance's life, but what choice did I have. I couldn't let those assholes find out about all of us.

"What are the terms of having Vance and me here?" I asked as I slowly stood up to sit back on the bed. I clarified, "Can we still do what we do, or are we stuck doing your shit?"

Demyan answered, "you can't leave. Vance? Well, we'll gauge his terms when he gets here."

Nikolaj commented, "you look worried. Interesting. You're stupid enough to follow us, but now you look worried at the mention of Vance coming here."

"I don't want Vance hurt. Clear? Hurt me all you want but leave him alone. Please," I pleaded as my world came crumbling down around me.

Nikolaj studied me like he was curious about how much pain I was willing to take for Vance. The truth was there was no limit to the amount of pain I would try to tolerate. Vance was my world. I would do anything, in our current situation, to protect him.

Demyan leaned his head into his hand and rubbed his lips with his finger while he surveyed me the same way Nikolaj was.

Demyan broke his trance and vowed, "you have our word. We won't hurt Vance."

Nikolaj offered, "if you are good, we won't hurt you either. Unless you want us to." He glared devilishly at me. I couldn't help but be curious about his innuendos.

Nikolaj's phone rang and broke the intense stare-down. He answered as he stepped out of the room. Leaving Demyan and me to clear up loose ends.

"How do we get a hold of Vance?" Demyan demanded again while he moved his leg to rest his ankle on the opposite knee. I watched him regretfully, and the tears welled in my eyes before giving him the number.

Demyan entered the number into his phone and pushed send. He held the phone to his ear while it rang.

I wiped the tears off my cheeks and tried to keep my eyes from watering. My nerves were on edge.

I heard Vance answer, "what?" The tone of his voice made it clear he was pissed.

"Is this Vance?" Demyan inquired with his thick Russian accent; a dead giveaway to Vance of who was calling.

Vance demanded, "where is she?"

"Who?" Demyan played, with a smirk on his face, as he rubbed his hand down his thigh and picked imaginary lint off around his knee.

"Don't fuck with me! Where is she?" Vance sneered.

Demyan laughed and directed his look to me. He charmingly explained, "she's safe in front of me.... on the bed." His eyes dropped to my body and scanned every visible part while his tongue darted out and licked his lower lip. I nervously curled my legs up into my chest.

"Safe?! No! Let me talk to her," Vance commanded.

"Of course," Demyan complied in his calm demeanor. He stood and handed me the phone, letting his fingers brush against my hand.

I put the phone to my ear and sucked in a breath. "Vance," I choked out in a panic.

"Fuck, kiddo! What the fuck were you thinking," Vance questioned.

"I needed to talk to Seth," I muttered sadly, focusing on his voice.

"No, you didn't," he growled, paused for a long moment, then continued, "what did you find out!? Nothing, I bet!" He's never been angry with me, but he was then. He had every right to be, too.

"Nothing. Except it's an organization. I don't know how many people it has. They find you if they want to work with you. They can get you anything for the right price," I rant out in a mumbled voice.

Nikolaj walked back into the room. He sat in his chair by Demyan, and his eyes burned with hate when he observed me on the phone.

"What's going to happen now, kiddo?" Vance asked quietly and softly. His voice was soothing to me.

"They won't let me leave. I told these assholes what you and I do. I hunt, and you collect data." That was my way of telling him not to say anything to those men.

"They want you to work from here with me," I softly confessed, knowing he would but not wanting him to.

The phone went silent, deafening, my throat went dry, and I was overwhelmed with the feeling of how bad I fucked up. I choked back my tears. I would not show those two weaknesses anymore.

"When do I leave?" Vance asked. My eyes closed, and a tear dropped down my face.

"When does he leave?" I whispered to the two men, not opening my eyes to look at them.

Demyan answered, "tomorrow. We will call him with more details later."

I repeated the information to Vance.

"Okay, kiddo. I'll be there with you soon," Vance reassured me.

The thought of him giving up our life for my stupidity, the sacrifice he was making for me, killed me. I couldn't hold it in any longer, and the tears streamed down my face.

"Okay. Vance, I am so sorry," I apologized and hung up.

I wiped the phone on Demyan's chest and headed to the bathroom. I slid the door shut and stared at the hot mess I was in my blood and dirt-covered clothes. What the fuck did I get us into? I took a deep breath and pulled myself together.

When I came out, both men were still sitting there. "Don't you two work?" I catechized.

Demyan chuckled, and Nikolaj leered at me. I couldn't stand the sight of those two men, and I wanted them out of my room.

"Rest. I'll come back shortly with food and a change of clothes. Don't try anything stupid," Demyan ordered and motioned Nikolaj to leave.

Once they left, I lay on the bed. Poor Vance. Maybe I could get them to let Vance go. Perhaps I could get them to let both of us go if we promised to be available when they needed us.

I just lay there, unable to sleep, unable to think straight. Vance was the only thing I could think of. It felt like I had sentenced my father and best friend to death.

Later that evening:

A light knock on the door, and Demyan walked in. His dark gray suit fit his powerful physique perfectly. He had a friendly grin as he walked over to me.

"Hey, M, can I call you M?" He questioned. I nodded as I sat up from the bed. I saw he had a plate of food, a glass of water, and clothes thrown over his shoulder. "We have Vance set to be here in the morning. He should be here at about 9:30 am," he explained. I lifted my eyebrows and nodded, trying to show some kind of appreciation.

Demyan sat in his usual chair, with his legs seated wide, and asseverated, "I know this isn't ideal for you both, but see it from our side. You snuck into our warehouse. Undetected! You skinned a man's arm, then stabbed him in the leg. You could be useful to us in the future. But then again, you could be a fucking liar, and you may know more about us than you let on." He held the plate on one thigh and the water on the other.

I didn't feel like saying a word to him, so I studied him as I sat there and fiddled with the comforter.

"You have our word that we won't hurt either of you unless you're lying; then we'll kill you," Demyan stated. His voice had a sinister way of threatening me in a calm, seductive tone.

I retorted back, "you don't scare me. I'm not yours to use how you want, and neither is Vance."

"Oh, but you are," Demyan grinned and licked his lips. I'm unsure why, but his demeanor and words tighten my core.

"Why do you need us?" I inquired, adjusting my position on the bed.

"Need? No! Want yes," he clarified.

"What could you want us for," I asked as I removed the comforter from my body.

"Anything. Everything. Whatever we want from you, you will do for us, understand?" Demyan demanded and smiled devilishly. I adjusted my position more and set my feet on the ground. He finally handed me the plate of food and the glass of water. I put it on the bed beside me.

"Where's your partner in crime?" I asked as I shoved a strawberry in my mouth.

"He's picking up a package," he stated calmly and composedly, watching my mouth. His calmness set fear down my spine. He was always too calm, which told me he was a dangerous psychopath.

"Oh, what kind of package? Drugs? Prostitutes?" I grilled him while I chewed some more fruit.

"Vance," Demyan retorted. The look on his face was sinister like he knew he had just earned my complete cooperation and he was going to ask me to do diabolical things.

I swallowed hard before expressing my threats to him. "Nikolaj better not hurt Vance. Not one hair on him!" The smile dissipated from his face, and we stared at one another for what seemed to last forever before that evil grin resurfaced on his face.

"He's safe with Nikolaj. I guarantee it," Demyan affirmed.

I took another piece of fruit and ate it. He watched my mouth intently as I chewed.

Did he have a fetish for people eating?

After a few seconds of awkward silence, I asked, "What *do* you two do? Mafia? Drug lords? MAFIA?" My eyes widened as I accentuated the word *mafia*.

He laughed, looked away from me for a second, and then disclosed, "no mafia. We do whatever we need to earn respect and money."

"Mafia," I eagerly countered in response with a mouth full of fruit. I swallowed the deliciousness and then drank the most refreshing water. The coolness of the water sliding down my throat felt amazing.

"We have ties, but we are independent of them," he clarified, tilted his head, and studied every movement I made.

"Yeah, okay," I sarcastically replied, but he looked mafia, and the mafia is mafia. I winked at him jokingly like I knew he was lying, but I dropped the subject.

I ate a few more pieces of fruit, and my eyes rolled to the back of my head, and he chortled while watching me.

"Who trained you?" He questioned. His face went serious, and he ran his hand through his hair.

Stunned at the question, I chewed slower and stared at him. I had to think up a quick response before he suspected me of lying.

"I learned through experience," I explained after I swallowed.

"No, no, no....M, no one is as good as you without training," he contended, leaned in closer to me, and said, "let's not start this relationship with lies." Leaning back, he smirked and winked.

"Relationship? I'm not going to marry you," I spat out. I might have wanted to fuck that sexy man but not marry him. Marriage was not in my life plan.

"Not asking you to. We're your bosses, and you're our employee. Don't be an employee we can't trust," he said, and I gulped hard.

I was starved and wanted to shove the whole plate into my mouth. So, I took another piece of fruit and asked, "do we have to discuss all this now?"

"No," he replied, leaned back, then said, "don't try to leave. You work here now. Think of it as an upgraded office with access to more than just you and Vance. We just want your skills when we need them. You can fight all the sickos you want. Deal?"

"Do I have a choice? No. So I guess it sounds like the deal is made," I sneered, then grabbed my sandwich from the plate.

"Hungry?" He asked, eyeing my mouth again as I took a bite.

"Yeah," I said with my voice muffled by the sandwich.

"There are major consequences if you try to fuck us over. Now, try to fuck us...." his voice weaned off, and I stared at him to finish his sentence.

"Here," he insisted and threw me the tee shirt and sweatpants draped over his shoulder. I caught it, and the scent of his cologne caught in my nose. *Fuck me*, he smelt amazing.

He started to speak again, which pulled my attention back to him. "Vance was told to pack your stuff as well. I'm sure you'd like to change into your own clothes sometime," Demyan explained as he looked me up and down as if he knew what I was thinking about.

I nodded as I held my stare on him. "So, Vance is home, then?" I asked.

"I don't know where he is, but he asked us to give him until morning to get everything together." He got up to leave, then turned back, "we are not bad people, M. You might like it here, with time," then walked out.

I would never like it there.

Present Milly

Chapter 37

I TRY NOT TO wake Vance as I scootch into the bed beside him.

"You are not as quiet as everyone says you are," he grunts, his eyes still closed.

I smile, just happy to hear him. "Sorry. How are you feeling?"

"Tired," he mumbles while lifting his arm to welcome me in. "I missed you, Kiddo."

"You have no idea how much I missed you," I reply with a chuckle and move into his embrace.

"Did I miss anything?"

"LOTS! But we will talk about that tomorrow." I sniff his skin deeply and state, "you showered."

"Yes! I figured you'd be in here. Didn't want to stink," he explains, then growls out a chuckle.

"Tell me what happened," I whisper as I stare at the ceiling.

"Tomorrow," he pleads, breathes deep, and closes his eyes.

I slowly open my eyes. I see Vance still sleeping, but I see something past him. I squint to make my tired eyes work properly. I quickly pop my head up when I realize it's the bosses and the doctor staring at us.

"Wow! You know it's weird to stand there and stare at people sleeping," I blurt out, and Vance starts to wiggle awake.

"We just walked in," Demyan clarifies and laughs.

The doc sets his stuff down by the bed. Vance moans, "already?! I haven't had coffee."

I kick off the covers, stand up, and walk to the foot of the bed to watch what the doctor is doing. He takes a long look over Vance, then grabs his stethoscope.

I feel something soft brush against my shoulders, and I look over to see Nikolaj wrapping his suit jacket around me. I realized then that I was in a tee shirt and panties. He leans down and whispers in my ear, "get some clothes on, now!" He kisses my temple sweetly as he inconspicuously moves my body toward the door.

"I'll be right back, Vance," I say over my shoulder. He doesn't say anything, just sits there with a look on his face.

I ran out of the room and into mine. Grabbed some clothes from the closet, threw them on the bed, and ran to the bathroom. I tear my tee shirt off as I brush my teeth, then run to the dresser to grab panties and a bra.

Toothpaste is running down my chin when I turn back to throw the items on my bed and see Nikolaj standing in my room. I bolt to the bathroom, spit, and wipe my face.

He enters the bathroom doorway smiling and inquires, "do you always brush your teeth wearing only panties?"

"I'm in a hurry," I blatantly state, bite my lip between my teeth, and put my hands on my hips. I stand there in only my panties for Nikolaj to stare at. His eyes cover every inch of my body, and I feel powerful knowing he likes what he sees.

"Why are you in a hurry?" He finally says as his eyes snap to mine.

"To get back to Vance," I snark to make another obvious point.

"The doctor needs some time to assess him," he states, moving closer to me. His brows pull together as he asks, "do you always sleep in Vance's room?"

"No. Just last night," I clarify, following his every movement with my eyes.

He nods, looking me up and down and rubbing his beard.

"Okay! I'll get dressed," I giggle, trying to move past him.

"No! This is good for now," he states, gently pushing me back to the counter, and my ass presses against the cool marble. He looks over my shoulder into the mirror. "This is the best spot to see all of you," he says seductively.

I look over my shoulder to see my ass cheeks resting perfectly on the countertop, making them appear plumper. When I turn my head back to him, I feel his fingers brush against my stitches.

He insists, "we will have the doctor look at this."

"Why? I'm fine," I scoff. I don't need a doctor to tell me to be more careful. On second thought, I jokingly add, "well, I guess he could. Maybe I could stare at his dick, too!"

Nikolaj pushes his hard body into mine, grabs my hair, and yanks it forcing my face to tilt toward his.

"You're not as funny as you think you are, my sweet Milly," he grits possessively.

"Are you crabby?" I smirk as I lay my hands on his chest, and his warmth sends goosebumps throughout my body.

"Are you looking for spankings?" His voice engulfs me with desire as he pulls my hair further, stretching my neck back. Running his teeth over my jawbone and down my neck, he suggests against my skin, "or would you rather I leave you hot and wanting me?"

"Neither," I whisper as I turn my head slightly to nip at his ear. He releases my hair, and I slowly pull my head up, nestle my face into his neck, and kiss it. His hands slowly rub up and down my back. I lift my leg, wrapping it around his waist as I push myself onto the countertop to better angle my center, still covered in the thin fabric of my panties, to his bulging cock begging to be let out of his pants.

"That is not an option. Now, I'll decide for you," Nikolaj replies with a low groan in his voice. His hands move to my naked breasts and twist my nipples. "I will leave you wet and aching for me all day long!"

He slides his hands into my soaked panties and cups my sex, careful to not touch me down there.

"So wet already," he kisses my neck, then bites at the sensitive crook, and I yip at the pain it causes me.

I sink my teeth into the shoulder of his shirt, but it doesn't faze him. He stays still, making sure not to move his hand against my soaked pussy. The anticipation of his hand hovering over me in my panties forces a desperate ache for his touch. I try to relieve the ache by moving my hips to grind my clit against his hand, but he pulls his hand out before any contact. I let out a frustrated huff as he held a long gentle kiss on my lips.

"Get dressed," he commands, giving me a devilish smile, before walking out.

Holy Fuck!!

I stand there naked with a soaked pussy and a complete mess for him.

When I walk back into the room, I see the doctor's done caring for Vance, and he's putting items into his bag. I leer at Nikolaj as I hand him his jacket, then walk over to the bed and sit on the edge next to Vance. I look back to see Nikolaj sliding his jacket on and buttoning, and I can't look away from his thick tattooed fingers.

"He needs rest and time to heal," the doctor announces to us, and it pulls my attention away from Nikolaj.

"Thanks, Doctor, I'll walk you out," Demyan says while motioning to the door for the doctor to follow him.

Nikolaj motions to me and insists, "let's give him time to rest. We'll discuss the details later." He brushes his hand over the small of my back as I stand up from the bed, then asks, "fair enough, Vance?"

Vance agrees, then lays down to go back to sleep. He looks broken, and it's killing me that I can't fix it for him.

Downstairs we see Sven and Gus waiting by the door. Neither looks happy. "Hey, boss, we need to talk," Sven demands in a panic while walking toward Nikolaj.

Demyan closes the front door after the doctor leaves and meets up with Gus.

"What's going on," Nikolaj asks in his deep, delicious voice.

"Hey, Milly," Sven acknowledges me, proving a point that I should not be there when they talk, then continues, "can we talk in your office, boss?"

The guards and Demyan start walking toward Nikolaj's office, and I walk toward the basement stairs. Nikolaj grabs my arm and whispers in my ear, "wet and horny," and then he disappears with the men into his office.

A stupid grin forms on my face, and I glide gleefully down the stairs until I see the weapons room door open. It's never open. Glancing in there, I hear rustling and banging.

"Hello," I hesitantly say and cautiously step into the room. A figure pops out from behind one of the gun safes, and I jump out of my skin before yelling, "Franklin! Jesus fucking Christ! You scared the shit out of me! What are you doing?"

Holding my hand over my heart, I scan the room and draw my attention back to Franklin. He's a weapons specialist with an icy personality and is antisocial.

"What are you doing here?" He snaps.

"Door was open. I came in to see why," I answered, defending my choice to be snoopy.

"Do you always walk through doors when they are open?"

"No, I was just...." I start, but his patience is already gone.

He argues, "you should mind your own business. Now get out!"

"Okay," I mumble and quickly turn to leave the room.

I run through the office door full force. "Hey guys," I demand their attention as I run over to them. Theo is perched up on Daniel's desk. "What's going on in the weapons room? Franklin's in there, and the door is wide open."

"No idea, but that's odd, though. The door is never open. And until now, I thought Franklin was a myth," Theo jokes, then laughs excessively hard at his own comment.

Daniel rolls his eyes, then retorts, "you're dumb! I knew he was real, and you've been here longer than me." The two bicker back and forth, and I see this conversation is over, so I walk over to my desk.

I have a few leads to work on from Enzo's computer, which is a better option than listening to ding and dong argue.

The office door slams open, scaring the shit out of all three of us, and the bosses charge to their desks with the guards in tow.

Nikolaj motions with his hand and barks out, "Daniel, pull up last night's feed!"

I peek from the side of my computer to see what is going on.

Daniel runs over to the control desk and starts clicking away. He looks frazzled. Demyan is hovering over him like a hawk. I don't know what they are looking at, but I hear Daniel say, "Static, boss. It's just static."

"FUCK!" Nikolaj growls, slamming his hands down on his desk.

Demyan throws a container of pens, walks over to Nikolaj, and says, "we'll figure out who it was, then kill them!"

Sven and Gus huddle with the bosses, and Daniel walks back to his desk while giving me a *holy shit* look.

Seconds later, Nikolaj storms to the middle of the room, demands our attention, and says, "does anyone know who is stupid enough to steal from our personal arsenal?!"

The three of us look at each other, astounded, and shake our heads.

"If anyone knows anything or saw anything, speak up," he insists, throwing a screwdriver from the table in the middle of the room.

"Nothing, boss. We know nothing," Theo stutters, getting off Daniel's desk.

Nikolaj's anger is fierce, godly, bone-chilling, and mesmerizing. I move and stand at the edge of my desk to watch him closer, my legs are shaking, and my pussy dripping from his intensity.

"Get out there and find something," he demands while motioning at Sven and Gus, standing next to his desk on the other side of the room.

I return to my seat and try not to look like the apparent creeper I am.

What the fuck is wrong with me? I'm completely turned on by his rage.

He returns to his desk where Demyan is waiting. I hear Demyan speaking Russian on the phone, but I have no idea what he's saying since he is speaking quietly.

I wonder who would take weapons from them?

Why?

When?

Was it an inside job?

If not, how did they get in?

Nikolaj was gone most of yesterday, but Demyan would never betray him.

Leaving, Nikolaj stops at my desk. I pretend not to notice him there. I wonder if I'm playing hard to get or too proud to let him see me completely turned on right now.

He spins my chair to face him, jerking me with it, then places his hands on either armrest of the chair. He towers over me, then leans down into me to say, "I'll see you tomorrow, da?" He leans further to my ear and seductively whispers, "remember, I want you aching for me by the time I get back."

He stands and follows Demyan out of the room.

I let out a heavy sigh. Nikolaj keeps me on edge, and my body reacts to it with desire.

I turned back to my desk, struggling to remember what I was doing before I was distracted.

My phone vibrates, and I jump, hitting my knees on the underside of my desk, getting Daniel and Theo's attention.

"Jumpy Today, Milly?" Theo asks with a chuckle.

"I guess," I responded, looking at my phone. My brows pull together, then I smile.

It's from Nikolaj. *'No fucking yourself tonight, either.'*

I start blushing instantly.

A second text from him. *'You're blushing, aren't you?'*

Is he going to fuck with me the whole time he is gone?

'Yes.' I text back.

'Good,' he replies. I set my phone down to get back to work.

Lunchtime, so I head upstairs to check on Vance and bring food for us to eat.

"Hey, kiddo," he grunts as he pushes himself up to a sitting position on the bed.

"Hey," I reply with a smile on my face. I am so happy to see my best friend here with me again. He looks more rested now than he did this morning.

"What's going on?" He asks as I set the plates down on the bed and crawl up with him.

"Lunchtime," I say, adjusting on the bed beside him, then handing him his plate. I take a bite of my sandwich and savor the fantastic meat and cheese combo in my mouth. I cock an eyebrow at him and say, "get this. Someone stole weapons from the boss's weapons room last night."

"No shit," he exclaims, then says, "ballsy! Maybe I should go help them."

"No! Doc said to rest. So, rest," I demand as I point my finger at him. I chuckle, then say, "yes, very ballsy. Oh, and Franklin isn't a myth." I take another bite while staring intensely at Vance to get my point across about Franklin.

"I didn't think he was," Vance says, with a mouth full of food and giving me a weird sideways look.

There's silence between us for a few minutes as we eat. I see Vance enjoying his small bites of food as much as I'm enjoying stuffing my face. I wonder what they fed him when he was their prisoner, or maybe they didn't feed him.

"Anything else I should know about?" He asks, staring intently at me.

"No." I shake my head, trying to play it cool. I know he wants to know about Nikolaj, but am I ready to admit it to Vance? It wasn't but a few days ago that I was sure he hated me.

"Bullshit! You are a shitty liar! Spill it," he yells and tosses a grape at me.

"What?" I tried to look innocent and unaware of what he was talking about.

"Don't *what* me. Nikolaj this morning. What was that about?" He sets his plate on the bed, and I see he has only had a few bites.

"Eat Vance," I grumble and roll my eyes.

"Talk, Milly," he grunts as he moves a bit. I shove some fruit in my mouth and chuckle at my attempt to not say anything. I laugh and lean into him.

I swallow my food and ask, "if I tell you, will you eat the rest of your food?"

"Yes," he says, grabs his plate, and takes a bite of his sandwich.

"Fine! It's a thing. I don't know. Came out of the blue. I don't understand it, and I don't know how to explain it," I quickly grumble, then shove a grape in my mouth and look at the ceiling.

"A thing? Milly do better than that," he demands. I stare at him like he just asked me to disclose my deepest secrets to the world. Not that he doesn't already know every secret I have.

I grunt out in frustration because I really don't know what is going on, but I'm enjoying whatever it is.

"One minute, I'm sure he hates my very existence. The next, he's.... I don't know," I say, shying away and eating some more fruit.

Vance finishes his plate, leans back on his pillows, and states, "I didn't think he could resist you much longer. He was breaking before I left."

"What?" I demandingly question. Confusion dazes me as I turn to face him better.

"Oh, come on, Milly! He's been obsessed with you since I met him," Vance states while rotating his neck before bringing his gaze to me and continuing, "when I met him three months ago, he had no interest in talking about me, but he asked a lot about you."

"What did you tell him?" I squint my eyes, feeling slightly betrayed that Vance would keep this a secret from me. If the big scary Russian boss is obsessed with me, shouldn't that be something I should know?

"Nothing. I wasn't sure about Nikolaj back then."

"Now?" I ask, gritting through my teeth. Feeling like I'm the inside joke, and no one is loyal to me.

"I talk to him here and there about you, Milly," Vance replies. He can see I'm starting to get pissed. He grabs my hand and explains, "look, I haven't said much about you. Nikolaj does most of the talking, and any questions he asks are answered vaguely."

"You two are always talking, so is it always about me?" I asked, glaring at him.

"Kiddo, you're not the center of the world. We talk about work, too," he answers jokingly, then releases my hand.

"I *am* the center of your world," I smirk and cock an eyebrow.

"You're not wrong there," he admits, takes a deep breath, and continues, "he's been fighting his feelings toward you for a while. He thinks you would be a weakness to him. That's why he tries to create distance between you two, but apparently, he caved."

"Oh. So, you knew Nikolaj would eventually kiss me?" I ask with a side glare.

"Eventually, yes. I figured he would fight himself a little longer," Vance snickers, then coughs, holding his ribs.

"Are you okay?" I asked, leaning over to get his glass of water for him.

"Fine," he replies, then takes a drink. He savors the cold water in his mouth before swallowing. He shuffles down the pillows a bit to lie down and says, "Milly, you deserve to experience every good thing that comes your way. So, if you want him, then go for it."

"Is that your blessing?" I sarcastically ask with a scoff and roll my eyes.

"Yep. You have my approval," he retorts and wiggles down the bed a bit more, trying to get comfy, then closes his eyes.

I sit there in a moment of silence, thinking about the information just disclosed. I've misjudged everything for the last three months, including Vance's ability to keep secrets from me. I should be elated with the news about Nikolaj, but somehow, I'm more confused than ever.

Vance opens one eye and looks at me, "he's bewitched by you, kiddo, accept it," he chuckles and closes his eyes again.

"Vance, no one says *bewitched* anymore," I groan, then shake my head laughing.

"I need my beauty sleep, so get out," Vance says.

"Alright. I'll be back in a few hours," I say while wiggling off the bed. Turning back to Vance, I warn, "don't do anything stupid while I'm gone."

I quietly click the door closed to his room.

My life just went from boring to holy shit in a few days.

My phone vibrates.

'How's Vance?' Nikolaj texts.

'How did you know I was with Vance?' I replied.

'I know everything.'

'Really? He's good. Resting.'

'Go to your room.'

'Why?'

'Do it!'

I can hear the demand in his text like he was saying it to my face. As I walk to my room, flutters build in my core. I can only imagine what he wants from me. Nudes!

I text back, with shaking hands, *'here'*.

My phone pulsates. Nikolaj's calling me, and a smile crosses my face. Phone sex it is!

"Aren't you busy?" I ask condescendingly.

"Do you always answer your phone with a question?" He asks, not giving me time to answer. He follows up with, "we're driving. Is your pussy wet?" He questions with a charmful raspy voice.

My center turns into knots, and I feel my cheeks warm. "Oh my," I whisper seductively.

"Well?" He deeply growls demandingly.

"I don't know," I stutter shyly, frozen. I'm soaked, but it's not easy for me to talk like Nikolaj. I can think of some nasty thoughts, but having to verbalize them is different.

"One," he says over the phone, and his deep voice vibrates in my ear.

I bite my lower lip, letting it drag through my teeth, getting lost in his memories. Realizing I'm taking too long to answer, and he will keep counting, I blurt out, "yes! Fine! Yes!"

His throaty groan rumbles over the phone, feeling like it's wrapping around my body and engulfing me. He demands, "slide your hand down your pants and rub your delicious cunt for me."

"What?" I questioningly choke out. "Sven is right there, isn't he? Oh my god," I say, cringing in total shock that he would talk like that in front of his men. What if they knew he was talking to me?

"Two," he responds calmly.

"I'll take ten, just don't make me do this when Sven's right there," I demand. There's silence for a second, and I know I just fucked myself with ten spankings.

"Deal! That's 12 for tomorrow," he points out, and I hear his chuckle over the phone.

"12! No! I said ten," I argue. No way was I taking 12 spankings!

"You earned two before you made the deal. So, 12. Tvoya zadnitsa budet krasnoy i moya," he growls.

"Yebena mat'," I whisper. He gives a throaty growl.

"You're good at whatever you are trying to do to me," I say breathily.

"I know," he says, then hangs up.

Past Milly
24-years-old

Chapter 38

THE FOLLOWING DAY, I'm semi-conscious when I hear the door to my room click open.

"M, good news," Demyan stated while closing the door, then walking into the room. I snapped awake and quickly sat up. "Oh," he laughed, "sorry, didn't mean to wake you up, but you have a guest arriving soon. Might want to get ready."

"Is it 9:30 already?" I asked as I stretched.

He walked to his chair with his eyes on my body as I lay on the bed. He squinted suspiciously as he sat down in the chair and pointed out, "it's 8:00 am, and I did bring you pants to wear, you know?"

I adjusted my shirt to cover my bare ass, then explained, "I was hot, so I only put the shirt on after my shower." I sat up and swung my legs to the edge of the bed.

He sensually stared at my bare legs. His tongue darted out and licked his lower lip. He smiled sweetly while he adjusted his position in the chair, then broke his trance and responded, "Niko picked him up early *for you*."

The way he emphasized his last two words seemed like I should be extra appreciative of the effort being made to keep me a prisoner here. What did he want me to do, swoon, because he did something *for me*? I don't fucking think so!

It was apparent Demyan was a ladies' man and used to being the object of desire for everyone. He had *fuck me* eyes and a fantastic smile. His build was just as superior as his partner's. The obvious difference between the two bosses was Nikolaj's demeanor instantly clarified he was very dangerous. Demyan's demeanor would bait you into his trance, getting you close to him, then he would show you how dangerous he was. Demyan was the real-life version of *Curiosity killed the cat*.

"Vance is here!" Excitedly, I jumped up and asked, "toothbrush?"

"All your toiletry needs are in the bathroom," Demyan pointed out, then stood from his chair. His gaze never left my body as I walked to the bathroom.

I looked through the drawers to find everything I needed to clean up for Vance. As I brushed my teeth, I spotted Demyan fixing and smoothing my bedding in the mirror.

With a mouth full of bubbles, I asked, "why are you fixing my bed?"

"Because it needs to be made," Demyan chuckled. His hands smoothed the comforter one final time before he smacked and placed the pillows. The force he used to hit the pillows made my body surge.

I spit, rinsed my face, then said as I walked out of the bathroom, "I'm only going to mess it up again, so what's the point?"

"You don't believe in a clean and organized place to live?" He inquired with a sideways look like an unfixed bed was the most disturbing thing he's ever heard.

I rolled my eyes, grabbed the pants from the chair, and slid them on, making sure Demyan could see my movements.

I knew I was playing with fire, taunting him, especially since I have never fucked anyone, but it would be a grand adventure to have him throw me on the just-made bed and rip my clothes off. Something about that man filled me with an overwhelming amount of desire.

To be honest, I had never thought about fucking anyone before. I was content with doing it myself, but the two men that manhandled me the day before had me twisted. Like their aggressiveness opened the door to some dimension in me that I had buried a long time ago.

I threw my shoes on. "Ok, I'm ready," I eagerly said.

Demyan walked past me to the door, and I followed like an excited puppy.

He led me down a hallway, around a corner to the stairs that led down to the next floor. The whole way, his scent lingered in my nose.

We reached the main floor. I saw a sitting room to my right with couches and a piano. As we turned left around the corner, I saw another sitting room to my left and to my right, a kitchen and dining room big enough for an army.

I looked straight ahead and saw luggage being rolled in, then I heard Vance's voice echo down the long corridor, "where is she?"

I ran and felt Demyan try to grab my arm, but I was too fast. The pants he let me wear were too big and started to slide down my hips, so I grabbed one side with my fist. I could hear his shoes hit the floor at the same pace as mine, so I knew he was running, too. Vance looked over to see the commotion and took a few steps toward me before Nikolaj grabbed his shoulder.

I sped up, and as soon as I got within reach, I jumped into Vance's arms, wrapping my legs around his waist, "kiddo," he sighed and squeezed me so tight it hurt, but I didn't care. I missed him so much in the two days I've been here.

"I'm sorry," I whimpered as I buried my face into his neck.

"Milly, did they hurt you?" He grilled, trying to set me down, but I didn't want to let go of him. "Let me see you," he demanded. I slid out of his arms, and he looked me over. Demyan's clothes were too large for me and made it impossible to see anything but my forearms.

"No. The Russians have been good to me," I confessed, grabbed his waist, and pulled myself into his chest.

"Goddamn it, kiddo. I said not to follow these men," he whispered with his lips on top of my head.

I opened my eyes to see everyone staring at us. Vance pulled away, leaned his head into mine, and grunted, "what a mess you got us into." He kissed my forehead and pulled me close to his side as he turned to Nikolaj and Demyan.

"Vance, I'm Demyan," he said with a smile, then held his hand out. Vance reluctantly shook it. "You've met Nikolaj," Demyan continued and pointed to his partner. Vance nodded, looking between the two men and the two men behind them.

"We have much to discuss regarding your living arrangements here," Nikolaj stated.

"Yes, we do, but first, show me my room, so Milly and I can unpack. You have my word we won't be trouble for you," Vance shmoosed.

Demyan complied, "of course. Follow me."

We grabbed as much luggage as possible, and the two guards grabbed the rest. As we headed to the elevator, Demyan explained the parts of the house we walked by.

On the second floor, we exited the elevator. Nikolaj pointed out, "your room is next to Milly's."

"I'll stay in her room if it's all the same," Vance suggested aggressively.

"It's not. You will stay in the room next to Milly," Nikolaj barked. Vance stared him down, and the tension started to rise. We were against the four of them, and Vance was no longer a fighter. I laid my hand on his arm. He nodded, knowing what I was trying to tell him. I knew he didn't want to be there, and we couldn't trust them, but there was no need to try and burn the place down over a room.

"Are there locks on the doors?" Vance asked and eased his glare.

"Of course," Nikolaj replied.

Vance turned to me, "use the locks at all times. We'll have a copy of each other's keys, so I can get in when I need to," he explained. Turning his attention back to our captures, he motions for them to continue to his room.

"We promise not to hurt either of you. We are men of our word," Demyan promised while unlocking the room Vance would be sleeping in.

Vance scoffed, "Of course you are. That's what I always hear right before the *honorable men* do something really shitty."

Nikolaj's eyes filled with rage as he took a step toward Vance, a move to warn Vance to watch what he said.

I looked over to see Demyan's usual calm look had been replaced with a bone-chilling look of a killer. His eyes grew angry and sinister as he stared at Vance as if pondering all the ways he would make him suffer if he got his hands on him. Then a smile crossed his face. He cleared his throat, then calmly asked, "what bags go in your room, Vance?" The change in Demyan's presence just reiterated how dangerous he really was.

"These three. The rest are Milly's," he directs, then turns back to me. Gus took the three bags to Vance's room. I see the majority of the bags were left in the hall.

"These are all mine? What did you pack?" I asked in shock that I had so many bags.

"Everything in your room," Vance said and made a weird face.

My eyes widened. "Everything?" I confirmed.

"Yep!" Vance said as he popped the "p" with his lips.

His look told me he had packed my sex toys from the drawer beside my bed. Well, that secret was out now. My face turned red, and my heart was beating in my ears. I looked around to see all the men looking at me. I wanted to sink into the floor.

In my defense, I was not about to fuck anyone I lived with in Chicago because they were considered my family. So, I settled with my toys, which did the trick.

Trying to get them to stop staring at me, I barked, "ok! Can we get on with it?!"

Gus walked out of Vance's room and looked at everyone looking at me. "Did I miss something?" He asked.

"NO," I snapped, pushed past everyone, and walked into Vance's room. I could feel the men looking at me as I looked around his room.

I heard the men start to shuffle around in the hallway. Then Nikolaj ordered, "Sven and Gus, take her bags into her room."

The men met up with me in Vance's room, which was identical to mine, except reversed. Our beds shared a wall.

"Look, now I can hear you snore through the wall!" I giggled and nudged Vance.

"I don't snore," he said sarcastically, scanning his room.

Nikolaj stated as he walked into the room behind us, "the walls are built quite well. You shouldn't hear much from each other's rooms."

Vance wheeled his bags to the bed as he asked, "where do we get the stuff we need?"

"What stuff would you need?" Demyan inquired.

"Shampoo, conditioner, and Milly will need things," Vance pointed out.

"We have people who shop for us. Make a list, and we will send them," Nikolaj explained coldly.

"We'll let you get settled. We can discuss your terms later, but just know Milly doesn't leave without Nikolaj or me with her," Demyan said, handing Vance the keys to his room. Vance nodded and glared at me with *what a mess we were in* look.

"Ok, Milly, let's see your room," Vance ordered, catching Nikolaj and Demyan's attention, causing them to stop in the hallway and turn around.

"Ok. Come on," I complied as I grabbed Vance's hand and pulled him out of his room. We pushed past the four men and headed to my room. I looked over my shoulder to see we were followed by Demyan and Nikolaj. I stopped and gave them a funny look but quickly moved my attention to Vance.

"Did you sleep in here, kiddo?" Vance asked with a confused, funny tone.

"Yes. Why?" I asked suspiciously.

"Beds made. Not your thing," Vance said with a chuckle, and I heard Demyan laugh behind us. I nudged Vance in the side, then wrapped my arms around his waist. I turned back and scowled at Demyan. He winked at me with a huge grin.

Nikolaj, stone-faced, sarcastically said, "I assume the room will suffice for Milly?"

Vance turned his head to look at him, "the room is excellent. Thanks."

Nikolaj nodded, then followed Demyan out of the room.

"He's intense," Vance whispers against my temple.

"Yep!" I said, popping the 'p.' I adjusted my arms to his shoulders and looked at his face, "I'm so sorry. I really fucked up."

He ran his hands through his curly hair, then hugged me. I was an asshole for forcing him to be there with me, but I was lost without him. I knew one thing; I would never disobey Vance's orders again.

"Stop saying sorry. This wasn't part of our plan, but we will adjust," Vance tenderly responded, then kissed my forehead. "Unpack! We only have an hour before the meeting," he ordered and nudged me.

He started to walk out of the room, then turned to say, "oh, I never want to talk about the drawer by your bed. Got it!"

My face turned red, and I winced. "Deal! Stop bringing it up, Vance!" He chuckled and walked out of the room.

I was unpacking my last bag, hurrying through, so I could talk to Vance before they came and got us. Vance was very organized when he packed my room. He had everything folded neatly, so it was easy to just set everything in drawers.

I tried to keep my room organized in Chicago, but shit would end up wherever. Vance, on the other hand, was military organized. Nothing was ever out of place.

"Are you almost done, kiddo?" Vance asked while walking in. "Everything put away, right? Or just tossed around?" He sarcastically interrogated.

He really did treat me like his kid. I could only imagine this would be the same kind of relationship I would have had with my real dad if he were still alive.

"Have some confidence in me," I joked, then asked, "how are you so normal? And I'm not a 'kiddo'! And I put everything away the right way!" I abandoned my suitcase on the bed, half-unpacked, and walked over to Vance.

"So, this meeting, we're not going to tell them anything about us, right?" I whispered.

"Right. I'll talk, though. You're clearly off your game," Vance insisted. Instantly annoyed, I furrowed my brows at his comment. "Don't get mad! You know exactly what I mean. You have taken beating after beating but never let a word slip out, but you split right open with these two men." He was wide-eyed and shook his head in disbelief.

"I've never had the threat of never seeing you or our family again. I knew I would go home those other times, but I'm a prisoner this time. I guess I panicked. Vance, you're everything to me. Our family is my world, but you're like the air I need to breathe." I felt the tears welling up in my eyes, so I hugged my best friend. I couldn't quit hating myself for what I did.

"They think it's just you and me, right?" He asked. I nodded against him. "Let's keep it that way," he whispered.

We heard someone walking into Vance's room, then we heard, "hey, Vance!" Realized it was Demyan, but before we could say anything, we heard his footsteps coming to my room. "Hey, there you are. Let's get this meeting done. What do you say, Vance?" Demyan asked while clapping his hands together.

"Where do you want us to go?" Vance asked.

"Us? No. Milly isn't invited to this meeting," Demyan snapped.

"She goes with me, or I don't go," Vance gritted through his teeth and pushed me behind him. I stood there watching Demyan's sinister look come through.

"Vance, you are not in a position to negotiate. She stays here," Demyan argued and moved closer to Vance.

I squeezed Vance's arm and feared he would be forced to fight. Vance had physically fought anyone in years, and his physique showed he stood no chance against the broad and muscular Demyan.

"Then the meeting is here!" Vance barked, holding his ground.

"You don't get to make demands here," Demyan yelled, stepped closer to Vance, took a deep breath, and then gave an evil grin.

"Fine. She comes with. If you don't meet our expectations, we'll kill her in front of you."

Shocked, I yelled, "what about your word not to hurt us?"

Demyan didn't take his eyes off Vance and said, "you are both the enemy until you're not. Don't mistake my kindness for weakness. Now, follow me." He turned on his heel and walked out of the room.

Vance grabbed my hand, pulled me close, and we followed him.

Nikolaj's office was across from the main entrance of the building. "Kakogo khrena, Dem?" Nikolaj barked while standing in front of his desk.

"On by ne stalbez neye," Demyan explained and walked ahead of us to his business partner.

"JESUS FUCK!" Nikolaj growled while he and Demyan sat on the other side of the desk.

The office was huge; bookcases full of old books lined the walls, a mini-bar in the corner by the desk, and a couch and some chairs.

"Sit," Nikolaj demanded and huffed out a breath before he continued, "there are no negotiations for her. She stays here at all times. Unless accompanied by Demyan or myself. Clear?" Nikolaj scowled at Vance.

"Fair enough," Vance said, glaring at me, and I slumped in my chair.

"Then why the fuck is she here?" Nikolaj angrily asked while he leaned into his desk. Vance leaned forward, unintimidated by Nikolaj's wrath.

"I'm all she has in this fucked up world. She is to be by my side at all times," he answered. He was so angry that he didn't realize he was squeezing my hand.

Demyan leaned forward in his chair. "Let's agree we don't know each other at all, and all our guards are up. But remember, we are not the ones that intruded into a warehouse they should not have been at." They all looked at me, and Vance looked at me with a cynical glare, then directed his gaze back to the men in front of us.

"Fine. You're right. Milly should have never followed you two, and because of her actions, we are now your captives. I understand that. Just understand Milly and I have been together for a long time. We have been through some major stuff together. We are bonded," Vance explained calmly while staring at Nikolaj.

"We understand that bond, and we'll honor it," Nikolaj agreed.

Demyan caught Vance up on our earlier agreements, "we've already agreed to let you two continue to hunt. What we want to know is what are *your* skills, and are you trustworthy?"

Vance adjusted in his chair. "I won't do anything to jeopardize Milly's safety. I will do whatever you want," he replied humbly. My heart broke in two, knowing I ruined Vance's life forever.

Vance went on, "I just want to make one thing clear. NONE of your men, including yourselves, are to touch Milly. Clear?"

Nikolaj instantly moved forward in his chair. "You think Milly will be raped and tortured by our men or us?" The look on his face could have set someone on fire. Clearly, we should never have questioned the honor of those men a second time.

Vance, on the defense, spat out, "I don't know you! She's mine to protect!"

"Great job protecting her when she walked into our warehouse!" Nikolaj retorted and threw a coffee cup across the room.

Vance didn't say a word. Instead, he calmly sat there, unaffected by the rage. I, on the other hand, quivered at the intensity of

Nikolaj. I knew how strong this man was. I knew how bad he could hurt me if he chose to, and the restraint he has not to kill me.

Composing himself, Nikolaj said, "we have no intention of hurting Milly. We are honorable men! Death is the consequence of dishonorable actions. Milly is safe. Safer here with us than alone doing whatever the fuck you two do!"

I stood up and yelled, "why are all of you talking like I couldn't defend myself?! As I recall, it took both of you to fight me. So clearly, no one is fucking me without my consent!" I slammed myself back in the chair and stared at the wall to my left.

Vance chuckled, breaking the tension, then snarked, "it took both of you to fight her?"

I whipped my head toward him. "VANCE!" I snapped.

"I don't doubt your skills, kiddo," Vance complimented and laughed.

"She is well trained. Now you know why we can't just let her go," Nikolaj boasted and leaned back in his chair.

Demyan added, "at the warehouse, she was inches behind us before we knew she was there. She ghosted right through our security detail. She's good."

Vance cocked a smile. "Yes, she is."

"You trained her?" Nikolaj asked with a suspicious tone.

"Yes, and experience," Vance said and leaned back in his chair.

It seemed like the tension in the room had subsided, and we could get to the terms of our stay.

I stared at the men across from us and wondered why they would be so worried about what I knew about them. I can guarantee they weren't Lazlo, or they would have killed Seth when he started talking.

Demyan cleared his throat and said, and I returned to reality, "let's get to the terms."

Nikolaj leaned back, folded his hands on the desk, and said, "I visited with you a little on the way here. I don't feel like you are a threat. I'm not a trusting man, but you have more to lose fucking us over than we do." He pointed at me, and he looked me up and down.

"Over here, big guy," Vance demanded firmly.

Nikolaj slowly rolled his eyes toward Vance, and his jaw ticked as he pushed his teeth together. Demyan adjusted in his chair, with his calm, smiling demeanor, and cleared his throat. Nikolaj relaxed his glare, and Demyan inquired, "what is it that you contribute to your team, Vance?"

I noticed that Demyan would interject whenever Nikolaj started to get angry. Was that because Nikolaj was all mouth and no action or short-tempered and quick to kill?

The conversation about what we do and how went on for a while. The information Vance gave was vague but had enough detail to satisfy the two men in front of us.

Demyan nodded. "Ok, you two do what you do, but under our watch. Milly doesn't leave here without us. She's too good but too much of a risk for us. She will have a phone with our numbers, our security detail, and your new number."

"My new number?" Vance asked.

"Yes. You will have a number specific to my team. Untraceable from the outside." Demyan clarified, then continued, "Vance, we could use your areas of expertise more often, prove yourself trustworthy and loyal, and we may give you more access and privileges."

"Deal," Vance said. I'm not sure why, but after the tension eased, it seemed like Vance was almost excited about his new life.

"You will work downstairs with Daniel and Theo. You will live upstairs in your own rooms," Demyan added.

"Does everyone on your team live here?" I asked.

Nikolaj looked my way and vaguely explained, "only our elite. Our best."

"Let's give you a tour. Hopefully, over time you will come to like our compound. Maybe even establish trust between us," Demyan said in a hopeful tone.

Past Milly
24-years-old
Chapter 39

THE TWO MEN SHOWED us the entire house, except Nikolaj's place. They showed us the office we would work in and our desks. The garage had at least six cars and a couple of motorcycles.

We met the kitchen staff and were told they make three meals daily; no requests. Eat what they make or starve.

We met the house cleaners, security detail, gardeners, maintenance, and everyone else that worked in the compound.

We toured the grounds, and Demyan pointed out his house, but we didn't go in.

The tour took about two hours. Then they led us back to the office we would be working in and left.

"Hey, you're both back!" Theo smiled.

Vance and I took in the whole room since the bosses weren't here to rush us. There was a wall of monitors covering every angle of the compound. I studied each monitor, searching for an escape route.

"Stop it, Milly," Vance firmly whispered as he walked up beside me.

"What? I'm not doing anything," I whispered back, playing innocent.

"I hear your thoughts! Stop looking for a way out. There's not a way out," he sternly insisted. I rolled my eyes because he knew me, and sometimes it sucked that he knew me so well.

"There's always a way out," I stated confidently.

"Stop it! We have their trust until we don't! Do not fuck this up, too," he demanded in a pissed-off whisper.

"WOW! Offensive," I retorted. He just glared at me before turning his attention to the monitors. "Fine. But there is a blind spot," I clarified in a whisper, then headed back toward the other two men working.

Daniel popped his head up. "Hey. Hi. Oh, here's your desk. I'm glad you two are here. It will be nice to have someone else to talk to other than Theo." He laughed.

"Hey, I'm great company," Theo clarified. I can't help but smile.

"What are you working on?" Vance asked.

"Oh boy! You are in for a treat," Theo exclaimed, then became a complete nerd on both of us. He explained every piece of what he was doing, then in full description, then of another piece of tech, then to another and another.

Vance relaxed a bit and took off his suit jacket. I admired how Vance tried to make the best of the shitty situation I got us in.

"Do you think they are okay?" I whispered to Vance.

"Yeah, just two nerds doing what they love."

"Oh, so we'll fit in with them," I stated, then laughed.

"We'll keep our info private until we know we can trust them," Vance said while running his hand through his hair. "Well, let's play robotics with these two," he said loud enough to get Theo and Daniel's attention.

"Yes," Theo said excitedly.

Daniel added, "Well, sometimes we must collect information for the bosses, but tech is our specialty."

"So, you set up the cameras on the property?" Vance asked.

"Yes! Not a blind spot to be found," Daniel boasted proudly.

Vance smiled, nodded, then scrunched his face, "but there is."

Daniel stood firm and argued, "no way!"

"Milly, show them," Vance demanded.

I stared at Vance for a long moment. I didn't know what he was doing, but I was pissed. That could have been our way out. "I didn't see one," I grit my teeth.

"That's because there isn't one," Daniel reiterated.

Vance changed the tone of his voice, "Milly, show them now!"

"Okay," I whispered, defeated, and betrayed.

We walked to the cameras, but our new bosses walked in before I could get a word out. Nikolaj stormed toward me so fast, making Vance jump in between us.

"What's the problem, big guy?" He asked Nikolaj.

"What are you doing with the monitors?" He growled. Demyan stopped beside Nikolaj, curious for the answer.

Daniel stepped in and said, "sorry, boss. She's showing me a blind spot in the camera view."

"Show us all," Demyan calmly said, moving closer to me.

My nerves amped up. My throat was dry as I walked to the first monitors. "Okay. Cameras 53 and 57 don't meet. See? There are missing views by the wall of the house and the bushes by the pool. This leaves room for someone to hide in the bushes and walk along this wall undetected until they get into view of camera 53, but by then, it's too late."

Daniel stared and analyzed all the monitors. "Holy shit! There is! Sorry bosses, I missed a few bushes."

Vance stood proud, "it's her job to find blind spots, so she can access buildings undetected. That's why she's the best." Vance nudged me with his shoulder.

"Those are just bushes, nothing back there to get in or out," Demyan said.

"I can get in and out," I smirked, trying to set up a challenge.

"No way," Demyan challenged.

"BET," I demanded as I stepped closer to Demyan.

"Let's go," Demyan entertained. "Niko, stand here and tell me if you see her."

"You won't," Vance said. I looked at Vance, and he nodded, "give them hell, kiddo!" he smiled.

I followed Demyan to the spot outside. He was on the phone with Nikolaj. "You can't see us... okay...Do your thing, M," Demyan said.

I analyzed the bushes, walls, and camera directions. I slid on the wall to the bushes, stepped over the bushes, and crouched down by the other brushes.

I analyzed my current position. I stayed low to the ground, sneaking between a gap between the bushes; I made it to thicker bushes and trees.

I walked a few feet down through those trees to the cement wall surrounding the perimeter. I slid behind a pile of huge rocks used for landscaping and crawled to another set of bushes covering the lower three feet of the wall.

I paused, listening to Demyan talking on the phone, but I didn't know what he was saying. I saw a small vent on the cement wall that I knew I could squeeze through.

I removed the screws of the vent cover with a hair clip, then squeezed through the vent hole. Once through, I pulled the vent cover back in place.

I turned around to look at my surroundings. There was nothing there but trees, fields, and grassland. Where the fuck were we?

I took off running to my left, remembering the compound's layout, and the front gate was to my left.

That was the longest fucking cement wall I had ever seen. It felt like I was running forever. I finally reached the end of the wall and turned left. More FUCKING wall!

I stood for a second to catch my breath and then ran again. I finally saw the metal gates. I picked up the pace and ran onto the road that led to the gates. I saw six men and Vance standing inside the closed gate.

"There's.... a....blind....spot," I huffed and puffed out and fell to my knees to rest.

"Come on, kiddo, was it that long of a run?" Vance asked and laughed as the gates opened, and the men walked to me.

"Why the fuck....do you have such a long.... fucking wall?" I flailed my arms toward the wall, still breathing hard. "Who the fuck.... are you trying to keep out?....The fucking boogeyman?"

Demyan walked over to me, laughing and shaking his head, and handed me a water bottle.

Nikolaj said, almost smirking, "we saw you once you got out of the wall. We would have picked you up, but we wanted to see if you would take this opportunity to run free."

I chugged the whole water bottle down, stood, brushed my pants off, then explained, "no way! Vance is here, so I'm here."

Sven and Gus stood behind their bosses, snickering at each other.

"What's so fucking funny?" I demanded.

"You're persistent," Gus joked, and I scoffed at him.

Sven added, "you need to work on your cardio." I glared at him.

"Oh, you got jokes? You run that fucking wall," I snapped back sarcastically.

"Nah, we take ATVs around here," Gus pointed out.

"Oh, so that's how you beat me to the gates," I bitterly stated.

"You think we are going to run? Nah, we work smarter, not harder," Demyan added to the banter.

I rolled my eyes at all this and plopped myself into one of the ATVs. Vance slid in beside me, and the bosses jumped in front.

"Guess we will have to fix the blind spot," Demyan said to Nikolaj. Nikolaj nodded, then called maintenance to fix the vent I pulled off.

We returned to the mansion, and the bosses let Vance and I return to our rooms to settle in. We didn't say a word until we were in my room.

"What the fuck, Vance?! That was our way out," I huffed and shoved my hands on his chest. He didn't budge, but it felt good to try.

"Your way, yes! My way, no! Look at me, kiddo! I don't exactly have the physique to squeeze through small holes," he clarified, rubbing his belly. "Seriously though, I was establishing trust. Showing them a weakness in their safety and giving them a chance to fix it. This is our life now. Like it or not. No sense being enemies with these guys."

I rolled my eyes, but Vance was right.

Vance giggled at my frustration at having to play nice and stated, "listen, I'm not saying we will brush each other's hair and sing kumbaya around a campfire. They have more ties to the world than we ever had, and we can use that. All we have to do is what they want when they want. Milly, we still get to do what we do, just with a different atmosphere."

I glared at him, then turned to grab some clothes from my closet across the room. I yelled to Vance as I walked to the bathroom, "it sounds like you actually like these guys and being here." I leaned against the door frame and waited to see what he would say.

"Just making the best out of an unpredicted situation," he chuckled.

I felt guilty bringing him here, and maybe I should play by his rules because mine didn't work out so well.

"I'm going to shower. Stay in my room! Do not leave!"

"I'll check for cameras and recorders," Vance said.

True to his word, Vance was looking for cameras and recorders when I walked out of the bathroom.

"All clear," he said as he turned to me.

"Okay. Good. By the way, that soap they gave us smells heavenly," I said, then laughed and sarcastically stated, "I'm just making the best out of an unpredictable situation." I wink at him, and he laughs.

"Good. I'm showering next. Stay in your room! Do not go throughout the house without me. Understood?!"

"Okay," I said and tossed myself on the bed.

Vance stopped at the table in the kitchenette and took the spare key off my keyring.

"I'll lock the door on my way out but try to take a nap."

I watched him walk out, then I closed my eyes.

Present Milly

Chapter 40

I slept in Vance's room again. Today he's up before me and ready to go to work.

"Should you be walking around?" I mumble as I stretch.

"I'm good! Let me get back to normal life," he insists with his coffee cup in tow as he walks to the bathroom.

"Okay. Mr. Grumpy pants," I joke as I jump out of bed. "I'm going to change. See you in a few."

"I don't need a babysitter, kiddo."

"Yeah, sure! See you soon," I said while closing the door. I look at my phone. There is a text from Nikolaj from a few minutes ago. *'I'm downstairs.'*

They're back already?

We may get details about who stole the weapons and Vance's capturers.

Vance and I walk around the corner of the kitchen just in time to see Gus throw an orange at Theo.

"I didn't miss much here," Vance jokes. Everyone froze to look at Vance, who was smiling ear to ear.

"Vance! Holy shit! Welcome back," Daniel says, putting his coffee cup and running over to hug Vance.

"I missed you, man," Theo says.

I lean up against the counter. Sven comes over to me with a shit-eating grin.

"Hi," he whispers and just stands there smiling.

"What?" I ask suspiciously.

"Don't '*what*' me...." He lingers. My eyes go wide. "Just kidding, Milly. Loosen up!" He nudges me.

Either he knows but doesn't let me know, or he doesn't. Nikolaj didn't use my name on the phone, so maybe Sven doesn't know anything.

"Did you find the weapons thief?" I inquire as we stand there, watching the chaos of bantering and bonding in front of us.

"Yes," Sven says before Gus chimes in, "fucking new guard here. He started last week. He was weird as fuck but dead now."

"Why would he steal guns from these guys?" I ask.

Sven takes a sip of coffee before answering. "He was a member of a group that tries to intercept gun shipments. Thought they would get the advantage on our supply by stealing from the bosses."

"Dumb fuck tried to sell the weapons to a group of Russians. They called Demyan while we were looking and told them they had the guy and would wait for us to show." Gus adds in.

"Wow," I say and take a drink of coffee.

"Vance! Good to see you up," Demyan states, walking into the kitchen and straight to the coffee machine.

The men start bullshitting each other, and I sneak out to Nikolaj's office. The door is open, so I peek inside.

"Come in," he demands, but I can't see him. "Shut the door," he orders, and I finally spot him behind the door putting some books on the shelves of the tall bookcases.

"Hi," I softly say. The sleeves of Nikolaj's shirt are rolled up, revealing his thick tattooed forearms.

"Hello!" He rasps, swooping me up in his arms. I wrap my arms around his neck, and his lips fall on mine, giving me a good morning kiss. His lips slightly parted, allowing my tongue to slip in to taste his delicious mouth, and my hands grabbed the back of his head.

I suck his bottom lip, then nip it with my teeth, making him growl. I smile against him, then his lips trail down to my neck, catching my sweet spot, and I whimper.

"MMM...You know everyone will find out you like me if you're not careful," I point out as Nikolaj devours my neck.

He smiles against my skin and clarifies, "they already know." He sucks and kisses my neck more, making me quiver.

I pull back just to admire his face. He groans and tightens his body around me as if stretching with me in his arms. "Long night?" I ask.

He releases me and pulls me with him to the mini-bar. "Always," he mumbles while pouring two cups of coffee. He mentions, "I noticed you weren't in your room this morning," handing me a cup, then taking a sip from his cup while eyeballing me.

"You were in my room?" I ask, arching my eyebrow.

"Da," he answers in a possessive tone.

"Why?" I ask naively. He looks at me with a seductive smirk. "Ohh. Were you in there long?" I question with my lips against my cup before taking a drink and letting the warm, bitter liquid fill my mouth.

"No. I knew where you were," Nikolaj replies, looks me up and down, then says demandingly, "I will expect you in your room tonight. You are not allowed in another man's bed any longer. Understood?"

"It's Vance's bed! Not just any man," I joke but realize he's not kidding. I start to feel my face turn hot, and I become defensive. "I was just worried about him. That's why I stayed there. We always take care of each other," I tried to clarify.

"No more sleeping in his bed," he demands as he walks to his desk to set his cup down.

"So, is this when you start to think you get to control me?" I snap, taking a few steps closer to him.

He sits down at his desk and leans back in his chair. "Milly, I am not about to be made a fool of in front of my staff because you're seen sleeping in Vance's room. No one here knows anything about you. I wouldn't want them to think you two are intimate when you are with me. I'm not controlling you, but to be with someone like me, you must follow certain rules and uphold certain standards."

"What are we?! I may not know how dating works, but I don't think fingering me makes me your property," I spouted out, walking closer to him.

"My property?" He questions with a tone. "No! I want you as my companion," he professes, staring at me with frustration.

"Companion? What does that even mean? Giving up everything I love to protect your precious pride!" I lean my hands on his desk.

He leans forward. "I am not a traditional man. It doesn't suit my lifestyle, Milly!'

He stands quickly and rounds the table to meet me. He doesn't touch me. He keeps a small space between us. "When I want something, I go after it. You know how I feel about you. I don't need labels or time frames to tell me what you mean to me. If you want to pursue this with me, then understand you must only present yourself as mine! Clear?!" He stands there, burning a hole in me.

My breathing is heavy. I want Nikolaj, but I won't give up my love for Vance. I take a deep breath, and my mind races to salvage this time with him.

"I don't normally sleep in Vance's bed, but he's hurt. I wanted to make sure he would be okay. He's been there for me for so long. I can't promise I won't stay with him again if he is sick or hurt. He's like my father. Wouldn't you stay with your father if he were sick or hurt?" I choke out.

He just looks down at me. "Go to work," he snarls.

Why is he being such a FUCKER?!

I storm to the door, then quickly turn around to ask, "can I be in here when you talk to Vance about his time away?"

His look turns cold. "Are you afraid he will tell us something but not you?"

"No. I just want to know what happened to Vance." He nods one time, then turns away.

Guess we are back to being an asshole.

I walk into the office to see Vance nestled in his chair, and a smile crosses my face. "Good to see you back at your desk, bestie," I joke, walking over to him.

"Good to be back."

I sit on the corner of his desk beside him, and we lean into each other. "What happened? Please, tell me. Nikolaj said I could be in the office when you talk to them, but I want to know now," I pleaded.

"Ambush."

"Who?"

"I don't know. We thought we had a lead on a Lazlo setup. Ended up captured. I'll explain more later," he whispers.

"Secrets are not okay, you two," Theo yells, making us both jump. "We missed you too, Vance! Where is our intimate whispering in our ears? Huh? Daniel, did you get intimate whispering in your ears?" Theo makes a scene. Daniel gives him a weird look. "Just kidding! Loosen up!" Theo laughs.

"You still have a bad sense of humor." Vance chuckles.

"You were only gone for like six days! You thought there would be major changes?" Theo banters.

"I just thought you would think the reason I left was you, and you would try to change," Vance jokes. I roll my eyes, scoff, and head to my desk.

I work most of the morning with Daniel on a better security and camera system for the weapons room, but my head is all twisted with Nikolaj's interaction this morning.

How can I go from wanting to hate him because I thought he hated me to wanting to be with him because he wants to be with me, back to hating each other?

"Milly! Are you here?" Daniel says while snapping his fingers in front of my face.

"Yes! I'm here. Sorry." I slightly shake my head. "Okay, Daniel, we are going to set up the cameras on two different networks, so if someone is stupid enough to try this again, we'll have two networks recording, but they won't know that."

"Perfect," Daniel says, fiddling with some wires on the new fingerprint scanner.

Demyan's walking down the stairs, "how's it going, you two?"

Daniel replies, "we are almost done."

"Good! I knew you two could do it," Demyan says. Daniel and Demyan stare at each other for a long second. I smirk and suspiciously watch this interaction.

Why are they looking at each other so long?

I clear my throat, "hi," I say softly. "Welcome back," I add with a chuckle.

"Okay. I have to talk to Vance. Keep up the good work, you two," Demyan says, pats Daniel on the arm, and heads to the basement office.

"What was that?" I whisper to Daniel.

"What?" He scoffs and looks back at the wires.

"Boy! Don't *what* me. That wasn't a good job, stare. That was a different kind of stare," I giggle.

He shakes his head. "You're reading into things. I'm not his type," he says, finishing up the wiring.

"How do you know? He could be gay, bi, or whatever he wants to be, and that looked like a LOOK," I laugh and gesture a hand job motion.

"Fuck off, Milly!"

"Okay, fine," I say, holding my hands up and nudging him to the office. We cross paths with Demyan and Vance.

"Have fun," I softly say to Vance. He smiles.

I look at Demyan to see him holding his look on Daniel, then noticing me and winking.

The office door closes behind us, and I shove Daniel. "Did you see him staring at you!? Seriously?!"

"No." Daniel gave me a look. "I saw him wink at you. Besides, I already said. I'm not his type."

"Whatever," I growl as I walk to my desk.

"What did I miss?" Theo asks.

"Nothing," Daniel answers, trying to kill the conversation.

"Just Demyan's appreciation for Daniel," I chirp with air quotes to emphasize appreciation.

"Oh, I've noticed he likes your work a lot," Theo says, understanding my meaning.

We both give Theo a weird look, though.

"What? I notice things, but I don't always have to say I notice things," he scoffs.

Past Milly
24-years-old

Chapter 41

Vance clarified to the entire crew that he and I would be off the grid for a while. Not to look for us or expect any calls from us.

They all knew I had gone to the warehouse. They knew Vance wouldn't leave me here alone.

It was difficult adjusting to my new setup. I had to be careful who was around when I talked to Vance.

The bosses had my computer set up so they could see everything I was doing. There was no way for me to speak to anyone outside of here.

It was suffocating.

I wanted to go out hunting.

I wanted to train with someone other than myself.

I wanted to be around my family.

Vance adjusted to this life a lot easier than I did. He got along with everyone, and it was annoying to share him with those people, but it was my fault, so I had no choice.

Theo and Daniel were okay nerds to be around. We worked with them as much as we could.

We also helped set up gear for Sven, Gus, and Aanya when they needed it.

Nikolaj hated me. Demyan was friendly and flirty, so I couldn't help but smile when he was around. The bosses loved Vance, but who wouldn't?

Nikolaj and Vance talked to each other whenever they could, but I didn't know what about.

Sven and Gus were always joking around with everyone and competing.

One day, I saw them working out in the gym around the corner of the stairs while snooping around the main floor. I stood outside the glass door, watching them bicker about the correct form for lifting. They remind me of the way Rosco and Adio always bullshitted each other.

I missed training with them and my family.

"Milly, you okay?" Sven yelled at me from inside the gym.

"Yeah. Yeah, I'm fine. Just lost in thought," I yelled back and looked around quickly to find an escape.

"Well, come in," Gus said. I opened the door and slowly stepped in.

"I wasn't trying to be weird. I just miss my old life, I guess," I said, running my hand up my forearm.

"I can't imagine what you are going through, Milly. I'm sure it's hard, but you put yourself in this predicament," Sven said.

"What the fuck, man! You don't need to say that," Gus said, hitting Sven's arm.

"What!? She's smart. She knows."

"Okay, well, I'm still standing right here, so maybe we can talk about something other than my stupid-ass decision," I said, looking around at all the equipment.

"Of course," Gus said.

"You work out, right? So, what do you like to do?" Sven asked.

"Well, I usually do weights and train. Like fighting," I shrug.

"You can work out with us. We'll even fight you if you want," Gus said and threw some punches in the air.

"Yeah. That'd be cool. Maybe it will help me get used to this place," I said.

"Cool! Let's start then." Sven motioned to the small fighting ring in the corner of the room.

"Or do you need to change?" He added, smirking.

"I'm always ready to fight," I scowled.

"What kind of fighting do you do?" Sven asked while we walked to the ring.

"Everything," I said.

"What's that mean?" Gus asked.

"It means show me what you got, and I'll defend myself," I clarified, taking my sweatshirt off and adjusting my tank top.

Sven stood in front of me first. He started to warm up, and I studied his movements. He was a few inches taller than me and solid-framed, but he didn't look fast or flexible. That should give me the advantage of speed and agility.

"Let's go," Sven demanded.

"Rules," Gus blurted out and stepped between us. "This is training, not personal. We don't hold grudges. Don't kill each other." We both nodded.

"Don't kick my balls, either," Sven said.

"Don't kick me in the vag, then?" They both looked at me funny. "Hurts women, too!"

Sven took the first punch, and I dodged it, then we were in full fight mode. He punched. I blocked. I punched. He blocked. I faked and uppercut him.

"FUCK," he yelled.

"You gonna live?" I banter with him. He smiled and came back to the fight. He went low, sweeping my legs out from me. I fell to my side. He took two kicks to my ribs!

"Easy, man," Gus yelled. Sven stepped back.

"No! I'm fine." I stand back up.

Our fighting went on for a long time. Intensifying with every second that went by. We were both bleeding in several spots, winded and tired.

"Ready to admit defeat?" I ask, out of breath.

"Nope," he responded.

"SVEN! What the fuck is going on?" Demyan yelled.

We both stopped dead. All three of us spun to face the door. Demyan and Nikolaj were charging at us with Vance in tow.

Nikolaj's eyes were rageful as he grabbed Sven around the neck and slammed him into the wall.

"STOP!" I yelled. "We are just training," I clarified, grabbing Nikolaj's arm.

He looked at my bloody face, then at my hand resting on his arm. His look was filled with fire, and he jerked his forearm like he was annoyed I was touching him. Slowly he released his grip on Sven.

"Training for what? We don't hit women! We are honorable men," Demyan yelled and stepped up to Sven.

"She wanted me to," Sven yelled back defensively.

Nikolaj glared at Sven.

Demyan looked at me.

Fear filled me. I didn't want to get anyone in trouble. I just wanted to fight and get a good workout in.

Vance intervened, stepping over to me, "this is the training she's used to. She needs to take hits and feel pain as well as give it. She can handle this."

Demyan looked between Sven and me, then nodded. Nikolaj looked like he was about to kill both of us.

"I'm fine. Really!! It looks worse than it is," I said, looking at the bosses and then at Vance, who smiled at me. He's used to seeing me bleeding or bruised. He spent a lot of years watching me train.

"Vance, you train with her like this?" Demyan asked.

"As best I can," Vance answered.

You could see them trying to piece things together in their heads. That comment may have just blown our chance at protecting our outside family.

I saw Vance calculating, in his head, how to correct the situation. He must sense them trying to put pieces together.

"She was orphaned at 12. She's 24. That's a long time to train. I'm not what I used to be, but I was something great when I was younger." This explanation seemed to appease them.

"So, you're good with her fighting our guards?" Demyan asked, but we could tell by his voice he was still not okay with Sven hitting me.

"Absolutely! Look at Sven. He's bleeding more than Milly," Vance said jokingly while pointing to Sven's face.

Which caused Sven to retaliate, "fuck that! With all due respect, Vance, she's bleeding way more than me."

Vance and I laughed and said, "you're lucky Demyan stopped us. I was about to KO your ass!"

Everyone, but Nikolaj, started laughing.

Gus rubbed his hand on top of Sven's head. "You aren't fast like her, and you're bleeding way more, old man!"

Sven swatted his hand away, "old man?! Who are you calling old? You're only four years younger."

"Are we going to finish this fight, or are we going to bicker about age," I spouted, positioning myself to kick his ass.

"This fight is over," Nikolaj demanded, adding, "Milly has work to do right now."

Demyan and his men caught one of the guys I was looking into about Lazlo. He was a perv, so it was easy to lure him in.

Tom Kraft was a social staple in the community. He was a perfect example of a human being to all those he deceived, but we knew him as a pedo.

I planned to take my time with that fucker.

I suit up in the basement office, and Vance advised me how to handle Tom when Sven walked in, "Ready, Milly?"

"Yep," I grabbed my hat off my desk and followed Sven upstairs to the cars. Demyan and Gus were walking to their car, and Nikolaj was sitting in his car on his phone. I slid in quickly, hoping he wouldn't get angry about waiting for me.

"Hi," I softly said. Nikolaj glanced at me, then his attention was back to his phone.

Sven sped around town with Gus on his tail.

We were headed to the warehouse that changed my life not too long ago.

This is a brutal reminder of my biggest mistake to date.

We pulled in through the big doors.

I reached to open my door when I was startled by Nikolaj firmly saying, "how many times do I have to tell you to wait!"

I looked at him wide-eyed as he got out of the car. Sven opened my door. "My lady!" He gestured with his hand for me to get out.

I rolled my eyes. "I can open my car door."

"Boss says no, so the answer is no."

We walked into one of the office rooms. Gus was standing by the door. "Good luck Milly. Hope you get your answers." I smiled at him.

Nikolaj met up with Demyan and Aanya, who were talking in the corner of the room.

I started to organize my tools on the table. Feeling ready, I grabbed the smelling salts and headed over to Tom Kraft, who was passed out in the chair.

I turned and waited for the bosses to tell me to start.

I saw Nikolaj and Demyan leaning against the table, Sven and Gus on one side, and the cleaners on the other.

Aanya was walking out.

Nikolaj nodded.

That was my signal.

I took a deep breath to level myself.

Showtime!

Present Milly
Chapter 42

VANCE IS BACK IN from his meeting with the bosses and walks to me. "We have a job tonight," he whispers.

"What?" I ask as he sits on my desk.

"There were seven men when I was captured. Nikolaj and his men only got six. The leader got away. Which means our family is in danger."

"Did you tell them about our family?" I whisper as I lean closer into his leg.

"I had to, Milly! These people were quick and deadly! They could ambush our house. We need the bosses' resources on our side," he says, rubbing his forehead.

I sit back in my chair. "Okay. What's the job?"

"Intel on the leader. If he is who I think he is, he'll be around this area. We need to look for him."

"Okay. I'm going with you," I firmly point out.

"Yes! I demanded it," Vance says, standing from my desk.

"Who's the guy?" I ask, turning my chair to face him.

"I think the man was Ricardo Menendez. Business partner to Christoff Gunter."

"Who are they?" I ask as I write their names down.

"Big-time criminals. The bosses know them. They are crooks to the core. Will do anything for money. They would sell their own family for money. So, the perfect lead for finding out more about Lazlo. Bosses called a meeting with them about the group that stole their weapons. It's at their office building, so we sneak into their office and get as much information from the files as possible."

"So, the bosses will distract the two men while we break into their offices and steal information?" I ask to clarify.

"Yep." Vance nods confidently.

The door swings open. Both bosses, and Sven and Gus, walk in. "Is she briefed?" Nikolaj asks Vance.

"Yes," Vance answers as he walks to Nikolaj.

"Great! Let's do this," Demyan says, walking backward to face us as he walks to Nikolaj's desk.

We stand around discussing the plan while we wait for Daniel to get blueprints of the building we are going to.

"Is this a real meeting about the breach of the weapon's room, or just a facade so we have time to go through files?" I ask.

Demyan edges himself on the desk close to me, "it's both. These guys either are responsible for our breach, or they know where we can find the guys responsible. We know they are part of a group, but we don't know who ordered the breach or how many were involved. They are loyal to no one! So, we have to make sure we play our angle right."

"They've been after our inventory and market for years now," Nikolaj adds, but I refuse to look over at him. He's being an asshole!

"So, your business is weapons and trading," I say, looking at Demyan.

Everyone is dead silent, so I look at Nikolaj angrily, glaring at me. I stutter out quietly, "I just...I have never been told what you do, so this is new to me."

"Everything seems to be new to you! Are you sure you can handle this mission?" Nikolaj says with anger and sarcasm.

I step toward Vance and Demyan while keeping my eyes on Nikolaj. He moves his attention to Sven and Gus to discuss their jobs for tonight. I feel relieved when he looks away, but I'm pissed that he was being rude to me.

Daniel finally walks in with the blueprints. Tossing them on the desk and unrolling them, he says, "these were not easy to get, and they are five years old. Hopefully, there isn't any new construction done to the building that isn't on them."

Nikolaj sits in his chair to look at the prints, then leans back in his chair. I step toward the desk to look at the images, and Vance says, "well, kiddo, figure out your plan."

I feel everyone watching me, including Nikolaj, as I study the prints. I try to ignore how uncomfortable I am with all eyes on me. "The ventilation system here would be an access point to the office," I say, pointing out the vents that lead to the office ceiling, "but getting to the 8th floor unnoticed? That could be tricky. The building is covered with security guards and cameras. Vance, you will need to loop the office footage, so they see the same footage of the office before I'm in there; that way, I'm not seen when I'm in there. There is a service elevator here, but I would have to cross your meeting room. That's too much of a risk. A stairway is an option, but I'll need a lookout ahead and behind me."

I rub my hand over the top of my head, grab my ponytail, twist it into a bun, and stick a pen through it to hold it up.

I glance up to see Nikolaj watching me. He looks kind, making me not want to be mad at him, and my body craves his touch, even if he is mad at me.

Should I be turned on like this because he is sitting here staring at me like he did the other night when he was fingering me? Or because I smell his cologne?

I realize I'm still staring at him and quickly jerk my eyes back to the blueprints. My face is red, and my breathing is slightly heavy. Hopefully, no one noticed me doing that.

"We could dress you in housekeeping, and you could just walk in," Demyan says, startling me.

"Not the worst idea, Milly," Sven says.

"Umm...Too easy. In my experience, easy isn't the best way," I respond while rubbing my forehead. "We can try it, though. I'll need a maid uniform, and make sure you guys are ready to save my ass if I get caught by other housekeepers." I laugh.

"You walked in blind to our building," Nikolaj says in a deep tone, sending chills down my back.

"My destination wasn't the 8th floor in your building," I smile.

He smiles back like the devil he is. Does Nikolaj know what he's doing to me without doing a fucking thing to me? He holds his gaze on me, and I feel my pussy start to get wet. He does know what he is doing to me. I lick my lips and smirk at him, hoping it might do something to him. "You know, a maid's uniform sounds fun." I seductively say.

"STOP! NOPE! I don't want to hear another word," Vance says, shaking his head.

Everyone busts out laughing, and a small crack of a smile crosses Nikolaj's face; then, he says, "the maid uniform is our plan. You will walk in as the cleaner. Sven and Gus will deter anyone who gets too close to you. You will leave before we leave the meeting room. You will change and walk out of the office with a trench coat and heels. Then you will look like an employee leaving for the night, not a maid cutting out early. Sven and Gus will escort you to the stairs and out of the building."

"Boss, you want mc to just walk around in plain sight?" I ask like this is the stupidest plan I've ever heard.

"Yes," Nikolaj replies.

"What about other staff?" Demyan asks.

"She will look like a cleaner. No one there will bother themselves with conversing with a cleaner. Daniel, find out which cleaning service they use and get a uniform," Nikolaj orders, and Daniel nods and then walks to his desk.

I state, "Boss, what's the plan b? What if this plan backfires? I think I should sneak in, out of sight, and leave the same way."

Vance puts his hand on my shoulder. "These men are nothing like we've dealt with before. The bosses know the men, so let's follow their plan."

I look up at Vance, who is looking at Nikolaj.

"M, we'll keep you safe no matter what. Otherwise, kick some ass, and we'll deal with the consequences later." Demyan chuckles and walks over to Daniel's desk.

"This is the plan, Milly. We leave at six. The meeting is at 7. Any questions?" Nikolaj states firmly.

"No," I softly say. I study the blueprints and listen to the commotion around me.

Vance says, "I'll go get into their camera system." He squeezes my upper arm. "You got this, kiddo." Then walks to his desk while yelling to Theo, "Theo, we need earpieces."

"On it, Vance," Theo responds.

Demyan says to Vance, "hey, you need to rest today, too. We need you ready at six."

"I'll get the cameras figured out, then I'll go up for a quick rest," Vance says.

Nikolaj leans into his desk and looks up at me. "Worried?" Nikolaj asks softly.

"Never," I assure him with half a grin.

"Good," he says, smirking.

"Milly, about earlier." He puts his hand on my hand that is resting on the blueprints. "I'm not asking you to choose between Vance and me. I'd never want to come between you two."

"I know." I look at him and smile. "I don't know how to explain how you make me feel, Nikolaj," I say softly while leaning over the desk toward him, "but whatever this is, I want it. Besides, I'm sure Vance will appreciate his bed back. I tend to move around a lot in my sleep." I wink at him, making him smile.

"Good! Come to my place for lunch when you're done looking at the blueprints," he says, standing and buttoning his suit jacket.

I watch over my shoulder from my leaning position as he walks away from me. His movements are smooth, powerful, and graceful. His suit fits deliciously over every body contour, slightly exposing his muscles through the fabric. His thick thighs make the threads of his pants work for their purpose. I bit my lower lip while staring at him until he finally exited the office.

I look at the prints for a few minutes longer, but the anticipation of having lunch with him is too much.

I turn to leave the room. "Oh, kiddo, you heading up for lunch?" Vance asks.

Oh god, is he going to ask me to have lunch too?

"Yes," I mumble.

"Good. I'll walk up with you. I'm going to lie down. My head is pounding."

"Okay."

"Hey, M, are you nervous about tonight?" Demyan asks.

"For what?" I say surprisingly. "Oh, the raid. No, I'm not nervous." I try to cover up. I'm nervous about going to Nikolaj's place for the first time.

"You okay, Milly?" Daniel asks.

"Yeah, I just forgot to eat breakfast, so I'm going to eat now."

"Okay. We'll be up in a few minutes," Daniel says.

"Okay." I walk out, following Vance.

"We can talk tonight about what happened. Okay?" Vance asks.

"Yeah, if we are not too tired after this mission." I smile.

We walked by the dining room. "Okay, I'll see you later, Kiddo," Vance says as he continues to walk upstairs.

I linger around the column by the dining room until I know Vance is upstairs. The longer I stand there, the more my nerves build.

Present Milly

Chapter 43

I SLOWLY WALK UP the stairs.

Getting to the 3rd floor, standing at Nikolaj's door, contemplating my next step like a dork.

The door opens, and he stands there with his shirt sleeves rolled up, drying his hands. "Were you going to stand there all day or knock?" He jokes, glancing up. I look up to see a camera.

"Um, hi. I.." Why does he cloud my thoughts so much?

"Come in. Lunch is almost ready." He motions and walks off to the kitchen straight from the entry.

I look around the place as I step in. Nikolaj's home is breathtaking. The view I can see from the floor-to-ceiling windows in the living room is like a picture.

The smell of his cologne intoxicates me, forcing me to bring my eyes back to him, watching me from the island in the kitchen.

"Wow!" I boost, raising my eyebrows. He smiles.

"Sit," he says, motioning to the dining room.

I glance around quickly. In the living room is a little sitting area with a piano and a balcony across the whole wall of floor-to-ceiling windows. The kitchen is open to the dining room and is as big as the one on the main floor, with a much bigger island.

The dining room has floor-to-ceiling windows as well. The table seats 10. There are two places set. I pick the spot on the side of the table, leaving the head spot for him.

He brings salad and sandwiches over.

"Wow! Do you cook for yourself?" I chuckle.

"Yes. Why?"

"I figured Trina and Sasha would be up here cooking."

He chuckles while putting salad and a sandwich on my plate. "Sometimes, but mostly, no. I like to cook. Besides, this isn't cooking; this is a sandwich and salad. I make more elaborate meals at dinnertime," he explains with a wink.

"Oh! Never pinned you for a chef," I banter.

"Chef? No. Food enthusiast? Yes."

I smile, watching him sit and serve himself. He nods for us to start eating.

I take a bite of the sandwich first. It's an explosion of sweet and salty. Mouth-watering good!

"So good! What's in it?" I say, covering my mouth full of food.

He tilts his head as he leans back in his chair, then says, "shredded chicken with apples and cranberries in dressing."

I swallow in a big gulp. "Wait! You're not eating. Did you poison it?" I ask sarcastically.

His eyes don't move from my lips, and I smirk. He's planning something. I can see it in his eyes. He rubs his lips with his finger as he leans forward in his chair.

"Maybe. But that would be too easy. If I was going to kill you, I'd fight you like that first night we met." He smiles.

"If I remember correctly, I beat you and Demyan that night," I point out.

"We weren't trying to kill you, just get you to settle down," he says and cocks his brow at me.

Leaving me to wonder, while taking another bite, just how good of a fighter he might be if he wanted me dead.

"I like watching you enjoy your food," he says while adjusting himself in his chair to eat.

"Okay. Well, I'm not particularly keen on being watched."

"Fair enough," he says before taking a bite of his sandwich. Now, I find myself staring at him. The ticks of his jaw as he chews have me memorized. He looks at me; I jerk my eyes away so he doesn't know I am staring at him.

"So, you live up here alone?" I cough out.

"Yes."

"Do you have family around here?" I ask.

Instantly tensing up when I see him staring at me with a scowl. Maybe I crossed the line by asking him about his family, but I was just making small talk.

He leans back in his chair, then says, "Yes, but they live in a different compound we built for them."

I relaxed after he answered.

"You made more than one of these places?" I inquire.

"Yes. I heard you also have a family," he says, trying to put pressure on me. Now I know how he felt when I asked. It's too personal to talk about family, but he did answer my question, so I'll appease the statement.

"Yes," I say softly, looking at my food.

"Any other secrets you have? I would like to know them all," he confesses with a smirk, leaning toward me and letting his hand rub over mine.

Can Nikolaj Fedorov really be my other half in life?

Can I tell him my story and not be judged? I guess I will find out.

"I have a whole life story, but this isn't the time," I say as I flip my salad around, then take a bite.

"Why didn't you come to our meeting with Vance?" He asks, glancing at me, then takes a bite of his sandwich.

"I was helping Daniel," I shovel salad into my mouth.

He chuckles, still watching me eat, but I'll allow it because the food is good.

Then he shakes his head, "Demyan said you had finished up when they came up." He watches me like I'm hiding something.

"I didn't want.... I figured..." I roll my eyes. "Vance will tell me about it later. I didn't want to return to your office at the time. Okay?" I shift in my chair and lean over to him. I can smell his cologne, and it's making me feral.

"Fair," he agrees with a nod and takes a bite of food. I take a deep breath to savor his scent and then return to eating.

"How old are you?" I ask. If we are going to do whatever we are doing, then I should be able to ask him anything, and he should answer.

I know he is older than me, and I don't care. It's just a question that he is clearly trying not to answer. I tip my head toward him and cock an eyebrow.

He hesitates, "older than you," he says with an eye roll as he tilts his head.

"Come on. Let's get to know each other. I'm 24," I chirp with a bit of wiggle in my seat.

"I know," he says, while his head rests on his hand and his fuck me eyes scan my body.

"Okay. Well......" I fold my hands under my chin, resting my elbows on the table, and stare at him.

"How was lunch?" He asks, not moving a millimeter.

"Really good! Thank you," I snarked at him, "stop trying to change the subject."

"Okay. 35. Happy?" He asks as he stands, grabs the dishes, and walks to the kitchen.

"Very! Thanks for asking," I say, bubbly as I jump up and follow him, but he quickly turns back to the dining room.

"How long have you had this mansion, and has everyone been here with you? Well, except Vance and I, of course," I ask, following right on his heels.

"Five years. Most worked for us in the villa before we built this place," he pauses at the table to answer, then grabs the placemats.

"Why did you build it?" I ask as I follow him back to the kitchen and look around at his place.

He stops, slightly turns, leans toward me, and says, "you have many questions. You know curiosity kills the cat."

I smile. "You can ask me whatever you want," I say but instantly regret it.

I know Nikolaj wants me to tell him my life story, but am I ready to let it all out?

Sure, I've said snippets of my life but never the details about my abuse, the scars, the tattoos, the people I've killed; every deep dark secret I have that burns at my soul.

I watch him as he works around the kitchen, then I see him start the sink water and flip his tie over his shoulder.

"You do dishes, too?" I joke as I get out of my head.

He just shakes his head in disbelief. "I'm capable of keeping my home clean."

His hands, soaked in hot soapy water, rub around the plates, and I don't think my aching pussy can take much more of his extreme sexiness.

"I didn't mean that," I stutter out as I squeeze my thighs together to relieve some of the need. "Just that you're you, and you strike me as someone who has people do things for him."

"I have people do housework for me, just not all the time. Twice a week. Irina and Sasha cook when I'm busy and freeze it for me."

I start drying the dishes as he washes them. "Okay, back to my question, why did you build this place?" I ask while nudging him a bit. Internally I hoped he would open up to me.

"When Demyan and I took over each of our family's businesses, we had big ideas, and money was our only goal. We grew additions to the businesses our fathers started and grew them fast. This created a lot of enemies. We agreed to build the compounds to keep our loved ones safe."

I smiled at him, relieved he would open up about his compound. This is a great start.

"What businesses?" I slyly ask.

"Milly!" He firmly says. Guess he's not ready to tell me everything yet.

"Okay. Okay. Have Theo and Daniel been here since it was built?" I ask, hoping to get this conversation back on track.

"No. Theo came two years ago, and Daniel came eight months ago."

I nod, then ask, "who was here before?"

"Two of my father's men. Theo replaced Marcus when he died, and Daniel replaced Anders when he died,"

"By died, do you mean...." I run my thumb over my throat.

He laughs. "No. They died naturally. They were both very old."

We finish the dishes. Putting the towel down, I say, "okay, back to work."

He takes a step closer to me. "You didn't come here just for lunch."

The way he is looking at me tells me I don't need to ask what else I came up here for, but I like to make him talk.

"I didn't? Then what else did I come up here for?"

He grabs me and leads me around the corner of the kitchen, down a long hallway to the room at the end.

I step inside, and the first thing I see is an enormous bed.

Nikolaj pulls me to him and explains, "you have 12 spankies due from yesterday. We'll get them done now since we're busy later."

He moves a piece of loose hair from my face. "Since I haven't gotten to hear you scream yet, we're doing them here where your sounds are not restricted," he smirks.

My face turns red.

He kisses my lips with force and ownership, making it easy to tell his desire for me is consuming him, too.

Present Milly

Chapter 44

I NIBBLE HIS NECK and earlobe as he carries me to his bed. He groans, palming my ass cheeks, squeezing them harder with every step.

My body is nervous and anxious about the marks he's about to leave on my ass.

He stops and pushes me off onto the side of the bed with a bounce. I lift back up onto my knees, facing him.

"Lay down," He snarls at me with a lustrous tone.

"Please, 12 is a lot," I purr as I move my way closer to him. "Maybe we can make a deal," I softly say, running my hands up his shirted chest and around the back of his neck.

He towers over me, but his high bed brings me closer to eye level with him.

"I won't make any more deals."

I tilt my head slightly, knowing if I argue with him, I will just get more spankings. This stubborn man ignites my desire and my frustration. "Fine!" I snap.

This is going to hurt my pride as much as my ass. I pull my pants and panties to my knees and flip over onto all fours. Facing my ass right in front of Nikolaj, exposing my wet slit. Turning my head to look at him over my shoulder. "Then get it over with, so I can get back to work," I demand.

He doesn't say a word while moving his hands up the back of my thighs. His thumbs brush my wet slit, making me shudder. He palms my ass cheeks, and I tense up when I feel one of his hands pull away from me.

WACK!

I let out a throaty scream as my head drops down.

"I want to hear you scream!" He snarls.

WACK!

WACK!

Nikolaj's hits intensify. I let out a scream through my teeth, and my breathing is heavy. I peek over my shoulder to see him hit my other cheek two times.

WACK!

WACK!

I scream into my shoulder.

He forcefully slides a finger into my soaked opening. I moan and grasp the comforter with my hands. He moves his finger in and out, then hits my ass two more times!

WACK!

WACK!

I scream as he shoves another finger into me.

WACK!

WACK!

Two more hits while he fingers deep in my wet pussy, as my ass cheeks sting and throb.

He pulls his fingers out and switches to his other hand. Two fingers fill me again. I moan out, "oh fuck!" Fisting the comforter harder as I try to sturdy my balance.

He slides the 3rd finger into me, stretching me as I scream out. I push myself back onto his fingers to feel him deeper in me. He fingers me so hard I can barely handle the intense pleasure he is forcing on me.

Just as I relax to allow for a deeper thrust, he concludes my spankings with three consecutive hits.

WACK!

WACK!

WACK!

I scream, moan, and struggle to hold myself up. I'm on the brink of the most satisfying orgasm ever; then Nikolaj pulls his finger out and stops.

My breathing is heavy, frustrated, and confused. I look at him over my shoulder and say between breaths, "I.... was....close....to....cumming!"

"I know," he purrs, "I felt you tightening on my fingers."

"Why stop then?" I ask with annoyance in my tone.

"I didn't want you to cum!"

Frustrated, I turn and gently place my sore ass on the bed. "Who says you have a say if I cum or not," I snap.

"ME!" He growls.

I'm so frustrated that I was built up to something I'd never felt before, and he stopped. Asshole!

"Fuck your games," I snap, sliding toward the side of the bed with my pants and panties still at my knees.

He smiles like he is happy to see me miserable and frustrated.

"Where are you going?" He asks with a deep, lustful voice, and his massive hand on my chest to hold me in place. The warmth of his skin gives me goosebumps.

"We're done here, right?!" I glare at him.

"No! Get back on the bed." He gently pushes me back, my glare softens, and I hold back a smile.

The lust in his eyes makes me obey his command. I turn my body as I slide up to lay my head on the pillows. He grabs my pants and panties and tears them from my body. He walks to the foot of the bed.

"Open," he demands.

I do as I am told and spread my legs for him to see my wet pussy.

He takes his shirt off, never taking his eyes off me. I sit up slightly to pull my shirt off over my head.

"What are you doing?" He growls with a rasp in his voice.

"I need this," I beg. "You need this," I pleaded.

His chest heaves: he pauses, then unbuckles his belt and pants, dropping them to the floor.

"Tell me what you want, Milly!" The desire in his voice rolls over me.

I swallow hard.

"I want to cum," I shyly whisper, too embarrassed to talk dirty.

He shakes his head, his eyes burning into me. "Tell me how to make you cum!"

I bite my lip as he climbs on the bed. His body was built by the devil himself, and his muscles flexed as he moved closer to me.

His enormous cock is hard, and the tip glistens with precum.

He runs his hands up my legs, over my thighs, squeezing gently. Tingles cover my body in anticipation.

Inching closer to me, he whispers, "Milly?!"

"I can't talk the way you do," I shy away, sucking my whole bottom lip between my teeth.

He growls so deeply the vibrations fill me as he nestles on his heels between my thighs, looking over my body.

"Fuck me," I breathe out. His eyes snap to mine.

I prop myself up on my elbows and say more confidently, "that's how I want to cum, by you fucking me."

His lip twitches.

His gaze darkens.

He has waited so long for me.

Now is his time to make me his.

He moves his body on top of mine. I feel his hard length rest against my wet slit. He licks my nipple and then raises his hand to pinch the other.

I moan out, "Nikolaj."

He smiles against my skin.

It makes me smile.

He moves his head further up, running his tongue against my lips, pushing his cock onto my clit, making me moan.

He puts his head against mine and whispers, "I can make you cum any way you want, but I don't want you to rush into this if you are not ready."

I push my lips onto his soft, full welcoming lips. His tongue takes my mouth. I moan, running my hands up his back, and pulling my legs up to his waist. His body size forces me to open my legs further, so he sinks onto me more.

He breaks our kiss and moves his mouth to my neck, biting it hard and making me scream in his ear, "I want to fuck you!"

His hand follows my curves as it moves between my legs.

He lifts his hips, aligning his massive cock to my entrance.

He retakes my mouth as he slowly slides the head inside me. The stinging pleasure makes me moan as his tongue muffles my sound.

My fingers dig into his back.

He pauses, only for a second, then mercilessly thrusts further into me. No longer with ease, but like the desire in him cannot hold back any longer.

I break our kiss as the burn of me stretching around his cock causes me to scream and throw my head back into the pillow. My nails dig up his back to his shoulders.

He groans, "so fucking tight!"

I moan as he pushes deeper into me. My legs tighten around his waist.

"Relax. Let me in," he whispers in my ear as my head pulls into his shoulder.

He slightly pulls out as I relax, then slams back in, fisting a hand full of my hair.

"OH GOD, NIK...." I scream, but his movements cut off my words.

He thrusts faster, harder, and deeper into me. The more he does, the better it feels. My body is stretching to accept him.

My nails dig so deep into him that I know I'm drawing blood. I pull my hands into his hair and grab two fists full.

He moans as he pounds into me, making my tits bounce with his movements. He comes up to kiss me, taking every ounce of breath left in me.

Electricity starts to build from my limbs, traveling to my core. My scream intensifies.

Nikolaj's movements are steady and hard. He bites my neck, sending me over the top, and I cum, screaming, "NIKOLAJ!"

My body quivers, and my pussy throbs on his cock, still fucking me. He doesn't stop. He fucks me harder and faster.

"Please, yes, Nikolaj!" I moan in his ear. My body tenses up as I build to another euphoric climax. Screaming out, "NIK..." as I release on his cock, again. He pulls out, pinning his cock between us, and cums on my belly as he grunts into my neck. I feel the warmth of his cum on me.

He moves his head to kiss my lips. Tingles are still covering my body, and our breathing is heavy.

He leans up and pushes two fingers inside me again. My back arches at the stinging pleasure returning.

He pulls them out, rubbing them through his arousal, glistening on my stomach, then says, "open!"

Still caught in a daze from what just happened, I open my mouth. Nikolaj shoves his fingers in for me to suck us off of him. Licking every creamy part of his fingers, which is fucking my mouth.

He shoves his fingers down my throat. Jerking, I slightly gag, and my eyes start to water.

"Sensitive," he says with a smile. "Good! I want your face a mess when I'm fucking your mouth later tonight."

He takes his finger out of my mouth and licks them himself.

"Oh my," I whisper. What have I gotten myself into because I'm all for it? It's exciting and new, and I'm obsessed with him.

"Come. Shower," he says, then flicks my nipple with his tongue. Sucking it in his mouth, then biting it. I moan as I arch up. Releasing it with a pull, he gets off the bed.

I lay there for a minute to register what had just happened. I hear the shower start and see Nikolaj walking back to me on the bed.

Sitting up to scoot off, I notice a light pink color on his white comforter.

"Oh my god! Sorry! I didn't think I would bleed since...." I say, mortified and not sure what to do.

He shakes his head as he grabs the corner of the comforter and throws it over the mess. "It's completely normal, Milly. It was your first time. I'm well endowed and didn't take it easy on you." He grabs my hand and guides me to the shower.

He lets the water hit his back to shield my face.

"Are you okay?" He asks kindly while he washes my body.

"I'm great," I responded with a chuckle.

"Was I too rough?"

"NO! I...WOW!" I stutter out as I grab the soap bottle, squeeze some in my hand, then wash his torso. Running my fingers over every protruding muscle he has.

I can't help but stare at his cock, soft but still huge. He grows and shows. I chuckle to myself.

"Touch it," he says, getting my attention.

"What?" I ask.

"You're just staring at it. So, touch it!"

I hesitate as I rub my hands around his waist. He laughs at my nervousness, while rubbing soap in his hands above my head.

"Okay," I softly say with an attitude.

I bite my lower lip and grab the length of his shaft. The skin is soft and smooth. I run my hand up to the head and run my fingers around the rim, causing it to jerk in my hand.

My body tingles with excitement.

I grab his balls with my other hand. I run my finger up the center of his head; it jerks again and hardens. I gently squeeze his balls.

"MMMM, be careful, or I'll fuck your mouth right now," he groans while washing the shampoo out of his hair.

"Oh," I gasp out a breath.

"Turn," he orders. I turn into the water as he washes my hair.

"You know I can do this myself, right," I banter. I'm struggling with him and this level of care he is giving me.

"I take care of what's mine," he says while paying attention to every strand of hair on my head.

"Am I yours?" I ask him.

He tilts his head down to look at me. "Do you want to be?"

Without hesitation, I eagerly say, "YES!"

He smirks. "Then I'll take care of you."

He dries me first as he stands there dripping wet and looking so sexy. My stomach flutters, and I can't help but run my hands on his cheeks.

"You are intimidatingly perfect, Nikolaj."

He scoffs a weird look at me, slaps my ass, and says, "get dressed, Milly!"

I smile as I return to the bedroom to gather my clothes.

"No panties," he says as he walks into the room completely naked. He grabs the comforter off the bed and brings it to the laundry basket.

"What? I have to wear them," I snapped.

"Why?!" He asks sarcastically, as he brings a fresh comforter to the bed and flips it on.

"Because..." I roll my eyes.

"You'll have to do better than that," he demands, adjusting the edges of the comforter.

I stare at his cock, freely moving around. "I would soak right through my pants all day long, and everyone would be able to see what you do to my body," I explain, still naked and walking closer to him.

He eyes my body. "Fine, but no panties when you are in my place!"

I smile so hard it feels like it will never leave my face.

Present Milly

Chapter 45

"Who are you?" I hear a voice say from behind me. The lady with big brown curly hair in a ponytail leans against the wall by the elevator I'm waiting for.

"What? Oh, I'm a stand-in. Someone called in." I shrug, waiting for the elevator door to open and adjusting my maid uniform.

"Must be Rachael. She's always calling in sick."

"I don't know. I just go where I'm told to go." I fiddle with some cleaning bottles on my cart, trying to avoid eye contact.

"Haven't seen you around here before," she says, leaning toward me a bit.

"I'm normally on Kitson and East cleaning." I look at the elevator floor to see how much longer I must wait.

"Oh, you clean rich people's houses. Office buildings are a lot easier," she points out, talking sassy with her hands.

"Yeah? Well, no one is around the house when I'm cleaning." The doors open, and I push my cart in and press the 8th-floor button.

"Ok. See you around," she says while walking back to the cleaning room.

I take a deep breath once the door closes. This is too fucking risky for me to be out in the open like this. Everyone can see me. Not to mention my ass and vag are sore from earlier today, and it's throwing me off.

I push my cart out on the 8th floor and see Nikolaj and Demyan walking down the perpendicular hall toward the meeting room.

FUCK!

I turn my cart down the same hall they are in, slow my strides, keeping my eyes down, but I know they saw me.

"Hey, sweethcart! Come here!" I hear a sinister voice say. I turn slightly to see a skinny taller man with greased back hair, an attempt at a goatee, and a scummy look on his face looking right at me.

"Me?" I ask, pushing my finger into my chest.

"Yeah. Come here," Christoff Gunter says, holding the meeting room door open.

I leave my cart and slowly walk over to him. He grabs my arm and pulls me toward him, in clear view of Nikolaj and Demyan.

"I haven't seen you around here before," he says, with his face close to mine. I can smell his disgusting coffee and cigar breath.

"Someone called in. I'm a fill-in." I look behind him and see Nikolaj and Demyan sitting at the table, intently watching our interaction.

He groans as he looks down at my body, and his hand runs down my side. I slightly jerk away. He quickly reaches around to grab my ass and squeezes.

"Nice and tight," he laps once at my lips, then smirks. "Be in my office next door in an hour. I'm going bend you over my desk and fuck that tight ass hole of yours," he demands and laughs, running his hand up my arm, then down the front of my uniform over my breasts.

I see Nikolaj's face burn with fury as Christoff turns and closes the door.

"Oh shit," I mumble to myself.

I return to my cart just as Sven and Gus round the corner.

Sven stops by me, turns his head slightly to pretend to talk to Gus, then says, "what are you doing, Milly? You're supposed to be at the office already."

I slowly start to push my cart and adjust a bottle. "Christoff wanted to talk to me," I scoffed without looking like I was talking.

"Why?" Gus says, looking at Sven.

"Want's to fuck my tight ass hole," I mumble sarcastically as I open the door to Christoff's office.

"What the fuck! Motherfucker! I'm going to kill him," Gus grits and turns to face Sven completely.

Sven moves his body to block the cart as he puts the bag on it. I pull the cart into the room and close the door and the blinds.

There are eight file cabinets along the office's back wall that adjoins the meeting room. Now, I have to be sure not to make any noise that the meeting room will hear so as not to trigger anyone coming in.

FUCK!

I search for any file that could be a hint to Lazlo or names of people we've hunted in the past, but nothing. All I see are business folders, accounting folders, and inventory folders. This is a lot of cabinets to just have these types of folders. There has to be something else. Something darker than everyday accounting.

The first three cabinets are complete duds. I open the 4th cabinet, the first drawer, and scroll through the files.

NOTHING!

I hear two knocks on the door. Gus's signal that Demyan texted the meeting is almost over, and I need to get out.

I pull open the other drawers and scan quickly over the labels. In the 3rd drawer on the 5th cabinet, I see a file that says 'Benecelli'!

WHAT THE FUCK!?

I take it. A folder a few files behind 'Benecelli' says 'Red.' I grab that file as well.

I run to the cart, pull my hair down, and open the bag Sven put on the cart. I tear my uniform off, dress in the silk button-up and black skirt and change my flats to heels. At the bottom of the bag was a trench coat. I throw it on, put the files in the bag, and slowly open the door.

Sven and Gus motion to hustle, and we practically run to the elevators, but the meeting room doors open before the elevator doors.

We hear the men talking. Sven rapidly pushes the button a few times, grabs a file out of the bag, and opens it.

Gust turns his body to block me and leans into me, giving the illusion we are kissing. The doors open, and Gus shoves me in, with Sven behind us.

"They saw us," Sven says, pushing the button for the parking garage.

"Fuck!" Gus says, running his hand over his face.

"Boss didn't look happy either," Sven says, laying the back of his head against the elevator wall.

"What choice did I have," Gus snaps and paces.

"What's going on?" I ask, looking between the two men.

"We are not allowed to touch you," Gus says, "and what the boss just saw was me kissing you!"

"But you didn't," I point out.

"That's not what the boss saw, though," Sven adds, "the bosses said from day one, HANDS OFF!"

"If he's mad, I'll explain it to him. You were protecting me, Gus," I exclaim.

The doors open, and we run to Demyan's car.

Gus drives out of the garage as fast as he can.

My phone rings. It's Nikolaj.

"Hi," I say softly.

"Are you ok?" He angrily demands over the phone, putting me on guard to defend Gus and giving me butterflies.

"Of course. I had Gus and Sven to help me," I chuckle, trying to smooth the tension.

"What was that about by the elevators?" He snarls.

"You all came out before the elevators opened. Gus had to shield me somehow."

He doesn't say a word. The silence causes my throat to be dry and my nervousness to rise. I don't see how he can be mad. I'm safe. But I will not let him hurt Gus for protecting me.

"That fuck, Christoff, is on his last days. Fucker couldn't quit talking about you. Piece of shit," he grits.

"Well, it was a tempting offer," I purr and laugh, fiddling with the strap of the bag I had to carry.

"Be careful, Milly!" He drops his tone, and it makes my pussy clench.

"Where are you?" I ask, trying to think of anything other than how much I want to touch him again.

"Behind you," he says. I look out the back window and see Nikolaj's G-wagon.

"Ok. Bye," I smirk and hang up.

A second later, a text comes through from Nikolaj, *Is that pussy of yours wet?*

I try to cover my face, so Gus or Sven don't see me blush.

'Yes. Stop. I'll see you soon,' I text back.

Leaning back in the seat. "Oh, Sven, do you have that file?"

"Yep, here. Who is Benecelli?" He asks while handing it back to me.

"Vance's last name," I say and stare at the file's cover.

"I never knew that," Gus says while focusing on the road.

Sven shakes his head, "me neither. Hey Milly, what's your last name?"

I look up at both men and reply, "Benecelli."

Sven turns slightly to face me. "Wait! You have Vance's last name, but you're not blood. Are you married to him or his son or something."

I chuckle, and explain, "no. When I was saved 12 years ago, we had to fake my death, so Vance changed my name to Milly Benecelli. Vance's quote-unquote daughter." I smile.

"So, you really are a ghost," Gus laughs, then says, "do you have a headstone?"

"Yes, in Chicago, by my grandmother and my father."

I stare out the window, thinking about my grandmother. It's been three months since I visited her grave.

Present Milly

Chapter 46

ARRIVING AT THE MANSION, I see Vance standing on the steps waiting. Gus opens my door, and I run to Vance with the files in my hand. "Look, these were in the office cabinets!"

"What the fuck!?" He mumbles, and the look on Vance's worries me.

I hear two car doors shut. I turn to see Nikolaj and Demyan talking to Sven and Gus. I hope Nikolaj isn't mad at Gus.

"Let's go dig into these," I say eagerly, pulling on Vance's arm.

Vance shakes his head. "Just wait. We have to find out what the bosses learned in their meeting tonight." Vance looks past me and says, "how did it go?"

"Let's talk in Nikolaj's office," Demyan says, rubbing the back of his neck. They start to walk into the mansion.

Nikolaj wraps his arm around my waist and turns me around. He is standing a step down from me but still taller.

"Are you ok?" He whispers gently with his lips on my forehead.

"Yes. Except for Christoff squeezing my ass cheeks, that hurt. They're sore, not to mention the offer to fuck my tight ass hole; yeah, not happening." I giggle.

"One," he rolls his eyes in annoyance, then smirks.

"For what? I was stating a fact. Not provoking you," I protest, then press my lips against his.

"Mmmmmm," he moans, "this fact is not worth repeating. So, you have one." He moves his mouth to my neck and shoulder, then growls in my ear, "the only one fucking that tight ass hole is me." His hands move down to cup my ass cheeks.

"Oh no, you are not, mister!" I snap with wide eyes and pull back from him.

He draws me closer to him again. Squeezing me just enough for me to melt into him.

"Someday, I will have you begging for me to fill every part of you," he whispers, running his bearded cheek against mine, then biting my earlobe.

"We'll see about that," I say, breathy and with desire.

His smile forms against my shoulder, pulling his teeth across my neck. I quiver, and a slight moan escapes.

"Two, Milly!"

"Wait! What?" I whisper in objection.

"Let's do this meeting before I bend you over on these stairs," he says, pulling me to the front door.

Entering his office, all the men have drinks. Nikolaj is handed his drink by Demyan, and Vance gives me mine after I take my trench coat off to lay it on the chair.

"Well, there's a lot of shit going on, and Christoff was more than willing to tell us for the right price," Demyan starts. "He knows who made the arrangements to get the new fucking guy on our security team to steal from us and who they paid off in our team to let it happen unnoticed."

Nikolaj, standing beside me, cuts in and says, "that's not any concern to Vance and Milly. What is, is who ambushed your team, Vance. It was Ricardo Mendez. Christoff was easily bought and snitched on him in the first five minutes of the meeting."

"Where is Ricardo now?" Vance asks, scowling.

"Christoff didn't know," Demyan answers.

"Or wouldn't tell us," Nikolaj says, running his hand through his hair, then taking a drink from his glass.

I grab Vance's shoulder and ask, "what if he is looking for you? What if he's at...."

"Maybe," Vance interrupts me to avoid hearing that everyone we love could be in danger.

I turn to Nikolaj, standing in front of him, "Nikolaj, if he is as dangerous as everyone says, my family is in danger." I grab his hand, he's staring down at me, and I see sincere empathy in his eyes.

Vance says, "Milly, they have safety in numbers. They will be fine. I will call them now to warn them." Vance squeezes my shoulder, looks at Nikolaj, then leaves.

The men continue to talk as I watch Vance leave. After the door shut, Nikolaj leans to my ear, "Vance knows...."

I cut him off, pulling my face to him, "let me go to Chicago."

"No!" He pulls back slightly, angry and furrowing his brows.

"Nikolaj, please, I'll be safe. I'll go with a guard. PLEASE!" I beg, grabbing his upper arms taught in his suit coat.

"I forbid it," he snarls, and I push away from him.

"I'm not your property," I snapped.

He looks up at the other men and demands, "LEAVE!" They do as ordered. Once the door is shut, he wraps his hand through my opposite arm and pulls me into him.

"Nikolaj..." I begged, turning my head to face him.

"Quiet," he snaps, startling me. He takes a deep breath, then says, "you think you have a say if you leave or not because we fucked? Your terms haven't changed." His jaw ticks angrily while he squeezes my arm.

I try to pull away, but I can't. Nikolaj's grip tightens around my arm.

"Don't be an asshole," I bark. Jerking my arm again. I snap, "us fucking isn't why I'm asking, you dickhead!" I roll my eyes and breathe deeply to calm down while choking back tears.

Turning, facing him, I softly say, "then come with me." Placing my hands on his cheek, his face softens, and I tiptoe up and gently kiss his lips. "Nikolaj, you built impenetrable compounds to protect your family. My family doesn't have that." I kiss him again, running my hand up his arm to his shoulder.

He releases my arm and wraps one arm around me, and the other caresses my cheek. "Milly, if anything happened to you, I'd burn this world down in vengeance," he whispers, his face pushing against mine. "I can't risk you."

I kiss his soft lips. He puts his hand up to the back of my head, pushing me into the kiss as he devours me passionately.

Unbelievable, the way his mouth demands me to submit to him, and I do every time. I feel his cock harden the tighter he holds me. My arms wrap under his and up his back.

He pulls away, leaving me gasping for air. I bring myself back to his lips to whisper, "fuck me, Nikolaj."

He obeys, taking his suit jacket off and dropping it to the floor. He lifts me up, and my legs wrap around him. I start sucking his ear and neck while he brings us to his desk. He places me down on his keyboard on his desk, sucks in my bottom lip, then bites it.

"First, two spankings." He pulls me off the desk, and my feet land on the floor. He turns and pushes me over so my hands land on the seat of his chair. He pulls my skirt up to my waist. He doesn't waste time with theatrics and delivers two hard, painful hits.

WACK!

WACK!

I don't have time to react as he pulls me up, spins me around so my back is to his chest, and sits in his chair, taking me down with him in his arms.

He places my feet wide on the edge of his desk. He leans back in his chair, pulling my back into his torso while he kisses the back side of my neck.

His hand slides down between my legs; the other hand unbuttons a button on my shirt and slides in to grab my breast.

Running his finger down either side of my wet sensitive nub and pinching it between them. His other hand slides under my bra, lifting and twisting my nipple. I lay my head back on his shoulder as the pleasurable sensation engulfs me.

I know the rules now. Not a sound anywhere but in his place. A challenge I will accept but cannot guarantee I can hold in my sound of pleasure.

Turning my head to catch his ear as my body pushes up on him from the desk. He works his way down, sliding a finger in me as he moves slightly for a deeper reach.

I bite my lower lip, holding in the want to scream at the feeling his fingers are causing. He bites my shoulder hard. I scream out uncontrollably.

"One," he grins, sliding his finger in and out of me.

"Not fair, cheater." I moan in my chest as his 2nd finger slides in.

He thrusts them in, filling me in the best possible way. I move my hand to my swollen clit, rubbing it to match his movements. He moves his other hand, twisting and pinching each of my nipples.

I feel the build-up of ecstasy pulling to my core. "Don't you dare.... fucking....stop....Nik!"

I hear him chuckle, and I release. Holding in my moan, pushing my head back into his shoulder, pulling my legs closer to me, as my body explodes with pleasure all over his fingers.

In one swift move, he moves me off his lap and pushes my torso down on his desk.

He kicks my feet together as he widens his stance and tears my panties from my body. The excitement increases in me as I hear his belt unbuckle, and he unzips his pants.

He covers my mouth with his hand while his other hand holds his cock as he pushes into me slowly past the head and stops. He moves his hand to my shoulder, as his other hand stays on my mouth and pulls my head back slightly.

Powerfully, he thrusts into me, lifting me off the floor. I scream against his hand. His other hand holds me in place as he slams into me repeatedly, stretching and filling me. Thrusting me forward, my thighs pinned between Nikolaj and the edge of the desk.

His movements become harder, unforgiving, and my screams muffled. I feel his cock forcefully and moving faster in and out of me.

My body moves up and down on his desk. Without warning, I cum! My pussy throbbing. My body is shaking, but he doesn't stop.

He slides his hand from my shoulder to my sensitive pulsing clit and rubs deep and steady as he fucks me.

I feel his cock so deep inside me. His balls were slapping against me. My screams are muffled, but I still scream, "NIKOLAJ!" into his hand, but my words are inaudible to him as my 3rd orgasm consumes my body.

I feel his cock building inside me. He pulls out to cum on my back, grunting, and his legs jerk and shake.

My breathing is heavy, and my body goes limp as the warmth of his arousal marks my clothes.

He slowly removes his hand from my mouth. I hear his pants zip back up. Pushing his thighs against me while buckling his belt.

"Stay!" His voice is so seductive and demanding. He sits in his chair behind me.

There is a long pause, no movements or words. Looking over my shoulder, I see Nikolaj admiring my bare, wet, just fucked pussy, and the marks from my two spankings on my ass.

"What.... Are....You....Doing?" I say, still trying to compose myself after the best, hardest fuck of my life.

He blatantly says, rubbing his beard in his hand, "looking at your sweet wet cunt!"

"Oh my god! Nikolaj!" I say as I push up off the desk, feeling almost embarrassed from being completely exposed and vulnerable.

"Where are you going?" He asks, leaning forward in his chair, bending me over his desk again with his hand splayed between my shoulder blades. With his other hand, he grabs my ass cheek and bites it. I scream out as I tense up.

"Two," he counts with his mouth against my ass.

I snap, "I'm not standing here for you to stare at."

He scoffs, slowly shoving two fingers in me, then twists them. I quietly breathe out a moan at the pleasure of him inside me returning.

"You'll do what you are told to, and I said stay," he demands with a tone of voice so deep and raspy it makes me quiver.

FUCK, he's so sexy!

I relax my chest back on the desk.

Nikolaj starts rubbing my ass, lightly licking the marks he left, then biting the other ass cheek. I scream into my forearm.

"You'll do whatever I tell you to do because you want to feel me in you." His voice is sinister as he twists his fingers in and out of me, sensually aggressive and faster.

I brace my hand on the desk, pushing my shoulder up as I hold in my cries of pleasure.

He slides the 3rd finger into me. I catch my scream in my throat and brace my other hand on the edge of his desk as I push my ass toward him, so he can be deeper in my cunt.

His other hand grabs my thigh, licking my wetness off his fingers as they move in and out of me.

His tongue drags up until he licks my back hole. I forcefully jerk myself straight up and forward into the desk.

"No! Nik," I demand breathily.

He thrusts his fingers in my wet pussy harder, filling me, owning me. "Please don't fuck my ass," I whisper in my pleasured state.

"Never without your consent," he says with his chin resting on my tailbone. I lift one knee onto the desk, bracing myself, and slide my hand down to rub my clit.

"You want to cum, my delicious Milly?" His voice rasps against my skin then he runs his tongue over my raised thigh.

"YES!" I moan as I throw my head back.

"Good! Cum!"

At his command, I explode into a rush of ecstasy. His finger still twisting and fucking me as I feel my pussy throb on them. My head goes light, my ears ring, I see stars, and my body shakes. I stop rubbing my clit to brace both hands on the desk and lower my leg.

Dizzy, I drop limply into his lap, and he wraps his arms around me to catch me. He brings my legs up over the arm of the chair. My head rests on his shoulder as I catch my breath. He leans over to the desk, grabs a bottle of water, and hands it to me. I take a considerable drink as he runs his hand through my hair.

"Not bad for someone who was just a virgin a few hours ago," he states in a low, calm tone.

I smiled against him and tucked further into his chest. "I definitely can't take much more, and I'm going to be sore."

"You'll soak in the tub and relax. That will help," he says, running his hand down my arm and back up again.

"Thank you," I whisper, then giggle, "I'll be ready for round two later."

He nuzzles his chin against the top of my head. "I'll go with you," he says, rubbing my leg.

"I can bathe myself, you know." I kiss his chest.

"I mean, I'll go with you to Chicago," he clarifies but sounds apprehensive about his decision.

"Really?! OH, THANK YOU!" I cheer, pulling up to give him a tight hug. "Thank you," I whisper into his neck.

I stand off his lap, pulling my skirt down from my waist, and I can still feel his cum on my back. I look down at him as he admires my legs, with his elbow resting on the arm of the chair and his hand nestling his head.

"How do I get upstairs without anyone noticing your cum on my back?" I inquire, squinting at him.

He laughs, runs his finger over his mouth, and says, "learn to swallow, and we won't have this problem."

"Oh my god, Nik," I breathe out and blush.

Present Milly

Chapter 47

I look for Vance downstairs in our office.

"Hey! Knocked on your door, but no answer. Figured this would be the only other place you could be," I say as I walk over to his desk.

He furrows his brows at me with a confused look. My hair is freshly wet, and I smell like Nikolaj's soap.

"I wanted to wash that asshole, Christoff's, hands off me," I shrug while sitting on top of his desk beside his chair.

"What did I miss?!" He asks as he leans back in his chair.

"Christoff grabbed my ass before the meeting started," I explained, scrunching my face.

"What the fuck!" Vance exclaims, rubbing his hands on his face.

"You weren't supposed to be seen by anyone. What went wrong?" He demands.

"Nothing. The meeting started a few minutes late, and I pushed my cart by the meeting room when the door was still open, and Christoff saw me. It's fine, Vance," I reassure him. I look over at the files he has spread on his desk. "Anything interesting?"

He leans up and hands me a folder, "lots!"

I pull my legs up onto the desk and crisscross them.

"That Benecelli file is a real lucky find, Milly," he nudged my leg. He grabs a second file and leans back in his chair. "I made copies just in case," he says and laughs.

"That's just like you," I reply, shaking my head with a smile.

I open the file, and the first thing in it is Vance's picture, then Frank, Jared, Grace...I flip quicker, Mary, Adio, Linford, and Rosco.

"Fuck Vance! What the hell is this? They know our whole team," I say with a panicked tone.

"I know, but not you. You're not in the file. Thankfully, but it gets worse," he says, leaning forward again and resting his head on my knee.

"How much worse?" I ask with worry.

"A lot." He doesn't move. I put my hand on his head and lay the file on his desk to flip through it one-handed.

He chuckles, keeping his head on my knee, "you following some Russians into a warehouse wasn't such a bad idea after all. If we are lucky, they will help us clean this mess up."

I flip through the pages. I see familiar names of people we hunted. Pictures of our warehouse, our house, even us in action, but none with me in them.

Some of these documents are from two years ago! Two years of data about us, our hunts, and anything they could find about us.

I look at some of the names and dates, then it hits me. "Fuck, Vance! These are the names and dates of the hunts that led us to Lazlo!"

He leans a bit, "yep, keep reading through it."

The last page in the file has last Friday's date on it. There are notes, times, and dates. This is what Jared needed Vance for. These fucks made it look like a big hunt, but it was a setup. They wanted Vance, and they lured him in.

"They've been watching us for years. Why were you the only one caught last Friday?" I somberly ask.

"It felt off to me. I told everyone to hold back. I didn't think it was a hunt on us, but maybe a police setup. I don't know." He runs his hand through his hair.

"Fuck," I huff out.

"They were at the hotel opening since Seth Jones is in this file. So, they knew we were looking for him. They should have known we would be there. Why didn't they see me or any of us?" I ask.

"They work with the bosses. They probably knew Nikolaj and Demyan would get to him first. They probably didn't waste their time watching for us. They didn't expect someone to follow two criminal Russians to who knows where." He laughs as he moves his chin to my knee and looks up at me.

"They have legit businesses, too," I joke. Vance nods and laughs.

I lean down, putting my head close to his, and whisper, "Vance, are the bosses with them or us?" Hoping I didn't lose my virginity to a man trying to kill the closest thing I have to a father.

"They are with us, Milly," he reassures me with a smile. I feel instant relief.

He leans back in his chair, and I say, "we were hunted the last two years while we were hunting. That's fucking twisted. Could someone on one of our teams have betrayed us?"

"We have a big operation, so it's hard to say," he answers while looking vaguely at the file.

I pick up the file with 'red' written on it. "What about this?"

"That file is a record of names, dates, amounts paid, and types of transitions."

"People?" I ask.

"I can't say for sure yet, but I think it's the records of Lazlo's transactions. By looking at the locations listed, more than one person is running the show."

"Have you checked our files? How many correspond with the dates in this file?" I ask eagerly.

"Haven't gotten that far yet." He smiles.

I hear the door to the office open and glance over. It's Nikolaj walking in wearing joggers, and I can see the outline of his massive cock through them. A tee shirt that hugs every muscle his torso has, and his neck tattoos peeking out of the collar. His arms are covered in tattoos, and stretch his shirt sleeves. He looks fucking perfect no matter what he is wearing.

His face goes cold as he looks at me, then I realize I am sitting on Vance's desk, in shorts and a tee shirt, with my legs crossed open.

I've never worried about how I dressed or acted around Vance because he's never looked at me like that. Old habits, I guess.

I move my legs to the edge of the desk, letting them hang down. I know I will hear about this later.

Nikolaj stops beside the desk. I glance up at him, and his eyes move from me to Vance. "Anything interesting in the files?" He asks, then looks down at my legs, back up to me, then over to Vance.

I can't help but lower my head, not making it evident that I want to look at every bit of him without being noticed.

All our encounters together, but I've never actually looked at him in all his detailed glory. His large hands are covered with tattoos running up his arms and down his fingers. His palms are tattooed. The right has an outline of a colt 45, and the left has a dahlia outline tattoo. His forearms are thick, guiding up to his perfectly muscular biceps, broad shoulders, and luscious wavy brown hair pulled to the back of his head in a bun.

The smell of his cologne intoxicates me.

Making my way to his face, I realize he is staring back at me. I drop my eyes and fumble with the folder sitting on my lap.

"They know everything about the last two years of our hunts." I clear my throat and nervously say.

"Except, Milly," Vance says.

"Milly isn't in the files at all?" Nikolaj lightly leans over to me to look at the file lying on my lap. Nikolaj asks, as his breath brushes my skin and his voice rumbles in my ear, "So no one knows who or where she is, then?"

Vance leans back in his chair, saying, "Guess not."

"We could use this to our advantage," Nikolaj says while moving away from me.

"NO WAY! She stays out of all of this," Vance firmly says, jumping forward to the edge of his chair.

"They wouldn't know to look for her. She would be a ghost," Nikolaj counters.

"NO! I don't know why this file exists, but these men are a step ahead of us and very dangerous. She stays out of it," Vance snaps, leaning back in his chair in a huff.

"I'm right here, you two!" I say, pushing off the desk and onto my feet. "I'm going to help my family!" I lay my hand on Vance's shoulder. "Nikolaj already agreed we could go to Chicago to help them," I say, looking up at Nikolaj.

"NO!" Vance says, rushing to a standing position. "I will not allow you to be a part of this. I will not allow you to be in harm's way."

He grabs my shoulders, and Nikolaj comes closer to me with his gaze locked on Vance.

"I will go with her. I will not let anything happen to her," Nikolaj says, touching Vance's upper arms.

Vance sneers back, "You let Christoff grab her ass!"

"VANCE!" I yell, slamming my hands on my hips.

"A mistake that will cost him his life!" Nikolaj growls, removing his hand from Vance.

"I've killed for her!" Vance snaps while moving toward Nikolaj's face.

"So have I!" Nikolaj towers over Vance.

"Both of you, stop!" I demand, pushing into Nikolaj and Vance.

"Vance, you can't protect me in your condition, and this situation is too dangerous for me to worry about if you're ok. You stay and rest. No option! Nikolaj will protect me. I know he will!"

Nikolaj places his hand on the small of my back and says calmly, "Vance...."

"She's my world, Nikolaj!" Vance interrupts him and sits back in the chair, resting his forehead in his hand.

"And I will do everything to keep her safe. Christoff and Ricardo don't have the balls to cross me. Maybe the balls to have someone do it for them, but never themselves," Nikolaj tries to reassure Vance.

I kneel to Vance, resting my hands on his thighs, and he looks down at me. "You and our family trained me. Trust my 12 years of training. I can do this. Now, go rest. I can tell you are sore by how you grunt when you move."

He smiles at me, kisses the top of my head, and whispers, "Ok."

I watch him leave as I stand by Nikolaj, still by Vance's desk.

The door clicks shut. I turn to Nikolaj, place my hand on his chest, and joke, "you'd better be right about Christoff and Ricardo, or Vance will kill you."

He does a throaty chuckle, "I'm not saying we won't be challenged, but you won't die." He cocks an eyebrow at me.

I banter, "reassuring. Can't wait! So, when do we leave?"

"In the morning." He steps closer to me, pulling his eyebrows together. "So, when I walked in, did I see your legs on his desk?"

Stuttering, I say, "y-y-yes, that's what you saw. Old habits. Sorry."

"Three," he growls with the most sinister look in his eyes.

"WAIT!" I lean into him and softly say, "my ass can't handle another spanking right now."

He leans in, looking at me, "then don't give me a reason to spank you."

Cocking my eyebrow, "fine. You get one, then!"

He smirks, "for what?"

Curling my lip between my teeth, I think, Milly, for what!

"Well, I'm waiting, Milly?" He says seductively, wrapping his arms around me and holding me to him.

"For being so fucking irresistible."

"No, that's not how this works." He shakes his head slowly.

"Fine, because you ruined a perfectly good silk shirt by cumming on it."

He laughs, "fine, but I already told you the solution is swallowing. I can't cum in you without a condom, and I don't just carry those around." He cocks his head down to me while running his fingers over my jaw.

"Maybe I could get on birth control?" I scrunch my face.

"No. That shit's not good for your body."

"What?" I look at him, confused.

"Let mother nature run its natural course with you. I'll worry about the condoms." He kisses my nose, "let's go to bed. We have an early morning."

Pulling my hand as he leads me out of the basement office and up the stairs. "Am I going to my room?"

He slightly turns to me and asks, "which room do you want to sleep in?"

"Yours," I smirk.

"Good. We can get those spankies done."

"Wait, maybe my room." I giggle as I try to pull away, but he tightens his grip on me.

"Too late!" He says, leading us up the stairs to his room.

"Are you hungry?" He asks while closing the door.

"Starving." I kick my sandals off and follow him to the kitchen.

"Any requests? Favorite food?" He glances at me while opening his double fridge.

"Vance usually cooks for me. He's Italian, so we ate a lot of pasta and stuff. I will eat anything, so you can make whatever you want."

He leans against me with a devilish look, "anything you say!" My face turns hot. "Blushing? I thought I would have fucked the blushing out of you by now." His words make my pussy ache, and I love it.

"Guess you should try harder," I taunt him with desire.

Leaning into my ear, he says in a raspy voice, "be careful what you ask for, Milly. I've been taking it easy on you, but those words will get you into something you are not ready for." He lightly kisses my cheek and then returns to his mission of making our food.

Walking behind him, I wrap my arms around his waist and rest my head on his back. I fantasize about all the things he could mean.

After covering the pan on the stove, he turns to wrap me in his arms. "We have a few minutes."

Before I can say anything, he turns around and pushes me down on the island. "What are you doing?" I ask, but I already know the answer.

"You know exactly what I'm doing," he says with a growl.

"How hard do you want your spankings, Ms. Try Harder?"

Ignoring how sore my ass is from earlier and letting anticipation and curiosity get the best of me, I say, "show me what you're hiding from me."

"Are you sure?" He asks, and I can hear the warning in his tone, and I should heed it, but I'm not one to show weakness.

"Yes," I say, and rest my face in my hands to prepare for pain that will turn into pleasure and hopefully a good fucking.

He slowly pulls down my shorts, caressing my marked cheeks as he leans into me. "Last chance to retract your words," he says against my ear.

"Are you scared?" I taunt him more.

A sinister deep chuckle escapes his throat, and goosebumps cover my body.

He steps back and grabs a wooden spoon from the drawer by the stove. Rubbing the spoon against the back of my thighs up to my ass cheeks, sliding it between my legs, he rubs the spoon against my wet slit and smacks it, leaving a stinging pleasure. I like how this is going so far, so I push my ass toward him.

He ties my hands together behind my back with a towel and gets ice from the freezer. He runs it down my slit, then over my clit. The cold of the ice and the warmth of his hands balance perfectly as he runs circles over my clit.

My body enjoys the sensation, and my moans grow into a hum the more intricate and faster he rubs.

He lightly spanks my ass with the spoon, and I feel the ice and fingertips at my entrance. Expecting he will gently stretch me like all the other times, I prepare to feel a single finger enter me, but instead, he slides the ice and three fingers inside my wet pussy all at once.

I moan as the intense stinging pleasure stretches me to accommodate his three thick fingers pushing further into me.

Feeling the cold of the ice inside me excites me, but my hands cannot service my clit, so I force myself into his fingers as a sign to finger fuck me harder.

His fingers thrust into me harder and harder, deeper and deeper. I lift my ass, so he can reach deeper into me. My screams of pleasure intensify as the orgasm builds.

"Do not cum until I tell you to," he commands, but it's too late. I feel the orgasm cover me. I can't stop it. He pulls his fingers out, but I'm cumming. I feel my pussy throb, missing his fingers filling me.

Breathing heavily, I try to apologize. I was too close to my orgasm when Nikolaj said it, but before I got a word out, the spoon hit my ass hard.

I pull myself up from the stinging pain. He slams my torso back down on the island, and I see him rubbing blood between his fingers.

"Did you make me bleed?" I demanded, but he didn't answer.

He slams his fingers back in me, I scream out, and he picks up speed. I feel his thumb circle my back hole. I try to move away, but he presses me to the island. "Don't move," he growls.

"Don't..." I start to say.

WACK!

WACK!

WACK!

Three hard blows against my ass cheeks. I thrust upward and screamed, "OUCH! That fucking hurts!"

"That's the point! I told you not to cum!" Admiring his work on my ass, "you bleed so easily. I'm going to destroy this body," he says, palming my ass covered in marks and blood.

"FUCK NIKOLAJ! What the hell?!" I yell out.

"You wanted to see what I could do. I showed you." Those were not spankings to turn me on and fuck me. They were spankings to prove a point.

I mess with the towel to untie my hands, then quickly pull my shorts up. Wiping the tears from my face with my back still toward Nikolaj. "What the fuck, Nikolaj? Those fucking hurt," I say again as I choke back my cries.

He turns me to him, leans down, and wipes the remaining tears from my face. "See, you are not ready for the things you ask for."

"You're right! I will never be ready for that," I snap, grab the spoon from him, and hit him in the arm with it. "FUCKER!" I yell, then storm to the bathroom.

What the fuck did I get myself into?

I pull my shorts down to see new marks on top of old ones and the blood smeared on my cheeks and clothes.

A gentle knock on the door startles me, "Milly, can I come in?" His voice is soothing and calm.

I pull up my shorts and slowly open the door. "What?" I whisper out.

"I'm sorry. I should not have done that. I knew you weren't ready for that intensity," Nikolaj says while pushing the door open more, studying my face while he puts a piece of my hair behind my ear. "I would never hurt you unless the pain causes you pleasure."

Pulling me closer.

"I'm ok," I say. "I'm sorry I hit you in the arm."

I wrap my arms around his waist and rest my head on his chest. His heart beating in my ear is soothing. I can't be mad at him. He gave me what I asked for because I asked for it, even though he knew I wasn't ready.

"Let's get your ass iced," he says with his lips against the top of my head.

"Just to clarify, I liked the ice part; no more drawing blood for now, and don't fuck my ass," I say with my face squished against him. I hear him chuckle.

"You will want my cock in your ass some time. I promise you, I'll have you begging for it," Nikolaj says, resting his chin on my head.

"Only if you try it first. I heard it hurts too much."

"I have tried it, and I like it. Hurt? Maybe a little in the beginning, but you'll stretch," he explains, running his hands through my hair.

"What? You like it in the...." I pause for him to answer.

"Yes, and if you want to fuck me first, then you can. I promise you'll love giving and receiving. But that's all for later. For now, you'll have to lay on the island with ice on your ass to help the welting. I have to finish cooking."

Gripping his shirt, I cringe. "Oh my god!"

"I can smear ice cream all over your ass and lick it off. Is that a better idea?" Nikolaj jokes.

"Nikolaj!" I shield my face as he squeezes me tighter and laughs.

Present Milly

Chapter 48

WE PARK BY THE jet on the tarmac. Nikolaj turns to me, "are you ready for this?"

"Yes," I reply and watch him get out of the G-Wagon to walk around to open my door.

As we walk in, Demyan, Gus, and Sven are already on the jet.

"Took you long enough!" Demyan banters to Nikolaj.

"Had something to do really quick," he replies, handing Demyan a briefcase.

QUICK?

There was nothing quick about waking me up this morning, devouring my wet center.

There was nothing quick about him pinning me against the shower wall and mercilessly fucking my pussy from behind.

There was nothing quick about how he pulled my pants down, bent me over by the front door, and slammed his rock-hard cock into me. He fucked me so hard I had to place my hands on the floor to stop from falling over. After I had two more orgasms, he spun me around, shoved me to my knees, and came all over my face.

The only thing quick about Nikolaj Fedorov is how quick his dick gets hard.

I take my seat by the window with Nikolaj beside me. There's a table in front of us, and Gus and Demyan occupy the two spots opposite us. Sven is seated in the single seat to Nikolaj's left.

"Have you ever flown before?" Nikolaj asks.

"Yes. Many times," I reassure him.

"Puke in the bag if you need to, Milly!" Sven yells out while pointing to the front of my seat.

I roll my eyes, "I'm fine! Thanks, Sven!"

The pilot announces our ETA for departure, and the flight attendants serve us scotch and walk around, securing the cabin.

Nikolaj leans into me, "want to learn how to suck my dick when we are in the air?"

"Nikolaj!? No! Not with everyone around!" I firmly whisper, looking out the corner of my eye to see if anyone heard.

"We would go to the sleeping quarters," he says.

"Oh," I say, smirking, and lean back.

"Is that a '*yes*'?" He growls into my ear as his hand twists into my hair. I see if anyone is watching us, but they're preoccupied with their conversations to care about what we're doing.

"Maybe," I whisper, bite my lip, and rub his leg.

"You're blushing again." He runs his finger down the side of my face.

"Doesn't your dick get tired?" I ask.

"I've wanted to fuck you for three months! I'm making up for the lost time," he purrs, moving his head to my neck and gently kissing it.

The door to the plane is closed, the pilots shut the entrance to the cockpit, and the flight attendant asks if we need to go over safety guidelines since I am new to the jet, but Nikolaj refuses.

Within a few minutes, we are taking off. I look over to see Sven holding the arms of his seat so tight his knuckles are white.

"Sven, if you need to puke, use the bag," I joke and point to the front of his seat, and the men at the table laugh.

He groans, "I never said I liked to fly!"

"You're such a baby," Gus says, while Demyan shakes his head and laughs, never looking away from a file.

I turn toward the window and watch the earth get smaller and smaller as we go higher and higher. It's so peaceful in the air, completely isolated from everything in the world. I wonder how a world so beautiful from up here can be full of such shitty people.

"We have a four-hour flight, so let's go over the files and get a plan formed," Demyan says and sets the file on the table for all of us to see.

"M, tell us about the people in the pictures," he says, spreading the pictures all out across the table.

I flip through them and put them in an order I can easily explain. "This is Jared and Frank; they are Vance's younger brothers. Jared and his wife found me when I lived in River's Bend, Iowa. This is Mary, Jared's wife, and Grace, Frank's wife. They are retired military, along with Vance and Jerad, and Frank is one of the best hackers in the world."

"He obviously isn't THE best, or else he would have known someone was watching you," Sven says while resting his head in his hand and looking over at me.

"Shut your crabby ass mouth, Sven," Gus yells.

"No, he's right," I say, "Christoff and Ricardo have a better hacker since Frank never noticed anyone watching us, and that's probably why we never could find information on Lazlo."

I rub my hand on my head, and my throat goes dry as I realize just how serious this is. "Can I get some water?" I ask Nikolaj, and he snaps his fingers for the flight attendant's attention.

After chugging a bottle of water, I continue my debriefing, "this is Rosco. He's one of my trainers and a hunter. This is Linford and Adio, brothers, and my other two trainers and hunters."

"Oh, now THIS makes sense," Gus states, "now I see how you could fight so well. I knew Vance couldn't train you like that. No offense to Vance."

"I'm sure he would agree," I laugh.

"What about the rest of the file, M?" Demyan asks.

I point to another picture. "The nine of us lived in this house together. We tracked and hunted out of the attic. Our weapons room was in the basement."

I point to another picture and say, "this is our warehouse, and whoever took this picture got our cleaners' cars in it, so they know who covered our assess."

I slump into the chair, feeling helpless and completely violated. "We had to be closer to Lazlo than we knew for them to take the time to follow us around collecting all this information," I state.

"Milly, do you honestly think your team had no idea they were being followed? This is a lot of information for someone to have and never be noticed," Nikolaj asks, pointing to the pictures.

"What are you saying? We would have known if there was a threat to any of us. It's how we worked. There were never secrets," I snap and lean up.

"It was just you nine that did this work?" Demyan asks.

"No. We have a huge organization. We have people all over the world," I reply, and I know where he is going with this. He thinks the same as Nikolaj, that it's an inside job.

"None of them would give information to Christoff and Ricardo?" Nikolaj insists.

"I can't see any of our people betraying us. I don't see how they could benefit from it," I say, pulling my eyebrows together.

"Tell us what they are like, their personalities, stop telling us what you think they are capable of and if you trust them or not. You trust everyone, and that makes you naive," Nikolaj spits out as he slams his hands on the table.

"So, you just want to think it's an inside job. You don't even know these people, but to you, they're guilty," I snap at Nikolaj, turning to face him better.

Demyan looks between Nikolaj and me and says, "Milly, it's a possibility, and without us knowing any of these people, we are taking a huge risk. We could be walking into a trap."

"What don't you understand? These people are my family, and the others I've hunted with wouldn't betray us," I yell, choking back my tears of frustration.

Why don't these men believe me?

Demyan tries to smooth over the situation, "it's not uncommon for people to sell information for money. Some people don't have a sense of loyalty. This is a lot of detailed information they have, so someone must have given it to them, M." His words ignited a fire in me.

"I need a minute," I say, jumping up and throwing a leg over Nikolaj and then the other to climb to the aisle.

The flight attendant sees me, "anything you need?"

"No, just going to the bathroom," I tell her in passing.

I rest my hands on the counter, staring into the mirror, and try to collect my thoughts. I must accept that betrayal could be possible, but who and why?

I wonder if Vance has Frank and Jared looking into our people. We are a prominent organization fighting for the same purpose, but it wouldn't be impossible for someone to join under the false accord.

A knock on the door startles me.

"What?" I snap, wiping the tears from my face.

"You good?" Gus asks. Why is Gus asking if I'm good? I open the door and give him a confused look.

"Nikolaj was going to come back here, but I talked him into letting me talk to you," he explains and puts his hand on the door frame.

"Why would you care how I feel?" I ask.

"Because I know about being betrayed. I mean, so do the bosses, but they've seen that stuff their whole lives. Their fathers were betrayed many times. It's part of their life. But I saw how hurt you were at the mention of it, so I knew they wouldn't help you with this adjustment," he says, smiling, moving his hands in his pockets.

"What adjustment? None of you know my family as I do. They wouldn't turn on any of us," I grunt and cross my arms over my chest, leaning against the door frame he was just touching.

"I said the same thing about my older brother back in Trinidad. I never thought he would do anything to hurt our family. I was wrong."

He leans on the wall opposite me and continues, "he was in deep with the wrong people. They robbed our parents' house at gunpoint. They killed our parents and our little sister. Took everything of value. Later, I found out it was my brother that pulled the trigger. Turns out he wasn't the good guy I thought he was. I still can't wrap my head around it, but I don't have to. What happened happened, and I can't fix it." He drops his eyes to the floor and shrugs his shoulders.

"Gus, I'm so sorry. That's horrible," I said compassionately.

"Don't feel sorry for me. I just wanted you to understand it could be anyone. Keep a clear head. Put the facts together. Keep your emotions and history with these people out of the equation. Trust me. It will help soften the blow if it's an inside job."

I nod and follow Gus back to the table.

"You okay, M?" Demyan asks as he stands, takes a few steps to greet me, rubs his hands on my arms, and smiles.

"Yeah, just a lot to think about," I say, smiling back at him.

"We don't have time for emotions, so let's get this file worked over," Nikolaj barks in annoyance, then stands to let me sit.

I look up at Gus as I step to my seat; he smirks and slightly shakes his head. It's good that Gus came to talk to me because I have a feeling if Nikolaj did, we'd be in a fight right now, or fucking, or fighting and fucking. I squeeze my eyes shut for a second to clear my head, then take my seat and flip through the file.

"Okay, these people, dates, and times are the ones we hunted within the last two years. They could correspond with the 'red' file. Do you have a copy of that, Demyan?" I ask, insinuating that I want Demyan to hand me the file, not Nikolaj.

I feel Nikolaj's frustrated eyes burn on me. Maybe I'm looking for trouble with him, or perhaps I'm pissed he's being so insensitive. All I do know is I just earned myself a spanking.

Demyan hands me the file, and I compare the dates of the transitions with the dates of our hunts. "A few of our hunting dates line up with Lazlo's transactions." I highlight them in yellow.

I compare our other dates to the 'red' file transactions. Some are lining up, but there are multiple transactions per day. I wish I had access to the files of our other divisions, so I could cross-reference their hunts to this file.

"I have your family staying on the top floor of one of my hotels in Chicago. We'll meet up with them there and see what they know," Demyan says and motions for another scotch and one for me.

"Is everyone from the house there?" I ask, then take a sip of my scotch, and let the liquor simmer in my mouth.

"I'm assuming so. Vance called them to set it up," Demyan explains, looking at me, then takes a drink. His long stare has me shifting in my seat. I look at Nikolaj to see him staring at Demyan, then he adjusts his position to lean an elbow on the table.

"Have your men stand guard throughout the hotel. We may need them ready when we meet this family of Milly's," he demands, breaks his stare on Demyan, slams his scotch, then glares at me from the corner of his eye.

I scoff and turn toward him a bit. "This family of mine won't hurt you if they don't have to, so don't give them a reason to by being a dickhead," I growl, slam my scotch, then feel instant regret. The burn in my throat makes me cough, and my face winces. Gus and Demyan laugh at me, making me chuckle while trying to compose myself.

Nikolaj is unamused and focuses on the flight attendant pouring more scotch into his glass. How she looks at him makes me wonder if they've fucked before.

"Blagodaryu vas," he says to her kindly, making me jealous. She walks away with a shit-eating grin, then he cocks his head slightly toward me. "You are out of your league if you are trying to fight me," he says with his cup to his lips.

"Challenge accepted!" I growl back and roll my eyes. I move, in my seat, to be as far as away from him as I can and stare out the window. He might be used to people betraying him, but I'm not, so he needs to ease off the *fuck you* attitude he is giving me.

"M, is there anything else you can tell us that might help us understand what is going on?" Demyan gently asks.

"I'll try to think of something," I sweetly say in Demyan's direction, smile, then go back to staring out the window.

"Maybe just talking about your past will give us some clues," Gus suggests.

I smile at him, set my hands on his, and say, "Gus, I would do anything to help you understand me better, but I doubt anything I say will ease your worries." He's wide-eyed and staring at the big bad boss man himself.

I toss a glare to Nikolaj, then look back out the window. I know I shouldn't play these petty games to try and make Nikolaj jealous, but he doesn't get to be an asshole to me. I'm not dealing with his shit today. He'd shoot everyone and call it a day if it were his way.

Demyan and Gus move to sit in the two chairs opposite the couch Sven was lying down on to help with his fear of flying. I watch them talking and laughing with each other, like ordinary people. I whip a glance at Nikolaj. He is staring at his scotch with a scowl and his finger tapping the side of the glass.

I snap at him, "what, no rude fucking remarks to say to me?"

He doesn't look at me, but he gently says, "I watched my father get shot by his right-hand man when I was 16." My whole body feels like it's dropping, and I feel like an asshole. "He lived, but his right-hand man didn't. I stared at that scar on his chest every time I saw it. It was a reminder of how close someone can get before they show their true self." He takes a sip of liquor.

I lean into my chair, facing him with my shoulder to the back. This is the first time he has opened up about anything like this. I'm not about to fuck it up by interrupting him.

"Demyan and I grew up together. We watched people betray our families over and over. Our fathers were naive, like you," he says as he looks over at me.

"Betrayal and loyalty are all we know, Milly. Loyalty is easy to fake. Betrayal is what will get you killed," he says, shifting in his seat to face me. "I can't lose you because I put my guard down and make a mistake or misjudge a situation."

He runs his hand over my face. "I hope everyone is as good as you say they are, but if not, I will kill them all to protect you and Vance."

He leans his head to mine. I melt into him and lay my head in the crook of his neck. He's not such an asshole. He's just been through so much shit that he can't put his guard down.

I whisper to him, "I understand. I'll accept that there is a chance it's an inside job. I'll keep my guard up, too."

I gently kiss his neck, wrapping my arm around his body and squeezing his upper arm, and say, "one question. Unrelated to betrayal," I pause, wondering if I should even ask it.

"What is it, Milly?" He asks. Such an impatient man.

I take a deep breath, lower my voice so no one else will hear me, and ask, "have you fucked any of the flight attendants on this jet right now?" I pull my head up to look into his eyes.

He looks down at me, furrows his brows, and says, "why? Would you be jealous?" He grabs my chin, tilts my head back, and then tells me, "don't think I didn't notice how friendly you got with Demyan and Gus after she left the table."

I smirk and squint my eyes, then demand, "answer!"

"Are you jealous?" He asks, grinning and cocking an eyebrow.

I pull my chin out of his grasp, scoot back in my seat, and surprisingly blurt out, "you have! Which one? All of them?" I feel my face flush, and sadness and jealousy fill me. Why does this bother me? Of course, he fucked them. He's fucked a lot of women before me. I know this, so why does it feel like a slap in the face.

He stares at me with a confused look on his face. Shakes his head a single time and takes a pull of scotch. "I wouldn't disrespect you by bringing you around women I've already fucked. So, no, my sweet Milly, I have not fucked any of these women. I do, however, use my manners. How she looks at me is out of my control."

I stare at him, and I feel embarrassment cover me. "I'm sorry. Maybe, I still think this thing between us is too good to be true, so I guess.... yeah, jealous," I explain, then reach for my scotch and take a drink.

I hear him chuckle. "Now, are we done fighting?" he asks. I nod yes, and he follows with, "then, how about that blowjob."

I snap my head up and smirk. "Seriously, is that all you can think about?" I insist. He growls into my lips as he holds my chin up again and lets his lips fall onto mine. "Okay," I say before pushing my lips back into his.

He grabs my hand, pulls me from my seat, and I follow him to the sleeping quarters. I sit on the bed, and Nikolaj stands in front of me, rubbing my jawline with his thumb as I look up at him.

I unzip his pants, pulling out his stiff cock and rubbing the tip against my lips. I look up to see the devilish look in his eyes and lick the tip to tease him.

"Open," he demands in a lustful voice.

I follow orders, keeping eye contact, while I take the tip of his cock into my mouth. Wrapping my hands around the shaft and licking around the sensitive ridge of the head.

He moans out, "excellent start!"

I close my mouth around his cock and suck it into my mouth further. He gasps in a breath, then palms my head, slowly moving me up and down the length of his thick shaft, careful not to go too deep at first.

He keeps a slow pace until my jaw relaxes. His eyes lock on mine as he pushes deeper into my mouth. The taste of his skin covers my tongue. I try not to gag when he gets to the back of my mouth, but I can't help it.

"Breathe through your nose," he directs, and it seems to help me take him better. He thrusts into my mouth, his cock hitting the back of my throat and going deeper. I flinch at the new sensation, then moan as he pulls back.

He thrusts harder and deeper into my throat, my eyes water, and spit lubricates my lips, dripping down my chin as he moves his cock in and out.

Twisting my hand around his shaft as he pulls out, then let it slide back through when he slams back into my mouth. My tongue explores the shaft of his dick, and I feel his smooth skin gliding through my lips, making my pussy clench with desire.

I move my other hand down the front of my pants to my soaked center and rub my wet, swollen clit.

He keeps his eyes on me. My eyes water, running down my cheeks from the movements hitting my throat. He moves his hand and curls it around my neck. "You look so fucking gorgeous with my dick down your throat," he groans, as his speed increases, thrusting further down my throat.

His cock fucks my mouth with the same intensity he's fucked my pussy, and I can barely get a breath in. My fingers rub my clit wildly as my orgasm builds.

The taste of precum fills my taste buds as I move my other hand to his balls and squeeze gently. "Fuck, Milly! You feel so good," he groans as he tightens his grip on my hair and neck.

My orgasm hits, and his dick muffles my scream of release. Feeling his cum hit the back of my mouth, I swallow every drop he gives me. But he quickly pulls out and rubs his dick to finish cumming on my face. The warm spurts hit inside my gaped mouth, my lips, chin, and cheeks.

He rubs his dick around my lips to smear his arousal on me. I lick the tip as cum drips down my chin. My fingers gently circle my clit as I come down.

I feel powerful, sexy, and naughty. I want to explore every part of Nikolaj. I side my tongue down his throbbing shaft, then gently suck his balls into my mouth one at a time.

"Fuck," he moans, rubbing my head, "my perfect fucking Milly!"

I look in the bathroom mirror, waiting for the water to warm up in the sink. Nikolaj stands behind me, looking in the mirror and admiring his cum on my face.

I can't help but smirk at him. He doesn't even have to touch me. Just his presence behind me makes me feral. I wiggle my ass against him and reach behind me to grab him.

"We should get back to business," he mumbles into the back of my head. His arms wrap around my stomach, and he pulls me closer.

"That's what I'm doing," I say as I rub my hands down and grab his ass.

"Hmmmm, unfortunately, I mean actual business."

"Nikolaj," I purr, "please," I moan, moving one of my hands to the front of my pants, and letting my fingers find their way back to my clit.

"I will give you everything you beg for later, but right now, we need to work," he orders, kisses the top of my head, then walks out of the bathroom.

Flustered, I cleaned up and met him back at the table. I hear Demyan yell from his seat, "are you two going to play nice, so we can get back to work, or is it a lost cause to attempt this debriefing again?"

"Let's get this done with," Nikolaj demands while motioning for them to return to the table.

Demyan sits down with his glass of scotch and asks, "are we going to get through it this time, or are you two planning another fuck frenzy?"

Sven grumbles from the couch, "the noises we heard from back there sounded like he fucked the attitude right out of her."

"Watch it, Sven, or I'll push you right out of this fucking plane," Nikolaj warns.

Sven surrenders his hands up and rolls over to face us.

Demyan pours more scotch into his glass as he chuckles at the nonsense around him.

"Are you going to be sober when we get there?" Nikolaj asks in a flat tone of voice.

"Are you going to be distracted?" Demyan retorts, looking over at me, winking.

To avoid further talk about what we just did, I adjust in my seat and say, "okay! story time!"

I give them every detail of my life as I remember it. Even the worst parts.

Present Milly

Chapter 49

THE SUV ROUNDED THE corner and pulled into the parking garage. We were escorted to a private elevator.

My palms are sweaty, my throat dry, and my stomach is in knots. I haven't talked to or seen my family in three months. Would they even want to see me after I disobeyed orders and got myself caught? Maybe they hate me for ruining Vance's life.

The ride to the top floor of the hotel seemed like forever. Sven and Gus are placed at the doors to look for trouble as soon as the doors open. Nikolaj and Demyan stood in front of me to protect me.

The elevator stops, the doors open, and Sven and Gus stand at the opening and look around. Gus motions to the bosses to hold, and Sven says, "what's your name?" He's very stern and very British about it.

"Boy, if you have Milly in that elevator, you'd better move out of the way," a woman's voice abruptly snaps.

It was Mary!

I try to get past the bosses, but Demyan wraps his arms around my waist. Nikolaj steps in front of me and blocks the entrance to the elevator.

"What is your name?" Nikolaj stands tall, his arms crossed over his broad chest.

I yell while still in Demyan's grasp, "MARY! Her name is Mary!"

"Milly?! Is that you?" She asks as she tries to look around Nikolaj. "Let me get to her, you big brute," she orders.

Nikolaj hesitates but finally steps out of the way, and Mary leaps into the elevator, tears me from Demyan's arms, and squeezes me so hard I can't move.

I take in her smell that I've missed so much. "Mary, you're going to squeeze me to death." I laugh, and she pulls away.

"Sorry. I've missed you so much, my sweet girl!"

The elevator alarm goes off from the doors being held open too long. "Let's go," Demyan says and motions for us to get out of the elevator.

Mary tightens her grip on me as we walk past Nikolaj and his men. Eyeing me as we walk down the hall, she says, "you look good. Taken care of. You have stitches! Why? Did they hurt you?"

"No, Mary, they haven't hurt me at all. I hit my own head. They've been good to Vance and me." I smile back at Nikolaj.

"Still clumsy," she shakes her head. She stares back for a second, then leans in as we walk.

"Well, at least they are good-looking," she mumbles and winks at me, "even I wouldn't mind a ride!"

"Mary!" I say, shocked at what she just said.

I laugh so hard that I trip on my feet and fall forward, but before I hit the ground, I feel solid, strong arms wrap around me. Nikolaj pulls me into him, my back to his chest, and I balance myself again.

"Good-looking and strong. Double win," Mary winks at Nikolaj with a half grin. "And you," she nods at me, then shakes her head, "really are still clumsy."

We enter the double doors to the suite. Mary's still holding me close. Sven and Gus search the room for any trouble while Demyan's on the phone, and Nikolaj lingers close to Mary and me.

"Where is everyone?" I ask, scanning the room myself.

"They are in the other suite."

"Vance stayed back to heal," I say and turn back to Mary.

"OH! Vance is coming here. He's on the plane now." Mary stares at me, confused, then asks, "you didn't know?"

"What?" I look over at Nikolaj, but I see confusion in his eyes. "You didn't know either?" I inquire.

"No." He walks to Demyan and speaks quietly.

"When will he be here?" I asked Mary, and she was still grinning at me.

"What?" I chuckle.

"I'm so glad to see your face again. I was so mad you didn't follow orders. I was so scared I wouldn't see you again, but here you are, protecting us from something we would never have known about if you hadn't disobeyed orders. Funny how that works, isn't it?"

"I'm just glad to see you again." I hug her closer than I ever have.

Commotion sounds in the hall putting all four men on guard. They move to stand between Mary and me and the door. The racket gets louder, and the doors bust open with a bang.

Jared storms through the room's doorway and snaps, "how long do we have to wait before we can see Milly!?" Behind him, Adio, Lindord, Grace, Frank, and Rosco came into sight.

Crowding into the suite uninvited but most definitely welcomed by me. Tears well up in my eyes as I see the family I have missed for so long.

For a minute, the threat on their lives is gone, the time gone by without them never happened, and I'm back with my family and happy!

Unfortunately, the happy feeling only lasted a minute, interrupted by the severity of reality and the threat to my family.

When the chaos calms, I take the time to introduce my family to the bosses and their men. The tension in the room is vile.

Adio stands close to me like he's about to grab me and run. Nikolaj stands closer to me, and the stare-down between them is endless.

"Adio! Nikolaj! I'm fine! Stop!" I want this to be a good partnership, so mistakes don't get made. I want my family to like the man I want as a partner.

"Mouse, your head?" Adio points to my stitches.

"I'm clumsy. You know that," I tell Adio, who is now glaring at Nikolaj, who is looking at Linford walking up behind Adio.

Linford pats Adio on the arm, then grabs me around the waist from behind and says, "Mouse, I've missed beating your ass in training!"

Nikolaj grabs Linford's arms and yanks them off of me.

"Nikolaj, stop!" I bark, walking closer to him. I put my hands on his chest, tiptoe to reach his lips, and press a gentle kiss on them.

The room goes dead quiet as I realize everyone is looking at what I'm doing. I slowly turn, grab Nikolaj's hand and wrap it around my waist.

"He's good to me. Vance approves. Please, we all must get along," I plead. "This is bigger than us, and Nikolaj and Demyan are here to help."

"Very well, Milly," Mary acceptingly says. The tension wasn't completely gone, but at least now they knew they were not a danger to me.

Jared walks over to Mary and says, "Milly's right. This is a big deal. Let's figure out how to stop Riccardo from killing us."

Present Milly

Chapter 50

"YOU'RE A SNEAKY SON of a bitch, Vance!" I call out from across the room. He chuckles, then hugs Frank, who meets him by the door. He makes his way through the room, embracing the rest of the family, then walks over to Nikolaj and Demyan.

"Vance, didn't expect you, but glad you're here," Demyan says, shaking Vance's hand.

Nikolaj steps in to shake Vance's hand and says, "you just couldn't stay away." The three of them laugh together, and this shows everyone they have formed a bond together

"And miss all the action? No way," Vance jokes while looking around the room.

I stand by watching everyone interact, planning an attack on Ricardo, and it feels good having my family and bosses working together.

Rosco walks over to me, "you're quiet," he points out.

"Just taking it all in," I say with a smile.

He nudges into me with his arms crossed over his chest. "So Nikolaj?" He smiles as he cocks an eyebrow and eyes me from the corner of his eye. I nod as I look down at the floor.

"Yep. I guess so," I answer, then look up at Rosco.

"Well, he's handsome," he nods, then laughs. I laugh and throw my arm around him. "Yep, he's a good guy, Rosco," I say, and now we both are staring at Nikolaj.

"If he ever hurts you, I'll wear him as a skin suit," Rosco says, and my facial expression screams gross and confused.

Hours of planning go by, I'm overwhelmed by all the commotion, and I need a break. I walk into the hallway, close the doors to the suite behind me, shut my eyes and take a deep breath.

The door clicks open, and Vance walks out. "Hey, kiddo, what's wrong?"

"Nothing, just need a break," I say and lean against the wall, and Vance leans next to me.

"Remember when we'd go to the cemetery when it was overwhelming?" He asks as he glances over at me.

"Yes!" I look at the ceiling, then finish, "I'd like to go there again."

He looks at me, "we will before we return to Tacoma."

"Okay," I say sadly because returning to Tacoma means I will be away from my family again.

We stand in the hallway together, embracing the quiet.

Finally, the day comes to an end. Demyan, Nikolaj, and I are sharing a suite.

"Okay, I'm going to shower. Are you cooking, Niko, or am I?" Demyan asks while loosening his tie.

"Cooking? There's food here?" I surprisingly ask.

"I always have them stalk my suite before I arrive," Demyan explains, then he disappears around the corner.

"Wow, you two live quite the life," I point out to Nikolaj as I admire the suite.

I grab a glass, pour some vodka, and take a long pull, then sit on the chair by the island and watch Nikolaj's movements.

He takes his jacket off, places it on the back of the chair beside me, rolls his sleeves up, then heads to the fridge.

He grabs a bowl of grapes, setting it in front of me, "here, munch on these." Then rubs his hand on the back of my neck.

I pop a few grapes in my mouth and enjoy the sensation of them popping open as I chew on them.

The potatoes and carrots boil, and the steaks sizzle on the skillet. The smell is mouthwatering.

Demyan walks to the kitchen, shirtless and wearing joggers.

"Our turn to shower," Nikolaj says while handing Demyan the cooking utensils.

I'm not sure what's going on, but Nikolaj made no effort to fuck me in the shower. He washed me slowly like he was distracted.

He and Demyan barely said a word at dinner. Now, they are both in their bedrooms sleeping.

Did I miss something in the other suite?

Well, Nikolaj may be able to sleep, but I need to relieve some stress before tomorrow. I lay on the couch and pulled my tank top up, exposing my breasts and perky nipples. I grasp both my breasts with each hand. Massaging and teasing my nipples, sending tingles straight to my center as I squeeze them harder.

I'm mindful not to make a sound. Demyan is sharing a suite with us, and I don't need him coming out and seeing me fuck myself.

I move my hand down my stomach to my soaked slit, tease the entrance with my fingers, then move them up to the sensitive nub.

I spread my legs wider to give my fingers all access to my body. I closed my eyes, wishing my hands were Nikolaj's hands.

My movements quicken as the sensations of pleasure encompass my body, my back arches off the couch, and I feel my orgasm on the cusp of consuming me.

Then as I'm about to be whisked away by the pleasure, I hear, "you're so sexy!"

My eyes snap open, and I see Nikolaj watching me from the back side of the couch.

"Hi," I whisper with a lust-filled voice, slowing my movements on my clit, and I slide my fingers inside as he watches.

He grins at me as he moves around the couch. "Do you need some help?" He asks as he slides his sweatpants off, dropping them to the floor, and his hard cock lingers, building anticipation in me.

I bite my lower lip, wiggle my shorts off, then yank off my tank top. I lay back down, tossing a leg over the back of the couch, and the other foot plants on the floor. My legs are spread wide open for my sexy Russian to see.

He climbs between my legs, taking my mouth as he settles on me. Moving down, he sucks my nipple into his mouth and bites it. My moan catches in my throat as the sharp pain subsides into pleasure.

"You're all wet and ready for me," he says against my nipple.

I watch him take the bud into his mouth and suck it again, sending an intense sensation through my core.

I quietly hum out and wrap my legs around his back. I feel his tip at my entrance then he slams it into me. I cry out in pleasure as he thrusts fiercely into me again. His cock stretched me in the best way. He groans, wraps his fingers into my hair, and tightens his grip.

I nip at his jawline, and he growls and licks my neck before biting it. I fight to hold in my cries of pleasure.

He slams his lips to mine, and his tongue takes my mouth. His movements quicken, and I feel him deep inside my center. My head is pushed into the armrest with every powerful thrust.

I claw his back as he slams harder into me. I moan when he pulls my hair, tilting my head back so it's pinned between him and the armrest, exposing my neck to him. He growls in his throat while dragging his teeth along my jaw and down my neck. It covers me in desire.

My sounds build in ecstasy with every deep merciless pound into me. He hits all the right spots, and I scream, "NIKOLAJ!"

In an instant, he pulls out, flips me over, pulls my hips up into him, and slams back into me. I grab hold of the armrest and push myself back into him as he pounds into me. His fingers wrap into my hips, and he pulls me further to him.

My scream quivers and I yell, "YES! FUCK YES!"

He fucks me so hard that I see stars, and my body starts weakening.

Wrapping his arms around me, he moves to a sitting position and pulls me with him, never letting his cock leave me.

I haven't been on top of him yet, and the sensation of his massive cock filling me intensifies.

I lean back, resting my head on his shoulder, and grind on him. He nips my ear and fucks me from below while I rotate my hips.

"Fuck Niko, you're making it hard for me to sleep with a fucking boner," Demyan grunts as he walks into the living room. He has no shirt on and gray joggers.

I quickly lean up to get off Nikolaj, but he doesn't stop his movements and fucks me harder. The change in my body angle makes him hit deeper into me, and I cry out in pleasure.

"Hmmmmm, that's a sweet sound," Demyan moans, walking to the front of the couch and standing directly in front of Nikolaj and me. He eyes us up and down as Nikolaj pulls me back to him and slows his thrusts.

Nikolaj orders, "look at Demyan."

I watch lustfully as Demyan stares at my body yearningly. Nikolaj rubs his hands over my breasts, and I resume grinding on his hard cock in my wet pussy.

Demyan's eyes fill with desire. He drops his joggers, and his big hard cock pops out. Equally sized as his business partner.

He grips it, and with his other hand, he reaches down, running his fingers down either side of my opening while Nikolaj pounds in and out of me. He growls, collecting my arousal that Nikolaj's cock pulls out, then smears it over the fat head of his delicious-looking cock.

He starts to stroke his length watching Nikolaj's cock spread me open and fuck me. I grind on Nikolaj, moaning with every powerful thrust into me. Demyan's lustful look and the sensations I feel all stimulate me in the best way, and I feel my core tighten.

Nikolaj's dick grows firmer inside me as I lock eyes with Demyan. My body implodes, and I scream in pleasure. My body jerks and tingles in delight as my orgasm rips through me like a wild animal.

Nikolaj thrusts into me a couple of powerful times before he pulls out. I grab his cock, stroking and massaging his shaft up to the head until it explodes all over my lower stomach. I moan as he bites my neck while I stroke his cock and rub my clit.

Demyan strokes faster and then shoots cum all over my tits while staring at me. His eyes tell me he wants more, but how much will Nikolja let him have. I turn my head to catch Nikolaj's mouth, then I turn to lock eyes with Demyan.

I continue to massage my clit. Not to cum, but to savor the power and desire I feel in this moment. The cum of these two men warms my skin, and I feel sexy as fuck.

I slide my arousal-soaked fingers up my stomach collecting Nikolaj's and Demyan's cum from my body. I slowly lick and suck the three of us off my fingers, making both men grunt in their throats in approval.

Present Milly

Chapter 51

"THIS IS THE STUPIDEST fucking idea we've ever come up with," Rosco snaps, clipping his holster to his leg.

"Yep," Adio agrees, sitting by me as I tie my shoes.

"Through the front fucking door! We're just going to walk in plain sight through the front fucking door," Rosco spazzes while pacing.

I lean up, take a deep breath, and reply, "Vance said it's the best way because they won't suspect an attack. You know, the whole wooden horse thing."

I look to see Nikolaj and Demyan studying a file with Vance and Linford. I can't help but stare at Demyan and wonder what the fuck that was last night. Will he do it again, and how far will he go?

It's wrong for me to want him, but it's not like Nikolaj stopped it from happening.

"Milly," Adio snaps, bringing me back to him.

"What!?"

"Are you going to sit there gawking at your lover boy all day, or do you think you can gear up, so we can kill some assholes?" Adio asks, then shakes his head.

Gus and Sven walk over laughing, and Sven says, "you should have heard them on the jet!" My face shutters and I see Adio and Rosco staring at me.

"SVEN! They're like uncles to me, so shut the fuck up," I snap.

"Ah, mouse," Adio grins, "we have all had our share of mile-high sex."

All four men laugh, and I slam my hands on my face, "ew!"

Rosco laughs, grabbing Adio's arm, "bro, remember that flight to Bali when we tag-teamed that flight attendant in the cockpit while the pilots watched?"

"I'm flying with you two from now on," Gus jokes.

I walk over to the weapons table and grab my gear. Gus walks over to me and says, "I like your uncles." I nod, smile, then grab the knife for my boot and shove it by my ankle.

"Yeah, they're great guys but aren't you a little young to be besties with them," I grunt out of jealousy. First, I have to share Vance; now, the rest of my family has to be shared.

"I don't think so," Gus says with a weird look, then smiles, looking back at Rosco, Adio, and Sven wrestling around, laughing and talking.

"They are in their 30's, and you're in your 20's," I say, annoyed. Hoping to deter Gus from taking them from me.

"I sense jealousy Ms. Fuck My Boss, Who is 11 Years Older Than Me. We are all just trying to get along, and we are, so accept it," Gus says, turning to face me.

I want to slap him, but he's right. If I want my family in my life, I need to share them with the men who tore me from them.

"Let's go," Vance yells to the group, and I holster my Glock and two extra clips.

Parked at the gates blocking the long curvy driveway to Ricardo's mansion on the hill, Vance, Nikolaj, and Demyan are talking to the guard in the booth. They have a meeting with Riccardo and are waiting for the guard to get verification they are supposed to be there.

Six of us are in the SUV parked half a block away, watching them, when Vance radios, "we're in!"

Linford pulls ahead toward the gate. Sven points his gun, with a silencer, at the guard in the booth, then the guard's head jets back, and he collapses.

Rosco jumps out of the vehicle and heads into the booth to open the gate.

We're not worried about being seen; hiding is not part of the plan. We are going into the mansion in plain sight.

Rosco jumps back into the SUV, and we pull up the driveway on alert for guards.

Gus uses his Glock and silencer to pluck off two guards walking in the trees.

"Two," he says while sitting back in his seat.

"Fuck that," Sven mumbles, which ignites the competition I have seen so many times between the two of them.

We pull up to the mansion. No guards.

This doesn't feel right. The front door of the estate is wide open. We file out of the car, watching all angels as we shuffle up the stairs and enter the foyer. Dead silence rings in my ears.

"What the fuck is going on?" Adio whispers while looking around. The giant staircase is to our right, living room, dining room, and kitchen to our left.

The curtains are closed, lights are off, creating a darker atmosphere for anyone to hide. This time it's not us in the shadows. It's someone else, Ricardo's guards. We see them coming out from behind furniture and walls and walking down the stairs.

6 of us to 30 plus of Ricardo's men. This is not the ideal situation we would want to be in, but it's not something we haven't experienced.

I notice none of the men have guns. This tells me that they want us alive. Beaten and unconscious, maybe, but alive.

"Surrender quietly," one guard yells to us.

"Where's the fun in that?" Adio shit grins, looking around at the men circling us. A group of eight guards comes closer, but the rest are scattered further back.

"Are they scared?" Sven asks, laughing.

"We have orders for a fair fight," the asshole guard says.

"Like gentlemen," Linford sarcastically states.

One guard steps forward, trying to intimidate us by showing off his karate moves. Rosco laughs, steps forward to counter him, and lays him out.

Another guard steps forward to take his place in the group of eight.

Oh, that's how this is going to happen. No more than eight fighters at a time. Obviously, these are orders from above.

We look at each as we figure out what's going on. Linford leans into us and says, "Milly, Gus, and Adio, take these eight. Sven, Rosco, and I will kick the shit out of the rest. Join us when you are done with these eight." We all nod in compliance.

Adio whips out his baton from his belt and whips one guard across the face, flinging him to the floor. "One," he yells, and the battle begins.

I lift my leg and kick straight into the guard's chest that charged me and knocked him down. Jumping on top of him, I shove my thumbs into his eyes. I feel them break through, and goo pours out of his eye sockets. I grab the knife from my boot and slit his throat.

Sliding my knife back into my boot, I hear the grunts and screams of the fighting around me. I stand, punch another man in the throat, and he drops to his knees.

I see Adio slice a guard's neck open from behind.

Gus repeatedly punches a guard in the head, and I grab the guard running toward Gus. I pull back on his shoulders, and he falls to the ground. I stomp on his face over and over. The feeling of bones breaking beneath my boot doesn't deter me. I won't stop until he is unrecognizable.

We join Linford, Rosco, and Sven, who are currently kicking the shit out of as many men as possible. Linford is covered in blood as he stabs a guard in the stomach.

"Any of that your blood?" I yell out as I sweep the legs out from a guard running toward me.

"Yeah! They got a few good hits on me," he replies, and the guard he is stabbing falls to the ground. I start to stand from the leg sweep I just did, but the guy I knocked down tackles me to the ground.

I'm facing down as he grabs the sides of my head, and slams my head into the ground, once, twice, three times, then I feel his weight jerk off of me. I look up to see Sven, whose lip is bleeding, slitting the man's throat.

I wipe the blood from my nose as I stand up. I pull the knife from my boot and stab the next guard in the chest, pulling the knife out and stabbing it into his eye, then burying it in his throat.

Rosco grabs a metal statue off a table and smashes it into another guard's face, splitting it wide open as his teeth fly. I stand to see all the guards down and the six of us bloody, beaten, but undefeated.

"That was too easy," Adio says, looking around and trying to catch his breath.

"Sure was, brother," Linford agrees.

I cautiously look in the kitchen to see if anyone is hiding. Clear. As I turn around, I hear yelling and see Sven, Gus, and Adio fighting more guards. Linford is charging at me, with Rosco on his heels, yelling, "watch out!"

I feel hands wrap around my waist and mouth and tighten before I realize what is happening. "SHHHH!" I hear in my ear. Trying to jab and fight my way out of the grasp. I see a guard tackle Rosco from the side, then Linford.

"Boss wants you," says the man holding me, then hurls me over his shoulder. I kick and hit this asshole, but it doesn't faze him. He walks cool and collectively to the basement with me jerking around on his shoulder.

He throws me to the ground with a thud. "What the fuck?!" I yell, quickly looking at my surroundings.

Concrete floors and brick walls, and Nikolaj, Demyan, and Vance are tied to chairs in front of me, grunting and trying to get out of their restraints.

I hear a noise behind me and slowly turn around to see Ricardo leaning against a stainless steel table. He is chewing on a toothpick and eyeing me up and down. "Christoff was right; you are deliciously fuckable," he says, staring at me.

"What the fuck are you talking about?" I snap.

"You thought Christoff wouldn't notice a cleaning cart and maid uniform left in his office? He watched the cameras and saw you," Ricardo explains, taking a few steps toward me. His face scrunches a bit while he asks, "oh, you thought you hacked all the cameras?" Shaking his head no and tsking his tongue.

"Fuck you," I grit through my teeth.

Laughing, he kneels down to me. He grabs some of my hair and smells it. "We didn't expect that Fedorov and Morozov were in on it, though. That's a problem for us. Two of the deadliest men we are in business with, and now we are enemies." He clicks his tongue. "Sad, we were such good business partners," he sneers behind at the men tied to the chairs.

I hear them scream through their gags at Ricardo. I move to my knees and yell, "FUCK YOU! Let them go!"

"NO!" He yells and stands, turning to the table. "I'm going to do what Christoff couldn't." He looks over his shoulder at me. "I'm going to fuck that tight ass of yours while your men watch, unable to stop me." He laughs and says, "I'm going to fuck you so hard over and over until you fucking die!" He turns his back to me again.

I jump up, charge him, and punch the back of his head. He turns to face me, undeterred. His pupils are blown! He's on some kind of drug.

FUCK!

He hits me twice in the face, and I stumble back. Shaking it off, I step toward him, then I feel a sharp sting on the side of my head, and everything goes black.

"Milly!" I hear in a muffled distance.

"Milly, wake up!" Desperation in the voice intensifies.

The voice sounds like it's getting closer, more prominent, but still muffled.

I open my eyes, and everything is blurry. I see Adio hovering over me with his hand on my shoulder. I shut my eyes again.

I feel something bump into me. I jerk my eyes open to see Linford's face right in mine. I see his lips moving in slow motion, but I can't hear him. He looks my body over as more muffled sounds fill my head.

Blinking slowly, I see Sven in the distance, stumbling toward Gus, who is lying on the ground but working on getting up. I struggle to sit up, so Adio and Linford assist me.

I see Demyan and Nikolaj pushing Vance to the ground. Stumbling to my feet, forcing my voice to work, I silently ask, "why is Nikolaj holding Vance down?"

I barely hear Linford talking in my left ear as he says, "Milly, Vance has been shot."

I feel the world drop around me

Time speeds up.

The floor feels like it opened up underneath me.

The noise quickly increased in volume and speed, hurting my ears.

My head starts to pound.

The scene fast-forwards.

Everyone's moving so fast that my eyes can't keep up.

My body goes numb.

I yell for Vance, but no sound comes out of my mouth.

I grab Adio's shoulder to straighten myself up more.

I see Vance cough. Blood shoots out of his mouth.

Nikolaj's yelling at Sven and Gus to get the car.

Demyan looks over at me, gets up from Vance's side, and runs to me. He grabs my waist, pulling me close to him.

I look over his shoulder to see Nikolaj shaking Vance while pushing a cloth to the right side of his chest.

Vance's eyes slowly close, and his body goes limp.

I take in a full painful breath. Forcing my voice out as a single word escapes my mouth, filling the room with my screams of agony reverberating off the walls.

"VANCE!"

Coming soon....

Evil Retribution

Book 2 of The Hunters series

Social media

Check out my website for social media links & book updates

www.raowenwrites.com

Acknowledgements

Thank you for reading my first published book! I hope you enjoyed it. Please leave a review on my Facebook page. I would love to hear your thoughts.

Writing has always been an interest of mine, and I am so excited to finally be doing something I have only dreamt I would do.

None of this would be possible without the support from my absolutely amazing husband, my children, and family and friends. Thank you all so much. I love you more than you will ever know. A special shout out to DJ and AG for being the first two to read my book. Your opinions and recommendations are priceless to me.

Special notes

Do not give up on what makes you happy.
Some days are harder than others,
but growth & success need both good and bad days.
Learn from your mistakes, don't take them personally, and don't
dwell on them.
Stay true to yourself.

CPSIA information can be obtained
at www.ICGtesting.com
Printed in the USA
BVHW092350181122
652278BV00021B/2175

9 798987 222805